LOVE AT Fellside

VOL 2

DANI ELIAS

Editor: Sofia Artola Diaz

Proofreader: Katie Rosenthal

Contents

Content Warning

All Fellside Mountain Rescue books are contemporary romance novellas which include scenes of a sexual nature. They are not a closed-door story.

The books may also contain some or all of these:

- Strong language
- Arachnophobia
- Death of a side character
- Infertility
- Child abandonment

- Alcoholism
- Falling during climbing
- Bullying / Gaslighting
- Domestic violence/abuse
- Violence and physical abuse
- Mental abuse
- Child abduction/kidnap
- Strong language
- Animal slaughter
- Infertility
- Deaths of side characters

If any of this serves as a trigger for you, please decide if this is the book for you.

Finally, the book is set in the north of England and British English spelling is used throughout. That means a lot of times you'll find an "S" where you may expect a "Z". And our ass has an extra Rrrrr to it ;-). Also get ready to learn new words like spotted dick and squirty cream.

Dedication

To all my readers. Thank you for making me want to write more!

A cause close to my heart

My Fellside Mountain Rescue Series is about the men and women of a fictional group of volunteers risking their lives to help those in danger in the mountains. My characters may be fictional, but many mountain rescuers around the world do just this every day and they deserve our respect, our support and, at the bare minimum, our thanks.

Thank you!

Read with Me

Dani Elias

Message from the Author

Dear Reader,

Thank you for choosing Read with Me as your next reading adventure. In this book, you will meet Olivia, who will talk about the challenges she faces as a neurodivergent. However, I have made a conscious decision not to explicitly mention the specific learning difficulty she is dealing with.

Let me explain why. When I was preparing for this book, I had the privilege of talking with several remarkable individuals who navigate learning difficulties, but I want to be transparent about my limitations. I am not an expert in this field, and I believe it would be inappropriate for me to delve into the intricate details without the proper qualifications.

Furthermore, I want to be honest about the limitations of the novella format. While it allows us a glimpse into Olivia's world, it may not provide the extensive coverage that this topic deserves. That being said, there are fantastic books available that provide a more comprehensive examination if you wish to delve further.

Ultimately, my aim in this narrative is to focus on the emotional impact Olivia experiences due to the absence of a support system. I want to emphasize the importance of understanding and compassion in the face of such challenges. By highlighting Olivia's journey, I hope to shed light on the significance of support and empathy for those who may find themselves in similar circumstances.

Warm regards,

Dani Elias

Chapter 1

Rob

Oh my god, I wish she hadn't had that cigarette. The smell and taste that lingers in her mouth makes me want to gag a little every time she pulls me down for another kiss. Her fingernails are digging into my back as I move above her.

"Oh, Rob, you beast of a man."

Okay, what the actual fuck did she just say?

"You take me to new heights," she moans.

Just don't listen to her. Think of... Kate Winslet. Now we're talking—Kate Winslet in Titanic. Here we go. I move faster and close my eyes. I conjured up that image plenty of times in my teenage years, I can do it again.

If only Laura would move a little. She is just lying underneath me, giving me the most annoying fake porn-style moaning and that's it. *Jeez, stop thinking about her. Kate on the sofa. Yes, Kate on the sofa.* I move faster. I hammer into her now like a jackrabbit, but I am past caring. I just need to come and this to be over with. I push deep and simultaneously circle her clit with my finger. Hey, I still have a reputation to uphold. If I come, so does she.

"Rob," she moans my name again. *Shut up, shut up, shut up.* When I feel her pussy contract around my dick, I let go. My orgasm hits me and I stop moving. I roll off her and try to catch my breath.

"Do you want me to clean you up, baby?" she whispers seductively, reaching out for my dick. I swear, when he sees her approaching, he shrivels up. *Well, mate, you got us in this situation.*

"I've to get rid of the condom. But thanks for the kind offer." *Thanks for the kind offer?* I sound like a fucking Scout. I roll away from her before she can grab me and in the dark, I walk barefoot towards the bathroom. In passing I grab my boxer shorts which are lying on the floor at the end of the bed.

"Come back to me quickly, tiger. I want another round," Laura calls after me.

I close the bathroom door behind me and when the familiar click of the lock reverberates through the cool room, I finally relax. I take the condom off and throw it in the bin. I look at the shower and the idea of washing this woman off me is tempting. I turn on the water and wait until it runs hot before jumping under it.

I bumped into Laura at Blue Night, an awesome party exclusively for emergency service workers. It's a quarterly thing that different emergency services in the county take turns hosting, and we all come together to blow off some steam and have a blast. It had been a while since my Fellside Mountain Rescue mates and I last attended Blue Light, but tonight we finally made it again.

Well, not everyone from our team was there. Phil and his pregnant girlfriend stayed home because she wasn't feeling well. And Alex, my other FMR buddy, and his wife Emma also skipped the party. So, it ended up being just me, Nick, Chris, Suzie, and Tommy, our leader, who made the trip.

Nick brought his girlfriend Charlotte, but they didn't hang around for long. Chris and Suzie left even earlier. It seems they've become an item now, despite my initial warning to Chris. I was concerned that it would affect the team if things didn't work out between them. But seeing them together earlier tonight, it's clear that yet another member of our group is off the market.

Tommy used a business meeting in the morning as an excuse to escape early, leaving me to represent our FMR unit. I had considered asking Tommy to give me a lift back to Fellside when Laura approached me. She made it clear that she was up for some fun and my dick just couldn't say no. After a steamy make-out session on the dance floor she drove us back to Fellside and we ended up in my bed together.

I rinse the last of the soap off my body and switch the water off. I step out of the shower and dry myself before sliding into my boxers. No way will I go back out there in just a towel.

I take a deep breath and lean on the sink, my fingers gripping the smooth edge. The mirror above it is steamed up and I use one hand to wipe the condensation off.

"Bloody hell, what's going on with me?" I mutter. Tonight was meant to be like any other night; hitting the town, on the prowl for a bit of excitement. But something is off. I'm just not getting that same buzz anymore. It's like my whole outlook is shifting, and I'm not all that fussed about another quick shag anymore.

I mean, back in the day, those flings used to give me a temporary high, a little escape from the mundane. But now, there's this niggling feeling, this sudden awareness that it's all a bit shallow and empty. I'm longing for something more, something real.

There was a time when I loved the chase, like a game I couldn't resist. But the thrill is gone, leaving me with this weird void inside. It's like I've had a total shift in perspective, where those casual encounters just don't hit the spot anymore.

To be honest, I think I know where this is coming from. My best friends (well, except for Tommy, the workaholic) are all blissfully happy in their relationships. But hey, no hard feelings here! Seeing their happiness warms my heart, even though it leaves me feeling like the only person still waiting for the acceptance letter to a certain magical school.

Our hangouts have evolved too. Gone are the wild nights of mischief; now we opt for an evening in the pub, sipping drinks like civilised grown-ups and devouring meals like sophisticated food critics. We even threw a bash for Suzie's son Max's fourth birthday. Who knew children's parties could be the new social highlight of my life?

I rub my temple. First and foremost, I need to get Laura out of my bed. I wish I could use work as an excuse, but tomorrow is Saturday.

I work at the local library, and that often surprises people. I don't fit the typical librarian image. I have this cocky sales rep look women seem to like, and when I'm not busy organising bookshelves, I volunteer as a mountain rescuer and drive my friends crazy with my first-class pranks. So, while I may not fit the mould of a quiet bookworm, I've learned to embrace my unique quirks and enjoy life with a good sense of humour. After all, I couldn't care less about what anyone thinks.

My colleague Helen equally doesn't fit the librarian stereotype. In her fifties, divorced, with a fierce spirit, she rocks comfy outfits all the time, especially her favourite yoga pants (she says they're forgiving even if you've had a lot of cake). Currently, she's on the hunt for her next husband on Tinder. Between the two of us, we run the small Fellside library, which is funded by the local council. We also have a chap called Colin helping from time to time. He is a pensioner and tends to be available to take over for me when I am called to a rescue mission.

I stare into my own eyes in the mirror. Helen will chastise me when she finds out I hooked up again. She keeps telling me that I am ready for the real thing. I may have told her a bit too much about how I admire the relationships my FMR mates have. So now she is convinced that I also want one and shouldn't waste my time with women like

Laura who are for one night only. She says I should be looking for my special person. Well, lately I have started to wonder if she might be onto something.

"Rob," Laura shouts from the bedroom.

"I'll be out in a minute," I reply. I had hoped she would have left whilst I was taking a shower.

"Rob," she shouts again a little more urgent.

"One minute!" *For fuck's sake, woman.*

"Rob," she screams. "Get out here. There is blue light everywhere!" *What the fuck?* I push myself away from the sink and open the door. The bedroom is illuminated by a blue light emanating from the top half of the wardrobe.

"What's that? What is that?" Laura is screeching. She is kneeling on the bed, clasping the duvet to her naked body.

"I don't know," I say quietly. It is an eerie dark blue light. *What the fuck is this?* We are both staring at the wardrobe and neither of us is moving. The room is dead silent.

"Can you see me?" The voice of a little girl echoes through the silence. Laura stares at me.

"Hello?" The ghostly voice continues before she starts singing, "Itsy bitsy spider..."

"Make it stop, Rob!" Laura shouts. I am finally able to move. I don't believe in ghosts. At least I don't think I do. I move towards the wardrobe. "Make it stop!" Laura shouts again, trying to drown out the little girl singing.

"I'm fucking trying, Laura," I shout back. Whilst I glare at her, I don't pay attention to what's in front of me and stub my toe on the foot end of the bed. "Fuck," I swear under my breath and hobble the rest of the way to the wardrobe. The singing seems to get louder and louder making it more difficult to pinpoint where it's coming from.

"I'm getting the fuck out of here," Laura shouts behind me. I turn and see that she has dressed herself at lightning speed and is legging it to the bedroom door.

"Don't call me," she says before leaving the bedroom. *Don't worry; I wasn't planning to.*

When I reach the wardrobe, I stare at it. It is too heavy for me to move to check where the light is coming from.

"...down came the rain." The voice is fucking creepy and makes my blood run cold. I shake the thought from my head and look around the gloomy room. I notice the outline of a chair and grab it.

"Can you see me?" The ghostly voice calls again.

I peek on top of the wardrobe where I keep my suitcase. I lift the case off. *Aha!* Behind the suitcase is a small night-light. Definitely not something I have put there. I grab it and switch it off. *Mistake!* Now the room is completely dark and the ghost girl is singing again. It makes my skin crawl.

I turn the light back on and use it to find my main light switch on the wall. The moment I flip it and light floods the room, the situation feels slightly less spooky. I switch the night light off again and turn it in my hands. It has a timer function. *Bastards!* I throw the device onto the mattress. Now it's time to hunt a ghost.

I listen carefully for the voice and then crouch down next to the bed. I put my face to the floor and peek underneath the wooden frame. *Gotcha!*

I reach under the bed and pull out an old battery-operated alarm clock. I had one like this when I was a teenager. You added a CD to it and it would start the CD at whatever time you programmed it to.

I press the power button and the ghostly voice stops. Leaning against my bed, I stare at the alarm clock. *These fucking bastards.* A laugh escapes my lips. Oh, they are so going to pay for this.

"Where's Rob?" I hear Tommy's voice through the open door as I approach the meeting room. We have our monthly FMR unit meeting today. It always starts as a formal meeting at the FMR centre, but we usually move it to the pub around the corner quite quickly.

"I'm here," I inform him as I step through the door.

"Excellent, so we can start." He points at the empty chair around the table for me to take a seat.

"Sure we can. Can someone explain this to me?" I ask as I pull the nightlight and alarm from my backpack and drop it in the centre of the table.

"What's that?" Nick asks and he deserves an Oscar for keeping a straight face.

"This scared the living shit out of the woman I was shagging after the Blue Night."

There are a lot of thinly pressed lips around the table as everyone is trying to hold back laughter.

It has been a few weeks since that ghostly encounter, but with everyone tense and on high alert because of Suzie's ex, I didn't think it was the right time to confront them all. But now that life has settled down again, the gloves are off.

"I nearly broke my toe on the bed frame when she kept shouting at me to make it stop." I try to sound angry, but they all know me too well. "She asked me not to call on her again."

Now there is no controlling them anymore. Nick is the first to crack and his loud belly laugh echoes round the room, setting everyone else off.

"Mate... we're... not sorry," Alex laughs.

"We did promise you payback," Chris chips in. I rub the back of my neck and drop into my chair.

"Arseholes," I say before joining in with the laughter. "This must have taken you guys ages to plan."

"Mate, you covered me in ink, you signed Tommy's work email up to mailing lists for all sorts of porn sites, and you drew a cock and balls on Phil's back with sun cream whilst he was sleeping in the garden. Do you want me to continue? We told you one day we'd get you back." Nick is still laughing. He was the victim of my latest prank and so he's taking the greatest pleasure in this. Fine, I deserved it. I've played many tricks on them over the years. I love a good prank. I just have two rules: firstly, the prank must not cause any harm—physical, financial, or mental—to a person; and secondly, there is a difference between being a prankster and a bully, and that's a line I won't cross.

"Sorry about scaring away the girl though," Chris says with a smirk. "Do you want me to talk to her and explain?"

"Nah, frankly, after she called me a beast of a man, that ghost girl did me a favour." That's all it takes for all of us to burst into laughter again.

Chapter 2

Olivia

I step into the library and the cool air hits me in the face. It's a warm day for early September, and so the cooler air inside the building is a welcome relief. I glance around the large room. All in all, the library hasn't changed much from my teenage years, but I can see that the kids' area has been moved to the front of the open-plan room and has some comfy multi-coloured beanbags to sit on.

My eyes drift to the counter where you check out your books, and a smile creeps onto my lips. The same dark hair, cheeky grin, and dark blue eyes. Admittedly, I can't see them from here, especially as Rob is looking at something on his desk, but there behind the counter is the one person that made my school days bearable.

Rob is the same age as me, so we had a number of lessons together, and we would hang out during break time and after school. We first met when I was eight. Miss Miller made me stay behind to practice reading aloud because she was convinced I was too lazy to practice at home. She didn't want to hear that I found it difficult. Nowadays, they would send a child like me to get tested for learning difficulties, and there are many methods to help. But when I was growing up, all this was in the beginning stages and certainly hadn't made it to a small village like Fellside yet.

"Learning difficulties" wasn't a term people used. They would call me stupid, lazy, or dumb instead. Even my brothers nicknamed me Pippi because they found it amusing that I couldn't read, just like Pippi Longstocking. It frustrated me, knowing that reading was hard for me while others found it easy. I hated feeling like I wasn't good enough and it made me resentful towards those who didn't understand the struggles I faced.

On that afternoon, when Miss Miller made me stay behind, Rob worked on a special project in her classroom. He was a popular person in school and a prankster, but he was also incredibly bright. And he always did special projects, which is why teachers usually forgave his pranks.

After Miss Miller had made me cry by shouting at me, Rob followed me to check if I was okay. We became friends there and then. We spent many afternoons exploring the surrounding hills, and when it was raining, we would sit in this exact library, and he would read the Famous Five books to me. Yes, I wasn't a reader, simply because it was too difficult, but I loved listening to the stories, especially when he read them.

I take a few steps towards the counter, and my heart starts beating faster. I left Fellside when I turned thirteen. My father accepted a job in Leeds, and so we all moved. Rob and I were just too young to keep our promise to stay in touch. My family moved back to Fellside a few years back, but I was helping run my aunt's outdoor clothing store at that time and was besotted with a guy (who turned out to not be that nice after all) so I stayed behind in Leeds.

Of course, I had been back to visit my family a few times throughout the years, but something always stopped me from getting in touch with Rob. Still, I always remembered him and our friendship.

I am about to call out to Rob when an older woman steps up to him.

"I meant to ask you. How's Max doing? He looked cheerful enough when they were here earlier." She leans against the counter next to him.

"He's doing okay, but they're now taking him to a therapist to help with his nightmares," Rob replies. Hearing his deep voice sends goosebumps down my arm and I am not sure why. When I left, he still had the soft voice of a boy. There is nothing boyish in the sound that hits my ear.

"Poor baby," his colleague sighs then she notices me. "Can we help you, Miss?" I freeze when she looks at me.

"Olivia?" Rob asks with some uncertainty in his voice. He stares at me. I'm surprised that he recognises me.

"Hey, Rob!" I give him a goofy wave. How do you react when you meet a childhood friend you haven't seen in forever?

He looks at me for a minute. As his eyes travel up and down my body, I nervously pull on the hem of my T-shirt. I've come straight from work and I am still wearing my black uniform. The sport shop where I work as a department supervisor really could do with something more exciting than black hiking trousers and a black polo shirt.

"Fucking hell, Olivia!" He rushes out from behind the counter, grabs me and pulls me into a tight hug. My hands slide around his waist and the first thing I notice are tight muscles under my fingers. He also smells incredible. There is a faint hint of aftershave, but there is also a lot of pure manliness. My senses go into overdrive and my heart beats wildly. When he eventually lets go of me, I miss his warmth immediately.

"What are you doing here? Helen, this is Olivia; we were friends as kids until she moved to Leeds. Olivia, this is Helen. She runs this place and bakes the best biscuits in the world. Oh, fucking hell, I can't believe you're here," Rob babbles before pulling me into another hug.

"Maybe let her speak for a minute?" Helen interjects with a grin on her face.

"Oh, sure, sorry, what are you doing here?" He asks again.

"I moved back to Fellside two months ago and—"

"What the heck, and you've only come to see me now?" He frowns and something in me wants to say something that brings the smile back on his face.

"It's been so long and I wasn't sure if you were still in Fellside." That's a lie. Thanks to social media I certainly knew he was still here, but he doesn't need to know that I was nervous to see him. "I ran into Phil's sister and she told me you are in Phil's FMR unit and work in the library." Fellside is a small village and so you kind of know everyone. Phil's sister Jane was my brother Liam's crush, and she would hang around our house. When I bumped into her earlier in the week, she dragged me off to a coffee shop and gave me a rundown on everyone she could think of that we went to school with and was still living in the village. I didn't even have to probe to find out what Rob was up to. She talked about him for a full fifteen minutes and told me how he is an eternal bachelor who is shagging his way through the ladies in town. I gathered from her tone and the details she added to his story that she would love to be one of those women.

"This is so crazy. Look at you," his eyes travel up and down my body again. I feel a blush creeping up my cheeks.

"I just wanted to pop in and see if you want to catch up sometime. And maybe take out a book or two." *Okay, why did I say that?* I still don't like reading, so why would I borrow a book?

"Hell yes to catching up. Tell you something, I am meeting up with the FMR guys after work. Come along. You'll know most of them at least by name."

"Guys night out, no thank you," I giggle.

"No, nothing like that. Most of them are in a relationship and their partners will be there as well. You can meet them all tonight, they're amazing."

"Oh, okay. That sounds nice actually. I haven't really made any friends since coming back."

"You have me," he grins, pulling me into another hug. Three hugs, huh? Maybe I wasn't the only one missing "us."

"Where should I meet you?" I ask as I step away from his embrace.

'Wait!' Rob exclaims and swiftly hoists himself up onto the chest-high counter. Leaning forward with his legs dangling in the air, he reaches down. I really hope whatever he is looking for is hidden somewhere and he won't find it very quickly because the view of his arse is perfection.

"Here, give me your number." He gets off the counter and holds out his phone. I take it with nervous hands and type in my details.

"I'll text you when I'm done here. Phil and Nick finish early today, so they'll check out the pubs and see where they can find a large enough table for us."

"Sure, okay." *Why am I so nervous?*

"I can't believe you're back." He grins at me.

"It's good to see you too, Rob," I chuckle and pat his chest. His blue eyes turn dark and, I might be imagining it, but it looks like his cheeks turn a little pink. "I better go. Nice to meet you, Helen," I say. "Oh, and Rob, you look good." *Oh fuck, I didn't just say that.* I turn on my heels and walk out of the library.

"See you later," I hear Rob shouting and I just raise my hands and wave behind me. I take a deep breath when I step outside into the heat. *Kill me, kill me now.*

Chapter 3

Rob

Her curly hair bounces as she walks briskly out of the library. *Bloody hell, Olivia is back!* I was gutted when her family moved away from Fellside. I remember sulking around like a miserable sod for weeks on end. My parents thought I was just going through the first rough patch of teenage rebellion. Looking back, I reckon there might've been more to it. Can't say I would have admitted it at the time, but I might have been developing a bit of a teenage crush on her.

Anyway, not having Olivia around felt like a right kick in the bollocks. I felt utterly lost and empty. I often thought of her and I would get lost in memories, thinking about the fun we had. But like you do as a teenager, eventually, you move on. This was all before the time of mobile phones or social media, so staying in touch would have meant writing letters, and what teenager really does that?

And now here we are, both grown adults. And what a grown-up she has become. There is nothing girlish when it comes to her curves.

"Earth to Rob," Helen pulls me from my thoughts.

"Sorry, what did you say?"

"You've some drool there," she points to the corner of my mouth. I roll my eyes.

"She's just an old friend." Doesn't take a genius to work out what she was implying. I step back behind the counter and return to the pile of books I had been scanning to mark as returned.

"I see. We're pretending you didn't just blush because she touched you." Helen laughs and crosses her arms in front of her chest.

"Didn't you give me a lecture after that disaster with Laura that I should stop fucking around?" I whisper the last words. We have a lot of ladies from the WI hanging around in the library and they tend to clutch their pearls when we use the F word.

"With women like Laura. Olivia is the kind of woman I want to see you with." Helen is an old meddler despite what she has been through. Two years ago, she discovered that her husband was cheating on her with her own sister. But now, she proudly declares herself as happily divorced. She's been exploring Tinder in the past few weeks, and she's definitely not holding back! The stories she shares would make anyone blush, but you can't help but laugh with her. She's got no filter, and her zest for life is contagious.

Since my mum and dad moved to Spain a few years back she has taken it upon herself to mother me and she is adamant that I'm ready to settle down. I won't admit that she is right, but I definitely know that one-night stands are no longer my thing.

"You don't even know her," I retort.

"I'm a good judge of character," she says defiantly.

"I'll say it again, Olivia and I are just friends."

"When did you see her the last time?"

"Twenty-something years ago. We were thirteen when she left."

"Ah, your first crush."

"I didn't have a crush on her; we were just friends."

"Fine, that was back then. What about now?"

"Helen, she barely said five sentences to me."

"You hugged her three times." *Yes, I know,* I am painfully aware of that, but for some reason, I just couldn't keep my hands off her. Weirdly, it also felt like no time had passed. I felt as comfortable around her as I did when we were kids.

"So?" I reply like it's not a big deal.

"You're testing an old lady's patience here." She gives me her most stern look and I chuckle. "Fine, don't tell me then. But do me a favour and open your heart when you meet her tonight," is the last she says before grabbing some books and walking off towards the crime section.

"We're just friends," I shout after her, which sounds very much like we are not just friends. I should have just kept my mouth shut.

My eyes drift to the clock. Three hours to go until I see Olivia again.

As I turn the corner onto Church Lane I spot her leaning against the bus stop. Fuck she is beautiful. Her golden locks shimmer under the warm sunshine. Sporting a pair of jeans and a sleek, figure-hugging black top, it accentuates her curves in all the right ways, leaving me absolutely captivated. I take a deep breath before walking over.

"Hey!" I bend forward and give her a kiss on the cheek. I'm not sure what made me do that. We have never kissed each other on the cheek before, but it felt natural.

"Are you sure it's okay for me to come along?" There is uncertainty in her voice.

I got a message from Nick earlier, saying the pubs are absolutely chock-a-block. Typical Friday night, I reckon. So, we agreed to a change of plans and we're meeting at his place instead. It has been a scorcher of a day and we're determined to enjoy every last drop of summer.

"Absolutely. Everyone is really chilled and we always have way too much food. What's that?" I point at an orange plastic container in her hand.

"Chocolate cake. Couldn't really come without anything," she shrugs.

"Oh god, please tell me it is your mum's recipe." I loved that cake so much that Olivia convinced her mum to make me one every year for my birthday.

"Might be." She grins.

"Let me have some." I reach for the pot, but she pulls away from me.

"No way, that's for your friends."

"I'm your friend, Olivia. Give me some cake," I demand with a chuckle.

"Rob, behave!" She laughs and turns her body away from me, clutching the container to her chest.

"Olivia!" I warn her. I slide my hands around her waist and pull her to me. Her back crashes into my front.

"No," she shouts in between gasps of uncontrollable laughter.

"Give me!" I say again and try to pull the cake from her grasp, but she is stronger than she looks. Her fingers grip the container tightly. Time for plan B. My hands slide to her side and I start to tickle her.

"Rob, no!" she snorts, but I don't stop. I am laughing so hard by now that my eyes start to water. Olivia wiggles in my arms, trying to escape me.

"Fine, fine. Stop tickling me and you can have some." The minute she finishes the words, I raise my hands as a sign of peace.

"You're such a child," she giggles before opening the container and picking a small piece of cake from it. She holds the chocolaty goodness out to me between her thumb and index finger. Instead of grabbing it, I bend forward and close my lips around her fingers. Her eyes go wide and I realise what I am doing but I will be damned if I stop this now. My tongue pulls the cake from between her fingers and then licks over them. I taste chocolate and Olivia. *Fuck me.*

Olivia pulls her fingers from my mouth. Our eyes lock and neither of us says anything.

" Are you getting the bus or not?" a voice shouts from behind me and pulls me back to reality. I turn and see that the bus has pulled up at the stop.

"No mate, we're good," I reply through a mouth of cake and give him a wave. I see the driver mumble something under his breath before he closes the door and drives on.

"Let's go." I swallow the last of the cake, place my hand on her lower back and direct her to Nick's cottage which is not far from the bus stop.

"Hey, come in," Charlotte greets us when we arrive.

"Olivia, meet Charlotte, the one who managed to rope Nick into a lifetime of commitment," I chuckle, introducing the two women. With a smile, I watch as they exchange pleasantries, their eyes twinkling with genuine interest. As expected, Charlotte effortlessly draws Olivia into our little circle, making her feel right at home from the get-go.

There's something about Charlotte's presence and she naturally puts people at ease. Within moments, Olivia's initial nervousness dissipates. It's as if they've known each other for ages.

Charlotte leads us deeper into the cottage towards the garden in the back. When we step outside, all eyes are on us. I'm sure Nick told everyone that I am bringing someone. My friends are nosy as fuck.

"Olivia. Great to see you again." Phil waves. Phil was in the same year group as Olivia and I, so of course he would know her. I am actually surprised they didn't become friends, given how both were the quiet kids in school. The thought doesn't sit well with me, even if this is irrational. *She was my friend!*

"Right, let me introduce you to everyone." I grab her hand and link our fingers. She gives me a shy look but doesn't pull away.

"This is Alex and Emma, you know Phil, and this is his girlfriend Christina."

"Fiancée," Phil interrupts me. I roll my eyes before pointing at Charlotte.

"This lovely person you have met. Then we have Chris and Suzie and Tommy, who managed to tear himself away from the love of his life, his work," I chuckle. Tommy flips me not so discretely the finger and everyone laughs.

"Nick is inside prepping food," Charlotte throws in.

"That's a lot of names," Olivia giggles when we finish explaining who is who.

"Don't worry, we're at an advantage. We only need to remember one name," Emma giggles. "Just ask us. We won't be offended. Emma, and this is Alex, my husband," she repeats, but I have a suspicion that Emma is saying that mainly for her own benefit because ever since they got hitched, Alex and Emma drop the wife and husband words wherever possible.

"Take a seat, and I'll get you something to drink. What would you like?" I gently push her towards Emma.

"Just a coke please."

"Coming up," I reply and give her a reassuring smile before stepping back into the kitchen.

"Mate, any chance of some drinks?" I ask Nick, who is washing a mountain of lettuce in the sink.

"Help yourself. The fridge is full." He nods towards the appliance.

"Cheers."

"So, who is Olivia?" Okay, we are starting the interrogation early.

"Just an old school friend."

"I see." He doesn't say anymore, but the tone tells me he is not finished with his questions.

"What does that mean?" I ask whilst pouring coke into a pint glass.

"Nothing." He drops the lettuce into a large bowl. "Just, you've never brought a woman to one of our get-togethers and Phil said you were inseparable in school."

"Excuse me? When have you all turned into a bunch of old gossips?" I avoid his eyes. He leans against the counter and crosses his arms in front of his chest.

"You don't want to talk about it?"

"I don't want to talk about it," I confirm.

"Fine. I tried, but let me warn you: Charlotte and Emma have been on a mission ever since Phil told them everything he knew about Olivia. They think she is perfect for you. So, if you are really not interested in Olivia, tell me now so I can get them to back off."

I put the Coke bottle back in the fridge.

"What if I'm interested?" I finally look at him and he has a smug look on his face.

"Correct me if I am wrong, but she only came back into your life today?"

"I tell you, mate, it was like… it felt like a missing piece of my life was back when she stood in front of me. There was no awkwardness. It just felt like we had never been apart."

"So, there was something going on between the two of you in school? Phil wasn't sure."

"No, there wasn't. Hand on heart. But I'm starting to wonder if there would have been if she'd stayed." Saying it out loud, I can hear that it all comes across as a bit crazy, even if it feels very right.

"Sounds to me like you should find out if there is something there." Nick grabs the bowl of salad and we both head back out in the garden.

Chapter 4

Olivia

My eyes move towards the fire pit. The garden wall I am sitting on feels rough against the skin of my palms. The laughter of the group drifts over to me. We have only been here for a few hours and I already feel like am part of their circle.

These are amazing people. They immediately accepted me into their group. Emma and I have already arranged to meet for coffee at the Cherry Pie bakery next week because we share a love for their éclairs.

"Why are you sitting in the back here all alone?" Rob's voice cuts through the night. It's so dark at the far end of the garden that I can only make out his silhouette.

"I just—" I'm not sure what to say. I wanted a break because how nice everyone is felt unusual and overwhelming.

"Came here to think?" Rob suggests before taking a seat next to me on the wall. He is so close to me that our sides touch.

"Something like that. Your friends are amazing," I reply.

"Yeah, they're my family." His face is pointing towards the house. "You know I have no siblings. And when mum and dad moved it was only me left here. They've been my saving grace, even if they can be a pain sometimes," he chuckles.

"How so?"

"For example, they've all been gossiping about us."

"What have they been saying?" I turn to face him, even if I can only vaguely make out his features.

"They were wondering if anything ever happened between us in school," he says quietly.

"Ha, no, we were too young and I didn't look at you like that back then."

"How about now?"

I stare off into the distance, lost for words. Rob has been at my side all evening and we kept the group entertained with stories from our childhood. At one point he put his arm around my shoulder and it didn't feel weird or strange but familiar and perfect.

I sigh. The night is alive with the laughter and chatter of his friends gathered around the bonfire. My heart pounds in my chest, torn about what I should do. Should I spill my feelings? And if so, how do I even begin? Honestly, I'm not even sure what all of this means myself. It's crazy to think that we only reconnected today. The longer I stay silent, the heavier the silence hangs between us, weighing down on me.

"Rob, we've only just reconnected today," I finally whisper.

"True, but we've known each other for over twenty years."

"We were kids back then. We've both changed. I know nothing about you." *Except what I managed to work out from your social media account.* Yes, I may have turned stalker on him.

"I'm pretty much the same," he argues. If only. Yes, he is the same kind spirit from back in school, but there is so much more to him. "But okay, let's get to know each other..., do you enjoy your job?" He couldn't have picked a more boring question.

"Well, it's not the most thrilling job. Don't get me wrong, there is nothing wrong with it and it pays the bills, but I don't really feel a sense of achievement."

"If you could have any job in the world, what would you do?" He briefly touches my back and the touch makes my heart skip a beat.

"That's easy. A teacher. I always wanted to be a teacher."

"What stopped you?"

"Rob, you know my challenges with reading."

"Olivia," he mimics my tone, "Plenty of people have learning difficulties and go to university. I don't know enough about it, but there are tools and methods you can use to help with your learning."

"Where were you when I tried to explain this to my family?" I chuckle, but there is a little bit of bitterness in my tone. After we had moved to Leeds, I did try to make an effort and asked my family for help, but I was told that there was nothing wrong with me and that not everyone needs to go to university.

"What did they say?" Rob's voice sounds cold.

"Nothing, forget it." I try to divert. A booming laugh drifts over to us. Someone must have just told a very good joke.

"Should we go back to the others?" I move to jump off the wall but Rob's hand lands on my knee.

"Not yet. Please. I haven't seen you in so long."

"Okay."

"Let's play truth or dare," he challenges me. I turn to look at him.

"Rob, be serious. Who plays truth or dare in their thirties?" I laugh.

"You're never too old for truth or dare. And you said we need to get to know each other again. No better way to do that." He gently bumps my shoulder with his before asking, "Truth or dare?" I guess we are doing this.

"Truth." Yup, I don't trust him with a dare.

"Did you check up on me before you came to see me today?" I can feel myself blush, but luckily it is so dark that he can't see that.

"I may or may not have checked out your social media," I giggle.

I expected him to tease me, but instead he responds in a strained voice, "Just so you know, I haven't posted anything in a year and I'm not that guy anymore." I assume he is referring to the countless photos of him and one woman or another.

"What changed?" I would be lying if I said I hadn't worried about his bed hopping and what kind of guy he might have become.

"I changed. I grew up, I saw my friends all finding this one person that gives them peace and happiness, and somehow, maybe, I started to think I'd like that as well." He shrugs, his gaze focusing on a point in the distance. Not much I can say to that. Having spent time with his friends, I can understand the appeal. They should all come with a warning label saying, "Relationship Goals."

"Truth or dare?" I break the silence.

"Truth."

"How many other women have you read stories to?" I ask, my breath caught in my throat. They were mine, treasured and replayed in my mind. Sometimes, this irrational jealousy would creep in, imagining him sharing those intimate moments with someone else, making our connection less unique. It's like a sharp sting that stayed with me throughout the years.

"Is that a euphemism?" He laughs out loud.

"No, you remember you always read stories to me because my reading was so crap." Had he forgotten the moments that meant so much to me? My heart starts racing and knots are forming in my tummy.

"Of course, I remember. The Famous Five were our all-time favourites. But that was never even a consideration with these other women."

"Because none of them were stupid." The words are out before I can stop them.

"How often have I told you that you're not stupid? Don't call yourself that." He sounds cross. He always hated it when I called myself stupid.

"I know. I... I'm sorry."

"Olivia, you've got to know that it never even crossed my mind to share those moments with someone else. It was our unique thing, something special between us," he says with conviction in his voice.

"Those moments meant a lot to me as well," I whisper. I wish I could see his face and the expression on it. It is difficult to know what someone really thinks if you can't see them.

"What do you read nowadays?" Rob asks.

"Nothing, really. It just takes me too long, which ruins the whole experience."

"How about audiobooks?"

"I thought about it, but I have never looked into it."

"If you had to choose an audiobook, what genre would it be?"

"I don't know. Not the Famous Five," I laugh. "Romance, maybe."

"Is that sweet, clean romance, or are we talking smutty, steamy romance?" He says it as a joke, but his voice sounds strained and almost husky.

"I think I am grown up enough to go for the latter." I feel the blush creeping up on my cheeks again.

"Noted," he chuckles.

"Truth or dare?" I try to move us on to a safer topic. We continue asking each other questions. Favourite food, best holidays, past relationships, first kiss. Nothing seems to be off-limits.

"Rob! Nick must have been furious!" I laugh out loud as he retells one of the pranks he played on his teammate.

"No harm, no foul," he replies before jumping off the wall. He positions himself in front of me and gently pushes my thighs apart so he can step in between them. He cups my face and makes me look at him.

"Truth or dare," he says in a husky voice. I swallow hard. Every cell in my body is cheering me on to be brave.

"Dare," I whisper. He never tells me what the dare is, he just takes it. He leans forward and brushes his lips over mine. Electric sparks seem to be in the air. One of his hands slides into my hair and holds onto the back of my head. He leans in further and that's when neither of us can hold back anymore and our lips crush together. My eyes are closed and I tilt my head to the side allowing him to deepen the kiss. I part my lips and his tongue licks his way into my mouth. Grabbing hold of his T-shirt, I pull him closer. My legs automatically lock behind his back. All my senses are honed in on this kiss and I feel an incredible need to be close to him. A small moan escapes me.

Rob breaks away and I want to protest. He leans his forehead against mine and locks eyes with me in the dark before saying, “I’ve been wondering what that would feel like.”

Chapter 5

Rob

Having her in my arms feels right. My heart is still racing. I hadn't planned to kiss her, but I just couldn't stop myself.

"What are we doing, Rob?" she whispers. Her eyes are still closed.

"I don't know, but I would like to see where it leads. I know this is new, but it's also familiar. Don't give it a name. Just give it a chance," I plead. I know this is crazy. Twenty-four hours ago, I didn't even know that she was back in Fellside. I can't remember the last time I thought about her. But something feels so incredibly right about this. I need her to give us a chance.

"Am I going to be another notch on your bedpost?" I guess it is fair for her to ask, but the words still hurt.

"No. I can't label this yet, but I can guarantee you, it is nothing like any other encounter with a woman I've had before." I mean every word I say. She seems relieved. "Please. One chance." I am not too proud to beg.

"Would it surprise you if I said I kind of want this as well?"

I pull her in my arms and her head nuzzles against my shoulder. Today has been one hell of a day.

I look at Nick, surprised. He's brought his school class down to the library and they are all huddled in the kids' section at the moment listening to Miriam, a volunteer who regularly holds story time at the library.

"You're fucking with me, right?"

"No, mate," Nick chuckles. He leans over the counter and grabs a biscuit from the plate on my desk. I try to swat him away, but he is too quick.

"Are you seriously asking me to be your best man?"

"Why not?" he says through a mouthful of biscuit.

"What about Alex? I would have thought he is the guy you would like to be best man." Alex and Nick weren't always friends, but since they helped each other to get their respective girlfriends, they have seemed thick as thieves.

"He'll be Phil's. Phil was his. Tommy will be Chris's. So—"

"Is that a pity offer?"

"No!" He genuinely seems concerned that I could think that. "Frankly, if I could, I'd have all five of you. You're all my best mates. But Charlotte will murder me if I turn our intimate wedding into a circus with five groomsmen and bridesmaids." He chuckles. "Besides, I was thinking, if you're in the wedding party, you'll be less likely to play a prank on me."

"I am hurt." I feign upset, but we both know that I have been thinking about it. Frankly the only thing that has stopped me from coming up with a plan is the fact that I am a tiny bit scared of the women in the group. They will castrate me if I mess this up for Charlotte.

"So, how about it?"

"And you're sure you wouldn't prefer Alex."

"Rob, you're my mate, just like Alex. I would like you to be there as my best man."

"Well," I cough, "I... of course, I'd love to." Nick shakes his head laughing and holds out his fist. I bump it like we always do. Yup, we don't do mushy stuff.

"So, Olivia?" He asks before stealing another of my Bourbon biscuits.

"Mate, cut it out!" I take the plate and put it out of his reach. "What about Olivia?"

"Well, you snogged each other's face off at my house and that was a week ago. So, what's going on?" I look at him suspiciously. That doesn't sound like him. We don't talk about stuff like that. The unwritten rule of the group: if you need advice with your love life, you need to ask and we are there for each other, but otherwise, we keep our noses out.

"Did Charlotte send you?"

"I wasn't that subtle, was I?" He nervously rubs the back of his neck. "Frankly, lately I have spent way too much time discussing your love life with my wife."

"Your *fiancée*." I love to rile him up. Nick is desperate to make Charlotte his wife.

"My almost-wife. She's worried about you and she's on a mission. She and Emma are convinced that the two of you are perfect for each other, but they want me to make sure you won't cock it up. I told them it will be obvious that the question doesn't come from me. We don't meddle in each other's business."

"You talked Emma into giving Alex another chance," I reply.

"That was one time."

"Alex talked Charlotte into giving you another chance," I smirk. *Well, hell, maybe we do meddle in each other's business.*

"What the fuck, mate? You sound like my wife."

"Fiancée. And what's wrong with me? Why are they worried about me cocking it up?"

"They think you are a man whore," he whispers so his kids don't hear it. I want to protest, but Nick raises an eyebrow. I guess I deserve that.

"I... I really don't want to talk about it. It's between me and Olivia."

"So, there is something going on?" He leans over the counter, "Mate, give me something, anything, so I can get my wife off my back."

"Tell your fiancée—"

"Tell Charlotte to give me a call and I'll answer all her questions." We both look at Olivia who is standing next to the counter, her arms crossed over her chest and a smirk on her face. Her curls are tied up in a bun, but some have come loose and are framing her face. The tip of her nose is still red from the sunburn she got when we spent our lunchtime eating in the park yesterday. Since the evening with the guys, Olivia and I have spent hours talking about our life on the phone, went to the cinema last Sunday (but don't ask me what the film was about because we were snogging like teenagers), and have made it a habit of having lunch together.

"Are you ready for food?" she asks me. In her hand is a takeaway bag from the Cherry Pie Bakery.

"I am. Unless Nick has more questions for me." I smirk at him.

"Hey, don't give me shit, complain to my wife. If you'll excuse me, I need to take care of my class." He pushes himself off the counter. "And Olivia, do me a favour: don't make it too easy for him." He laughs before strolling over to the kids' area, where his class is still engrossed in the story.

I walk around the counter and press a soft kiss on Olivia's lips.

"Hi," I whisper and cup her face. I lean forward and...

"No snogging in the library," Helen says with a stern voice before laughing over her own joke.

"I am heading out for lu—"

"Before we go, can you get me set up on the audiobook app from the library you told me about?" Olivia stops me.

"Sure!" I grab a temporary library card, enter the details into the computer and activate it. "You'll need this one to register for the service."

"Cool, I already have the app on my phone." She hands me her phone and I help her get set up.

"What book do you want to download?"

"I'm not sure." She nervously nibbles on her lip.

"Oh, get *The Unnatural Habitat of a Cat Lady*. You'll love it," Helen chimes in. I vaguely recall her telling me about it from her book club. "Trust me, it's funny and steamy."

"Oh, what's it about?" Olivia asks.

"That would be telling. Just see it as a 'A date with a book' thingy, just that it's an audiobook rather than a paperback." I am not sure if I like the tone in Helen's voice. It is way too chipper, and I know that means she is up to something.

"Okay, why not. No risk, no fun, right?" Olivia laughs.

"Okay, cat lady coming up." I search the library app and find the relevant audiobook.

"Thanks. As a reward, I have an éclair for you." She gives me a big smile when I hand her phone back to her. My arm slides around her waist and I pull her closer.

"Kissing you is reward enough," I groan and press my lips to hers.

"No snogging in the library!" Helen shouts from behind the counter. Olivia giggles like a schoolgirl and pulls me to the exit.

Chapter 6

Olivia

"Mark my words, Amelia, you will be mine. I know I have hurt you in the past. I was a first-grade wanker back then. But I've changed. I will prove to you that I have changed, and I will show you that you're mine. And when you finally admit how wet your pussy gets just from hearing my voice—" I pull a wireless headphone from my left ear and listen into the silence. In my right ear I can still hear Ben telling Amelia just how he plans on fucking her. This book is hot, but I am in the stock room at work and I don't need a work colleague to hear what I'm listening to. I know I'm paranoid, but I keep checking to make sure nobody else can hear. I am about to put the bud back in when my boss Will walks around the corner. I reach for my phone and stop the audiobook.

"Hi, Will." I grin at him weirdly. I feel like I got caught stealing something when there is absolutely nothing wrong with me listening to the book. Will doesn't mind if we have music on when we work in the stock room, and it is not like he knows what I am listening to. The problem is, I know and that brings a blush to my cheeks.

"Just grabbing a box of these." Will holds out a shoe box before disappearing back onto the shop floor. I relax a little as soon as I see his bald head disappear through the door. I grab the tablet where I record the stock, but before starting to match the inventory with the stock sheet I pick up my phone to continue with the audiobook. I unlock the screen and notice a message blinking.

Rob

So, how's the book?

Me

Book is fine.

Well, the book is hot, the narrator is not.

Rob

Just fine?

Me

The male voice is a bit annoying.

Rob

What are you doing after work?

If you're not doing anything, why don't you come over and I'll read the male part.

Me

What?

Rob

We'll listen to the female narrator and then I'll read the male part. I don't have an annoying voice. Some would say I have a beautiful baritone.

My heart starts beating a little faster. The thought of spending some more time with Rob does make me feel giddy. *You are a grown woman. Get a grip!* But what if I don't want to get a grip?

Me

Sure, I'd love to. But just as a -warning, it is a dirty book.

Rob

How dirty?

Me

He's introducing her to sexual submission.

Rob

Fuck, and I'm alone at the library, otherwise I would leave now.

Me

I'll finish at five-thirty.

Rob

Come straight to mine!

I laugh and then I realise what he'll be reading to me. A shiver runs through me at the thought of the dirty talk he will be reading. Rob has just the right voice for Ben.

The last time he read to me was on the day before I left for Leeds. Famous Five, of course, even if we were almost too old for those books by then. *The Cat Lady* book couldn't be further away from the Famous Five. I giggle to myself as I grab my clipboard to continue the counting.

"God, I couldn't wait to see you." Rob gives me a big smile as I arrive at his cottage and pulls me in his arms. He is wearing cargo pants and a tight T-shirt, and if I thought he looked hot in his dress shirt, it was nothing to how he looks now. He looks push-me-against-the-wall-and-have-your-way-with-me hot.

"This is a cute cottage," I say as I place my jacket on one of the hooks on the wall. As I turn around, I catch Rob eyeing me from head to toe. His blue eyes go dark with lust, and it is an incredible feeling to see a man react to me like this. I know I'm not the perfect shape but I don't mind my curves and by the looks of it, neither does he.

"Rob? Cottage?" I try to pull him from his trance.

"Oh, yes, thanks. My parents helped me to buy it when they retired and sold their house They moved to Spain because my dad suffers from arthritis and the climate here wasn't helping. The money they got for their house stretched to getting them a property in Spain and giving me a start with the deposit for mine."

"I'm jealous that you have a place on your own. Living with my parents isn't easy, but finding a one-bedroom flat to rent in Fellside is impossible."

Rob leads me to the small kitchen at the back of the cottage.

"I know. Most empty properties are snapped up as holiday homes. Want a glass?" He holds up a bottle of white wine.

"Just a small one, please." He grabs two glasses from a shelf behind him. I have to say he is very tidy. Or maybe he just cleaned up before I came?

"So, tell me about the book so far. Where are you up to?"

"Oh, the story is so good." I stretch the word "so" to show my enthusiasm. "Amelia is this forty-something woman with this boring life. Work, sitting at home, hanging out with her cat. Occasionally she goes out with her friends. She hasn't been in a relationship in like forever. So, her work colleagues and friends keep teasing her that she is a typical cat lady. But right from the get-go as a reader you get a different picture of her because of her inner monologues She's this mature, boring person in public and a completely different person in private. She's hiding her real self from others."

Rob leads me to the sofa and we take a seat as I ramble on.

"But when you hear her inner thoughts, you know that there is a vulnerable, shy soul there looking for someone she can trust to be herself with. Enter Ben."

"The annoying voice," Rob interjects, and I have to laugh.

"Yup. Her friends set her up on a BDSM dating app as a joke. That's where she meets Ben. She thinks he is just trying to catfish her because..." I ramble on and on about the book. I recap every chapter I have completed so far. I am surprised by how much I remember having only listened to it once.

"And now they're at this wedding of mutual friends, and she's still fighting him." I finally finish and I notice a small grin on Rob's face.

"Why are you smiling?" I ask.

"Because you look beautiful when you're passionate about something. I mean, you are always beautiful, but just now you looked so happy and excited. It just took my breath away." Oh wow. I am pretty sure I'm blushing and my heart is hammering. I grab my glass of wine and take a sip because my throat is suddenly parched.

"Okay, so which chapter am I reading for you?" Rob asks. I grab my phone and check the contents. He opens his copy of the book on the right page and sits back. I lean my head against the back of the sofa. God, he looks so sexy with a book in his hands.

"Chapter seven. Benjamin." Rob's voice definitely is so much more fitting for Ben than the narrator in the audiobook.

"Why should I dance with you?" Amelia crosses her arms in front of her. If she only knew how sexy she looks when she fights me, especially because her eyes betray her. They show me that she still wants me.

"The way I see it, you have two options. Pretend you are here with me or the bride will set you up with Mister Bad Breath. It's your call, Darling."

I put my hands on her shoulder and turn her so she can see the bride approaching with that weird cousin of hers who had creeped Amelia out during dinner.

"Oh shit," Amelia whispers. "Fine, you win, one dance!"

We'll see. I grab her hand and drag her past the surprised-looking bride. When I pull Amelia in my arms, my cock thickens. She feels so good and so right. I close the distance between us and start to sway with her in my arms. My fingers slide over her curves and when I cup an arse cheek, a little moan escapes her lips.

"Do you like that, Darling?" She doesn't say anything. I squeeze a little harder. "Answer me."

"Yes," she breathes.

"Good girl. Tell me how wet you are."

"I am not—" I stop her with a rough kiss on her lips.

"Don't lie to me." I can see the conflict on her face. I know she wants to fight this because she is worried that people will

judge her. But she is equally excited by the prospect of testing out where this leads her.

"I don't know," she finally says and lowers her eyes to the floor. A beautiful pink is spreading on her cheeks. I grab her hand and drag her from the dance floor.

"Where are we going?" she asks in protest.

"In here." I push open a small door to a room that I assume the hotel uses for meetings. It's dark, but the streetlamps lining the driveway to the venue cast a little light into the room.

I press Amelia against the wood panelling and kiss her hard. My tongue is dipping into her mouth and she moans. Yes, it feels that good.

"Spread your legs," I demand.

"What?"

"You heard me, Darling. Spread. Your. Legs. Now." She hesitates for a second, but when she sees the fire in my eyes, she slowly parts her thighs.

I kneel down in front of her, and my hands slide up underneath her dress until they find her knickers. My fingers hook into the material on the left and the right and drag them downwards until they pool at her feet. I stand up again and lock eyes with her.

"Let's see, shall we?" I pull the hem of the bottom part of her dress up until her pussy is exposed. Slowly one of my

fingers glides over her cunt. It is immediately coated in her juices.

"So wet," I groan, and my fingers draw lazy circles around her clit before two of them enter her pussy. Amelia moans loudly and her hands grab my shoulders.

"Darling, put your hands against the wall."

"Ben, I—" She stops talking and moans again when a third finger enters her.

"I said, put your hands against the wall. You have one second, or I'll stop." A shiver races through her body, but she is finally my good girl and presses the palms of her hand against the wall on either side of her hips.

"Yes, Sir," she whispers. Fuck, that made my dick twitch.

"Now, listen to me." My fingers pump lazily in and out of her wet pussy. "You are not to come until I tell you to. Do you understand?"

Amelia whimpers but eventually replies, "Yes, Sir."

"This is my body to control," I growl, and my free hand tightens carefully around her throat. "Mine."

"Yours, Sir," she confirms. Her eyes are closed, and her mouth is open. Her breathing is getting faster. I keep moving my fingers in and out of her wetness but add a little extra pleasure by starting to circle her clit with my thumb.

"Fuck," Amelia hisses and her hand grabs my bicep. I withdraw my hand and take a step back. Amelia opens her eyes and looks at me bewildered.

"No, Amelia. I told you I would stop if you moved your hands."

"Please, Sir, I am sorry, Sir." It is amazing how quickly she slips into her submissive role. I undo my tie and slowly pull it from my neck.

"Let me help you, Darling."

I grab her wrists, one in each hand and pull them behind her back before wrapping my tie around it. I secure it all with a knot.

"Hmm, I like that look on you," I whisper and rub my nose up and down her neck, breathing in her delicate smell.

"Please, I need more."

Chapter 7

Rob

I shift in my seat. I can feel her eyes on me as I read.

"Well, that's hot," I chuckle. I look up from the book and her eyes lock with mine. My already hard cock gets even harder. She lowers her gaze to where my dick tents my trousers. And then she adds the killer strike; she bites her lower lip. *Fuck.* An electric current shoots down my spine. My eyes are laser-focused on her lips now.

"But who actually does that in real life?" Olivia asks, her voice sounding breathy.

"True. Most women I know would send me straight to the hospital or prison if I ever said stuff like that," I chuckle, although it comes out a bit forced. My whole body is wound tight, and my eyes haven't left Olivia's face.

"No guy has ever asked me how wet I am," she whispers, the blush on her cheek spreading like wildfire to the rest of her face.

"No?" I don't like thinking of her with other men.

"No. Have you ever done something like that?"

"Dominated someone?"

"Yeah." A nervous giggle escapes her.

"Well, no. But then again, I've never been in love," I admit, rubbing the back of my neck. Olivia sits up, leaning forward.

"What's love got to do with it?" she asks, phrasing it like a question but sounding more like a playful taunt.

"This dom-sub relationship is fuelled by more than just lust. It takes a whole lot of trust, and we know Amelia doesn't trust easily. Trust doesn't really come to play when you have one-night stands." I try to explain my statement.

"Maybe you're right. But if that's what sex is like when you're in love, then I can confidently say I've never been in love." She leans back on the sofa.

"Yep, same here," I reply. We fall into a momentary silence, both of us lost in thought and staring into the distance.

"But hey, it was hot though, wasn't it?" Olivia giggles, breaking the silence with a mischievous tone.

"Yeah." What more can I say? We both saw the physical reaction I had.

"Can you imagine me saying stuff like that?"

"Like what?" *Don't say it, don't say it.* I am not sure if I can keep my hands to myself if she starts talking dirty and we are supposed to be taking this slow.

"Sir, I am all yours," Olivia whispers and looks at me from under her eyelashes. *Well, shit.* My cock twitches and I have to hold onto the back of the sofa to not jump her. Olivia slides closer and plays with her curls.

"Sir knows that I would do anything for him. Anything," she tries to add some extra seduction to the last word. There is silence and then Olivia breaks out in laughter. I try to relax my body and a deep chuckle escapes me.

"Ridiculous, right?" she says and pushes a strand of hair behind her ear. Her eyes are still locked on mine, and they are looking at me cautiously.

"Sounded rather sexy to me," I finally say.

I am not sure who moves first, but I hear the distant thud of the book hitting the carpet as our lips meet. I pull her into my lap, and she willingly straddles me. I gently grab her neck and pull her closer, allowing me to deepen the kiss. When my tongue takes its first lick of her warm mouth, I feel like I want to die. She tastes like heaven. I stroke her tongue with mine and she presses her pussy harder against my dick. She starts to grind against me, her hands cupping my face and her tongue exploring my mouth.

I grab hold of her arse cheeks and flip us over so she is lying on the sofa and I hover above her.

"Now is the time to stop me if you don't want this, Olivia." I have to give her the option to say no.

"I want this... Sir." *Oh fuck.* This time she sounds sincere. All humour is gone.

My lips take another hard kiss from her before moving along her neck down to her collarbone. She is rubbing her pussy against me, and we are basically dry-humping like teenagers.

I slide my fingers under her top and over her smooth skin.

"Rob, don't hold back," she whispers in my ear and then places little kisses on my neck.

My hand under her T-shirt slides up and cups her left tit. I can feel her stiff nipple under the lacy material and groan.

"Take your shirt off," I demand and lean back to pull my own over my head.

"Oh, fuck you are chiselled," Olivia says and pulls the shirt back down over her abdomen.

"Why are you covering up?"

"I don't have any of these," she pokes at my abs.

"Thank god," I murmur and pull her shirt over her head.

"Rob, I—" I don't let her finish whatever she wanted to say.

"You are stunningly beautiful," I reassure her before bending forward and sucking one of her nipples into my mouth. Her hands slide into my hair and grab on. For a moment I fear she is planning to pull me off her, but she isn't. She is actually pressing me to her.

"Olivia, your bra. It needs to come off." My fingers slide under her and try to unhook it, but Olivia is quicker. She lifts her shoulders from the sofa, opens the hooks on the back of her bra and slides the straps down her arms before throwing it on the floor.

I lock eyes with her whilst taking a lick of her right nipple. The moan she gives me is reward enough.

"More. Rob, I need more."

"You asked for it."

I gently bite her other nipple before kissing my way downwards. When I get to the waistband of her jeans, I let my tongue slide under it whilst unzipping the trousers. I press soft kisses at every centimetre of skin I uncover.

Olivia keeps stroking through my hair and the tender gesture is driving me crazy.

When she finally lies naked in front of me I take a break and just look at her. Self-consciously, she puts her arms over her soft belly. I grab her wrists and pin her arms next to her.

"Don't hide from me. You are so beautiful." She is soft and curvy and gorgeous. That's all I can say. I lower my head and gently push her legs apart. I can smell her arousal and my dick jumps at the thought of sinking into her. I have a ringing in my ears and can't remember the last time a woman had such an impact on me.

"Rob, your phone," Olivia moans. *Oh, shit*, so it wasn't a ringing in my ears. I reach for it on the coffee table and I am about to switch it off when I see it is the FMR emergency line calling.

"Fuck, sorry, Olivia, it's FMR. I have to take that."

"Oh, okay." She sits up and grabs her T-shirt. I frown because I don't want this to be over but my phone rings relentlessly in my hand.

"Hello," I answer the phone.

"Rob, you didn't confirm the call out. Are you coming?" Jonathan, who mans the emergency call line, replies. *Mate, I was close to coming*.

"Sorry, I didn't see the text. What's the mission?"

"Teenager fell on Langdon Pike and broke his leg and arm. The helicopter can't get to him because of the high winds, so your unit is going up to medevac him."

"Oh, okay, where's the meeting point?"

"Nook farm. Fifteen minutes." The farm is not far from me, so I should still make it.

"I'll be there," I confirm. Jonathan hangs up and I turn to Olivia. She is fully dressed again and disappointment is written on her face.

"I am so sorry about this, but I have to go."

"That's fine. No problem." She smiles but it doesn't reach her eyes. *I know, I fucking hate this too!*

"Let me make it up to you. Tomorrow I'm babysitting Max, Chris and Suzie's son. Come and spend the afternoon with us and after he gets picked up, I'll make us some dinner and we can continue where today ended." I give her my best puppy-eye look. She giggles.

"Fine." She grabs her phone from the table, "But now I'll leave you so you can get ready."

"Rob, be careful," she says when I open the door for her. Then she places a tender kiss on my lips. My arms slide around her hips and I push my tongue into her mouth. I am about to press her against the wall when she breaks our lip lock.

"Your rescue?"

"Sure, yes. Fuck. Tomorrow. I'll text you!" I stutter and my voice sounds like I'm in pain. Olivia gives me a last smile before walking off.

I hurry upstairs to get changed into my outdoor clothes. I usually love being a mountain rescuer, but today I hate it.

Chapter 8

Olivia

There is nothing tender in Rob's kiss, just pure passion.

"Rob, the doorbell." He seems to lose his connection to reality whenever he kisses me. I laugh when he swears and walks to the front door of the cottage. I return to my tote bag lying on the kitchen counter. Rob had unceremoniously dropped it there when I arrived at his house, before pinning me against the fridge to give me a "welcome kiss."

True to his word, he texted me yesterday after his mission, and what started off as harmless flirting very quickly escalated into phone sex. I can't say I have ever had an orgasm on the phone before yesterday. My cheeks start to heat up at the thought of it.

On the call, he also asked me again to come over this afternoon and of course, I said yes. I don't even mind that we will be babysitting as long as I can spend some time with Rob. And, to be honest, I am looking forward to meeting Max. I've heard some hilarious stories about the mischief he has got himself into and he sounds adorable.

"Uncle Rob, I brought Superman," I hear from behind me. Max strolls into the kitchen, followed by Chris and Rob. When the little boy sees me, he stops and just stares at me.

"Of course you did," Rob chuckles. "Max, this is my friend Olivia. She's going to play with us this afternoon if that's okay." The little boy assesses me with his big blue eyes. I give him a smile.

"Okay," he finally says before climbing on a stool next to the breakfast bar. Chris positions himself protectively behind Max. I am not sure if he's aware that he is doing it, but he clearly has some very strong fatherly instincts.

"Right, we should be back by five. And no pranks, Rob, I warn you." He points at his friend, who raises his hands in the air.

"Hey, I don't know what you mean."

"Sure you do. He tried to copy your salt and sugar trick, but unfortunately, he exchanged the sugar with washing powder," Chris says. He tries to sound firm, but there is a twinkle in his eyes.

Rob laughs and so do I when I see the innocent look on Max's face, pretending he doesn't know what the guys are talking about.

"Fine, I promise: no more pranks until he is old enough to copy them properly," Rob declares with a smirk. Chris shakes his head. I am sure that's not the answer he was hoping for. Then he leans down to Max.

"Hey, mate, I'm heading out. Be a good boy for Rob. And when I get back tonight, we'll make pizza."

"Yes, pizza!" Max cheers before holding out his little fist. Chris bumps it with his and ruffles Max's blond hair before saying his goodbyes to us and leaving the kitchen.

"Right, what shall we do first?" Rob asks, clapping his hands together with enthusiasm.

"Miss, do you know how to make chocolate chip cookies?" Max addresses me, his eyes are wide with curiosity. I lean forward, bringing myself to his eye level.

"Sadly, no. But I do know how to make an amazing chocolate cake," I reply cheerfully to sell him on my idea.

"Mummy says I can only eat cake on special days," Max says, his face scrunching up with concentration, as if he is trying to come up with a masterplan. "But I almost never visit Uncle Rob, so that makes today a special day, right?" That cheeky little monkey knows how to work his way around the rules.

"I guess so, squirt," Rob laughs, clearly amused by Max's logic.

"But are you sure Chris and Suzie won't mind?" I ask Rob cautiously, a hint of concern in my voice.

"Nah, they know that when they leave him with one of us, we spoil him rotten. So don't worry about it," Rob reassures me with a casual wave of his hand.

"Alright then, Mister Max, are you ready to embark on a grand baking adventure with me?" I say and wink at him.

"Well, he is a little whirlwind," I laugh when Rob drops the last of the plates into the dishwasher. Max kept Rob and me busy all afternoon. We made cake, we built a fort, we painted, we built another fort because the first one was not big enough. Rob's living room looks like a war zone.

"I know. He's a handful, but we're all just glad that the kidnap didn't do more harm to him."

"I heard about it when I came back to Fellside. Were you there?"

"Me and Chris chased the guy and saw when the car spun off the road. Max still has nightmares and I'm sure Suzie and Chris do too. They are all getting help from a therapist, though".

I pass over some cutlery for Rob to add to the dishwasher and lean against the counter.

"It must be tough."

"It is and it isn't." Rob closes the appliance and wipes down the counter with a tea towel. "They found each other in the process and believe me, they are the best advertisement for family life. I haven't seen Chris this happy and content in years."

Rob moves closer to me, stepping purposefully. His body aligns with mine, and I sense a gentle pressure as he leans me against the counter. He plants gentle kisses along the curve of my neck, his warm breath giving me shivers. He nuzzles against the sensitive spot beneath my ear, setting off a delightful tingle that dances across my skin.

"I think you and I have some unfinished business," he whispers in my ear whilst his hands stroke gently up and down on either side of my ribcage.

"Is that so?" I fake ignorance, but when he nibbles on my earlobe, I can't stop a moan from escaping.

Rob grabs my hips and lifts me onto the counter. He pushes my thighs apart and steps between them before devouring my mouth with deep sweeping strokes of his tongue. He takes his time kissing me before breaking away.

"I couldn't sleep last night after our phone call. All I could think about was the sounds you made when you came." His voice is husky.

"Rob—" I try to interrupt him, but when he grips my thighs and pulls me to the edge of the counter so he can rub his hard length against my core, I forget what I want to say.

"Olivia, please tell me you want this as well." *Oh my god, how can he doubt it?* I force my eyes open and gently push on his chest so he takes a few steps back. I giggle when I see the panic and disappointment in his eyes. I jump off the counter and kneel down in front of him, and the simple move turns the look of disappointment into pure lust. I let my fingertips skate over the very obvious bulge in his trousers. He groans. His eyes grow dark as I unbuckle his belt and slowly pull the zip open.

"Let me show you how much I want this," I say in my most seductive voice before pulling his trousers and boxer shorts down in one swift movement.

"Olivia." It sounds like a warning, but his fingers softly stroking through my hair tell me he doesn't mean it. I wrap my lips around his hard cock and suck the tip into my mouth. I circle it with my tongue whilst sliding my hand up and down his shaft. His breathing is ragged, and the fingers in my hair hold on tightly.

I look up at him, and when we lock eyes, I take him deeper into my mouth. So deep that his tip touches the back of my throat.

"Fuck," Rob swears and I can feel his dick twitch inside me. With my eyes still on his, I slowly withdraw before sucking him back in.

"Olivia," he growls. I don't want to stop. I explore the entire length of his shaft with my mouth. I can taste the saltiness of the pre-cum on my tongue.

"Olivia!" Rob gives me a final warning and steps back. His cock pops from my mouth with an audible noise. Rob pulls me to my feet, lifts me up and plops me onto the island in the centre of the kitchen.

"Be careful, the cake," I laugh. Without much care, Rob pushes the plate of chocolate cake that we baked to the side.

"Who needs cake when you can have this," he mumbles before kissing me hard. I feel his fingers on my zip. "Lift," he asks me to raise my bum. I hold onto his shoulders before raising my arse so he can pull my trousers and underwear down. We are both still wearing our T-shirts but are completely naked on the bottom.

"My turn," Rob demands before grabbing my knees and pulling me to the edge of the kitchen island., He latches on to my pussy like a starving man. My head falls back and a deep moan echoes through the kitchen. I think I am in heaven.

Chapter 9

Rob

Her taste explodes in my mouth when I take the first lick of her pussy.

I should really take her to the bedroom, but I don't want to stop and I don't think she wants me to either.

"You taste so good," I mumble before moving my tongue up and down her slit again.

"Rob, I need to come. Please!" She begs. Her hand lands on the back of my head and she tries to pull me closer.

I work my tongue in and out of her channel and she wriggles under me. My cock is painfully hard by now, but he will have to wait his turn.

I kiss my way to her swollen clit. As my tongue circles the little nub, she calls out my name.

I start gently and increase the pressure until I hit her sweet spot. I have her right on the edge. She arches her back.

"More" she whispers. So, I give her more. I push two fingers into her wet pussy and she cries out. I slide them in and out a few times before curling them up and rubbing with pressure over her most sensitive spot.

That's all it takes.

"Fuck, I'm, I'm—" She doesn't finish her sentence. Instead, she moans so loud it almost becomes a scream.

I take a few final licks before letting her rest for a moment.

I grab my wallet from the kitchen counter and pull out my emergency condom. Always be prepared.

"That was—" She is lost for words again.

"We are not done, baby," I say as I return to the island. She is lying there still trying to catch her breath with her legs dangling from the counter. I pull my T-shirt off and she does the same to hers. Then I position myself between her thighs and she locks them around my hips.

She reaches out, places her hands on my neck to pull me down. Our lips melt together, and we get lost in a kiss for a while.

"I think I'm ready for him," Olivia giggles impatiently and gently grabs my cock to guide me to her.

I align myself and push into her in one deep stroke. We both groan in pleasure. No woman has ever felt so good and so right.

I hold still for a moment and just look at her. Her eyes are closed and her mouth is slightly ajar. Her curls frame her beautiful face and her cheeks are flushed. I could look at her for hours. This is how I would like to spend eternity, physically and emotionally connected with the most amazing person in the world.

She opens her eyes and frowns.

"What's wrong?" she asks.

"You are so amazing. " We gaze into each other's souls and so much more is said in this moment than the words we whisper.

"Rob—" Eventually she pulls me to her into another searing kiss. The minute our lips connect, I start pumping into her. Every stroke feels so good that I have to bring up every ounce of self-control to make sure this is not over before it has even properly started.

"Look at me, Olivia," I demand. When our eyes are locked, I pin her hands above her head and speed up my thrusts. Every time I sink into her, I want to groan because it feels so good and so right.

Lost in her eyes I move faster, every stroke pushing me closer to my release. And just when I think I have enough control to hold on a little longer, she squeezes my dick with her pussy as another orgasm hits her.

"Olivia," I call out her name before I explode, my eyes never leaving her. I have never felt something so intense. I lean my forehead against hers and she cups my cheek, stroking softly with her thumb over my stubbles. I take deep breaths in silence for a moment, feeling her chest move up and down against mine, both of us trying to calm our breathing.

"Stay with me for the weekend." It is not really a question, more a demand. I just don't want to let her go yet. I need her close to me. It is an overwhelming need that I have never experienced before.

"Okay," she simply whispers and presses a soft kiss to my lips. "But I have a family dinner tomorrow evening." Well, that would give me at least twenty-four hours. It doesn't sound nearly long enough, but I'll take it. Or, if I am sneaky, I might get more.

"What if I come with you to your dinner and then we come back here." I place a last kiss on her lips and then step back to remove the condom. Olivia jumps off the kitchen island, grabs my T-shirt from the floor and pulls it over her head. *Fuck, I like her in my clothes.*

"You want to come and meet my parents?" There is doubt in her voice. She grabs a piece of kitchen roll and a spray bottle with cleaning solution I keep next to the sink and sprays the kitchen island, where a very obvious wet patch shows just how much she also enjoyed what just happened. I put my boxer shorts back on.

"Why not?" I slide an arm around her waist and press small kisses on to the side of her neck. She leans back against me and turns her head to look at me.

"Rob, we have been friends for a few days, and whatever this is," she points between her and me, "it is not at the stage of meeting the parents."

"We were pretending to be friends but we were much more from the minute you walked into the library." I slide her hair over one shoulder and start kissing her exposed neck. "I am crazy about you and I would like to know everything about you. That includes meeting your family. Besides, they already know me."

"As my school friend. Not as my... whatever this is."

"Well, they liked me as your school friend. They will like me as your boyfriend," I clarify and I have to admit, I like the sound of it. Now I get why the other guys keep throwing the words wife and fiancée around. I like declaring to the world that she is mine.

She drops the cleaning material on the kitchen island and turns in my arms to face me.

"So, what, you want me to meet your parents as well?" She still looks unsure if I am for real.

"Well, again, they already know you and they live in Spain, but you can join one of our video calls if you want." I mean what I say. For the first time ever, I want the world to know that this woman is mine. She looks surprised.

"Okay, you can come for dinner," she finally says.

"Okay," I repeat and smile before throwing her over my shoulder and carrying her towards my bedroom.

"Let me down, you caveman," she laughs.

"Nope! I only have twenty-four hours before we have to leave for your parents. And I need to make the most of it."

"Twenty-three hours," she replies in between laughter.

"Fuck," I chuckle and start running towards my bedroom.

"Come in, come in," Olivia's mum ushers us into the living room. Olivia may have inherited her eye colour from her mum, but definitely not her height, as Mrs Hunter is at least four inches shorter than Olivia.

"Rob, I'm sure you remember my husband, Jeff" she introduces me with excitement in her voice. The tall man in his late sixties rises from the sofa chair in the corner of the room and shakes my hand.

"It's nice to meet you again, Mister and Mrs Hunter" I say politely. Honestly, while I remember everything about Olivia, I can barely picture her parents from our school days, despite hanging out at each others houses all the time.

Olivia, who's holding my other hand, softly squeezes it. I'm not sure if this is to comfort me or herself.

"Please, call me Jim, and my wife is Paula," her dad says with a friendly smile. Not sure if he'd still be smiling if he knew that I've been shagging his daughter in every room of my house over the last two days. I smile politely.

"And this is my brother, Liam," Olivia points towards a guy who's now getting up from the sofa.

I've seen Liam around. I think he once beat Nick and Chris in a mountain race.

"Hey," I shake his outstretched hand.

"So, you're the one who's taken on our Pippi," Liam chuckles.

"Liam," Olivia's voice carries a warning, but her dad and mum chuckle. What did I miss?

"Let's eat," Olivia drags me towards the dining table.

"Pippi?" I ask, curious.

"Forget it," she whispers.

"A nickname she earned when we were younger. She was as bad with reading as Pippi Longstocking. It stuck, and let's face it, she's still a bit like Pippi," Liam playfully tugs at one of Olivia's locks before settling into a chair at the dining table. I vaguely recall hearing her being called that, but I don't think she ever explained why she had that nickname. Olivia releases her grip on my hand and takes a seat. Her cheeks are flushed, and she stares down at the table.

Chapter 10

Rob

I grab a bread roll from the basket Paula holds out to me.

"So, Rob, where do you work? I remember you were a bright boy in school. I always wondered why you were hanging out with our Olivia," Jim chuckles before taking a hearty bite from his own bread roll.

"I work at the Fellside Library," I say. My voice sounds odd and I think it is the anger that is slowly creeping up on me. When I say the word library, Liam laughs out loud.

"Isn't that a bit of a girly job?" he asks before adding some gravy to his plate.

"Liam," Olivia hisses at the same time as I stop cutting my meat and look at him. I am not sure if he is just clueless or a bit of a dick.

"Lucky for me, knowledge in literature is more important for the job than the pencil skirt and glasses you may have seen in porn," I retort and put a piece of meat in my mouth. I am not sure who gasps louder, Olivia or her mum. Olivia slaps me softly under the table, but I can see her also biting back a smile. Liam's ears turn red and I know I got to him.

"So, where did you go to university?" Paula asks, pretending I never dropped the P bomb.

"Manchester. It meant I could come home every weekend and hang out with my friends."

"Oh, I heard good things about Manchester."

"Or as Pippi would say, so she remembers how to spell it Man, chest, ergh," Liam laughs and Jim joins in. Olivia is bright red and I can see tears in her eyes. She is putting a big piece of broccoli in her mouth, almost as if she wants to stop herself from saying something.

"Don't you two," Paula tells the two laughing hyenas off, but there is no sincerity behind it, especially when she giggles herself. I am stunned. My parents would go through fire for me. No way would they ever take the mickey, let alone hurt me this way. Liam and Jim start talking about football, so I use the opportunity and turn to Olivia.

"Why do you let them talk to you like this?"

"Like what? They're just joking, Rob," she tries to smile, but it doesn't reach her eyes.

"None of these comments are funny."

"That's what families do. They tease each other."

"Mine doesn't."

"Well, mine does. Let it go! Please?" she hisses and then carries on eating. The rest of the meal is uncomfortable to say the least. Her parents are overly friendly with me, but the constant digs at Olivia are setting me on edge.

"Rob, maybe you can convince Olivia to read more since you're so into books. If she weren't so lazy and practised more, she could achieve so much more in life than being just a shop assistant," Jim remarks in between bites.

I take a deep breath, setting the dessert spoon down before rising from my chair. Suddenly, all eyes are on me, a tense silence enveloping the room.

"I'm sorry, but I can't take it any longer," I say, my outward demeanour calm but my tone laced with a dangerous edge. I place my napkin on the table. Olivia is shaking her head, silently pleading for me to stop, but I am furious and I won't sit by and listen to more of this.

"Olivia is an amazing person, and your belittling of her is absolutely debilitating. You may think you're just joking, but in reality, you're nothing but a bunch of bullies. Thank you for the meal, but I can't sit here and pretend that everything is hunky-dory when you treat her like this. You are her parents, and I..." I pause, catching myself before I say something that Olivia may never forgive me for.

"Olivia, I'll call you later," I add. I turn on my heels and leave the table, swiftly grabbing my jacket from beside the entrance as I make my way out the door.

My heart pounds rapidly, and anger courses through my veins. I'm so furious I can barely breathe.

"Rob," Olivia calls out behind me. I stop and wait for her to catch up before facing her.

"What was that?" she asks with annoyance in her voice and the fact that she has a go at me rather than the people who spent the evening hurting her fuels my fury.

"I'm sorry, but I can't sit there and pretend they're not hurting you. I can't," I shout.

"They are my family and they just want what's best for me. It is not their fault that I'm stupid." Her voice sounds shaky. I stare at her. *Is she for real?*

"Olivia, you. Are. Not. Stupid. But they are the reason that you think you are. I love you. This is really not how I wanted to tell you that I love you, but well, here we are.

I love you. I am crazy about you. And it kills me that you can't see what bullies they are."

"They're my family," she whispers, her voice filled with anguish.

"And I am the man who loves you. I'll do anything for you, but the one thing I can't do is sit by and watch others tear you down," I respond, my words resolute. We lock eyes, and a single tear escapes down her cheek.

"Are you breaking up with me?" she asks, her voice trembling.

"No," I say softly, gently pulling her into my arms. "But please, talk to your parents and let them know how they make you feel."

"But it will hurt them," she sniffles, her voice filled with worry.

"They've been hurting you for years. Promise me." I insist, my voice firm.

"What if I can't?" she asks, her voice sounding fragile. *What if she can't?* Can I simply stand by and watch them continue to hurt her like this?

"I don't know, Olivia," I finally admit, the weight of uncertainty heavy in my words. I hold her closer, pressing a kiss to her lips, and at that moment, I wonder if it could be our last. My heart breaks a little, but eventually, I step back and say, "Think about it and let me know." With a heavy heart, I turn and walk away, leaving the decision in her hands.

I pull my helmet on and close the chin strap to secure it in place. The head torch fixed to it lights up Alex's face.

"Mate, maybe don't shine it right into my eyes," he complains and holds up his hand as a shield from the bright light.

I was almost home when I received a text from FMR. Two climbers were missing on the north wall of the Pin Needle, a notorious climbing route. The helicopter has located them, thanks to thermal imaging, about halfway up the wall. But now we need to climb up and see what's going on.

I fix the belay device to my harness so I can belay Nick, who will be leading the first part of the climb. Alex and Suzie have teamed up as well and will climb to the left of us, with the plan that each group will eventually provide support to one of the climbers. Phil and Chris will prepare everything at the foot of the wall for the final transport and Tommy, as leader, will coordinate. We have practised this kind of rescue dozens of times.

I look up at the rock face and there is no light. Either the climbers are not conscious or they were unprepared and didn't bring headlamps with them. I return my focus to the rope and set up the belay.

I'm still feeling anger from earlier and there is another feeling. The whole way over here, I was wondering what that feeling was. Panic. Yes, that's what it is. Sheer panic that I'll lose her over this. *I can't lose Olivia over this.*

"Rob!" Nick shouts and I look at him in surprise. Everyone is staring at me. "I asked you to check my knots." It is a routine safety move to check each other's knots on the harness and the belay device.

"Sorry," I mumble and step up to him. I shine my light on this harness and confirm he is good. He does the same for me.

"Right, everyone, focus. It should take you about forty-five minutes to get to them. When you get closer, try to make contact and report back." Tommy gives us our last instructions before sending us off.

"On belay?" Nick waits for me to confirm that I am ready.

"Belay on," I confirm and he steps up to the rock face. I see Alex do the same thing about ten meters to the left of us. Suzie is belaying him. We have all gone quiet and the only noises I can hear are the scrapping of the climbing shoes on the rock and the occasional grunt from the climbers when they have to use some extra force.

It takes Nick about twenty minutes to climb to the end of the rope. He sets an anchor and I follow him. It is always easier for the person climbing second as the rope has already been secured by the lead climber, meaning any drop will be minimal. If you lead and you lose your grip, you will fall into the rope until the last safety you have set catches you. This can be quite a distance.

I step up on the ledge next to Nick whilst he coils up the rope.

"Rob, what the fuck is wrong with you today?" Nick says whilst preparing the rope for the next pitch.

"What do you mean?"

"I had to call for rope four times. You weren't paying attention."

"I was—"

"No, you weren't; otherwise, I wouldn't have been hanging from my fingertips for ages until you released some rope." I know he is exaggerating. He is an excellent climber and he knows how to make sure he has a good stand.

"Let's not talk about it. I'll lead," I indicate that I will take over the lead. We usually rotate the leading and so the next pitch is mine.

"On belay?"

"Belay on. And concentrate," Nick warns me. I don't reply. I'm fine. I've been a volunteer for over five years. I know how to run a mission. I don't need Nick to tell me how to do my job.

After a ten-minute climb, I hear a faint voice to the left of me.

"Hello?" I shout.

"Hello, we're here," a male voice calls back. He sounds alert but weak.

"I am from mountain rescue; we'll get to you as soon as we can!" I find a secure spot to stand and add a safety device before pressing the buttons on the radio attached to my backpack's shoulder strap. I report the location of the climbers before scrambling up to them.

Suzie reaches the two men at almost the same time as me. They are sitting on a small ledge and seem to be both injured. One is holding his arm at a weird angle.

"Right, let's get you looked at," I say to them in my calmest voice. I lean back, expecting the rope I have fixed to an anchor point on the wall to hold me secure, only that familiar feeling of the rope tightening on the anchor doesn't come.

Instead, Suzie's scream echoes around me: "Rob, you are not—"

I don't hear the rest because I fall backwards into the dark void. It's like I'm floating in nothingness. No gravity, just me drifting down through the empty space. It feels like time stretches out, making the fall seem like it lasts for ages. It's a weird sensation, being lost in the darkness like that. I seem to be in free-fall forever, but just as panic starts creeping in, the rope yanks tight and snaps me back to reality. My body turns and I start swinging, upside down, towards the rock face. *Oh, shit!*

"Rob, Rob, can you hear me?" Alex's calm voice is somehow invading my dream. Everything is dark. I have no clue what is going on. I—

"I think he is regaining consciousness," Chris says in the distance. Something tight is wrapped around my wrist.

"I told him to fucking concentrate," Nick shouts.

"Now is not the time, Nick. We need to get him down," Alex's voice fades and I suddenly feel searing pain on my left side. I scream. Well, I think I scream. I'm not sure about anything except that I need to see Olivia.

Chapter 11

Olivia

I watch as Rob disappears into the darkness, tears streaming down my face. Feeling lost and not knowing what to do next, I wipe them off my cheeks and head back to the house. I close the front door and lean against it for support.

Out of nowhere, my Dad's voice breaks the silence, calling me into the dining room. With a heavy heart, I go in and take a seat, dreading what he might say.

"Olivia, I'm really sorry. We... I didn't mean any harm" he says, sounding down and sad. Hearing him like that surprises me.

"It's alright, Dad," I mumble, but in my head, I hear Rob's voice yelling at me to tell them the truth.

"But you always laughed along when we made those jokes," my Mum says, kind of trying to justify their actions, her hands clasped together, full of regret.

"Mum, please don't be upset. That's why I didn't want Rob to say anything," I plead, trying to spare them from feeling guilty.

"No, I'm glad he did. I'm really sorry," my Mum says, getting up from her chair and coming over to me. She pulls me into a tight hug, shaking with sobs.

"It wasn't that bad," I whisper, trying to reassure her. But she keeps insisting.

"Olivia, stop. You don't have to protect us. We should have protected you. I'm sorry," she says again, her words filled with remorse. Then she looks at Liam and my dad.

"I'm sorry too," Liam mumbles softly, his voice filled with regret. Was it really that simple? Did it take an outsider to make them see the truth?

"Olivia," Dad meets my eyes. "I'm proud of you, proud of everything you've done," he says, his voice thick with emotion. He's never really acknowledged my achievements before. I mouth a thank you and smile at him.

"Okay, this is getting a bit like a soap opera. Can we just go back to dinner?" Liam interrupts, trying to lighten the mood. But I can see the genuine sadness in his eyes, his regret for hurting me.

"Olivia, you should call Rob," my mum insists. It stings to hear his name. I grab my phone from the table and find his number. With trembling hands, I dial it and hold the phone to my ear as I walk into the living room. It rings a few times and goes to voicemail.

"Rob, it's me. We need to talk. Please call me," I say, my voice shaking with uncertainty. What if he's changed his mind? What if he doesn't want to deal with all this drama? He said he loved me, and I couldn't say it back. I put my phone in my back pocket and return to the dining room, even though I don't feel like eating anymore.

I've been staring at a photo on my phone for what feels like an eternity. It's one of those moments Rob captured of us in his bed not even twenty-four hours ago, all cuddled up, beaming at the camera. I love that picture; it holds so much happiness.

The TV blares some talk show in the background, but no one is really paying attention. Liam's busy playing a game on his phone, and Mum and Dad are discussing their upcoming vacation. Meanwhile, I've tried calling Rob a couple more times, but still no response. Doubts creep in, and I can't help but wonder if he's ghosting me.

Just as I start to lose hope, my phone suddenly rings, and I see Charlotte's name on the screen. I answer, attempting to sound cheerful. She doesn't need to know that I am anything but.

"Hey, Charlotte," I say, forcing a bright tone.

"Hey, Olivia." There's something off in her voice, a hint of concern.

"Are you okay?" I ask, feeling a knot form in the pit of my stomach.

"Olivia, where are you?" she asks urgently.

"At my parent's house," I reply, my breath quickening. I glance at my dad, and the worry must be evident on my face because he sits up straighter.

"Olivia, I need you to listen. There's been an accident. The guys were on a mission, and Rob... he fell," she says; the words hit me like a punch in the gut. *No, no, no.* "But he's alive," she quickly adds.

He's alive. Relief floods over me, and I struggle to catch my breath.

"He's in the hospital. They took him to Windermere," she continues. Fellside is too small for a hospital, and Windermere has the nearest one.

"Charlotte, how is he?" I ask, my voice trembling with worry.

"I don't know, Olivia. Honestly, I don't know. The guys didn't have all the details when they called me. They're all in Windermere with him," she replies.

"I need to go to him. I need to see him," I blurt out, jumping up from the sofa.

"Olivia, you can't drive yourself," Charlotte warns. I'm about to hang up on her, but Liam grabs the phone from my hand.

"Hi, this is Liam, Olivia's brother. What's happened?" he says, taking charge of the conversation.

I need to get to Rob. I feel utterly lost, my mind is blank as I stare into nothingness. Overwhelming panic starts to consume me, and my thoughts race like a speeding train, one horrible scenario after another playing out in my mind. I don't know where to begin, and the confusion immobilises me. Time seems to blur, and I'm unsure how long I remain rooted to the spot until Liam's voice breaks through, calling my name and snapping me back to reality.

"Olivia, I'll take you to him. We'll pick up Charlotte on the way," he says, gripping my shoulders as if he wants to shake me back to my senses.

"Okay," I manage to respond, my voice barely audible. I let Liam lead me to the car, and he straps me in. I feel like a zombie, disconnected from everything around me. There's only one thought repeating in my mind—I have to see him. I have to see him.

I've lost all sense of time. I don't even remember when Charlotte joined us, but now she walks beside me as we make our way down the desolate hospital corridor.

The nurse points us towards a small waiting room, and as we enter, we're greeted by the sight of six exhausted mountain rescuers. They all look pale and worn out. Suzie is curled up in Chris's arms, tears staining her face. Alex, Phil, and Tommy stand near the vending machine while Nick sits on a chair, his head buried in his hands.

"Where is he?" My anxious-sounding voice echoes through the room.

"The doctors are still running tests. He'll be alright," Tommy tries to reassure me, his voice shaky.

"You don't know that," Nick interjects angrily. Charlotte moves to sit beside him, speaking softly, but he doesn't respond.

"We do know. We've seen climbers after accidents before. You can tell when someone won't make it," Tommy says, his words an attempt to reassure us, but we all know it's not that simple.

"What happened?" I barely whisper the question, but the silence in the room makes it audible to everyone.

"We went to rescue two injured climbers. When we reached the spot where they were stranded on the rock face, Rob failed to secure himself to an anchor point, thinking he had. He leaned back, believing he was safe," Alex says, his voice filled with a mixture of sadness and fear.

"I tried to warn him," Suzie says through tears. Chris pulls her closer, placing a gentle kiss on her forehead.

"I warned him to concentrate," Nick yells, his hands frantically running through his hair.

"Nick—" Charlotte attempts to calm him, but he avoids her touch, pacing the room in frustration.

"It's my fault. I shouldn't have let him take the lead. I could see he wasn't focused," Nick admits, genuine pain etched on his face. Charlotte persists in comforting him, and this time, he allows himself to lean into her, his face resting against her shoulder.

"It's my fault," I speak up, my voice stronger than I expected. All eyes turn to me. "Rob and I had an argument earlier tonight. Well, not a direct argument, but... it's complicated. In any case, it's my fault," I confess, tears streaming down my face. I sink into one of the chairs and let them flow. I don't have the energy to fight the sadness. I feel lost and helpless. Since he walked away from me, my mind has been consumed by thoughts of him and the scene at dinner. And he probably was the same. How could he not have been distracted? Liam sits down beside me, gently stroking my back, offering a soothing touch like you would to calm a child.

"It's nobody's fault," Tommy asserts loudly. "It was a freak accident. They don't happen often, but they do happen... Nick, your quick reaction prevented him from falling even further. You did your job." Nick doesn't respond, and I'm not even sure if he heard Tommy's words.

"Olivia," Tommy steps in front of me and Liam, his voice filled with conviction. "Listen to me. Life is always throwing things our way. But during missions, we've learned to put everything else aside. I don't know what happened up there or why it happened, but you can't blame yourself for this!".

I nod, though deep down I'm not entirely convinced. I lean forward, my gaze fixed on the floor. Someone hands me a cold bottle of water, and I absent-mindedly roll it between my hands. My mind feels empty except for one thought—I need to see him.

Chapter 12

Rob

I try to get comfortable in the hospital bed, though I am not sure how. My left leg is propped up and feels heavy with the cast on. I look down at my bruised body. I am the luckiest bastard on the planet.

"Rob!" Olivia's voice makes me feel better immediately. I look up and she is standing at the door with Nick, who has his hand on her back.

"Mate, I lie here suffering in silence, and you are making a move for my woman?" I chuckle, but the laugh dies on my lips when I see the look on their faces. *Okay, maybe this is not the right time to joke.*

"Rob," Olivia whispers again and then runs to my bed, cradles my face and presses her soft lips to mine. Something is hurting, but I can't pinpoint what.

"Carefully, baby, I just kissed a rock face. I might be a bit sore for a while. No wild make-out sessions," I try to lighten the mood again. Nothing. "Babe, I'm okay," I finally say seriously. I wipe a tear from her face.

"No, you're not. I am sorry, mate. I am so sorry!" Nick says from behind Olivia. He sounds different, pained.

"What are you talking about? Why are you sorry?" *Are there injuries the doctors failed to tell me about? Am I dying?* I panic for a second until I realise that it is madness.

"I should have taken the lead on that pitch." *Oh fuck.*

"Nick, that's crazy. We always alternate. I can't explain what happened because, frankly, I can't remember anything past the point when I radioed everyone that I found the missing climbers. But if it was anyone's fault, it was mine." I fix my eyes on him. Nick is pale and he doesn't look like he agrees with my assessment, but there is no way I will let him take the blame for something that was all my doing.

"Fuck, mate, I am serious. Stop it. I'm going to be fine." Olivia, who is holding my hand, is gently squeezing it. Nick runs his fingers through his hair.

"Bloody hell, Rob, when I heard Suzie scream, I thought we'd lost you. You fell nearly thirty feet because one of the hooks you set didn't hold. You crashed upside down not far from where Alex was belaying Suzie," he says but sounds a little calmer.

"What happened with the climbers?"

"Suzie belayed Alex so he could climb over to you and when he was secured to an anchor, she took care of the injured climbers until the backup team could climb up. They took over from us with the climbers and we handled your evac."

"They let you?" Because of the emotional involvement, usually a different unit would take over the recovery of an injured mountain rescuer.

"Do you really think they could have stopped us? Tommy had a shouting match with the other unit's leader, but he made it clear that you are our problem," Nick chuckles.

"Thanks, Nick. I mean it. Now give me a man hug and then go and get the others so I can thank them as well."

"They would only allow two of us to see you," Olivia says, "but if you want to see one of the other guys, I can trade places."

"Don't you dare," I growl. "Mate, tell the others I... I said thanks." Doesn't really feel like a strong enough word but I can't think of anything else to say. "They're letting me out of here tomorrow and then we can all catch up and you can all pander to my wishes because I won't be able to walk for a while." Nick laughs and I take a sigh of relief. He is back—well, kind of.

"Now go and kiss that fiancée of yours. I am sure she is worried about you, if you looked as miserable out there as you did when you arrived here."

"Almost-wife," Nick chuckles. He gives me a brief hug and then leaves us alone.

"I'm sorry," Olivia whispers.

"Babe, do I have to read you the riot act too? It wasn't your fault either. I wasn't thinking, I guess, and not paying attention." I shrug, but my tense muscles ache and I wince a little.

"But I was the reason that you were distracted. I'm sorry, I—" A tear is rolling over her round cheeks.

"Olivia, honestly, I can't remember exactly what happened. Was I distracted because of the dinner? Yes. But I have been doing this job for over five years. I should have admitted to Tommy that I was not one hundred per cent. I could have swapped with Phil or Chris. If there is anyone to blame, it's me. Please, babe." I sound desperate. I want to take that ridiculous guilt away from her.

"I love you," she finally blurts out.

"Sorry, what was that? I think my hearing may be affected by my injuries," I say unconvincingly and she laughs. I just need to hear her say it again.

"I love you." Her eyes are on me and her voice is firm. "And I am sorry about this evening. You were right. I spoke with my family. I... I can't tell you how much it means that you stood up for me."

I reach out with my right arm and pull her closer.

"I think I need another kiss," I demand.

"I thought you were too sore." She raises her eyebrow and smirks at me, that little minx.

"Just be tender, but please kiss me." I plead with her to give me what I need. Olivia bends forward.

"I love you," I whisper just before her lips make contact with mine.

Epilogue

Rob

I hobble into the living room where Olivia is stretched out on the sofa. My leg is getting better, but I still have to go to my physio regularly and I am far from being able to attend rescue missions.

"Rob, what the fuck is this?" Uh oh, sounds like I am in trouble.

"What is what?" I ask and drop into the seat next to her.

"This!" Olivia holds out a brochure from an adventure travel operator.

"You said we should book a holiday together and so I picked up a few brochures." Olivia sits up and crawls into my lap. "Hm, I like that," I groan, bend forward and nibble on her neck.

"Not so fast, Mister," she says and pushes on my chest until I am leaning against the sofa and she can look into my eyes. "You only had your cast taken off three weeks ago and now you want to plan," she opens the brochure at a random page and her eyes go wide, "white water rafting...," she flips to the next page, "...and bungee jumping. Are you out of your freaking mind?"

"You know what we said, we need to live life to the fullest," I grin at her.

In the aftermath of the accident, Olivia and I realised that we had moved at lightning speed with our relationship, especially after the drama of the accident. It was only natural, but we also knew that we had to step on the brakes a little if we wanted this relationship to last.

We spent countless hours talking, pouring out our souls and sharing our deepest fears and insecurities. We also spent many, many hours discovering each other in the bedroom. A highlight of our journey, if you ask me.

My recovery wasn't straightforward either, but we celebrated the small victories along the way, the moments when we felt we were moving in the right direction. Now that I am on the mend, we want to celebrate with a nice long holiday somewhere, but I have a feeling we may have different ideas of what that should be.

"What, don't you remember we said we would try something new?" I argue and try to pull her closer again so I can get back to kissing her neck because I can never get enough of that.

"Well, I thought we'd lie on a sunny beach somewhere, sipping cocktails. We are not going bungee jumping."

"No? How are you planning to convince me?" I smirk.

"Hmm, let's see." She bends forward and nibbles on my earlobe. My cock immediately stands to attention. "I could...," her fingers slide seductively over my chest, "... call Nick and tell him you are planning to jump off a bridge." That little minx knows exactly how to threaten me. Nick is still blaming himself a little, regardless of how often I have told him to knock it off. To make up for it, he has nominated himself as my personal chauffeur and if I need to go to a doctor's appointment or anywhere else, he drives me there. I've given up fighting him. I may or may not have taken the mickey a few times and made him drive me for ice cream or similar. Boy, was he annoyed with me, but I was kind of hoping it would get him off my back.

If he finds out that I am planning an adventure holiday he will be fucking livid.

"Or you could kiss me here." I point to my cheek and she presses her lips to it. "And here." I point at my mouth and she immediately kisses me passionately. "And finally, here." I point at my crotch.

"Rob!" She playfully smacks my chest. "In all seriousness, I want a beach holiday where we can lie in the sun all day, sip cocktails, and in the evening make passionate love."

"Well, you can certainly sip my cock...tail," I laugh.

"Rob!" she shouts.

"Fine! Boring beach holiday it is, but you have to make it up to me every night."

"Every night?"

"Practice."

"Practice for what?" she asks and there is confusion on her face.

"For when you move in here." My heart starts beating faster. I hate when I wake up in my bed and she is not next to me. I need her here every day and every night.

"What are you saying?"

"I am saying that I want you to move in with me."

"But I thought we said we would slow down a bit."

"We are. We have been dating for a few months now. Time for the next step. Olivia, I want you in my life. My favourite thing in the world is waking up with you in my arms. Please move in with me."

"Will I have to call you Sir?" She asks in a seductive voice and I know I have her. When she starts joking I have won the argument.

"You can call me whatever you want as long as you're here with me."

"Okay," she whispers and then slides forward on my lap and kisses me deeply. "But no bungee jumping."

"No bungee jumping," I agree. "How about crotch kissing?" Olivia laughs out loud.

"I love you, you crazy man."

And just like that, I am as happy as I could possibly ever be.

Bonus Chapter

Olivia

"Rob, I will murder you," I shout as I storm into the living room.

"What?" he asks from the sofa his face is a mask of innocence. But I know him too well by now. Rob and I have been living together for over a year and I can read him like a book.

"The cake was for Emma's birthday party tomorrow," I yell.

"I—"

"Before you come up with some mad story, let me tell you, you still have crumbs right there," I swipe my thumb over the corner of his mouth and present it like evidence.

"Babe, I'm sorry, but it's *my* chocolate cake." He actually sounds sorry. "We can buy Emma *a cake*." He looks at me with his puppy dog eyes and I almost feel sorry for him. *God, I love this man.*

"Or we can give her the second one I made. Alex picked it up this morning because neither of us trusted you," I giggle. Rob opens his mouth in surprise.

"I'm hurt," he says but he doesn't fool me. He reaches behind the sofa and pulls out the plate of the half-eaten cake. "Well, in that case, you won't need this anymore," he grins and stuffs another piece in his mouth.

"Rob—" I can't finish the sentence because he places the cake on the coffee table and pulls me into his lap.

"Olivia, I'm sorry, honestly, but I just couldn't resist." He looks at me sheepishly.

"Next time, ask," I say and cross my arms in front of my chest. I won't let him get away with it that easily even if my pussy is desperate for some attention.

"You always say no," he protests.

"Not if you ask properly." I raise an eyebrow and a big grin spreads across his lips.

"Oh, you mean like this—" He softly kisses along my neck, carefully sucking the tender skin into his mouth.

"That's a good start," I moan. His fingers slip under my T-shirt and pull it over my head. He captures my lips and kisses me deeply while his hands unclasp my bra.

"Rob!" I squeal when he smears chocolate frosting onto my nipple but he just bends forward and starts licking it all off again.

"Fuck, that tastes like heaven," he groans before reaching out for more cake. He pushes me onto the sofa and spreads chocolate between my breasts and down my tummy. Then his lips follow the same path with his tongue licking me clean. I can feel the familiar longing pool between my legs. You'd think that after a year of living together sex would be more routine, but with Rob it's mind-blowing every single time. I'm pretty sure the first lick of my nipple was enough to leave a wet spot on my knickers.

When the chocolate is gone he unzips my trousers and slides his fingers over my skin. I fight a shiver and try to focus on the task at hand. *Get Rob out of his clothes;* that's my only mission. I unbutton his shirt and push it over his broad shoulders ready to explore every centimetre of his perfect body. I am addicted to his taste and his smell and I can't get enough of it.

"Rob I'm warning you, don't get that chocolate anywhere near my..." I point towards my crotch when I see him reaching for the cake.

"Oh, I wouldn't. That's my favourite taste and even chocolate would ruin it." His voice is deep and husky as he pushes the cake out of harm's way. He pulls me to the edge of the sofa and pushes my legs apart. When his lips brush over my pussy I moan out loud. Not for the first time I thank all the gods that our neighbour, Mrs Warner, is deaf as a bat.

My hands grab onto his hair as his tongue licks my channel before sliding the tip along my folds to my clit. By now he knows exactly what pressure I like on that spot. He immediately sucks on the little nub and starts massaging it with his tongue.

"Fuck, Rob!" I arch my back. I am so close, so close. He holds me on the edge for a few moments before pushing two fingers into my pussy to trigger my orgasm.

"Did that work as a repayment for the cake?" He grins and wipes the remnants of my juices from his face with the back of his hand.

"I think I need more," I whisper and pull him to me for a kiss.

Rob

I close the door to the cottage quietly and toe my shoes off. It is silent so hopefully Olivia is still asleep. I tiptoe up the stairs and slowly open the bedroom door. A small gap between the curtains lets the first sun to hit the bedroom and in the dim light I can see her curled up. The duvet is tightly tucked in around her and she hugs her pillow and mine. Olivia always steals the pillow and the duvet, but it gives me great pleasure to fight her for them because we usually end up having fucking amazing sex.

The last year has been the best of my life. Olivia is all I was missing. Getting back enough fitness to return to work with FMR has been tough and I couldn't have done it without her. She provided comfort on days when it all got too frustrating, and she encouraged me on days when I wanted to give up. She's been there every painful step of the way.

I put the box I'm carrying on the floor and carefully remove its contents. My heart is hammering. What I am about to do has been on my mind for months and I just don't want to wait any longer.

I put the little grey kitten onto the bed. "Go, go to your new mummy," I whisper and try to shoo it towards Olivia. The little rascal starts playfighting with my hand instead. I pick the kitten up again and put her closer to Olivia. The furball starts sniffing and slowly moves to where I want her to go. When she gets to Olivia's arm she sniffs some more before licking her.

Olivia stirs. I nervously rub my hands on my jeans as I slide into bed next to her.

"What is this," she mumbles sleepily as she opens her eyes. When the kitten hears her voice it meows and playfully attacks on her arm.

"Oh my god, Rob, what have you done?" Olivia squeaks with joy and picks up the kitten. "It's adorable. Is it ours? Please tell me it's ours. I will be so cross if it's not," she giggles, kissing the kitten.

"She is ours; you just need to name her." I lean back on the bed. My heart is still racing . *Go on, baby, look closer!*

"Let's see, what name should we give you?" She holds up the cat with both hands and looks at the tiny ball of fur. Then she freezes. I am so nervous that it is hard to breathe.

"What's this, Rob?" Olivia asks and reaches out for the ring dangling from the cat's collar. I bend forward and carefully untie it to take the ring off, then place the kitten back on the bed where it scampers off to play with a pillow.

"Well, when I asked the kitten if she wants to move in with us she said she doesn't want to live in a house of sin and forced me to get you a ring."

"She is a very religious cat, then?" Olivia smirks.

"Very." I grab Olivia's left hand and slide the ring onto her finger. "What's do you say, will you make an honest man of me?"

"Rob," she sighs, cupping my face with her hands. "Yes, I will marry you." I can feel tears in my eyes and I am not ashamed of them. I don't think I have ever felt as happy as I do at this moment.

"I can't wait to be married to you, Olivia. I love you more than anything in the world."

"I love you too, Rob," she whispers and then pulls me down to kiss me.

Afterword

The Unnatural Habitat of a Cat Lady

If you were wondering about the book Olivia was reading, I have some good news for you. The Unnatural Habitat of a Cat Lady will be out on 28 May 2024!

The End

NEXT IN THE SERIES IS
TOMMY & ELLA'S STORY

Build with Me

Dani Elias

Chapter 1

Tommy

Loud laughter drifts over to me. I place my rucksack in the back of the Range Rover with the large Fellside Mountain Rescue logo on the side.

"Can you fucking cut it out and hurry up?" I yell in the direction of where the guys are gathering the gear. I am already late for a meeting with a supplier and I really don't need any further unnecessary delays.

How I have managed to combine my work with volunteering for FMR is sometimes a mystery, although it has become easier since Ella took over as my assistant. She uses some kind of magic or voodoo to keep business partners happy when I have to reschedule yet another meeting because some tourist has gotten themselves lost in the hills of Cumbria. Well, not magic really, but she cunningly hypes up my volunteer role with FMR, so much so that the person feels too guilty to complain, given that I am doing "such noble work". She even managed to get some of them to donate to FMR. She really is something special.

I untie my heavy mountaineering boots and slip my trainers on. I find it easier to drive in my trainers. Another backpack drops into the boot of the car. *Thank fuck, they're finally ready to leave.*

"Want to tell me what's wrong with you today?" Alex asks. In between tying my shoelaces, I glance at him as he leans against the side of the Range Rover with his arms crossed in front of him. He is still wearing his FMR jacket and a beanie to protect him from the cold autumn air.

"Nothing. I just have a meeting."

"Mate, you always have a meeting. But that's never stopped you from having a laugh with us at the end of a mission before."

"It's an important one." *Not true.* It's just another laundry company that wants to try to convince me to send my linen to them.

Alex raises an eyebrow. Of course, he is not buying that shit, he knows me too well. Alex and I are the longest serving members of FMR in our unit. We both joined as volunteers at the same time; I was twenty-three and Alex was nineteen. When I was promoted to unit leader I insisted that Alex was part of my team. The only other guy left from those early days is Nick. Over the years we added Chris, Rob and Phil to our unit and those five have become my best friends. During a mission I am their boss, but the rest of the time we are just six lads having a laugh —— if I'm not busy with work, that is.

Our latest member Suzie is currently not taking part in missions. She and Chris are expecting a baby and with all will in the world, there is no climbing for her now that she is in her third trimester.

Alex sits down on the edge of the boot. "I've drawn the short straw to find out what is wrong with you. So, if you want to get to your meeting in good time, you better spill."

I sigh and sit down next to him. "Fuck, I don't know, Alex. It's all getting a bit much." My fingers slide through my sweaty hair.

"Work and FMR?"

"Yes." It's only half the truth, but it is the truth.

"Why don't you take a break from FMR?" He is asking a valid question.

"Are you after my job?" I laugh trying to divert. Although we don't officially have a second in command at

FMR, Alex is kind of my unofficial deputy. He is calm under pressure and all of the lads respect him and look up to him.

"Bollocks to that," he laughs. "But I am willing to help out a friend for a while."

"I don't really want to give it up and I promised my dad I wouldn't," I try to explain. My grandfather played a role in the formation of the first rescue team in Fellside in the 1940s. Later on, my dad joined him and both were Fellside Mountain Rescue volunteers until the day they died. It meant a lot to them. So much so that my dad made me swear I wouldn't give it up when he saw how much of my life I sacrificed for my business.

"Nobody is talking of you giving it up. Why don't you take a month or two off from being a leader? I'll sub for you and you can still join our missions. But it means you don't have to worry about all the paperwork and all that shit."

"You hate the paperwork."

"That's the kind of friend I am," he chuckles. I look out into the distance. I can see the roofs of Fellside from up here. Somewhere beyond is my hotel where I should be having coffee with some sales guy trying to get me to sign a contract right now.

"Are you sure?" Somehow it doesn't feel right in my guts. Call me a control freak, but it is like passing on my baby. One of my babies, the other being my hotel.

"Definitely. Oh, and we also think you need to get laid," he adds matter-of-factly before standing up and starting to sort some of the rope bundles into the plastic crate we keep in the back of the car.

"Fuck off," I push back but really, he is not wrong. The minute he says the words, the image of a brunette in a tight pencil skirt is conjured up in my mind.

"What's that look on your face?" Alex asks with a smirk.

"I don't know what you're talking about." I sound defensive and I know that I just made a big mistake. I busy myself removing climbing gear from my backpack. The guys driving the Range Rover back to the FMR Centre will tidy it all away. I have my car parked lower on the mountain so I can head straight back to my hotel.

"Fuck, Tommy, we have been friends for over fifteen years. I have only once seen that look on your face and that was back when the she-devil put her claws in you." I stiffen when he mentions my ex-girlfriend. I was infatuated with her until I found out that all she was after was my hotel.

"You are shagging someone."

"I am most definitely not." I might wish I would be, but it's definitely not going to happen.

"Even better, there's a woman you are seriously interested in." He points at me and a cheeky smile appears on his lips.

"No."

"Tommy, stop fucking around. Tell me. Who is she?"

"It doesn't matter. I'm not going after her."

Alex sits down on the boot again.

"Why not?"

"She works for me."

"Who works for you?" Nick steps up to us and puts the casualty bag next to the ropes.

"Nobody."

"Bit difficult to run a hotel without staff, mate," he laughs about his own joke but he stops when neither Alex nor me join in. Alex has his arms crossed in front of his chest and is just looking at me expectantly. *Well shit.* There is no way he's going to drop the topic. I ruffle my hair and blow out hard.

"My assistant Ella." The minute I say her name I feel the tightening in my guts I get every time I am close to her.

"You have the hots for your assistant?" Nick blurts.

"Yes, fuck, it's stupid. And no, before you ask, nothing can happen!" I point at both of them. Alex raises his hands in surrender.

"Mate, I haven't said anything. But tell me, why did you hire her?"

"I didn't. My HR manager did." After complaining to Anna for the hundredth time that I needed more help, she finally went out and hired an assistant for me. I should have been in the interviews but as usual I was too busy and I thought I could leave it to Anna. Truth be told, she did hire the best person for the job. It's not really Anna's fault that I don't have my dick under control.

"So, you didn't hire her because you fancied her?"

"Fuck no. I didn't even see her before she started with me. I wasn't in the interviews and I would never hire someone because of the way they look. And if you must know, she is amazing at her job."

"So, what's the problem?" Nick asks and then takes a bite from an apple he has pulled out of his rucksack.

"I can't hit on my assistant. It's wrong. It could also get me into all sorts of hot water if she's not interested and make me look like a creep. And I don't want to lose her as my assistant."

"So, instead, you just take your frustration out on everyone else," Nick remarks which makes Alex chuckle.

"Fuck, was I that bad?"

"I think Gordon Ramsey swears less in a week than you did in the last three hours."

"I didn't realise—"

"It's okay, mate. We've all been there, but fuck, talk to us." Alex slaps me on the shoulder. "And think about my offer."

I nod and pull the zip up on my jacket.

"And I would think again about if you want to give it a try with your assistant. Not everyone is like the she-devil," Nick adds before peeking past the car to where Chris and Phil are waiting. "It's safe to come. He's in a better mood."

Every time I drive up to the hotel and see the elegant sign saying Greenview Manor, I am amazed that this is all mine. I worked in the hotel trade all my life. I finished school when I was sixteen and started as an apprentice when the hotel still belonged to Mr Sinder. He encouraged me to spread my wings and learn the trade by working in some other hotels as well. I did a couple of ski seasons in Austria and one dreadful summer in an posh hotel in Tuscany. But I always knew I wanted to come back here. I started on reception and worked my way up to hotel manager. And when Mr Sinder decided to retire, I used the money I had inherited from my dad as well as a very sizeable mortgage to buy it and make it mine. I have spent the last five years improving the standard of the hotel, and last year we were voted the number one venue in the Lake District. The phones haven't stopped since and there is hardly a day when we are not at at least ninety percent occupancy.

I park my car in my designated parking spot in front of the hotel and lean back in my seat. *Fuck, I'm tired.* The call for this mission came at five this morning. It is now ten and I haven't even had breakfast yet.

Movement to the left catches my attention. *There she is, the angel that haunts my dreams.* Ella steps out from the front entrance in her usual business attire of pencil skirt and blouse. She and I are the only ones in the hotel that don't wear the uniform of black trousers and polo shirt, and I'm glad she doesn't. With her chestnut brown hair casually pinned up and her curves accentuated by that damn pencil skirt, she is a vision.

I take a deep breath before opening the door to my car and stepping out.

"Morning, Tommy," she greets me with a big smile.

"Morning," I mumble. Did I forget to mention that ever since she joined us, I have turned into a complete arsehole? It's a defence mechanism, I guess.

"I've moved your meeting with the new laundry company to tomorrow. Otherwise, you are free until lunch time when you are meeting with Simon from King's Travel," she rattles off and holds out a mug which I assume has coffee in it. I take it from her and flinch a little when our fingers touch. If she has noticed my reaction, she is not letting on.

"Thanks," I grunt. Ella just gives me a small smile and looks down at her tablet.

"You might want to take a shower—"

"That's exactly what I had planned, thank you. Have the occupancy numbers ready for me when I come back down," I snap before taking a big gulp from the mug. *Fuck, that coffee is hot.* I feel it burning all the way down into my stomach and I try hard to not show the pain on my face.

"The numbers are already on your desk," she smirks and stalks off towards the hotel entrance. Before she pushes the door open, she turns to me. "Oh, and Tommy, the coffee is hot."

That little minx.

Chapter 2

Ella

The heavy entrance door closes behind me with a loud thud. As Tommy is not in his usual suit, he'll take the staff entrance at the back to get into the building. I know him, he is too much of a professional to be caught by his guests in his FMR gear. Not that he isn't proud of his volunteering, but he has strict rules for the hotel and he would never break them.

"Tommy is back, so the heads of department meeting this afternoon will go ahead. Please let everyone know," I say to Lindsey, the young receptionist, as I pass the front desk. She nods but doesn't reply as an elderly couple approaches her.

I love this place. Tommy has done an incredible job in transforming the hotel. The great hall next to reception is definitely my favourite part. Stained glass windows in the ceiling, beautiful woodwork, a feature fireplace, and elegant furniture all create a sense of grandeur transporting you back to Victorian times.

The wooden staircase leading from the ground floor to the first floor creaks under my feet. Tommy seems to be extra grumpy again today. He is an enigma. He can be incredibly kind one minute and a big grouch the next. Only last week he went out and purchased an insane amount of baby gifts for one of the waitresses who had given birth to a baby boy. Most staff look up to him and consider him a great boss, the guests love him and, despite his busy life, he gives up his time to volunteer for FMR. Rumour has it that he can also be a fun guy especially when he hangs out with his friends, but I have yet to see this side. All he has been with me since I started was grumpy.

I asked Anna once if he wasn't happy with me and I guess she must have spoken with him because for a few days he was a little friendlier but now we are back to Lord Grumpiness. Don't get me wrong, he isn't mean to me (believe me, I had my share of viciousness directed at me when working in my family's firm). No, Tommy is like a grumpy teddy bear. I don't think he could harm a fly.

After I passed my probation, I became a little braver and when he gets too arsy, like just now, I do give back. I love the shocked look on his face when I stand up to him. He doesn't know what to do with himself in those situations and just mumbles something before retreating to his office. It makes me giggle every time.

I step into the small room just outside Tommy's office where my desk is and drop my tablet next to my laptop. Both rooms were originally Mr Bryant's study, the wealthy owner who built this place in the eighteen hundreds. Now they are two boring offices with magnolia walls and beige carpets. But the furniture is chunky and old, giving the room a little character. And Tommy's corner office has stunning views, on one side of the mountains and on the other of Lake Windermere.

I walk to the small coffee machine on the credenza. Tommy doesn't allow himself much luxury, all his profits are reinvested on improving the hotel. But he insists on having one of those fancy coffee machines with capsules in the office. He prefers that brew even over the freshly made ones from the restaurant. I prepare everything so I only need to press the button when he comes down. He will want to have another cup after he was called out at five this morning; that's the time he texted me to let me know he would be late.

Tommy's small flat is in the attic of the hotel. He lives and breathes this hotel and he usually works seven days a week so staying on site makes sense for him. How he hasn't burnt out yet, I really don't know.

I glance at my phone where a message notification is blinking. Knots form in my tummy when I see who it is. I pick up the phone with shaking hands.

Lee

Just checking we are all set with the big boss.

I hesitate for a minute before replying to my brother.

Me

Of course. Your appointment is set for four p.m. on Tuesday as per my email.

Immediately the little moving dots appear and tell me that he is replying.

Lee

That's not what I meant. Have you been working him?

Me

What?

Lee

To make sure he hires us.

Me

He will choose whichever company is best.

My family has the most prestigious architecture company in the area but getting Tommy's hotel extension project would be a fantastic opportunity.

Lee

For fuck's sake, Ella, for once put the family first.

Me

I have! When I drew the plans for your proposal.

I throw my phone on my desk. Fear spreads through me. I shouldn't have said that. He is going to make me pay. I pick the phone up again.

Lee

You are lucky I'm not there.

You better make sure he likes YOUR plans as much as you think he will, because if we don't get this deal it's all your fault. And you wouldn't want me to tell him that you've been plotting behind his back. I thought you liked the job at that hotel.

I don't reply to Lee's message but my fear is replaced in parts by anger. I always put the family first. For five years I quietly worked in the background, creating design after design that secured project after project whilst my brother took credit for it. "It's for the family," I was told by Lee and by my dad.

Don't get me wrong, I am not a praise seeker but I would love recognition when I work hard. Eventually I had enough and decided to leave the family business. My brother, who always had a violent side, didn't take it well. I hid in Fellside whilst my bruises were healing. I couldn't really attend a job interview with a massive black eye.

I sent out CVs to different architecture firms in Cumbria but being a member of the Grange family meant that no other architecture firm would go anywhere near me. Whilst my dad's company had won many awards, within the industry the company was known for unfair business practices. My brother and my dad don't shy away from bribery or even threats and other dirty tricks but nobody has been able to prove it yet. Their bad reputation tainted my name as well.

When Lee eventually found me in Fellside (I still don't know how he did it), he tried to get me to come back with him. But I wasn't budging. My job here meant something to me, and I wasn't about to ditch it. Lucky for me, we were in a coffee shop and so he couldn't make a scene. He stormed off, and I stayed put for another hour, hoping he'd actually left, before I sneaked back to my flat.

I didn't hear from him again until a month or so later, when Tommy sent out a tender to architecture firms for the extension. I couldn't really stop him from including my family, as they are well known. Lee asked me to draw the plans for the extension. And now I am paying the price for not standing up to my family once again.

When I couldn't find a job as an architect, I applied for anything and everything just so I could stay in Fellside and I ended up at Greenview Manor. I love my job and I am the happiest I have been in a long time. Tommy is a handful, but the job is fun and interesting and I admire Tommy's business sense. He is incredible with people, except with me, and he deeply cares about the hotel.

If only he wouldn't make me nervous and giddy at the same time. Aside from being an amazing person he is incredibly attractive. I don't think there is a single female staff member who doesn't secretly fancy him. As of late he has become one of my favourite masturbation fantasies and I am pretty sure it is not okay to picture your boss giving you a good shafting almost every night. A small smile spreads on my lips and I can feel my cheeks heat up. No, I definitely don't want to lose this.

"Love, is Tommy here?" The voice of Ian brings me back to reality.

"He's getting changed, Chef," I reply and busy myself with printing some reports. I made the mistake on my first day to call Ian, the head chef, by his first name and was promptly put in my place by his sous-chef. It's ridiculous really. We even call Tommy by his first name. But when it comes to the kitchen staff, everyone thinks they are the next Monsieur Escoffier.

Ian leans against my desk and taps on the wood until I look at him.

"When can I take you out, love?" He asks in his thick Brummie accent.

"Ia...Chef, I told you before, I'm not interested." I give him my best stern look before returning my attention to my emails.

"Playing hard to get, are we? You know, I won't ask forever, I have other options." He gives me a cheesy grin. I very much doubt that he has many options and that has nothing to do with the fact that he always smells like chicken stock or that he tries to cover his bald patch by using way too much gel to hold his hair in place. No, it is all down to him being a creep. He is a brilliant chef which is why he is still here, but he has been warned a number of times by Anna.

"Ian, what are you doing here?" Tommy's voice booms through the office drawing both mine and Ian's attention to him. Yes, Tommy is allowed to call Ian by his first name. I would love to see someone tell him he has to call that creep Chef.

"Tommy, I've the menus for the VIP fundraiser."

"Leave them with Ella, I'll have a look at them this afternoon."

"Sure." There is an edge to Ian's voice. He hates it when Tommy puts him in his place. "See you at the department meeting." He waves a goodbye and leaves my office.

"Was he inappropriate?" Tommy looks at me and for the first time I see something else than grumpiness staring back at me. He looks... concerned, maybe, but there seems to be something else.

"No," I laugh, "He's just Ian. I've forwarded you an email from the bank you need to look at, please."

"Sure." He slides his large hand over the smooth top of my desk before walking towards his office. "Ella, tell me if he bothers you." His eyes find mine. They are caring and have lost their usual hard edge. I forget to breathe and his concerned look warms my insides. I almost wish he would return to being a grump.

I give him a small smile and say, "Don't worry. I can take care of myself." He doesn't reply and instead just gives me one last look before walking into his office.

I take a deep breath. I need to stop lusting after him, but he is making it bloody difficult.

Chapter 3

Tommy

My hand hovers over the door handle to Ella's office. *Fucking Ian again!* The voice and accent of my head chef are easy to identify. This is the third time this week that he is hanging out with my assistant. Even if I have no right to be jealous I can feel it deep in my guts. Trying to get control over myself, I take a deep breath and push the door to the office open.

"Ian, you're spending more time in my office nowadays than in the kitchen. Want to apply for an admin position?" My voice drips with sarcasm and Ian gives me a glare.

"Funny, Tommy," he says but there is no laughter. "I came to see if you want me in the meeting with the people from the VIP fundraiser." If Ian likes anything more than running after the female staff it's putting his face front and centre. I would have fired him a long time ago, but Anna keeps reminding me that disliking his attitude is not enough and there are employment laws to follow. Unfortunately, the female staff members never make an official complaint, I have yet to catch him in the act, and the guests love his food, so the feedback is first class. If I fired him now I would be in front of an employment tribunal in a heartbeat.

We managed to give him two warnings based on hearsay only, so Anna insists we need a proper reason for the final warning before we can dismiss him.

"That's fine, Ian, thank you. I've got it." I cross my arms over my chest. Ian is no taller than five foot eight and so I tower over him at six foot four inches.

"What if they have questions about the food?"

"Then I'll answer them," I reply firmly. My eyes drift briefly to Ella and I can see her biting her lips to hold in a laugh. "Ian, I've run this hotel for over ten years, I think I can handle a simple meeting." I know he hates to be called Ian, but I won't stand for this chef nonsense.

"Fine, it was just an offer. I'll see you later, love," he says looking at Ella and ignoring me. *What a prick.*

"Her name is Ella." My tone is cold. "She is your colleague and I expect you to show her the respect she deserves." Ian's face is turning red, but he doesn't reply. Instead, he just walks past me and leaves the office.

"What did he want?" My question sounds harsh.

"What he said. You interrupted before he could ask me out again." She looks at me with big eyes and I have to remind myself to breathe.

"You two are dating," I growl.

"God, no. No, no, no. I would rather run naked through Fellside," she exclaims and her cheeks turn pink. The image of her naked body flashes through my mind and I know I need to get out of here. *Fuck!* I slide my fingers through my hair just as the phone on Ella's desk starts to ring.

"Thanks, Tommy will be down in a minute. Can you please put them in the Oak Room?" she tells the person on the other end. The Oak Room is our ornate fine dining restaurant, and I prefer to conduct important meetings there when I want to make a strong impression.

"Virginia from the Rotary Club is here," Ella explains after she puts the phone down. I just nod. My mind is not really in the game today, and having to schmooze these people and convince them to hold their big fundraising gala in our hotel is the last thing I want to do. But I also know that this event is worth a lot of money and we need it to help finance the extension I am planning to add to the hotel.

We have a lot of large events but not enough bedrooms to put up all the guests and so adding twenty new rooms to the hotel is a no-brainer. I am meeting with some architecture firms next week to look at their plans before we decide on one and I can't wait. I have some vivid ideas for the extension which is why the tender document was thirty pages long. I wasn't sure if I should send it but Ella convinced me that there would be no point in holding back when I feel so strongly about what I want. I'd only set myself up for disappointment.

"Thanks, do you have the brochure for me please?" I try to give her a smile. *Don't be a grump, don't be a grump.*

"Here." She grabs the cream-coloured folder from her desk and stands up. Now I can see that she is wearing black trousers today rather than a pencil skirt and I almost comment on them until I realise it would be inappropriate.

Ella hands me the folder and softly says, "Wait." She reaches out and gently pushes my tie into place before pulling it tight. She is so close that I can feel her warmth and take in her scent. Our eyes are locked and I can feel my dick getting hard. *Jeez.* That's the last thing I need in the business meeting, a boner.

"Thanks," I say again but now my voice sounds strained. I take a step back before turning and leaving the office. This woman is going to be the death of me.

"It was a pleasure to meet you, Virginia." I shake her hand before Sheila, my Operations Manager, escorts her to the exit.

"How was the meeting?" I turn to see Ella standing at the foot of the oak staircase.

"I think we'll get the business," I grin. She gives me a big smile in return.

"That's amazing! That will be so helpful when talking to the bank for the loan." I love that she is as enthusiastic about my hotel as I am. I have met many phony people in my life and I know when someone is just blowing smoke up my arse.

"I know..., Ella, you have—" I point towards the dark spec in the corner of her mouth.

"What?" She wipes over her lips but misses what I suspect to be chocolate traces. She nibbles on that stuff all day long. I take a step closer and wipe with my thumb the crumbs away. Her breath catches when I make contact with her skin.

"There," I say before sucking the chocolate from my thumb. My breathing is faster and I am lost in her eyes. Ella just looks at me with a blush covering her cheeks.

"Tommy, there you are." A woman's voice makes Ella turn her head and break our eye contact. I feel like I have been ripped out of my happy place back into cold reality.

"Hi, Tommy," a second woman says and my eyes finally drift away from Ella and what I see causes me to panic. *Alex is going to be a dead man.*

"Christina, Emma... and Charlotte, what are you doing here?" I ask with dread in my voice.

"Well, Phil's sister is looking after Lilly; Jane loves to play the doting aunt. That means mum," she points at herself, "has the day off and so I convinced these two beauties to have a ladies' lunch. And where better than your hotel," Christina explains with way too much enthusiasm and I notice that her eyes keep darting to Ella. Emma and Charlotte, who both stand behind Christina look at me innocently but the blush on Emma's cheeks tells me there is much more behind this visit.

"You must be Ella," Christina introduces herself to my assistant. "We have heard so much about you." Yup, Alex or Nick or both definitely opened their big mouths because I have never mentioned Ella before to anyone else in the group.

Ella looks at me with a shell shocked expression and I just shrug. I'm not sure what else to do.

"Ella, these are Christina, Charlotte and Emma. They are the partners of some of my FMR mates." I point out my friends to her.

"It's nice to meet you," Ella says politely and she is greeted by three big, knowing smiles. They are definitely here to meddle.

"Are you from around here?" Charlotte finally speaks up.

"No, I'm originally from Manchester, but I moved here when I got the job with Tommy."

"And I bet our workaholic won't let you have time off to make friends," Christina laughs and slaps me playfully on the chest before linking her arm with Ella's. "You must have lunch with us. You don't mind, Tommy, do you?" She grins. Panic rises in me again. Christina has no filter, and I can't be sure what she will tell Ella, but what reason could I give for Ella not to take a lunch break?

"I... sure, no, that's fine if Ella wants to."

"Sure she does," Christina answers for her.

Ella laughs. "Apparently, I do. To be honest, Chef has a new pie on the menu that I have been dying to try."

"See!" Christina gives me a triumphant grin.

"Ella, please put the lunch on my tab," I offer.

"Oh, you don't have to," Emma tries to interject. She is clearly uncomfortable.

"Thanks, Tommy," Christina giggles at the same time. "Let's go," she commands and drags Ella off towards the restaurant with Charlotte hot on her heels. *Yes, run but you can't hide.* I gently grab Emma's arm before she can follow them.

"What did Alex tell you?" My voice sounds cold and I am sure I have a deep frown on my face.

"He..., I am sorry, Tommy. He told me what you said at the rescue and I mentioned it to Christina, and you know her."

"Yes, I do. You need to make sure she keeps this to herself, Emma. Please!"

"I'll try. I'm really sorry."

"I know." I give her a hug. Emma would never hurt anyone and I didn't mean to upset her. It's Christina I don't trust because she has a habit of putting her foot in it and blurting out things she shouldn't.

"We just want you to be happy, Tommy." she sniffles.

"I am happy," I declare trying to sound convincing but even I can hear that there isn't real conviction behind the words. "Now go and make sure Christina behaves," I usher her towards the restaurant.

I watch her walk down the long corridor. *Fuck!* I ruffle my hair again before pulling my phone from my pocket.

Me

I can't believe you told Emma.

The reply is immediate.

Alex

She's my wife.

Me

She told Christina.

Alex

Oh shit.

Me

They are here to have lunch and Christina invited Ella to join them.

Alex

You are fucked, man.

Yes, yes that I am.

Chapter 4

Ella

I can't remember the last time I laughed so much. Christina has been telling me all about how she pursued Phil, or Bambi, as she loves to call him. She hinted that both Emma and Charlotte had similar interesting stories on how they met their significant others but she left it at that.

I felt an immediate connection to all three of them. They are just the kind of people you want to have as friends.

"So, what about you?" Charlotte asks before putting a spoon full of spotted dick in her mouth.

"I'm single," I say but involuntarily add a sigh to it.

"Ah, but you don't want to be," Christina picks me up on it.

"Well, I wouldn't say no if the right person came along." Warmth rises in my cheeks. Of course, an image of Tommy in his FMR outfit pops into my head. I love the look of him in his mountaineering gear.

"The right person like a certain hotel owner?" she asks with a smirk on her face.

"No!" I almost shout but I also feel that my cheeks are full at blaze now.

"I know that blush," Emma grins at me.

"No, he is my boss," I whisper. Our staff are nosy and the last thing I need is for rumours to spread through the hotel.

"So? You wouldn't be the first two people who work together that fall for each other," Charlotte says and I appreciate that she keeps the conversation also to a whisper.

"Tommy is not falling for me."

"Ahem, did we not walk in on the two of you, mooning over each other with him wiping your lip and then sucking his thumb? Please! If Phil had done that when we started dating, I would have creamed my knickers."

"Christina!" Emma gives her friend a stern look.

"What? It's true," Christina laughs.

My heart starts beating faster. She's right. There was something so intimate about our interaction earlier, I nearly moaned when he slid his thumb over my mouth. But could he really be interested in me?

"He has been nothing but grumpy around me," I reply.

"Since when is Tommy grumpy?" Charlotte asks but then her eyes light up in excitement. "Or maybe he is grumpy to keep you at a distance because he thinks you are not interested and he's your boss. He's way too much of a good guy to abuse his position," she adds with glee and Emma and Christina nod in agreement. They jumped to that conclusion too quick. Did he talk about me?

"No way. I don't think so." I sound weak and my doubt of my own words is apparent.

"Ella, you're right, we don't know," Emma says. She stops Christina, who wants to interrupt, with another stern look. "But just consider the possibility. If you like him, watch out for signs and if you see them and the opportunity presents itself, don't let him slip away. He is a good guy and there aren't many like him. Trust me. I know."

Her words hit home. Did I interpret his grumpiness wrong? What if it isn't that he doesn't like me. What if it is the opposite. I take a deep breath and finally nod.

"Yeah," Christina cheers as if we won the grand prize in the lottery. "And you can test our theory tonight. Come to the pub with us. We are all meeting for our monthly get together, and Tommy will be there."

"I have to check if he is okay with it. I'd be invading his personal life."

"Pish-posh. I have invited you. That has nothing to do with Tommy," she interjects.

"I'll ask him," I reply firmly before waving the waitress over to get the bill ready so I can sign it for accounts.

After I've said goodbye to the ladies I walk back to my office. I carefully balance my tablet and a plate of food for Tommy whilst trying to open the door. Eventually I manage to push it open without spilling any gravy.

"Ella?" Tommy calls out the minute I walk through the door.

"I brought lunch," I reply. I place my tablet on the desk and then walk into Tommy's office. His door is open as usual. "Here you go." I place the plate with the roast chicken on his desk.

"A waitress could have done that," he says, his voice deep and growly.

"Sure, but I was coming this way anyway." I shrug and walk back towards the door.

"How was lunch?" Do I hear concern in his voice? I stop my walk and look back at him.

"It was lovely. They are a lot of fun. In fact, they invited me to the pub tonight," I add. Tommy's eyes widen for a second.

"If that's okay with you?" I ask cautiously.

"Sure..., why wouldn't it be?" he asks but there is an edge to his voice.

"Well, I don't want you to think I'm invading your personal life." Our eyes are locked and there is an electric tension in the air.

"You should come," he says finally. "I can give you a lift if you want."

"Oh, that would be great, thanks." I don't drive and I was planning to walk but if I can save myself the twenty-minute hike, I won't say no to that.

"Great."

"Great," I agree before turning and walking back to my desk. There are about a thousand knots in my stomach. Or are they butterflies? I can't be sure.

"Sorry we're late," a tall, dark and handsome guy says as he and his partner drop into chairs opposite me. Honestly, not sure what the entry requirements are for FMR but being hot must be one of them. I look around the table and every guy is handsome in their own way.

"Ella, this is Chris and his wife Suzie. They are the remaining members of our FMR unit. Now you've met them all," Tommy introduces me. He hasn't left my side since we arrived and shooed Christina away when she tried to take his seat next to me. This of course made her give me a knowing smile.

"Well, I am on a bit of a break from FMR," Suzie laughs and rubs her baby bump. Chris kisses her softly before placing a protective hand on her round tummy. Could they be more swoon-worthy?

"It's nice to meet you, Ella." Chris smiles at me.

"So why are you late?" Rob asks from the other end of the table. "We thought you wouldn't come at all."

"Mate, drama with Max."

"Max is our son," Suzie explains for my benefit. "And we now have a snail as a pet."

"Excuse me?" Alex asks.

"Snail Bail." Chris looks a little sheepish.

"Snail Bail?" Alex laughs so hard that everyone else starts laughing as well.

"And what, he was moving too slow back into the stable, is that why you're late?" Nick mimics the slow pace of a snail wiggling along on the table and everyone bursts out laughing again.

"No, me and Max were arguing that snails are not pets," Suzie explains, "There were tears and then this one," she points at her husband, "can't say no to him and now we have a snail in an old fish tank in the kitchen."

"Max was so happy." Chris just shrugs and grins. He clearly isn't sorry that he's given in. Everyone else bursts out laughing again.

I lean back in my chair and take everything in. They have the kind of friendship I have never had in my life. It feels more like a family than just friends. I almost envy Tommy for them, but then, they have somehow accepted me into the group and are treating me like one of their own, so maybe I don't need to be envious.

Tommy is different around them. He is relaxed and less serious. I have never seen him laugh this much. A while ago he placed his arm on the back of my chair and it has stayed there ever since. He doesn't really have his arm around me because he is barely touching me, but it still has set off a thousand butterflies in my tummy.

"Are you okay," he suddenly whispers in my ear. His warm breath blows gently over my neck and goosebumps form on my arms. I turn my head and look at him.

"Sure, why do you ask?"

"You looked lost in thought."

"I was just thinking how lucky you are to have such amazing friends," I say truthfully.

"They are my family. But I think they've adopted you as well. You are one of us now," he chuckles.

"Are you okay with that?" I am terrified he might think I am overstepping a line. His eyes are lock on mine and he takes a deep breath.

"Absolutely." It is just one word but there is more to this, I can feel it. Tommy turns to Nick who is sitting next to him and I let out a slow breath. When I look around the table, Christina smiles at me and gives me a wink. Of course she saw that.

"So did you have fun?" Tommy asks as he indicates to turn left. He insisted on driving me home even if it is only a short walk to my flat.

"So much fun! They are all hilarious."

"They liked you," he replies with his eyes fixed on the road.

"Well, I gave them all the gossip about you," I giggle and poke him in the shoulder. Tommy laughs out loud. It has been great to see him laugh and smile all evening. Jeez, if

I thought the grumpy man was hot, a happy and cheerful Tommy definitely made me, to quote Christina, cream my knickers.

"It's just over there, the small block of flats." I point to the left at the grey building. Tommy slides the car into a parking spot and turns off the engine.

"Ella, I think I need to apologise." He turns in his seat and looks at me.

"What for?"

"For being a moody arsehole since you started." He leans his head against the seat, but his eyes are still locked on mine.

"Well, I wouldn't quite put it like this, but I did nick-name you Lord Grumpiness," I giggle.

Tommy doesn't laugh. Instead, he reaches out and pushes a strand of hair behind my ear.

"I'm sorry."

"Why were you so grumpy to me?" I hold my breath waiting for his answer.

"I... I like you."

"And that's why you were grumpy?" I need him to say what I think he means to say. Absent-mindedly, he taps on the steering wheel and stares into the darkness through the windscreen.

"I like you, Ella. I like you a lot, but I am your boss and in order to keep my distance, I—" I stop him by gently cupping his face, turning it to me and pressing my lips to his. The minute we connect, he takes over. He slides his hands into my hair and turns my head to deepen the kiss. His tongue slowly strokes over my lip until I open up for him. I never thought a kiss could feel as loaded and intense as this kiss does. After what feels like an eternity and in equal measure like a fraction of a second, I move away from him. I need to get out of the car before I ask him to fuck me in the middle of the car park. I want him, he wants me, but it's not that easy. We work together. I need to get a clear head and think about this. I have fancied him for months now, but I never thought past the point of what would happen if we got together because it felt so impossible.

"Good night," I say before leaving his car and walking towards the building. Tommy waits until I open the door and only then starts his engine and pulls out onto the road. I don't dare to turn around, even if all I want to do is have a last glimpse of him.

Chapter 5

Tommy

Nervously, I straighten my tie for the fifth time. It has been two days since Ella and I kissed and I still don't know how I'll handle it when I'll have to face her in a bit. Whilst weekends don't really exist for me, Ella is off every Saturday and Sunday, so I haven't seen her since that kiss.

More than once over the last two days I have typed out a text message and every single one of them sounded stupid, so I deleted it again.

"Fuck!" I swear loudly before grabbing my rucksack and garment bag. Not only do I need to face Ella today, but we are also travelling to Manchester together to meet with different architecture companies for the expansion project. And we are staying overnight in the hotel of a friend of mine. The thought of spending so much time together makes my dick twitch with excitement and my stomach knot up with nerves.

"Morning, boss," John, our apprentice on reception, says when I walk past the desk. He grabs my keys and luggage and carries them outside to my car. He is a good lad and he takes on even the most menial tasks with an enthusiasm that is rare in today's youth.

"Thanks, John," I call after him before turning to the receptionist. "Sheila is in charge, but if there are any issues you can call me or Ella," I tell the young receptionist whose name I have forgotten. She has only been with us for a few weeks and with more than fifty staff working for me I tend to only learn people's names once I know they are really staying.

As I walk into the sunshine, I can see Ella leaning against my BMW X5. It is one of the few expensive things I have ever splashed out for in my life, but when I needed a new car I gave the Range Rover, which is so popular around here, a miss and opted for a bit more luxury.

"Hi." She gives me a small smile and nibbles on her bottom lip.

"Hey," I reply. I am glad that I am not the only one who is nervous. I briefly glance at my watch before accepting my car key back from John.

"You're in charge, John." I wink at him and he chuckles. He reminds me a lot of myself at his age and I can see him staying in the sector. He has the right mentality for it.

"We should go, there are some roadworks between here and Windermere," I comment before climbing into the car. I throw my jacket on the backseat and put the seatbelt on. Ella joins me and buckles up in the passenger seat.

Neither of us says anything as I pull out of the parking spot. A soft strand of her hair slides over my hand as I place it on the back of her chair when looking behind me to reverse. Immediately the image from Friday night is conjured up when I grabbed hold of her hair whilst kissing her. Ella is staring straight ahead and is not moving. Guilt hits me. I definitely made a mistake kissing her. She is uncomfortable now and it is my fault. *I can't lose her.* Not just because she is an amazing assistant but also because I rather have her in my life as just a friend than not at all.

After another five minutes of silence, I can't take it any-more. "Ella—"

"I'm sorry, Tommy!" she blurts out before I can finish my sentence. I glance at her as we drive along Lake Windermere. Fellside sits on one end of the lake and the town of Windermere at the other.

"What are you sorry for?"

"For attacking you in your car," she whispers and puts her head in her hands. I laugh out loud. I can't stop it.

"Well, I'm glad you find my embarrassment so funny," Ella says angrily. I indicate and turn the car into one of the many lay-bys tourists use to take photos of the lake.

"What are you doing?" she asks.

"Stopping so I don't cause an accident." I turn off the engine, unfasten my seatbelt and turn in my seat to face her.

"Ella, look at me." It sounds like an order and so I add, "Please?" She continues to avoid eye contact, so, I reach out and turn her face to mine. "Ella, what gave you the impression that I didn't like what happened on Friday night?" She pulls her bottom lip between her teeth again to nibble on it nervously. "I think it was my tongue in your mouth and not the other way round," I chuckle. A small smile flickers over her face and her eyes darken.

"Oh, Ella." I cup her face. " You've been driving me crazy ever since you started working at Greenview. But I am your boss. I didn't want you to feel uncomfortable so I would have never made the first move."

"And then I did."

"And then you did. Now I am not sure what to do. I don't want to go back to how it was before."

"Me neither. But you are still my boss."

"I know." I lean back against my seat and let go of her. "Let's get the next two days over with and then discuss how we handle this when we are back at Fellside. How does that sound?"

"Sounds like a plan," she agrees but I can see on her face that she is a little disappointed. "So, just to clarify, no kissing?"

"That depends."

"On what?"

"On you. Again, I don't want to make you uncomfortable." I look at her. I want to do the right thing, but I can't deny how much I want her.

"So, hypothetically, if we wanted to see if we are even compatible," she pretends to think very hard, "we could have a repeat of Friday night?"

"Hypothetically," I agree with a grin.

"Maybe even more."

"Maybe."

"I mean, we might just not gel. You might be terrible in bed," she giggles.

"Excuse me?" I mock indignation.

"I have very high standards." She twirls a strand of hair around her finger. "I mean, the kiss was promising but..." She leaves the rest of the sentence hang in the air. I laugh out loud.

"So, you want to use the next two days to see if we fit?" I ask more seriously. I need to hear it straight out.

"Yes."

"And what if it's a disaster?"

"Then we return to Fellside and pretend it never happened," she shrugs. If only it were that easy, but my need for her overrides all of my concerns.

"What happens in Manchester, stays in Manchester?"

"Exactly," she giggles.

"Okay," I finally agree, and Ella relaxes in her seat. My finger is about to push the start button for the car when I stop myself. My hand slides around Ella's neck and pulls her closer. When my lips meet hers, I relax for the first time since Friday. Kissing her feels like coming home after a long journey. Ella moans and I deepen the kiss. When my tongue slides over hers I groan. Nothing has ever felt so good. I take a last lick before breaking away.

"And just so you know, Ella, when I finally get you into bed, it will be fantastic." She locks eyes with me and laughs.

"Cocky much? Are you that good?"

"No, but the two of us together will be perfect." There is no humour in my voice and Ella's eyes widen.

I finally start the car and pull out of the lay-by.

Chapter 6

Ella

"Mr Hunter, it is a pleasure to welcome you to the Whitworth Townhouse Hotel," the young concierge greets us as we step into the lobby. The term *townhouse* in the hotel name is grossly misleading. It makes it sound quaint and small when it is everything but. Yes, it is made up of a number of old Georgian townhouses but that is really the only connection to that word. It is a grand and luxurious five-star hotel in the centre of Manchester. The fact that they have a concierge says everything, as this is definitely a job title on the way to becoming extinct.

I feel him glance at me. He must know that we have two rooms booked, but Tommy's hand on my lower back doesn't scream employer-employee relationship.

"Thank you, this is Ms Grange," Tommy introduces me. The concierge smiles politely, even if Tommy has failed to clarify who I really am.

"I hope you will enjoy your stay with us, Ms Grange." He ushers us to the check in desk and after we have signed our registration form, we are escorted to two junior suites on the top floor of the building. We did of course book normal rooms; Tommy doesn't like wasting money and we're only here for one day. But his friend, who owns this place, insisted on upgrading us.

Before we retire to our own rooms, we agree to meet for dinner in an hour, which should give me just enough time to wash the day off and get ready.

Tommy and I spent all afternoon with two architecture firms who have put forward a tender for the hotel extensions. The designs were not bad, but I could see on Tommy's face that he wasn't particularly taken by either. Deep in my guts I know he will choose my family's design. Not because they are my family, Tommy is way too professional for that. No, he will love the design. I know what is important to him in the hotel and I made sure it's all integrated in the design. A wave of guilt hits me again. I should tell him the truth.

My phone rings and I see Lee's name on the display. Perfect timing. It is like he can feel me fighting my conscience. I could ignore him but he will just keep calling until I answer. With a shaking hand I pick it up.

"Hi, Lee."

"How did it go to today," he barks down the phone.

"I can't—"

"Ella, don't fuck with me. You know how important this is for the business. If we don't get this contract we are done for. So, tell me. Did he like any of them?" Despite the firm having had many successes in the past, Lee and my dad are not good with money. They also lost a number of significant contracts after I left and Lee had to take care of the creative side of the company. Snagging the contract for Tommy's extension would really help them out financially.

I sit down on my bed and try to calm my breathing.

"He didn't like them."

"Are you sure?"

"Yes. They were not bad designs but very modern. It wouldn't fit in with Greenview Manor's concept."

"Good. I want you to work on him tonight."

"What?"

"Convince him we are the best option."

"Lee, he knows it's my family. He will tell me it's a conflict of interest."

"Ella, don't be stupid. Do it in a subtle way. I'll see you tomorrow." He hangs up before I can reply. *I won't do it. No, I won't do it!* I am shaking with anger, and frustration and fear. *No, I won't do it.*

I sigh when I look at myself in the mirror. In my naivety, thinking we would ignore Friday and act all professional, I only brought a business outfit for tomorrow and a casual jeans and T-shirt combo for the evening. And that's all I have to wear now. There is nothing seductive or sexy on it.

A knock on the door stops me from wishing for a miracle Cinderella-like transformation. I grab my simple black handbag and open the door.

Give me strength, how does he look so effortlessly hot? He is also just wearing jeans and a simple long-sleeved T-shirt but, in his case, he looks like a sportswear model. His T-shirt clings to his body and I can see the outlines of his muscles. *Am I drooling? It feels like I'm drooling.*

"Hey," he greets me and places a soft kiss on my cheek. He smells fresh and clean with a hint of aftershave. Just breathing in his scent makes my pussy tingle.

"Hi, sorry, we may have to go somewhere casual for dinner. I didn't think of bringing anything fancy." I can feel heat in my cheeks. Tommy's eyes move up and down my body.

"You look perfect in anything." *Oh boy.* He helps me into my jacket and then slides his hand in mine and links our fingers.

"Come on."

"Where are we going?"

"The most exclusive place in Manchester," he replies with a wink.

"Tommy, I told you—" I pull him to a halt.

"Ella, trust me, you are perfectly dressed for where I'm taking you." He pulls me along the corridor but bypasses the lift and pushes the door open to the stairs.

"Is the lift broken?" I really don't fancy fourteen floors of stairs, even if it is descending them.

"Nope," he chuckles as we step into the staircase. "We're going up and there is no lift." We climb a few stairs until we reach a door with a sign warning that access is for staff only. Tommy pulls the door open and we step outside into the cool air. I freeze at the spot. We are on the roof of the hotel. In one corner there are air vents and air conditioning units, but at the other end, with a view overlooking Manchester, is a small table under a pergola covered in fairy lights. There are outdoor pyramid heaters placed around it to give some warmth and their flames add to the romantic setting.

"This is amazing," I whisper.

"It is, isn't it?" Tommy smiles. "I can't take credit. Nick proposed to Charlotte up here and asked the hotel to set this up for that moment. Well, slightly less elaborately. The hotel's marketing team loved the idea and they have kept it and offer it as an exclusive dining experience to VIP guests."

"We are VIPs?" I smirk.

"No, but I have friends in high places," Tommy chuckles and pulls me to the pergola. "I know it's chilly today, but I thought we could at least try it and if it gets too cold, we can move the dinner to one of our rooms." He shrugs and insecurity flashes over his face.

"It's perfect," I say and yank him to me before placing a soft kiss on his mouth. His hand slides around my waist to align our bodies.

"Ella—" he sighs. "Let's eat." I am sure that's not what he wanted to say but I'll let it go.

The food is as amazing as is the setting and the view. By the time they bring a fancy version of Eton Mess, I am not sure if I can take another bite. Tommy has been relaxed and flirty all evening. He doesn't seem to be able to stop touching me and I don't want him to.

We share the dessert. There has been a spark in the air all night, but nothing compared to when he feeds me the sweet meringue. If the waiter hadn't interrupted us, I think Tommy would have pulled me into his lap then and there.

The staff quickly clear our food away before discreetly disappearing again. I give him what I hope to be a seductive smile before walking to the railing surrounding the hotel roof and looking down at the blinking lights of Manchester.

"What are you thinking?" Tommy steps up next to me.

"This has been an amazing evening," I reply as I place my hands on the railing. Tommy takes a few steps, slides his hands around my waist from behind me and pulls me close. My back collides with his chest. He places his chin on my shoulder.

"Now it's perfect," he whispers.

I don't reply. I just melt into his embrace. His warmth seeps into me and I wish I could stop time. In this moment all my problems seem so far away: Lee, the fact that Tommy is my boss, Lee... No, I don't want to think about this.

"Not quite perfect," I finally say into the night air.

"What would make it perfect?"

I swipe my hair to the side to expose my neck. "Your lips right here." I point at the sensitive spot under my ear. I have dreamed about him kissing me there.

Tommy chuckles and leans forward. However, he doesn't give me what I want, at least not right away. He places soft kisses where my collar bone ends and my neck starts and then ever so slowly slides his lips up. His stubble scratches softly over my sensitive skin and the tender touch makes my clit tingle. When he finally licks over the spot I showed him, I moan.

"Tommy, I need more," I sigh and push his hands from my hips towards my pussy. I have been waiting for this for months. In this moment I don't care that the waiters could return any minute. I have lost all sense of reality.

Tommy lifts one of his hands and uses it to grab by chin and turn my head. He captures my lips in a searing kiss whilst his other hand pulls my zip open and slides inside my trousers. His hand is cold from the night air and causes me to shiver when it makes the first contact with my skin.

"More," I mumble. And he finally gives me what I want. His thumb swipes over my clit and two fingers dip into my pussy. He is not tender or building my arousal slowly. He must also be aware that we could get discovered any minute.

"Fuck," I hiss as he finger-fucks me. I press my arse into him and I can feel his hard cock. Of course, I assumed that this would arouse him as well but to feel the evidence so clearly pushes me over the edge. I scream his name and it echoes over the roof tops of Manchester.

"Oh shit," I whisper as if I could take the scream back and place my hand over my mouth. Tommy chuckles and pulls his hand from my jeans. I turn just as he licks two of his fingers clean. I scrunch up my face.

"What?" he asks.

"You could have just wiped that on—" I am not sure what on.

"Are you mad? I have been dying to taste you. And you taste amazing," he replies with his eyes dark and hooded by desire. "Try." He holds out his thumb.

"Eew, no!" I slap him gently on his chest. He shrugs, licks his thumb clean as well before pulling me into a kiss. *Bastard.* I can taste myself on his tongue and I have to admit it actually arouses me. But over my dead body would I tell him that.

"See," he smirks when a noticeable shiver rushes through me.

"Tommy, take me to your room," I reply. That wipes the smirk of his face.

"Are you sure?"

"I have never been more sure of anything."

Chapter 7

Tommy

The minute the door closes behind us, I press Ella against it. Our eyes lock with a fiery intensity, and I can feel the desire burning between us. We are drawn to each other, unable to resist the strong attraction. I cup her face and our lips meet in a passionate, electric kiss. Our hands find each other, and we explore each other's bodies with urgency, wanting to be as close as possible. Time seems to vanish as we lose ourselves in the intensity of that kiss. It's a moment filled with raw passion, and I know it will leave a lasting mark on my heart.

Then Ella softly pushes me back and steps from my embrace. She gives me a shy look over her shoulder as she walks towards the bed before lifting her T-shirt over her head and dropping it on the floor. As she reaches the bed, she turns and locks eyes with me. I hear the zip of her jeans as she slides it down. She slowly pushes her trousers over her hips and steps out of them.

I swallow hard when I take in her perfect beauty. She is standing there with a cautious smile on her face wearing nothing more than green lacy knickers and a bra.

I rush to her, ripping my own T-shirt over my head, and throwing it behind me. The second I reach her I pull her back into my arms and melt into another kiss with her. Her fingers slide over my chest and, fuck, do I need her.

I lift her and gently throw her onto the mattress. She giggles, but the giggles turn into a moan the minute my lips land on her neck. I kiss my way downwards whilst my fingers push the cup of her bra aside. My thumb strokes over one of her nipples before I catch it between my lips and softly suck on it.

"Tommy," she whispers and her hands find their way into my hair.

"Tell me what you need, babe."

"I need you to fuck me," she moans and tries to rub her lace covered pussy against my crotch. Instinct takes over and I push my hard dick against her.

"No, naked, you need to be naked," she says through hard breathing. *Fuck!* I am basically dry humping her. I move from the bed and strip of the rest of my clothes. When my eyes land on her as she wriggles in need on the bed, I absent-mindedly grab my cock and pump it one, two times.

"Tommy!" She holds out her hand and waves me back to her. I step up to the bed, hook my fingers into the each side of her knickers and pull them down. I am about to crawl over her when I suddenly remember.

"Shit," I swear loudly and Ella's eyes widen in surprise. "Condom," I explain and walk over to my bag. Fine, yes, I brought some with me, just in case.

"You have a mighty fine arse, Mr Hunter," she giggles. I look over my shoulder and see her sitting on the bed. I grin and playfully shake my backside. Ella throws her head back and laughs out loud.

I grab the foil packet, rip it open and roll on the condom as I walk back to her. I bend forward and kiss her deeply.

"How do you want it, baby?"

"I don't care as long as I can look into your eyes," she sighs as she touches her forehead against mine. I scoop her up and place her into the centre of the bed before leaning over her. I align myself and push into her warm pussy. *So, this is what perfection feels like.* I groan deeply and hold myself above her. I want to make this last as long as I can, but Ella doesn't agree with that.

She places both of her feet on the mattress and lifts her hips up to meet me head on. I take a deep breath and match her rhythm. I pump into her and her pussy squeezes me hard every time I pull out.

"Fuck, Ella, I won't last this way, you need to slow down," I say through clenched teeth.

"No fucking way, don't hold back, please, I need this. I waited so long for it." *Shit*, her admission that she has also wanted me for much longer than just the kiss on Friday makes me lose all control and I push into her hard and fast. I can feel the tightening at the base of my spine.

"I touched myself so often picturing you doing this," she whispers with her eyes locked on me. She slides her hand between us and starts to circle her clit. "Like this."

That's too much for me. I hammer into her, my eyes always on her. Just when I feel I can't hold any longer, she calls out my name and I follow her with my own orgasm.

I am paralysed for a few minutes with my head in the crook of her neck. I can feel her warmth under me, her smell engulfs me and my mouth remembers her sweet taste. Then I realise that my whole weight is on her.

"Fuck, sorry, baby." I push up on my arms and look down on her.

"What's a better word than perfect? I really feel perfect is not enough for what just happened," she smiles at me and gently strokes my sweat-soaked hair from my face.

I give her a soft kiss and then roll off her. I dispose of the condom in the bathroom bin and grab a towel. I wet it under the tap with warm water and return to the bedroom. Ella hasn't moved. The only indication that she hasn't fallen asleep on me is that she is playing with a strand of her hair. I switch off the light and walk back to the bed in the dim light filtering through the curtains.

"Open your legs, baby," I whisper softly and I wipe her with the towel before throwing it through the open bathroom door.

We crawl under the duvet and I cuddle up behind her. She pulls the arm I have draped over her waist higher and snuggles her face into my palm.

"Can we stay here forever?" she asks into the darkness.

"Imagine all the brilliant things we'll miss."

"Like what? This feels pretty great to me."

"It is, for the lack of a better word, perfect," I chuckle. "But I would like to do so many things with you. I want to show you my favourite spot in the hills. I want to take you for éclairs at Cherry Pie, I want to cook my favourite food for you, I want to have an argument with you so we can make up like bunnies." My last comment makes her laugh out loud.

"Or bungee jumping?"

"You want to bungee jump?" I ask.

"Maybe, although I'm scared of heights."

"I'll take you bungee jumping, if that's what you want."

"You are too busy for all of that, Tommy," she giggles, but immediately a heaviness descends on this conversation.

"I would make time for you." And I mean it. The thought of sharing life with her, not just this stolen moment, makes me feel a deep happiness.

"Are you sure about that?"

"To be honest, I wonder if my long hours are down to me having nothing else in my life. Well, except for the guys and FMR, but hanging out with them lately has been difficult because it reminds me that it is just me. It has been just me since my parents died."

"No other woman? I heard rumours of a she-monster or something."

"She-devil. No, she was when my parents were still alive."

"Want to tell me about her?" She softly strokes over my arm.

"Not much to tell. I thought I was in love with her. My dad warned me that something didn't seem right. Turned out that she was after the hotel. She thought if she married me she would be the boss. But that's not how things work. She quickly found out that me having the hotel meant a lot of debt and not a lot of money to splash around. She dumped me after I told her to stop using the staff as personal slaves." I pull Ella closer and take a deep breath to draw her scent in. It's driving me crazy.

"I'm sorry, Tommy, it must have been hard to lose someone you loved like that."

"I didn't love her. I realised that afterwards. I loved the feeling of being with her. But when she walked out of my life, I didn't miss her. I was actually glad she was gone."

"And then you started to call her *she-devil*?" Ella laughs.

"Nope, it was Alex who came up with that. She tried to get me to drop FMR and he lost it. Even if I would have never done it. I promised my dad."

"I'm glad you didn't give up FMR. It gets you out of the hotel once in a while."

I laugh. She's right, it does.

"What about you?"

"What about me?"

"You know everything about my life, and I know hardly anything."

"Firstly, I don't know everything. And secondly, Lord Grumpiness, whose fault is it that we haven't had a single non-work-related conversation until a couple of days ago?" I pinch her gently in her side and she squeals. She's right though.

"It was safer."

"Safer?"

"Fuck, Ella, the minute you walked through my door I was a goner."

"Yeah, you're right, being grumpy in that case makes total sense," she muses.

"It did. I didn't think it was appropriate for me to drool over you."

"What about now?"

"We'll make it work, if you want to give us a chance." Ella turns in my arms and cups my face.

"I don't want to be anywhere other than with you. We can't help who we fall for and nothing inappropriate has happened."

"Not sure everyone will see it that way and I am willing to die on that hill. But you know it is always the woman that gets blamed. It's ridiculous, but—"

"People will always talk, Tommy. Especially in Fellside. But we know and our friends know the truth ." I place a soft kiss on her mouth.

"Now we are talking about me again! Tell me something about you." Ella shifts to turn her back to me again.

"What do you want to know?"

"Why Fellside?"

"Manchester was just not for me. I felt trapped here. There was no place for me in my family's business and I hate city life. When I came to Fellside for a break, I fell in love with the village and I knew I had to live there. Then I saw Greenview Manor and what you created there is amazing."

"I can't take all the credit. Mr Sinder started it all."

"But you gave it the soul that people love so much."

"Maybe. What about your friends, lovers?" I try to bring the attention back to her.

"I didn't have many friends in Manchester. My last relationship ended two years ago. It just fizzled out. No drama. I am not trying to be cryptic, Tommy, but there really wasn't much in my life before I came to Fellside. This is the first time I've felt at home somewhere," she sighs. Despite her reassurance, I have a feeling there is a lot more to say about this but she snuggles back into me.

"I think we should sleep; we have three presentations to listen to tomorrow." Ella ends our conversation. She turns her head for a final kiss and, as I pull her closer, I promise myself that I will do everything to make this work.

Chapter 8

Ella

I drop another sugar cube in my black coffee and try to stifle a yawn. We are in meeting two of three and I am struggling. Tommy woke me up at six with his face between my legs and after another round between the sheets we ended up giving breakfast a miss and rushed straight to the first meeting.

The only thing that is keeping me from dropping off is the thought that the meeting with my family is next. A look at Tommy is telling me that he is also struggling. He is quieter than he was in the meetings yesterday and his expression lacks enthusiasm.

"This was all very interesting. Thank you so much. As I said, we will take all the proposals away and discuss them with our sales and legal teams." I have to suppress a chuckle. By sales team he means Frank the Head of Sales and by legal team he means the one local lawyer we occasionally ask to check our contracts.

When we get out of the building, Tommy's hand lands on my back and he guides me along the busy pavement.

"They were worse than yesterday," he says with frustration in his voice. "Did anyone read the brief we gave them? Our building is Victorian, and they give me lofty, sleek and modern." My tummy is in knots. When he sees my family's plans, he'll know I was involved. I should have told him yesterday. It was the perfect moment when he asked me about my past. But instead, I just closed up.

Tommy drops his hand from mine when we step into the glass building. I have been through the lobby a million times, yet it feels different now that I enter it as a customer.

The receptionist is new and she doesn't recognise me. Tommy gives his name and she hands over two visitor badges and directs us to the lift. We step into the lift and after the doors close, Tommy takes one of the stickers saying "Visitor" and sticks it to my chest. He taps it once, and a second time and I swear when he does it the third time, he swipes his thumb over my nipple.

"Tommy," I laugh and slap his hand away. He gives me a smirk and puts his visitor pass into his pocket. "No way, Mister, you have to wear it," I protest and reach in his pocket. I pull it out and peel it off before reaching out for his chest. He tries to avoid me and I end up chasing him through the lift.

"Tommy," I shout in fits of laughter just as the lift pings and the door opens. I turn and the smile on my face freezes. Tommy takes the sticker from me, crunches it up and puts it back in his jacket pocket.

Lee gives me an evil smile before directing his attention to Tommy.

"Thomas, it is so nice to meet in person," Lee says in his best sales rep voice before nodding at me. For business connections Tommy always uses his given name.

"Lee," Tommy greets him and shakes his hand. We follow my brother to the boardroom. I don't recognise any of the staff that pass us, and I left less than one year ago. But the firm always had a problem with staff retention, thanks to how my dad and my brother treat them.

After Lee introduces us to some associated staff he has asked to join, we take a seat in the boardroom and Lee serves us tea. I am a little surprised that he is doing it himself. In the past, he would have had a secretary take care of us.

I am fighting hard to keep my anxiety in check. My leg is moving up and down nervously under the table and I feel every pointed look Lee gives me. Tommy glances at me occasionally and when they turn down the lights for the video presentation, he places a calming hand on my thigh. I try to draw strength from his touch.

I have to admit, they have done a great job at putting my drawings into a 3D model. It looks stunning and exactly how I had envisioned it. When the lights come back on there is excitement written all over Tommy's face, but he quickly catches himself.

He leans back and slowly flips through the pages of the folder with the proposal documents. All eyes are on him except for Lee's, which bore into me. I try to avoid him and luckily Tommy starts to ask questions.

When it is clear that there is nothing else to talk about, Tommy gives them the same run down of the next steps he gave everyone else and we leave. For one moment I was scared Lee would pull me aside but Tommy led me straight to the lift and so he didn't really have an opportunity to do so. I could feel his eyes following us though as we left the boardroom, and even Tommy's protective hand on my back couldn't calm me down.

When we step outside the sky is covered with dark clouds. I pull my jacket close and we head towards the car parked in a car park nearby.

"What happened between you and your family?" Tommy breaks the silence.

"Nothing."

"Ella, please. You were anxious the whole time and your brother barely acknowledged you." Tommy stops me and gently turns my face so I have to look into his eyes. I take a deep breath and fight the tears.

"There's no place for me in my family. Just leave it at that. I—" This is the right moment to tell him, but I can't. He will be so angry with me and I will lose him. "Let's go, it will rain any minute." I grab his hand and drag him towards the car.

I only slow down when we step up to the BMW. My hair is damp because it had started to rain as we were approaching the multistorey car park. Tommy unlocks it and opens the boot. He throws his jacket on top of his garment bag and pulls his tie off. I grab a hair band from my bag and tie my hair back. I am about to walk to the passenger side of the car when Tommy's hand lands on my tummy.

"Ella—"

"Seriously, leave it."

"No, this is not about your family. What about us?" My heart starts to beat faster at his question.

"What about us?" I whisper. Is he going to tell me that we have to stop seeing each other? I know I had suggested we could just forget all about it when we return to Fellside, but having spent time with him last night, I don't think I will be able to.

"I don't want this to stop." His eyes are locked on me and I can see the same uncertainty that is in my mind.

"But?"

"But I would prefer if we don't make it public at work until we've had time to explore it." His eyes are pleading but he has nothing to fear. My lips tilt into a smile.

"So you want to keep seeing me?"

"Fuck, Ella, of course. I wanted nothing more for months. But I don't want you to feel like you are my dirty little secret."

"The way I see it, I kissed you first and I asked you to fuck me last night so I think you are my dirty little secret," I sass which causes Tommy to throw his head back in laughter. "But, joking aside, we're adults. I'm sure we can behave ourselves at work and in the evenings, when you can pull yourself away from work, you can come to mine. I have a nice little flat with only holiday lets as neighbours." I place a soft kiss on his mouth.

"Just do me one favour—"

"Yes?"

"No more pencil skirts. I can't guarantee I can keep my hands to myself otherwise." He presses his lips to my forehead and walks to the driver's side of the car.

"I make no such promises," I tease him with a smirk and pull the seatbelt over me. There are butterflies in my tummy and I have a cheesy smile on my lips but deep down there is a dark feeling trying to rise to the surface. *I need to tell him the truth. I need to!*

Chapter 9

Tommy

I can hear Ella on the phone. The door to my office is closed, simply because otherwise I wouldn't get any work done. Ella and I have been secretly dating for two weeks now and I just can't get enough of her. I stay at her flat most nights and return to the hotel in the early morning. I am not sure what my staff think, but I am convinced that rumours are flying around about me having a new person in my life that keeps me out all night.

Only they haven't guessed yet that it's Ella who I spend my evenings with.

"Fuck," I mumble and rub the back of my neck. I desperately want to call her in so I can kiss her. That woman is like an addiction.

We have settled into a routine of being professional at work and then ripping each other's clothes off at home. It is crazy, exhilarating but also exhausting. I don't want to keep her a secret anymore. I want the world to see how amazing she is.

"Tommy," Ella says as she knocks on the door before opening it a gap. "Alex is here."

"Send him in." I give her a small smile which she returns before stepping aside. Alex glances at her and then me before smirking. He drops in the chair in front of my desk.

"I'll get some tea," Ella says and excuses herself.

"So, you did make a move," he grins knowingly.

"What are you doing here, Alex?" I ignore his question because I really don't have time for this. Me mooning over Ella has already put me behind schedule.

Alex doesn't answer and just crosses his arms defiantly in front of his chest. He is a bloody master in just stubbornly waiting until you spill your guts. He could work for MI5.

"Okay, yes, we are dating. But nobody in the hotel knows," I whisper and can't help it when a smile spreads over my face.

"You look happy." I sigh at Alex's statement.

"Very. Mate, I... I really can't describe it."

"No need. Don't forget I married the love of my life. I get it," he says before scratching his chest.

"So, what do you want? You didn't come all the way out here to chitchat."

"Rob called. His doctor said he is out for another eight weeks."

"Fuck!" My words echo around the room. Rob had an accident on a mission a few months back and his leg got badly damaged. With him out of action and Suzie about to give birth, our unit is on the verge of being understaffed. That means that if anyone is on holiday or ill we won't be called on.

"Why did he call you?" I'm the leader of the team; Rob should have spoken to me.

"He called me for advice on how to best tell you. I promised him I'd tell you because I have a solution." He scratches his left peck again.

"Why do you keep scratching yourself? Do you have a rash?"

"No, but this is kind of the reason why I am here. I have a tattoo and it's healing at the moment." He looks at me sheepishly.

"You have a tattoo?" I raise my eyebrow in question.

"Yes, why is that so surprising?"

"Well, for a start, I didn't know you were into tattoos."

"I wanted one for Emma and when the tattoo shop opened in the village—" I stop him mid-sentence when I can't hold back a chuckle.

"Are you telling me the conservative twats of the chamber of commerce allowed a tattoo shop to open in the village?"

Alex leans forward and whispers with a smirk on his face, "Smack bang in the middle right opposite the church." We look at each other for a minute before bursting into fits of laughter.

"Boy, how did the WI take it?"

"Don't know yet. I think they are still in their war council. Anyway. Ryan, the guy who runs the shop, and I got talking when he was doing my tattoo. He was a climber in his youth. He has started again now he moved to Fellside and I thought we could take him on as a trainee."

"I take it he is interested."

"Yes, and he understands the time commitment. He has someone working with him who can cover."

I lean back in my chair. Having another person on the team would definitely be great, even if it is just a trainee. He will only be able to do the basic tasks in the beginning, but it will be a great help nonetheless. And it would solve the staffing problem.

"Why not," I shrug. "Bring him to the meeting next week and I'll have a chat with him."

"Excellent, well, I'll leave you to your work."

"You know you could have just called me."

"Your head housekeeper sent for me; something about a broken headboard or something. I'm heading to housekeeping now, but I wanted to talk to you first." Alex is our go-to carpenter when we need repairs at the hotel. Not because he is my friend, but because he is the best and most reliable.

"Thanks, mate."

"No worries."

"Alex," I stop him as he is about to open the door, "What tattoo did you get?"

"A blossom with Emma's name in it." He has a loved up look on his face. Yes, he definitely found the love of his life. The minute I think this, Ella's face pops into my mind.

"How very romantic of you," I chuckle but he knows I am just teasing.

"Hey, I'm Mr Romantic," he replies with a smirk before waving goodbye and closing the door behind him.

I stare out of the window. I love Greenview Manor but lately I've been wondering if there isn't more to life.

"Tommy?" Ella's soft voice brings me back to reality. I swivel in my chair and see her standing in the door.

"Ella, would you mind coming in and closing the door please?" I ask in my best boss voice. A small smile tilts her lips and she does as I asked. I hold out my hand to her and she crosses the room to give me hers. I pull her into my lap and the minute she is in my arms I feel relaxed and content.

"Tommy, " she giggles quietly, "What if someone comes?"

"They wouldn't enter my office without knocking," I whisper against the skin of her neck before placing soft kisses there. A small moan escapes her when I hit the spot right behind her ear that she likes so much.

"Are you going to come over today?" she asks before sliding her hand over the front of my trouser where my hard cock is straining to get out and play.

"A thousand angry hotel guests couldn't keep me away from you."

Ella giggles and then slaps me tenderly on the chest.

"Hush, don't jinx it. We have been complaint free for four weeks." It doesn't matter how perfect a hotel is, things will go wrong and guests make sure you know about it. And even if nothing goes wrong, some still think "The guest is the king" and behave like my staff are their personal servants. It sometimes amazes me how people who are perfectly decent in normal life can turn into complete and utter arseholes the minute they book themselves into a hotel. Common decency and politeness are left at home.

"I don't want to talk about our guests now," I mumble before pulling her to me for a deep kiss. My fingers slide up her thigh and under her pencil skirt.

"Tommy!" She softly pushes off me and stands up. "Not here, you naughty man." She tries to reprimand me, but the lust in her eyes tells me otherwise.

"I told you, if you wear these skirts, I can't be held responsible for anything." She laughs and steps up to me again. She cups my face and places one long kiss on my lips. "That has to be enough until later."

"Fine," I grumble.

"Well, Boss, I am heading home for the day because it's five o'clock," she says loudly even if there is nobody around, before winking at me. As she opens the door, I can see Sheila hovering outside.

"Sheila, do you need anything?" I call out. She gives Ella a smile before stepping into my office looking a little nervous. "Is everything okay?" I ask again.

"Yeah, yes, sure. I have the staff rotas for you." She holds out a few pieces of paper. Yes, we are still old school here but Sheila recently showed me an app we can use and I signed off the order for it yesterday.

"Thanks." When she doesn't move, I add, "Anything else?"

"I—" She stops herself, walks up to the door and closes it. "Tommy, I have been working with you for three years now and I hope we have a relationship where I can be open with you?"

"Sure," I lean back but I am getting nervous. Is she planning to resign? Sheila is a superstar and losing her would be a massive blow.

"Are you and Ella dating?"

"What?" Shock must be showing on my face because she nervously rubs her hands together.

"It's just that you are different since the two of you are back from Manchester. Or should I say, you are back to your cheerful self. Ever since Ella joined us you were so moody; staff had started to talk thinking that the hotel is in financial trouble and that they could get fired any minute."

I take a deep breath. I hadn't realised how I had come across.

"Shit, I don't want staff to worry. I'll talk to them." Sheila nods.

"You should talk to them, but you should tell them the truth."

"About?"

"You and Ella."

"Sheila—"

"No, Tommy, please, as a friend, let me tell you. Nobody will care. You didn't date her before she came here. She has no advantage by dating you, it's not like you can promote her above anyone. She is widely liked. So, nobody will care. If anything, they'll be happy for you. But by being honest you stop any rumours from spreading. I mean, I noticed because I'm observant," she giggles, "but in the long run you won't be able to hide it. Better out in the open and everyone will forget about it."

I run one hand through my hair. "We were waiting until we know if it's serious."

"From what I've observed, you're both smitten."

"How? We were so careful."

Sheila laughs out loud.

"Please! Whenever she walks into a room, your eyes seek her out. You watch her interact with others and you have this small smile on your lips. And your door has been closed every time I've come to the office in the last two weeks." I should be embarrassed but all I can do is smile.

"I'll talk to her and we'll announce it in the next few days. I'm just worried staff will think I am a hypocrite."

"Because of Ian?" Anna caught the head chef making inappropriate advances on a female apprentice whilst I was in Manchester and fired him on the spot.

"Tommy, don't be silly. That's completely different. Ian was a sleaze who behaved highly inappropriately toward a number of women. I don't need to know the details of your relationship to know that Ella wants this too."

"She does."

Sheila nods and gets off the chair.

"Trust me, nobody will judge the two of you because everyone will see this isn't a seedy affair but a lot more."

"Thanks, Sheila."

"Not at all. That's my job."

"What? Watching out for my love life?" I chuckle.

"No, supporting you in making this hotel a success. The team holds you in high regard, Tommy. We have one of the lowest rates of staff turnover in the area and that's because people love working for you. Everyone will be happy for you and then move on. And I'll make sure they don't gossip," she says with a final laugh before leaving.

My eyes drop to the expansion plans on my desk. My lawyer had a look at the proposal from Ella's family and found a few points in the contract to query but otherwise it looks fine. I really should be preparing a reply to them but instead I push the papers into one pile, grab my mobile and my car keys. I need to be with Ella.

I walk pass reception to let them know that I'm leaving for the day and head to my car. As the car rolls along the driveway my heart starts hammering faster. She left less than an hour ago, but I miss her already.

Chapter 10

Ella

I pull the towel into a tight turban on my head to keep my wet hair from dripping. The bedroom looks a bit like a bomb site with Tommy's bag in the corner overflowing with clothes. I reach for some T-shirts that seem to be fresh and put them on a hanger in my wardrobe.

He spends almost every night here and has made it a habit to leave clothes at mine to change into. And it makes me weirdly happy. It feels domestic, it feels permanent. I throw some of his dirty clothes in the laundry hamper in the corner and add my clothes from today on top of it, before putting on some yoga pants and casual top.

I am past that stage where I feel embarrassed about not wearing a bra in front of Tommy. He has seen my breasts plenty of times, and he knows they are not as perky as those of a twenty-year-old, but he doesn't seem to mind. I grin. *No, he doesn't mind at all.*

I drag the hamper to the kitchen and load the washing machine with our clothes. My hips are swaying along to the music filtering through the speaker on the kitchen counter. I love some music when I do housework. I am just wondering if I should drive to the supermarket to do some shopping when the flat door opens. Tommy has a habit of working late so I have given him a key to my flat to let himself in late at night.

My eyes flit to the clock on the wall. It is only just after six. He is early.

"Hey, babe," he says before dropping two full shopping bags on the kitchen counter.

I lean back against the cabinets.

"What's all this?"

"I saw food was low and I thought we could cook together," he grins at me. But then something changes in his face. He crosses the distance between us and smashes his lips on mine. His kiss is urgent.

"Fuck, you look hot," he mumbles in between kisses. I laugh out loud and softly push him off me.

"Tommy, I am wearing yoga pants, towel turban and no underwear. I don't think hot is the right word."

"You are right, you look amazingly hot," he says; his eyes are dark and full of desire. "Wait, did you say no underwear?"

"Maybe." I can feel the heat in my cheeks.

"Fuck, let me see." He reaches out and grabs the waistband of my yoga pants.

"Tommy!" I laugh out loud but I don't stop him when he pushes my trousers over my hips. The soft material slides to the floor. Before I can say anything else he gently places me on the kitchen counter and steps between my legs. My towel turban falls off and my damp hair uncoils.

"I need you, Ella," he whispers with his warm lips sliding over my neck whilst his fingers dip between my legs.

"I'm not stopping you," I reply and Tommy growls deeply. He places my legs around his hips and when I lock them, he lifts me off the counter and carries me towards the bedroom.

"I'll tell you now, Ella, this won't be slow or tender. I need you hard and fast today."

"Hard and fast is good," I moan, nibbling on his earlobe. He loves it when I do that.

When we get to the bedroom, he drops me onto the bed. The minute I hit the mattress, he reaches for his trousers, unbuckles his belt and slides them down. I take my T-shirt off and then lay there waiting on the bed for this amazing man.

After taking off his clothes, Tommy crawls onto the bed and whispers in my ear, "Turn around." As I move to be on my front, he pushes a pillow under my hips and starts kissing a trail down my spine.

"Fuck, Tommy, you said hard and fast. I need you in me now," I complain. My fingers are grabbing the sheet underneath me tightly. I hear the familiar sound of a condom package being ripped open.

Tommy slides his body along mine and then enters me from behind. I love the angle he gets when he takes me this way. His hands slide along my arms and our fingers lock. He anchors us to the mattress and then pushes into me ferociously. With every thrust his hard cock hits my G-spot. My orgasm builds too fast. I don't want this to be over, but Tommy doesn't slow down. He groans and sucks on my neck.

"You feel so amazing, Ella. Being with you is the best feeling in the world," he whispers in my ear. Leave it to this man to say the sweetest thing in the hottest moment.

"Tommy!" I cry out as the orgasm washes over me. He keeps moving until he finds his own release and his thrusts keep my orgasm raging until he slumps down on me and stills.

He rolls to the side so his weight is no longer on me and takes me with him. His arms close around me and he holds me tight. This right here is my favourite place in the world.

“Baby, I forgot to get milk yesterday,” Tommy calls out from the kitchen. He was supposed to make us a cup of tea whilst I get ready for work.

“We can always have a cuppa at work, " I call back. Tommy appears in the bedroom door. He is already in his shirt and trousers, but his tie is hanging loosely around his neck.

“That’s fine, I’ll just pop to the corner shop,” he says before placing a small kiss on my neck.

“Okay,” I smile and he leaves me alone in the bedroom. I reach for one of my smart black trousers. I need to get some work done today and Tommy tends to distract me more when I wear my skirts. I feel the familiar warmth spreading through me. It’s the feeling I get every time I think about him and me. He wants to tell the staff today. We talked about it a lot last night, and I can see the point. Frankly, I don’t want to hide anymore.

The doorbell pulls me from my thoughts. I pick up my suit jacket from where I had put it on the bed and walk to the flat door. I pull it open expecting a sheepish looking Tommy because he has forgotten his keys yet again.

Instead, a strong hand grabs me around the throat and presses me against the nearest wall. I hear the door slam shut.

"Lee, you're hurting me," I croak out. My head stings from where it made contact with the wall, and his fingers press painfully into the sides of my neck.

"You don't even know how much I can hurt you. What the fuck are you playing, Ella? Why have we not received the yes on the project yet?"

"He's still working on your proposal," I sputter. My fingers grab his hand and I try to push him off me. Reluctantly, he lets go of me and I slump against the wall.

"Ella, I've fucking had enough. We need this deal. We need the signature on the paper by the end of the week or the bank won't extend our loan. Make it happen," Lee shouts and points his fingers at me. I try to move away from him but he has me cornered against the wall.

"Do you fucking understand?" he roars. I nod just as the door opens.

Everyone freezes for a moment.

"What's going on?" Tommy asks.

Lee's eyes dart between me and Tommy. Concern briefly crosses his face before he takes another step back.

"Thomas," he greets Tommy, "I was just in the village so I popped by to say hello to my sister." His tone is cold but not unpleasant. His stance is wide and his arms are crossed in front of his chest. "We haven't heard back from you on the proposal yet." There is a smirk on his face. "But I guess you have been busy." When he says the last word, his eyes look back at me where I am leaning against the wall.

"We'll let everyone know in the next few days," Tommy replies politely but the tone of his voice makes it sound like a threat.

"I see... I didn't know you and Ella are living together," Lee looks straight into Tommy's eyes. My heart hammers in my chest and the fear I feel is making it hard to breathe.

"We're not," I whisper drawing the attention of both of them to me. Lee slowly turns his head and his eyes bore into mine.

"Well, it's not really my business," he finally says. "I'll see you later." He puts an emphasis on the word later. Tommy, who had been blocking the flat door, takes a step aside, allowing Lee to leave.

When the door clicks shut and I know he is gone, I can't hold my tears back any longer. I slide downwards until I end up sitting on the floor sobbing.

"Ella?" Tommy's voice is laced with confusion and worry.

"I'm so sorry, Tommy. I am so sorry," I cry out in between sobs. I'm not looking at him, instead my head is buried in my hands. Tommy scoops me up and carries me to the sofa where he holds me close.

"Tell me what happened."

"I should have told you the truth," I whisper. I can feel him stiffen under me.

"What do you mean?" he asks. He sounds more agitated now. I lift my head from his chest. I notice that my hands are shaking and I press them together in the hope to make it stop.

"Lee wants me to convince you to choose my family's business," I say in a small voice. Tommy just stares at me and says nothing. He lifts me of his lap and stands up.

"What are you saying Ella. I don't—" He paces the living room before heading for the kitchen and returning with a piece of kitchen roll. He holds it out to me and I take the paper towel with shaking hands. I wipe my tears away and blow my nose, but I am not sure what good it will do as my tears are still rolling uncontrollably over my cheeks.

Tommy is just staring down at me. "I don't believe this. Explain it again to me. When I sent out the tender invitations you said you had nothing to do with your family's business!" He looks confused and stressed.

"Lee... Lee made me draw up the plans for the hotel because he knew I would know what you would like. And then he wanted me to convince you to sign the proposal. Tommy, I'm sorry. I'm so sorry."

"You took this job to manipulate me? And what for? To serve a family you told me you don't feel you belong to?" He crosses his arms in front of his chest and his facial expression has changed from confusion to anger. His last sentence hits me hard.

"No, no. I didn't know anything about the expansion when I accepted the job. I told you that I moved here to get away from my family."

"Then what? You started this relationship," he puts the word relationship in air quotes, "to get me to do what you want?"

I shake my head. Of course, he would think that. That's exactly what it looks like, but I would have hoped he would trust me more.

"No, I kept telling Lee I wouldn't do that to you. But Lee kept threatening me. I told him you have to make up your own mind. But—"

"But what?" He sounds cold and hurt.

"I did draw up the plans they showed you, there's no denying it. Lee's ideas are crap which is why the firm is in trouble. I did most of the planning behind the scenes in the past, and Lee took credit for my work. Both my brother and my dad kept telling me that I should stop being self-centred when I asked that projects have my name on them. It was all for the family. That's why I left. And when Lee found out about this project, he and dad, well—"

Tommy's glare makes me cry more. I am shaking and I feel like something is dying in me. I stand up and walk to him. I put my hand on his arm but he moves away from me.

"In short, you used your knowledge of me to draw up plans that you knew I would like to give your family's firm an advantage."

"Yes," I whisper. "And no. When I drew the plans, I wanted you to have the build you had envisioned. I love this hotel and I wanted it to be right. But, yes, I knew it would also help my family. I hoped they would then leave me alone."

"Fuck, Ella!" There are so many emotions in his voice but the anger and hurt are unmissable.

"I wanted to tell you a number of times over the last couple of weeks, but I was worried you would despise me."

"Ella—" His fingers roam through his hair and he looks to be in pain. "Ella, I... what is this?" He stops what he wanted to say. Instead he tenderly takes my chin between his thumb and forefinger and turns my head.

"What is what?"

"You have bruises on your neck. They weren't there earlier." My hand shoots up to cover them. "Ella, how did you get the bruises?" His eyes are locked on me.

"It doesn't matter."

"It matters to me. Was it Lee?"

I don't reply and that is answer enough for Tommy.

"I am going to fucking kill him," he growls before walking towards the door. I grab his arm and pull him back.

"No, Tommy, leave it."

"You need to at least report him to the police."

"He's family." I can't report Lee. He and my family will never let me forget this. Never.

"Fuck, Ella, no. That is not an excuse."

"Please, Tommy," I plead with him. "Tell them today that you won't hire them and he will be out of our life, your life."

Tommy's hands are in fists and his breathing is laboured.

"Please. I'll pack my stuff and move somewhere else and you don't have to deal with any of us again."

He puts his hands on my shoulders.

"What are you talking about?"

"I know I hurt you and I am so sorry that I didn't tell you the truth, but please believe me: none of my feelings were a lie. I know what I did is unforgivable, but I just want you to know that." More tears are flowing over my face. I feel tired and empty. I just want to curl up in a ball somewhere and cry until the pain stops. Silence fills the room as we look into each other's eyes.

"Ella, I love you," Tommy finally says. "Am I happy that you didn't tell me the truth? No! But I can now see why." He slides his fingers over the spot where Lee had pressed his fingers into my neck. "Baby, I love you." He places his forehead against mine. The anger has disappeared from his face. "Just promise me from now on, no more lies. If you are scared, you'll tell me."

"I am so scared, Tommy," I whisper.

"What about, baby?"

"Of losing you." I sob and he finally pulls me in his arms. I slide my hands around his waist and melt into his embrace.

"You're not losing me, Ella."

Chapter 11

Tommy

"Mr Hunter, Mr Compton, they are ready for you now," the young secretary says. I drop my phone back into my pocket and Nick and I rise from our chairs in the waiting room of Lee's company. I have been fighting my anger since Lee left Ella's flat but I can still feel it burning in my guts.

I could have sent them an email rejecting the project but I needed to see them in person to make sure they leave Ella alone. Nick has tagged along as a witness but also to stop me in case I need to be held back. Any of the FMR guys would have been here with me, but Nick, who is a teacher, is on half term at the moment, so it was easy for him to join me on a meeting during the week.

"Thomas, it is so good to see you again." Despite his words, Lee doesn't sound happy to see me again. His eyes are coldly staring at me when he holds out his hand. I grab it and squeeze it as hard as I can. For a brief moment he shows the pain on his face but then he is in control again. Oh, the things I would like to do to this man. I had to promise Ella to leave the police out of it and to not engage in any physical violence. This family has put her through so much but they still have a hold on her. It's some weird form of Stockholm syndrome and I want to get her some help to work through this.

Truthfully, she didn't need to worry. I am not a violent person. I don't think I have ever had a fist fight, not even in school. But for Lee I would make an exception. Nobody hurts Ella. Nobody.

"Let me introduce you to my father." The older man in the room rises from the chair and comes over.

"Pleasure, and who is your associate?" the older gentleman asks. He looks very much like Lee. I can't see anything in his face that would remind me of Ella.

"This is my friend Nick." I leave it at that and neither Lee nor his father ask more, even if I can see that they are curious.

"Should we take a seat?" Lee tries to guide us towards the boardroom table where a few staff members sit, just like the last time.

"I don't think that will be necessary," I stop him. "I am just here to tell you that your firm won't get the contract." The fake smile drops from both their faces. I can feel Nick taking a small step closer. He is telling me he is here.

"I don't work with people who use and abuse their own family members."

"But—" Lee tries to interject.

"No," I shout and my voice booms through the meeting room. "You listen." I take a step closer and Nick is again right behind me. "If you ever so much as look in Ella's direction again, I will go to the police even if I have to break I promise I made her."

I wait but neither of them says anything. The other people in the room shift nervously.

"Well, fuck you and your hotel," Lee finally hisses.

"Mr Hunter, I think it is best if you leave now." I can see anger in the old man's face and I am almost losing it. Neither of them is showing any kind of remorse.

"She's your daughter; you should have protected her," I shout before turning to Lee, "She is your sister, how can you treat her like that?"

"Please leave," Ella's father says. "I don't want to do business with someone who accuses us of practices like this. Especially not someone who is abusing his position to seduce a vulnerable woman. I wonder what your guests and staff would say about that," he grins at me like he just landed a blow.

I feel Nick's hand on my shoulder and I'm glad he is there. I try to calm my breathing because I am close to a heart attack with the rage flowing through me.

"My staff know that I'm in love with your daughter." I can see his self-assured smile slip for a minute. "And my guests only care if their poached eggs are runny." Nick snorts behind me. I'm not even lying. I rounded up all our staff yesterday and I made a very brief speech. They all cheered and then went back to business. Sheila was right. Nobody really cared.

"Don't threaten us because you won't win that game. I have way more information on you than you will ever have on me. Not that I have ever behaved in a way that could be harmful to my or Ella's future, like you have. Stay away from Ella, best stay away from Fellside. Only because she asked me, I haven't called the police...yet. But if I ever see you in Fellside again, I will get the police involved." I point at them both before turning around and stalking to the door of the meeting room.

"It was not nice to meet you," Nick chuckles behind me to everyone in the boardroom before catching up with me.

"Tommy, take a few breaths before you keel over," Nick demands.

"Can you fucking believe them?" I shout, causing a young guy who is standing in front of the lift to drop a pile of papers. He quickly scoops them up and scurries away.

"No. But then I can't imagine threatening my own sister."

"Your sister would kick your arse if you tried," I reply as we step into the lift.

"True," he chuckles, "But seriously, Tommy, I could never do something like that. They are two twisted fucks and not worth your breath."

"Let's go back. I need to see her."

"Fucking hell, a four hour round journey just to yell at two first grade arseholes. At least get me a coffee," he chuckles.

"I'll get you a takeaway," I laugh before adding, "I need to see her."

Nick drops me off at the hotel and I jog up the back stairs to my flat. After sharing our relationship with the staff, I asked her to stay with me until I felt confident that Lee wouldn't trouble her again. To my surprise, she agreed without putting up a fight. This makes me think she's still scared, even though she tried to reassure me that Lee would back off.

"Babe," I call out as I enter the flat.

"Bathroom," Ella replies. I drop my jacket on the chair, toe off my shoes and follow the voice.

"Can I come in?" I ask.

"Sure," she giggles. I open the door and steam hits me in the face. The room is dimly lit with only two of the wall lights on. Ella is sitting in my large bathtub covered by bath foam with a book in her hand. She gives me a half smile.

"Hope that's okay? I thought it might help me relax." She looks at me concerned.

"Of course. Can I join you?" Her eyes light up and that's all I need to strip off my clothes. When I step up to the tub, she drops the book on the floor. The warm water immediately calms me as I slide in behind her, but I only relax fully once she leans back against my chest and I can put my arms around her.

"How did it go?" she asks with worry in her voice. She let me leave after I had promised that I wouldn't call the police.

"I hate them," I hiss. She doesn't reply to my statement. Instead, she starts to gently stroke my arm. "Your father threatened to give our relationship away to create some scandal."

"What scandal? Who the heck would care?" She laughs bitterly.

"That's what I told him. I—" I take a deep breath.

"Tommy, tell me."

"I am sorry that you belong to a family like that."

"I never really belonged in that family," she whispers, and then presses tighter against me.

"I am so sorry about everything you have been through."

"Thank you. And thank you for standing with me, even after I lied to you."

"Ella—" She turns and presses a soft kiss on my mouth. "Make love to me, Tommy."

Chapter 12

Ella

I glance at my watch as I walk up to Tommy's BMW parked at the back of the FMR building. He had to attend a team meeting and I used the time to do some shopping, but he should be almost finished. I place the large heavy bag with my hiking boots next to the car. Tommy wants to take me up on Fellside Horseshoe next weekend and I wanted to make sure I have the right footwear. I will struggle enough as it is because my fitness is not the best, so at least I want to make sure my feet will be comfortable.

"You bitch." I recognise Lee's voice but before I can react, he grabs my hair and pulls me with him. He drags me near the wall of the house, out of sight of the road. The only way someone would see us here is if they walked out of the building.

"Lee, please, let me go," I plead.

"No. It's about time you get what you deserve. I have been following you all morning and now I finally get you alone."

My eyes dart around but I can't see anyone. I notice a window open on the upper floor. Maybe if I scream someone will hear me. I open my mouth but Lee puts his hand over it and presses me up against the wall.

"No, no, Ella, no calling for your knight in shining armour." I can smell alcohol on his breath. And it's not just a hint, he smells like a brewery. Panic rises in me. Lee is unpredictable at the best of times, but when he is drunk there is no bargaining with him. When I was younger I ended up in hospital with a broken cheek bone thanks to him. My mum told the doctors a random man attacked me on the way home from the pub. Afterwards she said that it must have been my mistake. I must have provoked him because otherwise he'd never have hit me that hard.

"We are ruined and all just because of you. Dad is furious. You already spread your legs to him, what was the big issue? We just asked you for a small favour but no, you couldn't do that for us." His hand slips a little and is now only half covering my mouth. I use the opportunity to open my lips and bite his hand hard. He yelps out in pain and pulls it back.

"You stupid cow," he shouts and I feel an explosion on my face before his fingers squeeze my windpipe again. I am gasping for air.

"Hey!" I hear someone shout. Lee's hand drops from my throat. I can finally breathe again.

"What the fuck did I tell you about showing your face here," Tommy booms. Lee takes some steps back and Tommy is next to me in instant. When he sees my face where, judging by the pain radiating from my cheek, Lee's hand imprint must be visible, he turns around to face my brother.

"You fucker, I'll kill you," he growls. Lee just glares at him. Before Tommy can start towards my brother, I reach out and softly grab Tommy's arm.

"Don't, he's not worth it," I whisper. He looks at me. I can see the anger and the pain in his face. This time he's not angry with me, but he's in pain because of what's happened to me. He gently cups my face.

"Baby, I can't let him get—"

"Watch out!" a voice shouts from behind Tommy. We both look at Lee and see him charging forward something silver in his hand. Tommy turns back to me and cages me against the wall protecting me with his whole body. Our eyes are locked and in slow motion I wait for him to react to Lee slamming into him but he doesn't. Instead, there is a scream next to us, and a tall, tattooed guy is pinning Lee to the floor.

"Get off me!" My brother tries to wriggle free. "That's assault!"

"Shut up," the guy sitting on him says and presses Lee's head against the tarmac. His bicep, which is covered in tribal symbols, flexes under the power he's using to restrain Lee. "What do you call what you just did to her?" he hisses at Lee.

"I did nothing to her. Ella, tell him." He must be delusional. Nick kicks the knife lying on the floor away and kneels down next to Lee to pin his legs down.

"Well, sadly for you there are two CCTV cameras up there, I'm pretty sure they'll tell a different story," Alex replies calmly as he puts his phone in his pocket. He looks at Tommy and adds, "Police will be here in five minutes."

"Tommy, take care of your girl. Nick and Alex can help me with this fucker," the tattooed guy says and gives us a reassuring smile.

Tommy nods at his team and guides me into the building. He takes me to a small kitchen on the upper floor of the FMR centre. Without saying a word, he lifts me to sit on one of the counters before grabbing an ice pack from a small fridge freezer. He wraps it in a tea towel and gently presses it against my face.

"How are you?" he finally breaks the silence. His voice is quiet but there is an edge to it. I take a deep breath and wait for the tears to come, but there are none.

"Tommy, I need to tell the police," I finally whisper. I know I said I wouldn't but I have to. I can't live like this anymore and I can't risk Tommy getting hurt either. Enough is enough.

"Yes, baby, you do and I'll come with you." Tommy looks relieved that he doesn't have to fight me on it. Ever since the incident in my flat he has been trying to get me to go to the police, but something held me back. Was it the shame or fear, or maybe the knowledge that if I take that step then I definitely no longer have a family? I don't know. Maybe it was a combination of all three.

"Thank you." I don't need to explain what I'm thankful for. He put himself in harm's way to protect me. I don't even want to think about what could have happened if the others hadn't stopped Lee. But Tommy didn't hesitate. He put his life on the line for me. A sob escapes me.

"Any time. I love you, Ella, and I'll do anything to make sure you are safe." I nod at his words.

"Who was the guy who stopped Lee?" I ask.

"That's Ryan. We were deciding if he can join the team as a trainee and I think he just qualified." He steps between my legs and I snuggle up against him.

"How are you feeling?"

"Hurt, sad, but also relieved. I am sorry I dragged you into all this drama."

"I'm not. I don't care what happens in your life, the only thing I care about is that I'm part of it." A lone tear rolls over my cheek. This time it's a happy tear.

"Sorry to interrupt." Alex has appeared in the doorway. "The police are outside and they would like a word with both of you. I'll send them upstairs if that's okay?" Tommy's eyes remained on me as Alex was talking, but now he turns his head.

"Yeah, that's fine," he replies. Alex nods and pushes himself away from the doorway and turns.

"Oh, and Alex," Tommy shouts after his friend. When Alex looks at him, he adds, "Tell Ryan welcome to the team." They both grin at each other.

Tommy turns off the main light before joining me in bed. He slides under the duvet and pulls me into his arms. As I reach out for the bedside lamp to switch it off he stops me.

"Wait, I know you are tired, baby, but you have barely spoken since we've been back. Are you okay?"

Am I okay? How can I be when I just filed a police report against my brother for physical assault? After the police took our statements at the FMR building they asked us to come to the station to take a full account from me. I was there for two hours telling them everything that's happened.

Tommy wasn't allowed to be with me, and I would have needed his strength. But he was waiting outside for me. The minute I walked from the room he pulled me into his arms and I felt safe again.

"I don't know," I admit. We had promised each other that there would be no more secrets. He frowns and pulls me closer. He is lying on his side and his head is propped up on one hand. His other hand is drawing circles on my tummy

"I think we should take a holiday. Just you and me. Two weeks relaxing in the sun somewhere," he finally says. I study his face. He looks sincere which makes me burst out laughing.

"Why are you laughing?"

"Because you can barely find time for lunch. How are you going to make time for a holiday?"

"I have been thinking. I'll promote Sheila to General Manager. Hell, when Mr Sinder owned the hotel, he hired me as a general manager. And it worked well. He carried the big decisions and I took care of the day-to-day problems. I think it's time to do the same."

I cup his face and softly stroke his cheek. "Are you sure you're ready for this?"

"Ella, I've been working since I was sixteen. In the last five years I've barely had a day off. I'm the one who constantly cancels on my friends."

"They understand."

"Yeah, they do. They've never held my no-shows against me. But they're my family and I want to make time for them. And I need to make time for you. And I need to make time for me. I'm tired, Ella."

I smile at him. "In that case, it sounds like a very good plan. What about the extension?"

"Well," he bends forward and places soft kisses on my collarbone, "I'll speak with the bank and ask if we can delay the loan by six months. This gives us enough time...," he places a kiss between my breast, "... for us to go on a nice holiday and for me to train Sheila up. Oh, and for you to draw up new plans."

I place my hands on either side of his head and make him look at me.

"Me?"

"Yes, regardless of what happened the plans you did were part of your father's company's proposal, so legally we could get into trouble using them. But I'm pretty confident you can come up with an even better concept," he grins. I sit up, excitement coursing through me.

"Actually, I was thinking. If you are interested, how about adding a few self-contained cottages down at the lake, with a main building including a yoga studio and a library? We could offer it as a retreat area. We had an enquiry from a group of authors last week who want to hold a writing retreat and that's how I came up with the idea. They could shut off down there and if they need a little bit more luxury they can walk up to the hotel for dinner."

Tommy just stares at me.

"If you hate the idea, that's okay," I mumble, sliding back under the duvet.

"No, baby, I love the idea," he assures me before placing a soft kiss on my lips. "I was just wondering what I did to deserve you in my life." With this, he pulls me back to him and kisses me long and hard. I'm pretty sure I should ask the same question but I'm just glad we found to each other.

Epilogue

Tommy

"Ella, look at me. You can do this, baby." My voice is as calm as it can be. Ella is shaking in my arms. Her eyes are filled with tears and her fingers are digging into my back.

"Are you ready?" the instructor asks. Ella presses her head against my neck and shakes her head, but I give him a smile and a thumbs up. Ella is strapped to me and I slowly walk us to the edge of the platform.

Ella and I are in New Zealand. Our short two-week holiday in the sun turned into a four-week trip around New Zealand in a VW minibus. We have been whale watching, been on some amazing hikes, and have camped at some beautiful spots. Now we are on the South Island for Ella to fulfil one of her bucket list dreams: bungee jumping. She made me swear on my life yesterday that I'd make her do it regardless of how scared she felt.

"Baby, look at me please," I whisper. Ella meets my eyes, a lone tear running down her cheek. She is hyperventilating. "Breathe, baby. Copy me." I take a deep breath, and another. She tries to copy me and her breathing slows a little.

"Are you sure you want to do this?"

"No, Tommy, you promised," she says between deep breaths.

"Okay, let's go, baby." I lift her in my arms and she locks her legs around my hips. I stand on the edge, my heart racing like I just finished a marathon, stealing a quick glance at her—she's a mix of wide-eyed excitement and trembling nerves, and it tugs at my heart.

"We got this," I say confidently and give her a big smile. She nods but her nails digging into my back tell me that the fear is still here. "I'll keep you safe, baby."

And then, I jump. We are hurtling into the unknown together, the world below turning into a swirling sea of colours. The wind roars in my ears, drowning out everything else. As the bungee cord bounces us back, a wild cocktail of love and exhilaration courses through me. Our fingers weave together and in that suspended, weightless moment, it hits me—this jump isn't just about the fall. It's about us, about discovering something incredible in each other's company, something that transforms the simplest moments into memories we'll cherish forever. And I now know for sure that I want a forever with her.

I watch Ella in the side mirror as she tries to guide me into the little parking spot. We are on the shore of a beautiful mountain lake and after handing over a generous tip, we were allocated the most remote and most romantic spot on the campsite. There is not a soul around. Ella had read about the campsite on an online blog and I was determined to get that spot for us.

When she gives me the stop sign I cut the engine put the handbrake on and jump from the vehicle.

"What an amazing view," Ella says as she steps up to me. I put my hand around her shoulder, pull her into my side and place a kiss on her head.

"It's even better because you're here." This is week three of our holiday and I haven't checked in with the hotel even once. Sheila was over the moon with her promotion and we quickly worked out a system that works for both of us. I have full confidence in her.

"Come on, Romeo: dinner." Ella pats my abs and walks back to the minibus. She slides open the side door and jumps onto the mattress. Frankly, there isn't much in that minibus. We store most of our stuff at the rear of it and the main section is taken over by a massive mattress. We eat on it, sleep on it, and have had incredible sex on it in some of the most remote spots we've visited. Luckily this minibus has curtains on the windows, even if it doesn't have much else. It's simple but we absolutely love it. So much so that we extended our holiday by a fourth week. Am I concerned? Not a bit.

I sit down next to Ella and take my take away box from her. We picked up burgers and chips on the way here. They are cold now but we're watching an amazing sunset over a crystal-clear lake. Who cares if the burger is cold.

We don't say much. We just watch the spectacle nature is providing us. When we have finished our meal Ella stuffs our containers in a shopping bag that is hanging from the open door and slides back onto the mattress where she places pillows against the opposite side wall of the minibus. This way we can lie down and still watch the sunset.

I take my shoes off and crawl over to her. When I settle in next to Ella, she places her head on my chest and we just lie there in silence. This is what happiness feels like. Could I be any happier? Yes, I could.

"Ella?"

"Shh," she whispers. Her hand is under my shirt on my stomach. She loves to feel my skin even if we just lie there and read or watch a movie.

Since she won't let me talk I decide to speak with actions. I reach into my pocket and put the little blue box onto my stomach right above where her hand is currently placed under my shirt. Ella stiffens, then lifts her head and looks at me.

"What's that."

"I'm not allowed to talk," I joke.

"Tommy! What is this?"

I take the box, sit up and pull her with me.

"Ella, I didn't have a life until you. Rob joked once that work was my true love but I know now I was just hiding behind it. You brought laughter, happiness, and joy into my world and I can't imagine not having you in my life. So—"

"Tommy, we have only known each other for what, just under a year? We've only been together for a few months."

"So?"

"So, aren't there rules? Shouldn't we date first for a year, a year and a half, then live together for a while and then—"

"Ella, you've been living with me since the incident." That's what we call it. The incident. "And who made these rules? All I know is that I need you in my life. Every day, every night. I love you." I open the box and show her the platinum ring with small sapphires. Ella hates diamonds, but she loves blue.

"Will you marry me, Ella?"

She sobs and looks from the ring to me.

"Yes, yes I will," she whispers before pulling me in for a kiss. After I slide the ring on her finger, she leans against me.

"Oh no, we missed the best part of the sunset," she exclaims, and I look at the lake. The sun has set behind the horizon and now all that is left is dusk.

"Well maybe we just have to stay another day. And for now, we can—" I crawl to the door and slide it close. "For now,we can celebrate our engagement. Time for my dessert, baby."

Bonus Chapter

Tommy

I sigh loudly. Report two done, three more to go. Serves me right for not doing the reports straight after each rescue mission. Instead, I waited until the end of the month and now I only have today to go before I get another telling off for submitting them late.

It doesn't help that the little office I share with other team leaders is the most miserable place in the whole building. It's tiny with a desk, a filing cabinet and no windows. The light bulb is weak and it always feels like it is late at night.

"Hi, Tommy." Ella's voice pulls me from my thought. She is leaning against the door frame in her pencil skirt and a blouse, but unlike when she at the hotel, the top two buttons of the blouse are undone and I can see her purple bra underneath it.

"Ella, what are you doing here, baby?" I lean back in the office chair and smile. This woman does get more beautiful by the day. It has been a year since we went to New Zealand. We got married straight after we returned and the last twelve months have been the best of my life.

"I missed you, Tommy," she says in a sultry tone. She steps into the office and closes the door behind her before turning the key in the lock.

"Ahem, Ella, what—"

"Shh, I'm in charge today." She smirks and walks behind the desk. She pushes my chair backwards so she can kneel in front of me. I am not sure what's come over her but I would be mad to stop her.

She pushes my legs apart and moves between them. Looking at me from under her eyelashes she reaches out for my trousers. The noise of the zip being pulled down is the only thing breaking the silence.

I hiss when her fingers grip my dick and pull it from my trousers. It is hard already.

"Ella, we shouldn't be doing this here."

"Maybe, but nevertheless we will." She winks before closing her lips around the tip of my cock. She swirls her tongue around it, and I groan loudly. She takes me in deep and then pulls back up. And again. When she swallows my dick up for the third time it hits the back of her throat. I grip the armrest of my chair.

"Fuck, Ella." I close my eyes and draw in a deep breath. I can feel a tightening and I know I need to stop her. "Ella!" I gently grasp her by the shoulders and pull her off my dick. "I need you, baby," I whisper and press my lips against hers. My hands roam over her arse and push her skirt upwards whilst my tongue explores her mouth. Why does kissing my wife feels so amazing?

As I slide her skirt over her hips, I notice something missing. I pull away so I can look at her. My fingers stroke over her mound, a mound not covered by knickers.

"Where's your underwear?"

"I didn't think I would need any," she sasses and grins at me. She sits down on my desk and opens her legs.

"Fuck, Ella, why are you doing this?"

"Because..." she grabs the front of my T-shirt and pulls me down, "because I love you and just really wanted you today." There is something her eyes that tells me there's more, but when she pulls me closer I forget all about it.

She lies back on the desk and I enter her in one smooth thrust. *I am in heaven.* My lips slide over her neck as I move faster and harder. My spine tingles and I feel a tightening in my guts. I need to come so badly, but not without her. Ella moans underneath me. Her eyes are closed and her back is arched. I reach between us and gently stroke over her clit. A shiver races through her and she pulls me to her for a kiss. I move faster and just as I think I can't hang on any longer she explodes and I let go. I push in one last hard time into her and then collapse on top of her. My breathing is heavy.

Suddenly the floor is pulled from under me. With an almighty bang the desk collapses under us and we both roll onto the floor. I try to turn us so Ella lands on top of me.

The little minx burst out laughing and I can't help but join in. I lie back on the floor with Ella on top of me and we both just laugh.

Suddenly there's another loud bang.

"Tommy, is everything alright?" Ryan's voice filters through the door.

"Fuck," Ella giggles and scrambles of me. She pulls her skirt down and tries to straighten her clothes. I jump of the floor and tuck my dick back into my trousers.

"All okay," I shout. Ella smirks.

"Open up, Tommy," Alex calls out and there is concern in his voice.

I look around the room. Ella and I are half presentable, but the guys will know what happened. It's not like we can hide the broken table.

When I hover unsure near the door, Ella walks up to it, unlocks it and pulls it open. Alex and Ryan both stare at her.

"Hi, guys. Tommy, I'll wait outside for you," she says in the most confident voice ever and then walks past the two of them.

Their eyes land on me.

"Did you just—"

"Yes," I cut Ryan off.

"What was the crash?" Alex asks and I point at the desk.

They both grin at me.

"Can you fix that desk please Alex?" I ask, sliding my fingers through my hair. I would rather not have to explain why our desk had collapsed into a pile on the floor to the other FMR leaders.

"Sure, after you've cleaned it. I'm not touching that until then," Alex frowns and Ryan bursts out laughing.

"Cleaning material is down there," Ryan points to the cupboard at the end of the corridor and they both walk off.

"Thanks so much," I shout after them, and I can't stop grinning.

Ella

My heart beats faster when I see Tommy stroll from the building. I am leaning against his car and just take him in as he walks towards me. It is almost overwhelming how this man makes me feel whenever I am near him. I feel safe, I feel loved, and I am happy.

"Ella, what was that, baby?"

"I told you." I'm anxious and it is obvious in my voice.

"No, come on, tell me. Something's going on." He puts his finger under my chin and lifts my heads to make me look at him.

"Let's go home and I'll tell you there," I try to get him to move.

"No, I want to know now." He looks worried.

"I just felt like celebrating."

"Celebrating what?" I take a deep breath and walk to the boot of the car. I pull out a small gift bag I'd been hiding in midst of all the shopping.

"That's for you," I hold it out for him.

"It's not my birthday."

"I know. Open it." I nervously bite my lip. My heart is hammering. It seems to take him forever to open the bag and pull the tissue paper aside. Finally, he pulls out a tiny baby beanie very similar to the one Tommy wears on rescue missions.

"No! No!" he says over and over but the joy in his face tells me all I need to know. "Are you sure?" He pulls me close to him with one of his hands protectively placed over our growing baby.

"Yes, the doctor confirmed it."

"We're having a baby," he whispers before placing a kiss on my lips.

"We're having a baby," I confirm and give him a big smile.

"Is it crazy to say that I love that little thing already?"

"Maybe a little bit," I giggle but the look in his eyes tells me that he means it.

"I love you, Ella, and I'll promise to love you and our baby forever."

"We love you too, Tommy."

The End

Next in the Series is
Dan & Rose's story

Wrap Up with Me

Dani Elias

Prologue

Alex

"Emms?" My voice echoes through the cottage.

"I'm in the kitchen," she shouts back. I drop my sweaty mountaineering stuff in a pile on the floor ready for me to take it through to the utility room and walk towards the kitchen. The sweet smell of baking greets me, followed by a big smile from my beautiful wife.

"You're back early," she comments whilst drying her hands on a kitchen towel.

"The wind was too cold, we couldn't be bothered anymore," I reply before pulling her in my arms. As a volunteer with the Fellside Mountain Rescue team, I regularly meet with my unit for training sessions. We've welcomed a new team member recently so we've increased the frequency of our practices. However, considering it's mid-December, these sessions often feel more like torture than fun.

My lips slide over her exposed neck up to her earlobe, which I gently pull between my teeth. "I'd much rather be home in the warmth with you."

"Alex," Emma sighs but moves closer. "This will have to wait, I have to make one hundred Christmas cookies," she protests with a giggle.

"What for?"

"The bake sale for FMR at the carol singing event tomorrow." Her tone is impatient. "Remember?"

"Fuck, can we not just buy some?" I really didn't plan on spending the afternoon in the kitchen with my wife baking.

"Alex!" she warns me before placing a soft kiss on my nose. "If you help me, I'll be finished a lot quicker and we might be able to have some fun with the left-over icing." She tries to sound sexy but she immediately blushes deep red. I chuckle.

"I'll hold you to that but let me take a shower first and then I'll come and help you," I reply and reach into my pocket to retrieve my mobile to place it on the kitchen table. A message is blinking, so I swipe the screen to unlock the phone. I don't just have a message; I also have some missed calls. I click on the text message first.

Dan

> Alex, I'm fucked. I need your help.
> Call me when you are free.

"Dan tried to get hold of me." I hold out my phone to Emma and she reads the message.

"That's weird, he hasn't been in touch for ages."

"I know," I say with a frown.

Dan and I know each other from when we were still in nappies. Our parents were neighbours. Or I should say my parents and his mother. His dad left shortly after he was born.

We quickly became inseparable best friends and Dan spent a lot of time at our house. His mother had some serious problems with alcohol and didn't really want to take care of him. When he turned eight, she disappeared completely. My parents became Dan's foster parents, and so we grew up almost like brothers.

When he was twenty-five, he moved to London to work as a stockbroker, but we always stayed in contact. Only, since I started dating Emma, he has withdrawn a little and has been in touch a lot less.

I press the dial button and Dan answers after just one ring.

"Thank fuck, Alex. I need your help." He sounds panicked and tired. There is the loud wailing of a child in the background.

"Dan, where are you?" I shout louder than I need. Emma drops the cookie dough on the kitchen counter and looks at me.

"Shh," he hisses in my ear, "Shh, Maisie." *Who the fuck is Maisie?*

"Alex, I'll call you back," Dan says in a rush before the line goes dead.

I stare at my phone.

"He said he'll call me back." I lock eyes with Emma but she looks as confused as I feel. "I think there was a baby in the background."

"A baby? I didn't think his awful friends had any children." When Emms and I started dating we went to London so I could introduce her to Dan. He took us out for a dinner with his so-called friends. Really they were just some first class city wankers and I almost ended up in a fist fight with one of them when he insulted Emma.

"I don't think they—" The ringing of the phone interrupts me. I accept the call and put the phone to my ear.

"Alex, hi, sorry about that."

"Dan, what the fuck is going on? Are you okay?"

"Yes. No. Shit, I don't know."

"Who's Maisie?"

There is silence on the line.

"My baby." His voice sounds small and sad.

"Come again."

"She's my baby." I close my eyes and take a deep breath before opening them again. Emma is staring at me with anticipation.

"How old is she?"

"A bit over three months," he sighs.

"Don't you think you could have called to let us know that you were expecting a baby?" I know we've been in contact a lot less but we are still the only family he has, and it irritates me that he pretends we are no longer part of his life.

"Fuck, Alex, I didn't know I was until someone dropped the baby off with me two weeks ago."

"What?"

"Long story short: turns out when they say condoms are not one hundred percent effective they bloody mean it. It was a one-night stand nine months ago."

"What about the mother of the baby?" I ask and Emma's eyes widen. She steps up to me and I pull her against my chest before pressing a button on my phone. "Dan you're on speaker. Emms is here."

"Hi, Emms." I hate it when someone uses my nickname for Emma. She is my Emms and Emma to everyone else but I let it slide this time. He doesn't sound like the Dan I know. He sounds small and defeated, and I don't think he needs me to go all alpha caveman on him now.

"Hi, Dan," Emma greets him.

"Dan, the mother?" I repeat my question.

"There were complications at birth and Kelly didn't make it. Her parents are too old to raise Maisie so they dropped her off with me."

"I'm sorry, Dan." Emma says.

"Thanks. I really feel for Maisie, knowing that she'll never have a chance to meet her mum." I can't read the emotions in his voice.

"And Kelly didn't tell you when she was pregnant?"

"Fuck, Alex, it was a one-night stand. It's not that we exchanged numbers or anything. She knew my first name and she eventually found me but wanted to wait until after the birth. Listen, I need your help, please."

"Sorry, Dan, sure. What can we do to help?" I have so many questions but he's right. He called me for a reason and we'll have time for questions later.

"I want to come back to Fellside."

"Mate, I'm not the king of Fellside, you don't need to ask me for permission," I chuckle.

"Funny. I need help. I have no clue what I'm doing with the baby and I have nowhere to stay. She won't bloody stop crying. Alex; I haven't slept properly in a few days. I chucked in my job and I need somewhere to stay."

"Woah, woah, that's a lot. Slow down. You left your job?"

"Yeah. They told me they could give me one week off to find a solution for Maisie but they want me back on the floor doing my usual sixty plus hours. How can I do that with a new baby? I would never see her awake." At his words I've to smile a little. He cares for her already, that's good.

"I thought if I come back to Fellside... your mum and you and Emma can help me. Alex, I'm fucked. I am so out of my depth. I have no idea what I'm doing." His voice is shaky. Dan has always been a confident guy who knows exactly what he wants. To hear him so vulnerable and defeated doesn't sit well with me.

"Come home, Dan. Today, tomorrow; we're here for you, mate."

"Thanks." There is some relief in his voice. Did he really think we wouldn't be there for him? Maybe I should have made more of an effort over the last few months.

"Of course. Do you need me to come down and help you move?" He just needs to say the word and I'll grab one or two of the FMR guys and we'll get him packed in a day.

"No, that's okay. But I need somewhere to stay that isn't a bed and breakfast full of tourists who won't be able to sleep when Maisie won't stop crying at night. I tried Tommy, but his receptionist said the hotel is full and he isn't there." In the background the baby starts crying again.

"Dan, of course—" Emma starts but I interrupt her.

"Of course you can stay with us. But I have a better idea." Emma gives me a questioning look but I put my finger to my lips and grin. This is probably the best idea I have had in years.

"Oh, okay. Do you think one of the other guys..." I actually feel sorry for him because he sounds so small and forlorn.

"You can stay at Rose's. Her bed and breakfast is being remodelled so she hasn't taken in any guests for the winter. You can stay with her for a month or two until you've got yourself sorted. She has lots of space which will be a lot more comfortable for you and Maisie than staying on our sofa."

"Rose... I'm not sure that's a good idea."

"Of course it is. Mate, if you prefer, you can stay with us but I just think you would be more comfortable at Rose's where you'll have your own room," I explain. I know I sound a little like I don't want him with us and gesture Emma to help me.

"Rose is very good with kids. You know, she worked in a nursery once," Emma adds but the expression on her face is utter confusion.

"Do you think she'd be okay with it?" Dan sounds more upbeat.

"Of course. I'll call her now. You pack up your little one and come home. Pop by our house first so we can meet Maisie." The thought of having Dan back makes me happy. The guys from FMR are my best friends, especially Phil, but Dan will always be my brother from another mother.

"Okay, if you are sure."

"Definitely."

"Great. Thanks, Alex. We'll see you tomorrow. I'll head out around nine-ish so we should probably get there in the early afternoon."

"Drive safely, Dan," Emma adds before we say goodbye. This is just perfect. I'm not concerned about Dan. He will be a brilliant father, I'm sure of it. He just needs some help. Of course, we've got his back, but setting him up at Rose's could really make a difference for my sister too. I can't wipe the big smile from my face.

"Care to explain why you just arranged for Dan to stay with your sister?" Emma has crossed her arms in front of her chest.

"Emms, Rose has been lost since her divorce. She needs something to bring her back to life. Dan needs help and who better than Rose. The two of them need each other. This is genius."

"Genius?"

"Sure! They fancied the pants of each other when we were in our twenties. How they never hooked up is beyond me. So maybe they can help each other and, in the process, fall for each other. Think about it. They will be together in her cottage, just the two of them. And it's Christmas! It will be romance pure. And she can help him with the baby. And one thing leads to another..." I wiggle my eyebrows.

"Alex, you are a weirdo. Shouldn't you be trying to scare every guy away from your sister?"

"Emms, we are not in one of these romance books you read." I pull her back into my arms. "My sister went through hell with this arsehole she married. As a brother, I don't want the next one to be a wanker too, true. But I don't need her to become a spinster cat lady either. I want a good man who respects her and makes her happy. Dan was my best friend growing up. How can I not want him to be with her?"

Emma places her hands on my chest. "Don't you think Dan has bigger problems at the moment?"

"No. You heard him. He's already worried about Maisie and has made her his number one priority. He will have that father thing down to a T in an instant. I know him, he just needs to find his confidence. And Rose can help him with that."

"You are just one big old romantic softy, aren't you?" I chuckle.

"You know how romantic I can be." The innocent words cause her to blush and I just have to kiss her. I love it when she goes all shy.

"And you are sure that's a good idea?"

"What's the worst that can happen? They've known each other since childhood. They always got along. So, worst case, he will just stay there for a few weeks until he finds somewhere to live and they part as friends."

"Maybe you're right." She smiles softly. I place a last kiss on her forehead before walking to the kitchen door.

"Where are you going?"

"Shower and then I'm going to get you dirty with some icing." I wink.

Chapter 1

Dan

I push the controls on my steering wheel and the beam of the headlights illuminates the road in front of me. It's only late afternoon but the gloomy sky means I need to have the lights on.

It's quiet in the car, but I don't dare turn on the radio in case it wakes Maisie. I have been struggling to get her to sleep ever since her grandmother dropped her off with me. Who knew that driving around in a car would put her to sleep?

My phone rings and I fumble with my Bluetooth earbud I keep in my cup holder. I hurry to place it in my ear so I can accept the call.

"Hello?"

"Hey, Dan, it's Alex. Where are you?"

"Hey, we're just leaving Windermere." I hear some little grunts from the backseat and I tense up. *Shit, I don't want her to wake up.*

"Cool. Listen, I forgot it's the village carol singing event and FMR have a stand, so we're all going to be down at the market square."

"Oh, okay."

"Come and meet us here. Just behind the market square is a gallery. It belongs to Charlotte, and you can park your car in the courtyard there. Nick and Charlotte will wait for you." The FMR guys have adopted me as an honorary member so I know them and their significant others fairly well. As well as you can get to know someone if you only see them once or twice a year.

"Mate, I can just—" Well, what can I do? If they're all at the square there's no point heading straight to Rose's as she'll be with them and the coffee shops will be rammed.

"Dan, come and hang out with us. It will be fun and everyone wants to see you and meet Maisie." I should have known that he would let the guys know about my baby.

"OK. I should be there in thirty minutes," I finally agree. I take a deep breath and try to focus on the road. That's the last thing I wanted to do today. I'm exhausted and I'm not sure how well Maisie will react to a busy carol singing.

"Dan, we're with you," Alex says as if he can hear my doubts. "We're here to help and support you and Maisie. You're not alone in this. Phil and Christina, Suzie, and Chris, they all have children so if you need advice they'll be the right people to ask. And we can't wait to see you. Trust me, we're with you on this."

"Thank you, Alex. Thank you, that's all I can say." I can hear the emotions and the tiredness in my voice.

"There's nothing to thank me for. You're one of us and we always watch out for each other. We can't wait to see you both."

"Okay, mate. See you in a bit." I reply before hanging up. Traffic is light on the road along Lake Windermere and we make quick progress. There's not a peep from Maisie in the backseat, and I'm amazed at how my little girl, who has been vocal about how she hates being with me for nearly fourteen days straight, is now sleeping like a little angel in my car.

These have been a few emotional weeks for me as well. When Maisie's grandmother unexpectedly showed up in my office and confronted me with the fact that I'm now responsible for this tiny little girl, it sent me into a state of panic. I had never considered becoming a father. I dated; I dated, a lot, to be honest. But I have never really found a woman I wanted to spend the rest of my life with let alone have a child.

Well, that's not quite true. Of course, there was Rose. My Rose. Or should I say Alex's younger sister Rose. As I grew up in the Harris household after my mother abandoned me, I've known Rose for almost my whole life. She always tagged along with me and Alex when we were little. She's two years younger than we are, so it was just natural that she would hang out with us. That is until we became teenagers and our interests changed.

I was lucky enough to get a scholarship to attend Leicester University but after graduation I wasn't sure what to do with my life so I returned to Fellside. I found a job in a bank and when I wasn't working I hung out with Alex. We joined FMR together, played rugby and went on the pull. Rose was often part of the group of friends we spent time with, and I think it was when I came back from Uni that I started to see her in a different light. I was completely smitten by her beauty. Whenever we crossed paths there was this playful banter and teasing but deep down, I couldn't help but remember she was Alex's sister.

I just didn't want to risk my friendship with Alex and so I kept my hands to myself even if I really wanted more.

Rose wasn't just beautiful; she was an amazing human being. Warm, kind, always there to help others. I always wondered if I decided to move to London because I felt that I couldn't have her. A small smile appears on my lips when I remember my last night in Fellside before I moved to London.

Thirteen years earlier

"Why are you sitting out here alone?" Rose's voice pulls me from my thoughts. I glance in her direction and see her leaning in the pub doorway.

"I needed some air." It's not a lie but it's also not the whole truth. I know I'm supposed to celebrate moving down to London, should be happy about the great job I landed. And I am happy, but there's also a nagging feeling in the pit of my stomach and I am not quite sure what it is.

Rose takes a seat next to me on the beer garden bench.

"Are you sad to be leaving?" she whispers into the cold autumn night.

"What could I be sad about? I have this amazing job—"

"Dan, it's me." She places her hand on my arm and the simple touch sets me on fire. Fuck, I want her so much.

"Okay, maybe I'm a little sad. I'll miss Alex and FMR."

"And me?" She raises an eyebrow.

"And you, of course." I chuckle. We both peer into the distance, surrounded by quiet except for the muted sounds drifting from the busy pub.

"I'll miss you too, FYI," Rose finally breaks the silence.

"Yeah?"

"Yes." She turns her head and our eyes meet. I'm not sure who moves first but suddenly my lips are pressed against hers. Fuck, she feels good. She opens her lips a little and licks her tongue over mine. That's enough for me to slide my hand into her hair and pull her closer. I deepen the kiss and I don't think any kiss has ever been as good as this one.

"Dan," she says breathy and cups my face. "Take me to bed." It's not a question, it's a demand.

"Rose, I don't think that's a good idea." It's a fucking brilliant idea, my hard cock protests. "I'm leaving tomorrow." I attempt to reason, unsure if this argument is intended for her or if it's meant to convince me.

"I know. Give me one night. That's all I ask for," she whispers and her eyes are pleading with me.

"Are you sure?"

"One hundred percent." My eyes drift to the pub where I left Alex flirting up a storm with some tourist. He'll kill me when he finds out, but I want this so much. I've wanted this for so long.

"Okay," I finally reply and pull her from the bench. We walk to Rose's flat which is only a few streets away, stopping twice to snog like two randy teenagers pressed against random walls.

When we finally get to her place we rip the clothes off each other.

"Fuck, you're so beautiful," I whisper as my hands slide over her naked thighs.

"Dan, no talking, more fucking." She puts on a front but there is something in her eyes that tells me this is much more than just a random one-night stand for her, and that alone should make me stop. But truth be told, this is much more for me too.

I lift her into my arms and carry her to her bed. The minute we land on her mattress I kiss a trail over her neck down to her tits. I lick over her tender nipples and then move further down.

I can smell her arousal telling me she is enjoying this as much as I am. Every time my lips connect with her skin she moans, and it is driving me crazy. My cock is twitching and precum glistens on its tip. I want to sink into her so much, but first I need to taste her. I swipe my tongue over her clit and I am in heaven.

Chapter 2

Dan

Little gurgling noises from the backseat bring me back to reality. Apparently someone is awake. I brace myself for another crying session but Maisie just babbles happily. At least I now know how to get her to stop crying. Take her for a drive.

In the distance I can see the first sign telling me I'm entering Fellside.

"We're here, baby girl," I tell Maisie like she actually understands what I'm saying. I have to admit that she has taken hold of my heart in the last days, screaming or no screaming.

I manoeuvre the car through the crowded roads until I find the gallery. I park my car and turn off the ignition. *I am home.* I take a deep breath before unbuckling my seatbelt.

"Let's do this. Time to meet our friends, Maisie," I say, but it's more for my benefit than hers.

As I open the door cold air hits me in the face. Nick exits the gallery and waves at me. As he strolls over to my car he pulls a beanie onto his head.

"Mate, it's been bloody ages." He pulls me into a manly hug and pats my back.

"I'm glad to be back." As I say the words I realise that I mean them. I haven't been to Fellside for ages, but today I don't want to be anywhere else but right here in the village I grew up in.

Nick studies me and frowns. I wonder what he sees. Do I just look tired or are the worries I have been struggling with visible on my face?

"So, introduce me to your daughter." Nick peaks over my shoulder towards the backseat of my car. There's no judgement in his voice and I really appreciate that. I walk to the door behind the passenger seat and pull it open. Maisie is strapped into her infant seat which is clicked into the base and doubles up as a car seat. She greets me with her blue eyes and a peaceful look on her face. I unclip her carefully and pull her out, placing her against my chest. This is certainly an improvement considering that in the beginning I didn't even know how to hold her.

"Would you mind giving me the blanket that's on the backseat?" I ask Nick and point with my chin in the direction. He squeezes past me and grabs the pink blanket that her grandparents gave Maisie. I drape it over her.

"Mate, maybe you should put a jacket on first?" Nick chuckles and I realise then that I am standing in the cold December air in nothing else but jeans and my long-sleeved shirt.

"Shit!" I tense up, and immediately Maisie starts to wiggle.

"Give her to me," Nick says and holds out his arms.

"What would you know about holding a child?" I mumble and sound like an ungrateful prick.

"Oh, is papa bear protecting his little girl?" he chuckles. "I'll have you know, I'm one of baby Emma's favourite uncles." Nick crosses his arms in front of his chest. I frown but eventually shift Maisie and hand her to Nick. I'm a bit annoyed when I see how expertly he holds her, blanket tightly wrapped around her, after I've been struggling for the last two weeks. She snuggles into him, completely content. Nick gently rocks her up and down in his arms and strokes over her back. She starts to close her eyes and falls asleep in his arms.

"What kind of magic shit is that?"

"What do you mean?" Nick looks at me puzzled, gently rubbing Maisie's back.

"All I got from her since she was handed over to me is wailing and crying, and you come along and get her to fall asleep within two seconds."

"Mate, even I can sense your frustration. You're tense. Babies pick up on that. It upsets them."

"Who are you? Mary bloody Poppins?"

"Told you, I'm everybody's favourite uncle." He chuckles. The door behind him opens and Charlotte, his wife, steps out of the building. She gives me a big smile as she joins us.

"And who is this gorgeous little girl?" Charlotte softly strokes Maisie's hair.

"Hi, Charlotte," I greet her, placing a soft kiss on her cheek. She flashes me a warm smile before motioning for Nick to hand my baby girl over to her. He can never say 'no' to his wife, so he reluctantly hands Maisie over to her. Charlotte snuggles my little girl against her chest and starts cooing. My daughter's an absolute angel. I can't help but feel even more like a failure than I have in the past few days. Maybe Nick's right. I've been a bundle of nerves, stressed and terrified lately, and Maisie probably sensed it. But I can't just switch my feelings off.

Nick, Charlotte and I slowly walk to the market square and find the stall FMR has set up, selling cakes and biscuits to raise funds for their operation.

I say hello to all the guys and they welcome me, like they always have, as one of theirs. Maisie is an instant hit, especially with the women of the group. But Charlotte, who's been hoping for a child herself, isn't keen on letting anyone else hold Maisie.

It's a rare chance for me to take a break from worrying about my daughter. I know every woman in this group will look out for her. I take a deep breath and finally start to relax.

"She's amazing, mate," Alex says as he hands over a cup of tea.

"Yeah, but don't be fooled. This is the first time she's not crying. I've never felt like such a big failure as I have ever since she came into my life." My hands slide through my hair and I take another deep breath. Deep breathing is the only thing that has kept me going.

Alex looks at me with concern but before he can reply a loud voice makes us both turn around.

"Dan! My boy, it's been so long." Alex's grandmother, the matriarch of the Harris family, steps up to us with a plate of cookies in her hand. I place a tender kiss on her cheek. She and Alex's parents have always treated me like I belong to their family.

"Hello, grandma Harris," I greet her.

"I've seen your daughter, she's gorgeous." Despite her kind words, I instantly sense that familiar feeling of failure creeping back in.

"Oh, don't look at me like that, Daniel, things happen for a reason. This little girl happened for a reason and nobody will or should judge you for that." I give her a grateful smile. I've always liked her and I know I can come to her for help no matter what. She holds out the plate of cookies to me and I pick one up, but before I take a bite I look at it closely and freeze.

"Is that..." I have to bite my lips to avoid laughing out loud.

"It's Santa's boxers." She smiles at me.

"Santa's boxer shorts?"

"That's right. Enjoy." She holds out the cookies to Alex and when he doesn't take one she walks off towards another group of people.

"Is that a dick?" I point at the outline of a hard cock clearly visible under the red frosting on the cookie.

"Apparently she saw a video on social media on how to make these and we couldn't stop her. So now we have dick cookies," he laughs and I join in with him.

I look at the biscuit, not entirely sure if I want to sink my teeth into it.

"Where's Rose?" I ask and finally take a bite.

"She doesn't really do big crowds since the divorce." His brow furrows. "She's become a bit of a recluse so I'm glad you'll be with her for Christmas. Which reminds me, she asked me to tell you to pop to the supermarket on the way to hers, please. Saves her from having to come into town." He shrugs.

"Was she okay with me staying at hers?" I feel a knot forming in my stomach. I've been nervous about meeting Rose ever since Alex mentioned her yesterday.

"Absolutely. She wouldn't have it any other way." He gives me an encouraging smile but there's something in his eyes that makes me suspicious. Something isn't right. But I really don't have any other choice.

Chapter 3

Rose

Why am I so nervous? For the fifth time I'm walking through the cottage to make sure everything is tidy and neat. My heart is hammering. *Stop it!*

I haven't seen Dan since before my divorce. But I never really stopped thinking about him. Not since our night together over ten years ago. Dan always had a special place in my heart.

I obsessed over him when we were growing up. First, when I was a small girl, it was just the kind of childish obsession you have for someone you look up to. But when

I hit my teenage years he definitely became the object of my dreams.

My eyes drift to the clock in the kitchen and I see it's past six. The weather forecast for tonight and tomorrow is horrendous. Just the warning of a little snow usually means chaos but for the next two days we have been warned of unprecedented snowfall. Even up here in the north of England we're not really used to snow, so, when it happens, life stops and all you can do is stay at home.

This is why I asked Dan to pick up groceries from town before coming up. I hate going into Fellside. Maybe hate is too strong of a word, but the constant gossiping behind my back since I got divorced has definitely put me off from heading down into the village. Luckily, my bed and breakfast is in a small hamlet up in the hills and that means I can avoid most people if I want to.

A knock at the door causes my heart to skip a beat.

"He's here," I whisper to myself. I walk to the door and place my hand on the door handle but I don't open it. I take a deep breath and another. *Get a grip!* I am behaving like the grim reaper is waiting to get me. Another knock on the door makes me jump a little and I finally pull it open.

The first thing I see are Dan's chocolate brown eyes then the smile that is lifting the corners of his mouth.

"Rose," he says in this deep voice that always gives me goosebumps. Our eyes are locked and I'm frozen in time. Just seeing him brings up a whole range of feelings. A little cry from the baby girl strapped into an infant seat in his hand pulls me out of my trance.

"Dan! Oh my god, I can't believe you're here! And look at her." I softly stroke over the little girl's head. "She's gorgeous, Dan."

"Can we come in?" He gives me a cautious smile.

"Of course! Come in, come in." I step aside to let Dan pass me. Closing the door to keep the cold winter air out, I take another deep breath before turning to face him.

He has placed the car seat on the floor. It's one of the things that you can click into a base in the car but also carry around. Dan hangs up his jacket on a coat hanger before picking up the seat.

"Come in," I say again and point to the back of the cottage where I have my private rooms which bed and breakfast guests can't access.

"I see you still like Christmas," Dan chuckles as he follows me into the living room. I mean, okay, he has a point. I go overboard each year but I love Christmas. A large tree covered in all sorts of Christmas ornaments is in one corner near the window. I have a large cardboard gingerbread house on a chest of drawers to the left of the fireplace. There are Christmas ornaments, fairy lights and Christmas garlands everywhere. The coffee table is covered with a Christmas tablecloth. In short, wherever you turn, you see Christmas.

"What's this?" Dan points at my pride and joy.

"Picture covers, let me show you." I skip to where he's pointing at one of the many festive pictures around the room. I was sick and tired of having to take frames down, display pictures for Christmas, and then replace them again after Christmas so I crafted covers that slip over the picture frames making it look like there are Christmas pictures up.

"That's genius," Dan says and gives me a big smile.

"Dan, it's so good to see you," I blurt out. He stills and then pulls me into his arms for a long hug. I am immediately engulfed in his heat and his delicious manly scent. My ear is pressed against his heart which is beating fast. This moment feels so perfect.

"I'm glad to be here too, Rose," he whispers but before I can reply, a little cry from his daughter draws his attention.

"Right, let's get you out of this seat," he mumbles and takes a step back from me. He bends over the infant seat. My eyes automatically stray to his arse. And what a nice arse that is. *Great, he is taking care of his little baby and I have nothing better to do than to perv over his bum.*

Dan fiddles with the straps securing the baby and when he finally manages to get them undone he lifts her carefully out of the seat. He looks tense as he does so.

"Maisie, this is my friend Rose," he introduces me to his little girl. When he says the word friend a knot forms in my tummy. Yes, that's what we are. Just friends.

"Hi, Maisie, it's nice to meet you," I coo and give her a smile. Maisie wiggles in his arms and then starts to whimper.

"I think I need to change her," Dan mumbles and I can see a frown on his face. For the next ten minutes he works quietly to try to get his daughter to feel comfortable. He changes her, and gets a bottle ready. Every so often, he mumbles "Work with me, Maisie!" but doesn't say much else.

It's clear he could do with a cuppa so I put the kettle on and get two mugs ready in the adjacent open plan kitchen. I have a larger kitchen at the front of the building where I cook breakfast for the guests, but this small, galley style kitchen is just for me.

"I should unload the car, I need her playpen for her to sleep," Dan suddenly says from behind me. "Would you mind watching her, please?"

"Of course not." My eyes drift to Maisie who is strapped back into her seat. She doesn't look happy and wiggles around a lot.

Dan nods, gives his daughter a last glance and steps out of the living room.

"Right, Ms Maisie, I don't think you want to be strapped in, do you?" I giggle before unclipping her and lifting her into my arms. She makes some small cooing noises before looking around the room. The twinkling lights seem to fascinate her so I step up to the Christmas tree so we can look at them close up.

"See that, these are my favourite Christmas lights. They blink like real candlelight. Do you see that?" I babble whilst gently rocking her in my arm. She gives a little grunt and then leans her head against my chest. Okay, I think my ovaries just exploded. I stroke over her soft, blonde hair and breathe in her sweet baby smell before placing a gentle kiss on her head. I just couldn't resist.

"Was she crying? Is she okay? Why did you take her out of the seat? Was she crying?" Dan's voice is panicked and I feel Maisie react to it with tension.

"Everything's okay, Dan," I say calmly, "Ms Maisie just wanted to look at the Christmas lights. Didn't you," I giggle and gently sway her again. She relaxes against me. "Dan, what is all this?"

He has a folded up playpen in one hand and a baby bathtub in his other hand. I can see at least four suitcases behind him and a big box with some toys sticking out.

"I... I just got what the sales people told me I needed. I didn't want to buy a bed for her until I find a house for us so I got her a playpen travel cot to sleep in for now." Insecurity is showing on his face.

"Oh, Maisie, you need to look out for your daddy because the cunning salespeople are taking advantage of him." She gives a little grunt like she is agreeing with me.

"Great, another thing I did wrong," Dan mumbles.

"Dan, look at me." I'm not having this. What happened to the confident man I know? "You've done nothing wrong. You are a first-time dad who didn't have nine months to get ready for this little princess. You're doing the best you can, so stop frowning and join us for a cup of tea." Although my words are demanding, I say them quietly and calmly.

"Let me unpack first. Where do we sleep?" is all he replies.

"Take the stairs to the first floor, it's the door I left open. But leave the playpen here so Maisie can lie down whilst we drink tea?" I suggest. He just keeps staring at me, like he's trying to figure out if my idea is a good one. Eventually he drops the playpen and heads back into the hallway.

"Right, Maisie, you and I have to have a word," I whisper, taking her through to the kitchen. "You need to give your dad a bit of a break because I have a feeling he is about to crack." She responds by creating tiny spit bubbles. I shift Maisie so I hold her in one arm and can pick up the kettle with the other. Whilst I pour water onto the tea bags already inside the mugs and finish making the tea, Maisie grabs hold of my cardigan and stuffs it in her mouth.

"Oh, darling, I don't think you are going to like wool. Let's see if you have a dummy somewhere."

I leave the tea to brew and search the infant seat.

"Aha." I hold out a little baby soother with daisies on the wide plastic bit. I rinse it under the tap before pressing it gently against Maisie's lips. That's all it takes for the little girl to pull it in and suckle on it.

"Alright, here's the food. I wasn't sure what you'd need." Dan joins us back in the kitchen. He drops four massive shopping bags on the kitchen table.

"Dan, that's amazing, but they are forecasting snow for two days not two months," I giggle whilst softly stroking Maisie's back. She is resting against my shoulder with her dummy bobbing in and out.

"Alex didn't say anything about snow. He just told me you need food," he frowns again and looks concerned.

"Hey." I hip check him. "At least we have the choice." I hold Maisie out to him. He hesitates, but then takes her from me and puts her against his shoulder. Maisie wiggles a little but eventually settles down.

"Tea?" I ask.

"Sure," he shrugs. "Oh, your granny gave me some biscuits for you." He pulls out a metal tin from one of the shopping bags. I recognise the metal tin immediately. My granny has kept her Christmas cookies in an assortment of metal tins for as long as I can remember.

I take the tin and pull the lid off.

"Is that a dick?" I feel my cheeks blushing when I look at the sugar cookies in the shape of a man's boxer shorts with a very clear outline of a hard cock underneath.

"Shh! Not in front of Maisie!" he whisper-shouts, appalled.

"Oh please, she hasn't got a clue what I am talking about. Dick, dick, dick," I laugh. Dan is trying to hide it but a small smile is playing on his lips and I can see that the tips of his ears have turned red.

"Alex said your grandmother saw the recipe online and they couldn't stop her from making them," Dan explains. Our eyes meet again and we both burst into laughter.

I place a few dick biscuits on a plate and take the tea bags from the mugs. I might have left them in a bit too long but nothing a good dollop of milk can't fix.

I place a mug and the biscuits in front of Dan who has taken a seat at the table before grabbing my own cup.

"They do look lewd," Dan chuckles and nods towards the cookies.

"I'll tell you what's lewd." I grab a cookie and try to lick the icing from it exactly where the outline of the penis is. Dan's eyes widen. Okay, I thought this might be funny, but it doesn't feel funny. It feels everything but funny. I stare at him as I slide my tongue over the biscuit dick and..., *fuck, I need to stop!* I stuff the cookie in my mouth but I underestimate how big it is and how dry. *Bloody hell.* Biscuit crumbs fill my mouth and when I try to swallow them I almost choke.

My cheeks are burning.

Dan leans forward and whispers, "I never thought I'll see you choking on a dick." He winks and gets up from the table. "I think Maisie needs a bath." He takes a last sip from his mug and leaves me alone in the kitchen.

Oh fuck, this is going to be a long month.

Chapter 4

Dan

"Maisie, come on, work with me," I plead with my little girl but she couldn't care less. She's screaming bloody murder and her face is scarily red. She keeps gasping for air but as soon as she's filled her lungs she cries so loud that I'm certain it can be heard in Fellside. *I can't do this. I can't do it.* I am failing and I don't know what else I can try. She deserves so much better than me.

I put her back on my chest, cradling her head on my shoulder, and rock her to see if this will calm her down. Nothing. I can feel tears of frustration filling my eyes.

"Why is the little princess so upset?" Rose says from behind me. I turn and find her leaning against the door frame, watching us. Sheer desperation takes hold of me. I walk up to her.

"Take her," I demand.

"What?"

"Take her." Rose gives me a concerned look but gently takes Maisie from my arms. The minute I know my daughter is safe, I turn around and march to the front door. I wrench it open, step outside and let it fall shut behind me.

Freezing air hits me in the face. As forecasted, it has started to snow and a thin layer of white has already covered everything. I bend forward and breathe in the cold air. One breath, another breath.

I can't do this.

I sink onto the snow-covered bench next to the entrance to the cottage. Slowly, the snow underneath me melts and seeps into my jeans, but I don't care.

I am not sure how long I have been sitting here when the door opens and Rose steps outside. She is wearing a bulky winter jacket and woolly hat.

"Here." She holds out my coat. I stare at it and eventually take it and put it on.

"Wait, where's Maisie?" I make an attempt to get up but Rose stops me.

"She fell asleep. And I have this." Rose holds up the baby monitor. "Now, want to tell me what happened?" she asks and sits down next to me. "Fuck that's cold," she jumps back up as soon as her bum hits the snow-covered wood. She wipes the snow off her arse.

"Here." I pull her onto my lap. She yelps but settles down with an arm draped around my neck.

"So?" she prompts me.

"I can't do this, Rose."

"Do what?"

"Be a father," I whisper into the night. Saying the words out loud breaks my heart and I can feel tears forming in my eyes again.

"Says who?"

"Me. I can't even calm down my baby. All she does with me is cry. I'm not a parent. What do I know about parenting?"

"Dan, most people don't know what they're doing with their first child. You need to stop putting yourself under pressure."

"How can I? She only has me. If I don't do this perfectly, she only has a failing parent."

"Let me tell you what I've seen. You willingly left your job and career for a baby you hadn't planned for. You moved back home to make sure she has family around as she grows up. I've just witnessed a remarkable father who made sure his daughter was safe in my care before he took off. A father who instinctively prioritized her being safe the moment I stepped out. Dan, you are an amazing dad. Just remember to go easy on yourself."

"Maisie's grandparents suggested I could give her up for adoption as long as I guarantee them visitation rights." My words hang in the air.

"Would you like that?" It's a simple question and I don't detect any judgment in her words. I take a deep breath. *Would I?* Regardless of what I have been through, I know the answer to this question.

"No. I was abandoned by my mother. How could I do the same thing to Maisie?"

"You're nothing like your mother, Dan."

"I hope not," I laugh bitterly.

"I know so. For a start, your first concern is your daughter, not your pleasure."

I don't reply, just stare into the distance. Rose leans her head against my shoulder.

"Dan?"

"Yeah?"

"Your bum must be frozen by now," she giggles.

"A bit." I laugh.

"How about we go in, I'll make you some hot chocolate and then you go to bed? I'll watch Maisie tonight. You need one night of proper sleep, and you'll see the whole thing will feel a lot less daunting." My eyes find hers and she gives me a big smile.

"Do you have whipped cream?"

"Do I have whipped cream?" she mocks me. "Do you know who you're talking to? Only the best squirty cream for you."

"And maybe even a dick cookie."

"Oh, do you want to lick icing off a dick now?" She puts her hands over her mouth the minute she says the words. "I can't believe I said that."

"I think you want to make it onto Santa's naughty list." I wink.

She jumps off my lap and I immediately miss her warmth, and not just because it's bloody freezing out here.

"Let's go and lick icing off Santa's dick," she giggles and pulls me off the bench.

"I've put up the playpen in your room. Are you sure you're okay to watch Maisie tonight?" Something doesn't feel right about handing my daughter over, even if it's to Rose.

"Absolutely. Now sit and have a hot chocolate." She puts a mug topped with a big dollop of cream on the table. I glance at Maisie, asleep in her baby carrier, before taking a seat.

"So are you going to tell me what happened?" Rose takes a seat opposite me. "Alex told me that Maisie is the result from a one-night stand and that you gave up your job to move back here because you need help."

"That's it in a nutshell, really," I reply. I scoop some whipped cream off the hot chocolate with my spoon.

"Dan," she calls for me to look at her.

"Really, there isn't much more to say. Kelly, Maisie's mum, was someone I met on a night out. We had sex, condom must have broken, although I didn't realise it back then, and that was that. We hadn't exchanged numbers or anything and I didn't expect to hear from her again." I take a sip. "When she found out she was pregnant, Kelly was trying to track me down by checking out websites for companies like mine. Finally, she stumbled upon my company profile, but then she wasn't sure if she should reach out."

"What changed her mind?"

"Nothing. She died during the birth. There were some complications the doctors had missed." I slide my fingers through my hair. It's weird to talk about the death of someone and not feel completely sad about it. It's awful that Maisie will never be able to meet her mum, and I feel sad about that. But I didn't really know Kelly so whilst it seems like I should be upset, I feel... neutral, for a lack of a better word.

"I'm so sorry, Dan," Rose whispers. I shrug.

"I'm sorry for Maisie. Kelly's mum, Joanne, came to my work two weeks ago. She and her husband are in their seventies and think they're too old to care for Maisie. They tried after Kelly died, but after a few weeks, they had to admit it was too much for them. They eventually found my details in Kelly's belongings."

"And they just left her with you?"

"No," I laugh but I feel some bitterness. "For them, and honestly, for my sake too, we decided to do a paternity test. It took a few days before we got the results. Joanne stayed with me to show me the essentials, like how to change nappies and feed her. But then Joanne had to go back home because her husband has a medical condition and needed her care. It's just been me and Maisie since then."

"Shit, that can't have been easy," Rose says and puts her hand on my arm. Her touch gives me some comfort and I relax into my chair.

"Well, work told me I can have a week off to find a nanny but then they expect me back. Rose, I was working sixty hours a week on average. How could I possibly do that and raise a daughter? I don't want a nanny to raise her. Although lately I think maybe that would be a better solution."

"I told you, Dan, don't be so hard on yourself," she admonishes me. I raise my hands in surrender.

"I know, I know. To be honest, the minute work made it clear that they won't agree any other adjustments that would help me take care of Maisie, all I thought about was coming to Fellside. I knew Alex and Emma, your family, the guys, and you would all help me."

"Hell, yes we will," she giggles and picks up my empty mug. "Do you want another?"

"No, thanks," I reply and stifle a yawn. I watch Rose as she washes the two mugs in the sink. She is wearing black yoga pants and a Christmas T-shirt with a burgundy cardigan over it. She's swaying her hips to the music that's playing quietly in the background. Her blonde hair is in a wild bun on top of her head. I can't help but remember running my fingers through her hair that one night, years ago. I suck in some air to get a grip of myself. I really don't need to take that walk down memory lane and to get a hard on.

"Are you okay?" Rose asks and looks at me with a frown.

"Yup, yes, yup," I stutter. Rose watches me and then shakes her head.

"Right, mister, bed!" she orders.

I laugh. "You're sending me to bed?"

"Yes, I am," she giggles before stepping up to me. "Get some sleep; you need it, Dan." She gently strokes over the dark circles that I know are under my eyes.

I stand up, which brings me a lot closer to her. Although she's tall, she has to lean her head back to look at me.

"Night, Rose."

"Night," she replies and swallows hard. I tuck a strand of hair behind her ear. It would be so easy to just lean down and press my lips to hers. Instead, I walk past her to Maisie. I place a gentle kiss on my daughters' forehead before walking to the door.

"Are you sure you're going to be okay with Maisie?" I ask one more time leaning against the door frame.

"I am. And if there are any problems, you're just asleep upstairs." She gives me a big reassuring smile.

"Rose, thank you. I haven't said thank you yet, but I really am so grateful that you took us in."

"Dan—" she doesn't say more instead just gives me another smile.

"Night," I say again.

"Night."

I walk up the stairs with a big grin on my face. For the first time in two weeks, I am starting to feel that maybe all will be okay after all.

Chapter 5

Rose

"On the first day of Christmas, my true love sent to me," I sing along to one of my favourite Christmas songs whilst chopping peppers. Maisie is babbling away in her playpen that I have put up in the living room. A fire is roaring in the fireplace and outside a thick blanket of snow is covering everything. I mean, this all screams kitsch, or as I call it, *picture perfect Christmas*, and I love it.

"Fiiiiiivvvveeeee golden rings," I loudly join the Spinners whilst putting chopped onions into the hot pan.

“Good morning,” Dan’s voice makes me shriek and some of the onions land on the floor. I glance at him leaning against the doorframe in jeans and a tight grey T-shirt.

“Good morning,” I mumble and my cheeks heat up. He strolls to where Maisie is lying wiggling with her arms and legs in the air.

“I fed her and changed her so you should have a happy baby on your hands.” He gives me a grateful smile and then lifts his daughter from the playpen.

“Good morning, baby girl,” he whispers and places a soft kiss on her forehead. She cuddles happily against his shoulder and grabs hold of his T-shirt with her dummy bobbing in and out of her mouth.

“How are you feeling?” I ask gently.

“Better. I... thank you for watching her last night. Did she wake you up a lot? I should have warned you that she doesn’t sleep more than one hour at a time.”

“She slept all night.”

“Excuse me?” He frowns but gently strokes over Maisie’s back.

“Dan, I think you both just needed a good night sleep. She was as stressed as you and the lack of sleep didn’t help anyone.” I can see him tensing up. “Dan, chill. Relax and she will be relaxed. Here—” I walk up to him and slide my hand over his eyes so he closes them. “Take a deep breath.”

He does as I tell him to. "And another." His chest expands as he draws in a lung full of air and as he does Maisie also breathes deeply.

"Oh my god, did she—"

"Yes, she copied you. If you're stressed, she gets stressed. That's it. And there is no need to stress. We are snowed in until at least tomorrow. There is nowhere to go and nothing to do but chill out." I give him a big smile.

"This is your Christmas dream, isn't it," he chuckles.

"It's perfect. But I also know it won't last. The weather forecast says rain for Christmas Eve." I shrug.

"So, let's make the most of today."

"Exactly. Shakshuka?" I ask.

"Pardon?"

I laugh at his confused look.

"Shakshuka. It's a middle eastern breakfast dish. Emma taught me how to make it and Alex loves it."

"Alex loves everything Emma does," Dan chuckles. He carefully places Maisie back in the playpen and holds out one of the chew toys he bought her.

"True. They're sickening sometimes, but I'm just glad my brother found someone that makes him so happy."

"Yeah, he's a lucky bastard," Dan mumbles before adding, "Right, tell me what this Shuka thing is."

"Shakshuka. It's just chopped onions and peppers. Some spices. You cook that down with tinned tomatoes until it is fairly solid and then make dents in the sauce to crack eggs in it. You put the lid on and cook that a little and then, voilà! Shakshuka."

"So tomato sauce with eggs." He wrinkles his nose.

"Don't be so British. It sounds weird but it is delish. Can you pop some bread in the toaster, please?" I ask him whilst I stir the onions and peppers and add the tomatoes.

"What's your favourite Christmas song?" Dan asks as he pulls plates from the shelf next to the sink.

"This one—" I scroll through my phone and press play. The first notes from Shakin' Stevens "Merry Christmas Everyone" fill the kitchen.

"I like that one," Dan says and starts bobbing a long whilst dancing to the table with the two plates. Yes, this Dan is the Dan I know. He just needed to relax.

We both start singing whilst dancing through the kitchen preparing our breakfast.

"Snow is falling," Dan sings along with Shakin's Stevens

"Snow is falling," I join the background singers that follow and we both burst out laughing. Dan locks eyes with me and I forget to breath for a moment.

"I think your shukashuka stuff is boiling over," he brings me back to the room.

"Shit," I swear and stir the pot, "and it is called Shakshuka. Say it."

"Shakshuka," he replies.

"Good boy," I mock praise him and Dan gently pinches my side which makes me laugh. I crack the eggs into the little dents I have made in the sauce and cover the pan.

"Right, take a seat; the eggs only take a few minutes." I order him whilst continuing to sway my hips to the music. I love Christmas music. If it weren't weird I would listen to it all year round.

I notice Dan give Maisie a cautious look to see if she is okay before taking a seat. I smile to myself. *Can't do it – Bollocks.* He is going to be a doting dad to that little girl. She couldn't be luckier.

"So, what are we going to do today?" Dan asks before taking a sip of tea. The pan is heavy when I carry it to the table.

"Watch telly and eat shitloads of food?" I grin whilst spooning some tomato sauce onto his plate and placing two eggs on top before putting the rest of the food on my plate.

"Sounds like a plan. And looking at your Santa's grotto," he looks around my living area, "you'll probably suggest some Christmas movie."

"Hello! It's Christmas!"

"You know what, I don't think I've watched a Christmas movie in ten years or so."

"That's blasphemy," I gasp in shock causing Dan to laugh out loud.

"Well, I'm happy to be educated. What's the first one we'll watch?" he asks whilst pushing his food around on the plate. I raise an eyebrow and he finally puts a spoonful of food into his mouth.

"Fuck, that's actually good."

"I know! I can't believe you doubted me," I giggle. "I think we should watch *Bad Moms Two*,"

"Is that another attempt for you to convince me that I'm a good dad?" he grimaces. I don't know what it is about him but whenever he frowns, all I want to do is make him smile again.

"No, it's because it has a hot stripper in it."

"Excuse me?"

"And he gets his balls waxed," I explain and then almost choke on my food when I realise what I just said. Dan throws his head back in laughter.

"Rose, what is it with you and the male crotch area these days. Is someone horny?" he teases and winks. I feel the blush creeping up my cheeks.

"No," I splutter. Dan returns his attention to his breakfast but the little smile on his face tells me that he is still thinking about what I have said, and that smile was worth me putting my foot in my mouth again.

Just as we finish our last bites, Maisie gives a little wail. Dan tenses up and the frown is back but I'm not that easily defeated. I put my hand on his arm.

"It's normal for her to whine from time to time. She probably just wants her daddy to pick her up." Dan's eyes are on mine and I can see his worry and fear. "Take a deep breath and then show your daughter that her fun dad is here." He closes his eyes and his chest rises and falls as he sucks in deep breaths. He tries to give me a smile as he gets up.

"Where is my little Maisie?" he coos. There is still an edge to his voice but his body seems more relaxed. He lifts the baby and she happily kicks her legs. He bounces her gently in his arms and a tiny smile appears on her lips.

"She's smiling," Dan exclaims with excitement and his eyes light up.

"See, she was just missing you," I grin. Dan softly strokes his hands over the back of his girl before quietly singing along to the Christmas song. Okay, my ovaries may have just exploded again.

"So, what do you think?" I look over to Dan who is lying next to me on the sofa. We have a blanket draped over us and our feet up on the little foot stool. Maisie is sleeping in her playpen.

"The stripper reminded me of your granny's cookies," he smirks. I gently slap his chest.

"I admit, it wasn't bad. Definitely prefer it over the cheesy hallmark movies." He leans his head against the back of the sofa and looks at me. "Do you ever think about it?" His voice is just a whisper as if he is scared to say the words out loud.

"About what?" Butterflies fill my stomach because I know exactly what he is talking about.

"Our night together."

"Where's this coming from?" I nervously tuck a strand of hair behind my ear. I would be lying if I said that I hadn't also thought about our night together at least a million times since he stepped into the house.

"I was just wondering," he says but his eyes are dark and I know there's much more behind his question.

"Have you?" I whisper.

"All the time. It was nothing short of spectacular." His admission catches me off guard and I gasp. I thought I was the only one who had kept this one night up on a pedestal. It was the best night of my life.

"Dan," I sigh but turn away from him. He sits up and gently grabs my chin to turn my head and make me look at him. He's so close. I can feel his breath fanning over my face. Just a little closer, just a little. I want to kiss him so badly.

Dan leans forward and I slide one of my hands around his neck. I never wanted anything more than him.

"Why have you never said anything?" I need to know the answer to this.

"We grew up with each other, I was basically a member of your family. And then there's Alex."

"What's my brother got to do with it? Please don't tell me he made some idiotic pact with you or something." I'm already plotting to spill some embarrassing secrets about Alex to Emma in revenge.

"No, he never said a word about you. How he never clicked on to me pining over you is beyond me."

"Pining?" I giggle about his choice of word but Dan just shrugs. "Why then?" I push for an answer because I need him to explain it just so I can start believing that there could be more than just one night between us.

"I don't know." His head drops. "It just... I really liked you but I also felt I needed to leave Fellside, needed to get away from everything that reminded me of my mum. We were both really young and who thinks about the happily ever after in their early twenties? It doesn't change the fact that I have never stopped thinking about you or the night when I last felt truly happy."

We both sit there silently. *Tell him that you're crazy about him. Tell him.* I don't know what's stopping me. He's just made it clear what he feels for me. Why am I still hesitating? Actually, I know exactly what's stopping me. If we give it a shot and it goes horribly wrong I'll lose him forever. Somehow staying just friends sounds so much safer.

"Want more hot chocolate?" I ask and my voice sounds strained. I get up from the sofa but Dan's hand on my stomach stops me from walking towards the kitchen. He stands up as well and pulls me into his arms. My heart starts hammering wildly and the world around us goes blurry. *Let it happen!*

Chapter 6

Dan

I cup her face and caress her lips with my thumb. The anticipation of finally kissing her again is thrilling but is also driving me crazy. I drop my head and touch my lips to hers. She hesitates for a second, but then she melts into my embrace and an incredible happiness washes over me. Like when you find something you thought you had lost forever. My tongue slides over her lips and a little moan escapes her before she opens up and allows me to deepen the kiss.

I drag her closer to me and then move backwards. She willingly straddles me when I drop onto the sofa and pull her into my lap. Her hands slide into my hair when I trail kisses down her neck.

"Dan," she moans, but then moves backwards before looking at me. "What are we doing?"

"I don't know." I ruffle my hair and take a deep breath. Her scent is the only thing I can smell and it is intoxicating. I take comfort from the fact that she hasn't moved off my knees. I've been waiting for this for ages and I don't want it to end. Hell, I have imagined a future with her a thousand times.

"Rose, my life is a shit show at the moment. I am in theory unemployed and homeless. I have the means to keep me and Maisie in a comfortable life for a few months but I have no plan yet for what comes afterwards. I'm a single dad, which means I have responsibilities I have never even thought about. But the truth is that I always wanted you, Rose. Always." I blow out a long breath and my eyes drift away from her up to the ceiling. I don't want to look at her and see rejection.

Rose gently cups my face. "Oh, Dan, I—"

"Holy fuck," I gasp, grab onto Rose's arse and lift her with me as I swiftly get off the sofa and sprint into the kitchen. "Fuck, fuck, fuck."

"Dan," she laughs and holds on tight with her legs locked behind me, "what are you doing?"

"There is a monster spider on your ceiling." I hate spiders. No, I despise them. I look at the distinct black spot. It is slowly crawling towards the area above Maisie.

"Maisie!" I scream like a dragon is after my daughter. I slide Rose off me and race to Maisie. She startles when I pick her up and starts crying.

"Dan," Rose is bent over with laughter. "It's just a small spider."

"Small? It's not small!" I squeeze Maisie closer. Okay, maybe I have an irrational fear of these eight-legged demons but I can't help it.

Rose shakes her head and giggles as she reaches for a glass.

"What are you doing?"

"Catching it."

"Kill it!"

"I'm not going to kill it, Dan." Rose rolls her eyes at me.

"What the fuck, Rose? Kill it."

"No, I'll catch it and put it outside."

"To freeze to death?" My words seem to make sense to her.

"Fine." She grabs a broom and walks over to the spider. She pushes the broom upwards but instead of squashing the eight-legged freak, it drops to the floor and starts running at high speed towards the kitchen. Instinct takes over and I hop up on the kitchen counter pulling my legs up.

"Kill it!" I shout again. Maisie cries a little louder in my arms. "Sorry, baby," I whisper.

With a whack, the broom comes crashing down. Rose turns it and I can see the squashed spider stuck to the bristles.

"There. Happy?" she asks and gives me a smirk.

"Thank you." I slide off the kitchen counter and sway Maisie gently. She quickly stops crying and bumps her head against my shoulder.

"Maisie, another job for you. You need to protect your daddy from itsy-bitsy spiders," Rose coos and strokes my girl's chubby cheek. Maisie squeaks in reply like she is agreeing and then grabs my shirt again. I gently stroke over her hair and plant a kiss on her forehead.

Maisie stuffs a bit of my T-shirt in her mouth and starts sucking on it.

"I think someone is hungry." Rose eyes us as she is cleaning off the broom. "Why don't you take her to the sofa and I'll make up a bottle?" she suggests.

"I can do it."

"Dan, it's okay to accept help." She winks at me.

"Rose?"

Her eyes find mine.

"Thank you."

I close the door to the bedroom. Maisie kept us entertained for the last couple of hours with her facial expressions and grins. After a bath, which I have to say is quickly becoming my favourite time of the day given how much she enjoys it, I put her to bed in my bedroom so she can hopefully have a restful sleep. *Maybe I am not that bad as a dad?*

More Christmas music drifts towards me from the kitchen as I head downstairs. With the baby monitor in my hand I lean against the door frame and watch Rose, who is making us more hot chocolate. She seems to be addicted to that stuff.

She is swaying her curvy hips and singing along to a song I don't recognise. I place the baby monitor on the coffee table and quietly walk towards her. My arms slide around her from behind and I sway along with her. She startles, but then melts into my arms.

"Dan," she whispers and presses against me.

"I wasn't done talking about us when the monster attacked."

Rose snorts, "The monster?"

"Yeah." I drag the tip of my nose up and down her neck.

"In that case, shouldn't you have protected me? Damsel in distress and all." Her voice sounds breathy. She drops the tea towel she had used to wipe the counter.

"Nah, this is the twenty-first century. Women got it all covered." I place a kiss on the point where her neck meets her shoulder. Rose lets out a soft moan and turns in my arms. She pulls me closer and melts her lips to mine. I move her backwards until she's pressed up against the kitchen counter.

"I want you so much," I whisper between kisses.

"You were always the one that got away," she admits, and her words hit me deep in my chest. So that one night was more than that for her as well.

"Stop thinking, Dan, get me naked," she demands and places soft kisses on my Adam's apple. My cock is painfully hard and pressing against my zip and all I want to do is sink into her. But first I need to explore every inch of her. It's time to reclaim what was mine for one night.

Chapter 7

Rose

Dan carries me towards the sofa. Like every time he has kissed me, my whole body comes alive under his touch.

"Rose, you are incredible," he breathes. He undoes the buttons of my cardigan, slipping it down my shoulders, and then, with a smooth motion, pulls my T-shirt up and over my head. Gradually, he coaxes me until I'm lying flat on my back, his body draping over mine. My hands find their way to his shirt, right over his toned abs, and I tug him closer, pulling him down towards me.

His lips slide along my throat before fluttering over my cleavage. He drags my bra cups down and my big breasts pop out. I have always been blessed with big boobs, but the way they are now pushed up is almost obscene.

Dan's eyes go dark and he whispers, "So beautiful," before clamping his lips around one of my pebbled nipples. He sucks on them until I let out a loud moan. When his hand travels downwards and cups my pussy through my jeans, he causes a fire to race through my veins. It is almost painful how much I want him to remove my trousers and put pressure directly on my clit. My fingers slide into his hair and I pull him back up because I need to kiss him.

My tongue peeks out and tangles with his. What starts off slow quickly turns into a wild make out session, like two teenagers who've finally managed to be alone together.

I pull at his T-shirt and whisper, "Take it off." Dan sits back on his haunches and strips off his top.

My fingers trace the outline of his six pack. Dan had always been in good shape, but this is insane.

"Work out much?" I ask.

"Going to the gym is almost like a rite of passage in London. You're not part of the in-crowd if you don't have a gym membership," he shrugs. "And, to be honest, I needed it to work off my stress."

"Two reasons I would never move to London," I giggle. I don't really work out and I certainly don't want a stressful job like Dan's. No, thanks.

"I really don't want to talk about London now," Dan growls before sucking one of my nipples between his lips again. He gently scrapes his teeth over it and a shudder races through my body.

My fingers find his belt buckle and I free the clasp before reaching for the button of his jeans.

"Not so fast," Dan stops me. He takes off my trousers so I am left wearing my bra which is tucked under my breasts and my cotton knickers.

He pushes my legs apart and then slides a finger slowly up and down my covered pussy. Up and down and up and down.

I squirm and moan, "Don't tease me!"

"Why not, you seem to like it," he smirks but eventually relents and drags my knickers over my hips. I am lying bare in front of him but instead of feeling embarrassed or ashamed of my curves, which has happened in past relationships, even with my ex-husband, the look that Dan gives me makes me feel like a bloody sex goddess.

"Fuck, you are more stunning than I remembered and believe me, you were already perfect in my dreams." I feel my cheeks heat at his words. Dan bends forward and places tender kisses on my mound and the inside of my thighs.

"Dan, no teasing," I warn again.

"I'm not teasing," he mumbles. "You taste delicious here." He kisses the inside of my thigh. "And here." He licks my skin a centimetre above where he just kissed me. "And here," he groans and finally his tongue touches my outer lips. He takes a thorough lick before circling my clit. *Oh my!* I remembered the night having been good, but I don't remember him being that good. My core tightens and I am starting to feel my orgasm build. I place my hands on the back of his head and push him closer to me. Dan chuckles and the vibrations create an intense sensation that has me moaning out loud.

"Do you need to come, Rose?"

"Yes," I breathe.

"What if I won't let you?" he chuckles before blowing gently on my clit.

"Fuck!"

"Say please."

"Please, pretty please, please!" I beg. Dan gives me one heated look before bending forward and sucking on my clit. Not gently but like a man on a mission. And just when I reach the peak he pushes two fingers in my pussy and curls them upwards to massage my sensitive spot. I cry out and I feel my back arch and lift from the sofa.

“Shh, Rose. If you wake Maisie, this fun will be over.” Dan places more kisses on my tummy before standing up and taking his trousers off. Yup, I definitely remembered how big his cock was. The minute he pushes his boxers down it bobs up and points at me and I just want to wrap my fingers around it.

“I don’t want to ruin the moment but do you have a condom?” He looks sheepish.

“In my bedroom,” I point in the direction adjacent to the living room. “I’ll get one,” I say and get up from the sofa. I unclip my bra and drop it to the floor.

Dan grabs me around my hips and pulls me into his body.

“Let’s move this to your bed,” he whispers against my ear before placing kisses along my neck. He grabs the baby monitor and drags me to my bed, but before he can push me onto the mattress I slip from his grasp.

“Sit down,” I point at the edge of the bed, pulling open the bedside table. I take out a condom and rip it open. Dan holds out his hand for it, but I gently slap it away and then kneel down in front of him. He draws in a sharp breath.

“Hello, my old friend,” I giggle before circling the tip of his hard cock with my tongue.

"Did you just call him your old friend?" Dan asks through clenched teeth.

"Mm-hmm, I definitely missed him," I try to sound seductive but it just comes out breathy. Dan groans as I slide his erection into my mouth before pulling up again. As I move upwards I drag my tongue along the underside of his cock. I bob up and down, over and over again until I feel his fingers grip my hair. It isn't painful, but it is determined.

"You have to stop," he pleads before pulling me off and pressing his lips to mine. He kisses me deep and urgently whilst lifting me onto the bed.

He rolls on the condom before aligning his body with mine, but then there is nothing stopping him.

His dick nudges the entrance to my pussy and I spread my legs wider in invitation. Dan groans again before sliding in, slowly and determined.

"Oh fuck, so much better than I remembered," Dan whispers before pulling out and pushing in again. When he is full seated in me, he stills. I roll my hips but he doesn't move.

"Is everything okay?"

"Yeah." He kisses me deeply but still doesn't move. "This just feels... it feels like I am back to where I belong."

Yes, we belong together! I don't reply and instead just kiss him deeply.

He links our fingers and puts our joined hands next to my head. He locks eyes with me and then moves. Every thrust feels better than the last. This is not just sex, this is more. It's intimate and emotional.

Dan moves faster and I push my hips up to meet him on every stroke. We don't need to talk. He must be able to feel my channel tightening because he speeds up. My orgasm hits me like an explosion and Dan follows straight after. But at all times our eyes are locked and we look into each other's souls.

As our breathing slows down he leans his forehead against mine. We are both slick with sweat.

"There's not enough words in the dictionary to describe how amazing this was." He places a searing kiss on my lips before rolling off me. I know I should say something romantic back. But what? The only thing that comes to my mind is "I love you" and let's not scare the shit out of him just when he found his way back to me.

Instead, I say the next best thing: "Stay with me tonight."

I put the toothbrush in the holder and rinse my mouth. The woman looking back at me from the mirror looks different. She looks happy. I haven't felt happy in a long time. I haven't been unhappy, but not happy either. I just lived.

When I step into my bedroom, Dan is already under the duvet.

"Is she sleeping?" I ask. Dan nods and I can see the baby monitor on the bedside table. We decided to stay in my room and leave Maisie in Dan's room rather than waking her again.

I crawl under the duvet and Dan pulls me into his arms.

"Dan, I hate to be this woman, but you have Maisie, you live with me and my brother is your best friend. It's not as easy as when we were younger and decided one night will do. This can get complicated real quick. Do we need to talk what this is?"

"I want you, Rose."

"Sure, now—"

"No, not just now. Fuck. Whenever I dated anyone, I always knew it couldn't be more than just one night because she wasn't you."

"Is that why you stayed away so much in the last few years?"

"You were married." His answer makes me sad. He and Alex were like brothers growing up. I hate to be the reason that he stayed away.

"What about before?"

"When we had that night together, we said it would only be one time, and I had grand plans for my life in London. I thought I could leave it all behind and be happy." His fingers slide under my pyjama top and start stroking my tummy. "And then you married that wanker and I really didn't want to see you with him."

I roll my eyes when he brings up Greg. Yeah, nobody in my family really liked my ex-husband either.

"Can I ask you a question?" Dan asks.

"Sure."

"Why did you ever marry Greg?"

"He asked me. I know it sounds stupid but in my twenties I thought the important thing was to get married. That's all my friends were talking about. When I started dating Greg he was really nice to me. It didn't take long for the arguments to start, but I assumed that's just how relationships were. You argue, you make up, you carry on. When he popped the question I should have said no. I mean, he proposed in the most cliche way."

"Ring in a cake?"

I giggle. "Almost. He took me out for Valentine's Day dinner and proposed in the restaurant."

"So I guess, he didn't really know you. You hate Valentine's and you hate public proposals," Dan chuckles.

I turn to look at him. "How do you know?"

"Ha, you made me and Alex watch these cheesy rom-coms when we were younger. And more than once you went into a rant about how much you hate public proposals because they're just for show."

"You remember that?" I whisper.

"Of course. And you hate Valentine's Day. You always said that if your boyfriend needs a commercial holiday to show you he loves you, he doesn't really love you." His expression is serious and there is an edge to his voice.

"That's right." I softly cup his face. His stubbles are scratchy on my palm.

"Do you remember when you and your friend staged a Valentine's Day protest in school?" he asks.

I laugh out loud. Sarah and I were two years under Alex and Dan in school. When I was sixteen, the school decided to hold a Valentine's dance. We pinned slogans over all the posters and turned up at the party dressed as Suffragettes. We may have taken it a bit far back then.

"She's married now and she and her wife live in Bath. She still despises Valentine's Day and every year she sends me an anti-Valentine's card." I grin. He draws lazy circles on my tummy and silence fills the bedroom.

I could look at him for hours. He is no longer just the pretty boy he was when we were younger. He is manly, ruggedly handsome, and irresistibly charming. And he still has a heart of gold. Lying here in his arms just feels as perfect as it gets.

"Can I ask you something else?" I nervously nibble on my lip.

"Sure."

"You said earlier that you moved away because Fellside reminds you of your mum and everything that happened. But now you're here."

He sighs deeply.

"It's funny. The first thing I thought about when I had Maisie in my arms was that I needed to bring her to Fellside. Not because I needed help, but because I wanted Alex and your mum and you to see her. And I realised then that, actually, Fellside is home because your family made me feel at home."

"Did you ever find out what happened to your mum?" I ask cautiously. Dan is quiet for a minute but pulls me closer as if my presence gives him strength.

"She died five years ago. I never saw her again. A couple of years back I paid someone to find out about her, but they could only tell me that she had died."

"I am sorry."

"Thanks. But you know what? I didn't really feel that much. She was never really part of my life, was she? I called Alex and he came down to London to hang out with me for the weekend. We were waiting for me to get sad or have a breakdown. And when I didn't have one, we went to watch the rugby instead." I know he's trying to joke but his voice is sombre. "I think we should try to sleep. Maisie will need feeding soon," he finally says and switches off the lamp on the bedside table.

"I'm glad you are both staying here, Dan. Even if this is only for the next couple of weeks, I am glad I get the chance to spend this Christmas with the two of you." I just had to say it. I had to let him know that I am okay with whatever this is.

"Me too," he whispers before kissing me deeply.

Chapter 8

Dan

Maisie's little cries pull me from my sleep. I reach for the baby monitor in the dark and turn it down so as to not wake Rose. She is curled up against me, her blonde hair spreading out behind her on the pillow.

I place a gentle kiss on her head and then carefully slide out from under her.

I tiptoe naked out of her room because my clothes are somewhere in the living room. Thank fuck she doesn't have any guests yet.

By the time I enter my bedroom Maisie is really pissed off and is telling everyone who wants to hear.

"I'm here, Maisie," I say and flip the light on. Her crying calms down a little and turns into a whimper.

I pull on some boxer shorts and a white T-shirt before lifting my very hungry baby girl from her playpen.

"I know, I know, you want some of that disgusting formula, right?" I coo whilst rocking her in my arms. I tried that stuff once and it is revolting.

Maisie bumps her head against my shoulder.

"Right, let's go." I drape a blanket around her. Although Rose left the heating on low throughout the night it is still a little chilly in the cottage.

I flip on the light in the kitchen. The bright beam startles Maisie and she whimpers. It shouldn't take too long to warm the bottle of formula I prepared yesterday evening.

"Almost there," I whisper and place a kiss on her forehead. She makes a little grunting noise and then smacks her lips. "Daddy has to talk to you, Maisie." I sit down on the sofa and lay her down my thighs. "What do you think of Rose?"

Maisie just grunts again and makes more lip-smacking noises.

"Yup, I like her too. I more than like her. I really want her to be part of our life, what do you think?"

Maisie excitedly wiggles her little arms and legs, and I take that as a resounding 'yes.' I can't help but chuckle and then let out a sigh. Yeah, this is definitely not how I pictured my life going.

I put Maisie back up against my chest and go to grab the bottle from the kitchen. When I am confident it's warm enough I head back to the sofa. I carefully put Maisie in the feeding position, cover her with the blanket, and hold the bottle to her tiny lips.

She latches on like she hadn't been fed in weeks.

I watch the rhythmic movement of the bottle for a moment. One of her hands is still grabbing my T-shirt like she wants to make sure I won't leave her and I can't describe what that does to me.

"I can do this, baby girl. I can be the dad you need me to be. I promise," I whisper. Maisie gives me a crooked smile before sucking on her bottle again.

"This girl is lucky to have you," Rose's voice makes me jump a little.

"Why aren't you sleeping?" I ask. She just shrugs.

"I woke up and you were gone and I thought maybe you two would like some company."

"Oh, Maisie and I will never say no to you keeping us company." A smile forms on my lips. *Fuck, she's beautiful.*

Rose gently strokes Maisie's nose before taking a seat next to me.

"You're so good with her. Did you and Greg never want children?" I am not sure if the question is appropriate but I feel we are close enough for me to ask .

The smile disappears from Rose's face.

"I did want to have children, he didn't. And to be honest, considering the divorce and what an arse Greg is, I am now glad we never had any." There is pain in her voice and I'm not so sure she really is glad.

My phone, which I had put on the kitchen table, starts vibrating. Rose and I both stare at it.

"It's three in the morning. Who calls you at that time? Booty call?" she jokes.

"Nope. Would you mind taking Maisie?" I pass my little girl to her. Maisie briefly stops drinking, but the minute she is snuggled in Rose's arms, she starts her rhythmic sucking again.

I grab my phone and frown.

"It's Alex." Immediately there is concern on Rose's face. "Hey, mate, all okay?" I ask after accepting the call.

"Yes, all fine. Well, we are okay, but I am calling to ask you for a favour."

"At three in the morning? Shoot."

"We have been called to an emergency. Apparently two young lads went for a snowshoe hike last night up on Fellside Pike and they haven't returned."

"Oh shit."

"Yes! Two teams have been searching for them since ten last night but now we've been called in too. They want us to head up from the Kirkstone Pass side, so not far from you."

"And you want us to have hot chocolate ready for everyone," I chuckle and give Rose a big grin. She relaxes when she realises that Alex is okay.

"We won't say no to that, but no. I was hoping you would join us."

"I haven't been on a rescue in years, Alex." I joined the volunteers in our twenties but then I wasn't in Fellside enough to ever really take part in rescues.

"I know. But Tommy left for New Zealand earlier this week and Chris is snowed in on the farm. Ryan is pretty new, so that just leaves me, Rob, Nick, and Phil who have rescue experience. We could do with an extra person. There's no climbing on that side up onto Fellside Pike and the most you'll have to do is help us carry them down. We can cover the first aid."

"Sure, okay," I say nervously, but he's right. I have run up to Fellside Pike from the Kirkstone side a million times and there's no climbing involved.

"Thanks, Dan! We'll pick you up on our way to the starting point and we'll have snowshoes for you. Do you have your outdoor gear or do I need to lend you something?"

"No, I have my gear with me." When I packed up in London I emptied my wardrobe. I'm not planning to go back.

"Wicked, mate. We should be there in forty minutes."

"Okay." I guess I'm going on a mountain rescue.

Fuck it's cold! I pull my beanie lower. It's stopped snowing and apparently is supposed to be raining tomorrow, but it doesn't feel like that up here. The beam of my head torch illuminates the soft snow in front of me. We've been out here for almost two hours and just as we got to the summit of the Fellside Pike, Alex, who is filling in as leader in Tommy's absence, received a call that one of the other units found the missing guys. The two lads are in bad shape but I really hope, especially with Christmas just around the corner, that they will be okay.

We are now walking back down and frankly I can't wait to get back to my two girls and not just because it is warm there.

"Did you enjoy our nightly hike?" Nick grumbles next to me.

"Sure, mate, but next time can you guys call me in the summer, when it is warm?" I chuckle.

"Seriously, where were these boys' parents? Why the fuck would you let them go to the mountains in that weather?"

"And I thought Tommy was the grumpy one." I joke.

"How's it going with Maisie?" Nick changes the topic.

"I think I'm slowly getting the hang of it."

"How difficult is it?"

"What?"

"Being a father."

"It's the most terrifying thing I have ever done. Why do you ask?" Nick stops and holds me back by my arm.

"Don't tell the others, but Charlotte and I have been accepted as adoptive parents for a baby," he has the biggest grin on his face.

"Congratulations Nick!" I give him a brief hug. Everyone in the group knows how much the two of them want a baby.

"We're not telling anyone because we're worried something could happened." I mime zipping my lips.

"You know I said it's the most terrifying thing?" I whisper. He nods. "I've also never felt such incredible happiness." This makes Nick smile happily and I can see in his eyes that he can't wait to be a father himself. We follow the others and soon catch up to the group.

"How's Rose?" Alex asks.

"Good," I reply nonchalantly, or at least I hope it sounds like it. Guilt nags me. Maybe I should talk to him.

"Is she driving you crazy with all the Christmas shit she has everywhere?" Alex chuckles. *Oh, mate, she is driving me crazy, that's for sure. But in a good way.*

"No, it's fine."

"She is, isn't she? You can tell me," Alex pushes.

"No, really. I don't mind"

"Don't hold back, man. I always tell this one when his sister's driving me up the wall," Ryan points at Phil.

"Oh my god, can you and Jane please leave me out of this," Phil whines.

"She's a bloody pain in the arse, mate." Ryan argues.

"What am I missing?" I ask Alex as Ryan and Phil bicker.

"Jane works in the shop next to Ryan's tattoo studio and she seems to be leading the WI war council on a mission to get Ryan out of the village." My eyes grow wide. If the Women's Institute is after him he's in for a real fight.

"Don't worry, my granny and Emma's grandma are leading the counter offensive," Alex chuckles. "So, everything okay with Rose?" he asks again. Does he know something? Or am I just paranoid?

"Yes, yesterday she saved me and Maisie from a spider." I'll take public humiliation about my arachnophobia any day over having to tell my best mate that I shagged his sister and that I am counting the minutes until I can climb back into bed with her.

I watch the FMR car roll away into the dark before quietly opening the front door and I see a light on in the back of the house where Rose's living room is. I hang up my hiking jacket and take off my boots. I am frozen to my bones and the warmth of the house feels good.

I tiptoe into the living room where Rose is lying on the sofa with Maisie cuddled up against her chest. She has a blanket draped over them both and as I walk closer my little girl opens her eyes and lets out a little grunt before smiling at me.

"Hey, baby girl," I whisper and gently pull Maisie from Rose's chest.

"What," Rose startles and sits up. Her hair is sticking up wildly and she looks disorientated for a minute.

"It's just me," I say softly and snuggle Maisie to my chest. She squeaks happily.

"You're back... Did it all go okay? Did you find them?"

"We didn't. One of the other teams did. They've taken them to the hospital. It looks serious."

"Shit, and so close before Christmas."

"I know. But they still have a chance," I reply and gently bounce Maisie in my arms. "Why did you both not go to bed?"

"Oh, we did, but missy here had other ideas."

"Did she cry?" I frown and place a small kiss on Maisie's forehead.

"No, but she wanted to have a chat," Rose giggles before walking to the kitchen. "How about a cuppa?"

"That would be great," I reply, looking at my daughter, "So you didn't let Rose sleep, hmm. Well, I think we need to have a word about this because we don't want her to kick us out," I joke and Maisie just gurgles happily.

"Never! I would never kick you out," Rose objects from the kitchen. "Turns out your daughter likes the Christmas lights because, after we settled down on the sofa, she just stared at the fairy lights and I think that's when we both fell asleep."

"Maybe she has your Christmas spirit?" I ask as I step up to Rose and put a hand on her back.

"Good morning," I whisper before capturing her lips in a long kiss.

"Good morning," she sighs. Maisie squeaks again in my arms.

"And good morning to you too," Rose coos at Maisie and places a kiss on her cheek as well. *Fuck, we are a Hallmark movie.*

Chapter 9

Rose

Dan pushes through the people, his hand protectively on Maisie's back where she is strapped to his chest. The very "helpful" salespeople had talked him into one of these baby wrap sling thingies. It "only" took us forty-five minutes to work out how to use it. In the end, Dan refused to take it off again. Instead, he zipped up his jacket around Maisie and sat in the back of the car with Maisie strapped to his chest because that was "a safer seat for him and her in case of an accident."

We are meeting Chris, Suzie, and Max at the Christmas market in Windermere. Neither me nor Dan wanted to leave the house, really. I don't like big crowds anymore having lived a hermit's life for a while, and Dan is concerned about Maisie. That's when Chris and Suzie pulled out the big guns and put Max on the phone who told us in a very sad voice that he was really, really looking forward to show us his favourite Christmas tree. Frankly I'm no longer surprised that Chris can't say no to him.

"There they are." I point towards a stand selling mulled wine and German sausages. Max, Suzie's five-year-old who is wearing a tiny elf hat, is longingly staring at the market stall worker who is putting sausages in buns.

"Dad, pleeeease, I'm so hungry," he whines just as we get closer. Chris scoops him up in his arms and steps up to the stand to order some food.

"So, I guess Chris still can't say no?" I giggle as I hug Suzie.

"No, but this time it's okay. We had planned to have our lunch here. Hope you guys don't mind?" she asks. Dan places a kiss on Suzie's cheek.

"Not at all, I'm starving as well. Rose, want one?" he asks.

"Sure," I smile at him, bending down to the pushchair to greet little Baby Emma. Emma is named after my sister-in-law as a thank you to her for protecting Suzie and Max from Suzie's evil ex. And so we don't get Emma and

Emma confused, we all have started to call the little one Baby Emma.

"How is Dan settling in?" Suzie asks and there is a twinkle in her eyes.

"Good, yes, fine," I reply and I am glad when Chris, Max and Dan rejoin us. I take the massive sausage from Dan's hand.

"Max, don't you want to say hi to Rose?" Suzie reminds her son.

"Hi, aunty Rose," he wiggles his little fingers. "I have a whole sausage to myself." He grins as he climbs onto the bar stool next to one of the big barrels which are used as tables. Suzie looks horrified by the idea of her son eating one of these massive sausages on his own, but before she can protest Chris subtly shakes his head to tell her that this is not actually the case.

"They're amazing," Dan says before taking another bite of his sausage bun.

"Watch ou—" before Suzie and I can finish the sentence a small dollop of ketchup drops onto Maisie's head. Maisie, none the wiser, keeps looking around in awe at all the excitement.

"Wait." I dig in my handbag for a tissue. Just as I pull one out Dan bends his head forward and licks the ketchup off Maisie's hair.

"Dan!" I call out.

"What?" he asks confused. Chris and Max both laugh their heads off and Suzie is also giggling.

"You can't lick her!"

"Why not? It's just some ketchup."

"Yes, but you're not a bloody cat," I laugh and step up to him. I wet the tissue with my spit and gently wipe away the rest of the ketchup from Maisie's blonde hair.

"You used spit as well," he protests with a smirk on his face. I roll my eyes and then notice the speck of ketchup on the corner of his mouth.

"Wait," I gently take his chin in between my fingers and dab at it. Dan's eyes turn dark and bore into me. The look he gives me makes heat pool in my core.

"Dan, your sausage," Chris pulls us from the moment. "The one in your hand," he clarifies with a chuckle. Heat rushes to my cheeks whilst Dan readjusts his sausage bun to stop the meat from sliding to the floor.

I take a step back and grab my own bun which I'd placed on the table.

"So, you and Dan?" Suzie whispers as Max drags Dan and Chris into a conversation about all the presents he's asked Santa for.

"What? No..."

"Oh, please! There was some major eye-fucking going on just now." She rolls her eyes at me. "Question is if you've shagged yet." I can feel my cheeks getting even warmer.

"Aha, so you already did."

I nod. What's the point of denying it.

"Listen, you can't tell anyone," I beg.

"Why? Everyone will be thrilled."

"Everyone? Do you think my brother will love it if he finds out one of his friends is shagging me?"

"I can't see Alex having an issue unless Dan hurts you." Hm. She might actually not be wrong, but still.

"Being as it is, I'd rather he hears it from me than through the grapevine. Besides, I don't even know what this is between us." A big sigh escapes me.

"That's love, my dear," she smirks and her words cause a thousand butterflies to set off in my tummy. I don't reply. Instead, I grab the wrapper my sausage was in and walk off towards the bin.

I'm about to return to the group when I notice something on the market stall next to the bin. A big smile spreads on my lips.

When I rejoin the others five minutes later, Chris and Dan are helping Max to finish his sausage. Of course, it was way too big for the little squirt.

"I have a present for you and Maisie," I giggle as I step in front of Dan.

"What?"

"Look how cute they are!" I squeal and pull two beanies out of the shopping bag in my hand. One is baby sized and one for an adult but otherwise they are identical. They are brown with a red dot on the forehead and little antlers sticking out. I carefully slide the smaller one over Maisie's head and she looks adorable.

"I'm not wearing antlers," Dan protests and tries to move away from me.

"Dan, don't be a child, wear the beanie," I demand.

"No!"

"Yes, look how cute Maisie is!" He glances down at Maisie who, as if on command, looks up at him with her little bottom lip sticking out. I take the opportunity to pull the beanie over his head. Chris, who had just stuffed the last of his lunch in his mouth, almost chokes.

"You look adorable," he says between bouts of laughter. Dan rubs his nose with his middle finger not so discreetly.

"You two look so cute," I giggle. I pull my phone from my handbag and take a sideways photo of Dan and Maisie both looking at me in their reindeer beanies. "See," I hold out my phone and show him. He tries to frown, but his lips tilt upwards.

“Take another one where we smile,” he finally says. I grin and take a step back. “Maisie, brrrrrr.” She always smiles when Dan makes this noise and just as her lips lift Dan smiles at me as well and I take the shot. Perfect!

Chapter 10

Dan

The mattress dips as I crawl back into bed.

"How often did she cry tonight?" Rose yawns.

"This was the fourth one, but to be honest she had properly shat her nappy this time. I would have complained too," I laugh before placing a soft kiss on her neck. And then another one a little lower. I push the duvet down and the cool air in the room makes her nipples pebble.

"What are you doing?" she sighs.

"Oh, as we are already up and Maisie is asleep for once—" I groan before gently licking around her left nipple. One of my hands slides under the duvet and gently strokes over the seam of her pussy.

"Dan," she warns me, but doesn't make any move to stop me.

I take another lick of her nipple before sliding even lower. For years I had thought I remembered every taste and scent of her, but what I remembered was some cheap imitation of the real thing. This, here, I can't get enough of her.

I slowly slide a finger into her warm pussy. Then a second one. She is squirming and I know what she needs, but I won't give it to her yet. We've been together every night this past week and I can read her body by now.

I slowly withdraw my fingers and push them back in.

"Oh fuck, please. Please, stop teasing me."

I love it when she begs. I add a third finger and curl them upwards.

"Yes," she hisses and tries to ride my hand but I pin her hips down to the mattress and lean forward.

"Say please again," I groan.

"Please," she cries out and I latch onto her clit. I feather my tongue over it before blowing softly on it. Rose shivers and grabs my hair so she can press me harder against her. I finally take pity on her and suck the little nub into my mouth. My fingers move faster and faster and it is less than a minute before she explodes on my tongue.

When I look up at her she has a pillow pressed over her face.

"Rose, what are you doing?" I chuckle.

"I didn't want to wake Maisie," she says, still breathing heavily.

"Give me that," I pull the pillow from her hands and throw it behind me on the floor. I'm about to reach for a condom when a little whimper comes from the baby monitor.

"See," Rose exclaims and sits up.

"No, she didn't hear you," I laugh and try to get up from the bed. Rose grabs my arm, pulls me back and then gets off the bed herself.

"I'll go. You get this..." she points at my hard cock," under control."

"How? Especially with you so deliciously naked," I groan. Rose pulls the oversized shirt she sleeps in over her head.

"Take a cold shower," she laughs and saunters out of the bedroom.

I walk into the adjoining bathroom and turn on the hot water. No fucking way am I having a cold shower.

Although the snow has been washed away over the last few days, it is still wintery cold outside.

I step under the spray and enjoy the warm water tickling down my back. I squirt shower gel in my palm and start soaping myself up. My hand automatically finds its way to my cock and I start stroking it. I lean against the shower wall with my other hand. In my mind I see Rose sprayed out in front of me with her pussy glistening. My hand moves faster as I imagine licking through her folds. I want to devour her. I can almost taste her on my lips. There is a tingling at the base of my spine and then the orgasm hits me. I draw in some deep breaths and finally open my eyes.

Oh fuck! My spunk has not only covered her shampoo bottle, which is standing on the floor of the shower but also her bath mesh sponge thingy which is dangling from the tap. I grab the bottle of shampoo and rinse it. Then I grab the sponge but the water just seems to push it further to the centre of the mesh. *Fuck.*

When I step into the living room, Rose is sitting on the floor next to Maisie who is on the playmat under the baby gym I bought her yesterday in Windermere. She absolutely loves it. It has stars and moons dangling down and she is fascinated by them. It was supposed to be a Christmas present but she is less than four months old; it makes no difference to her if she gets it on Christmas or not.

"I owe you a sponge thingy," I admit whilst throwing the soiled one into the bin.

"Why?" I can feel Rose's eyes bore into my back and my ears warm up.

"I took care of—" I point at my crotch.

"You fucked my sponge?" Rose's eyes go wide.

"No!" I exclaim. "And don't say f, u, c, k in front of my daughter."

Rose laughs. "Dan, she is a tiny baby. All she knows is that you and I are her personal servants who cater to her every whim." I shrug. "So, do I want to know what you did with my sponge?"

"I kind of... came on it. Accidentally."

"So, wash it off."

"I tried, let's just not talk about it and agree that I will buy you a new one."

I'm about to sit down next to Maisie when my phone rings. I pull it from my back pocket.

"It's my old boss," I announce to Rose before accepting the call. "Hi, Naz."

"Dan, how are you?" His greeting immediately makes me suspicious. Something's up. Nazim never ever wasted so much as a minute on pleasantries when I worked there.

"I'm good, thanks, and you?" If he can hear the suspicion in my voice, he doesn't react to it.

"Good, good. Busy. Dan, I just wanted to check in and see if you have found a new job yet."

"No." I mean, come on, give me a chance to get my head around this first.

"Well, I had a chat with HR and we think we could potentially make this work a bit better for you, if you want to come back." *Wait, they want me back?*

"What does that mean?"

"We could agree to forty hours a week over four days. This should give you enough time with your child."

I don't say anything. My eyes move to where Rose sits and plays with Maisie on the floor.

"For the same salary as before." Nazim's voice brings me back to the call.

"Same salary?" Rose looks at me and for a brief second there is a frown and then her expression is neutral again.

"Yes, and we will either pay for a nanny or if you want to keep the child with your family up north you can shift your extra day off around so you can have long weekends.

So, work Monday to Thursday one week and Tuesday to Friday the next giving you a four-day weekend."

"I don't know what to say Naz." And I genuinely don't. The job was incredibly well paid. This is money I can never make up here, and it is money that could ensure Maisie has a great future.

"Why don't you come down this week, just for an overnight trip, and we can discuss the benefits we are offering in detail ."

I swallow hard. " Sure, okay."

"Okay, great," Naz sighs relieved. "We'll email you the train ticket."

I nod. "Thanks."

I end the call with Naz as I take a seat next to Maisie. I poke one of the moons so it starts swinging above her and she waves her little hands excitedly.

"They offered me my job back," I say quietly.

"Oh, how do you feel about it?" Rose replies. Neither her expression nor her voice give away how she feels about it.

"I don't know. He says I can work shorter hours and I can shift it so I could come back up here every two weeks. It's a lot of money and it would ensure a secure future for Maisie." I try to catch her eye but she avoids me and gets up from the floor instead. She starts busying herself in the kitchen making tea.

"That's great, Dan," she says and finally looks at me. Her lips tilt up, but the smile doesn't reach her eyes.

"Want one?" She holds up a tea bag.

"Sure." I get to my feet and join her. I slide my arms around her waist from behind and put my chin on her shoulder but she stiffens a little.

"Rose, I need to at least check it out. I'm going down to London later this week just for one night."

Rose turns in my arms. "Want to leave Maisie with me?" Again, her expression doesn't give anything away. I wish she would tell me what she is thinking.

"Would that be okay? I'll take the train down and it would be a lot of stress for Maisie."

"Of course." She presses a kiss to my lips before turning back to the counter to finish our tea.

Knots are forming in my stomach. Why do I feel someone just burst the protective bubble around me?

Chapter 11

Rose

The smell of bacon fills the air and my eyes move to the clock on the kitchen wall again. The ladies should be here any minute. All of the girlfriends and wives of the FMR guys have become my friends. They are a bunch of crazy ladies, and it is rare that we all manage to get together except for the monthly FMR meeting. They all either have jobs, or are busy with other things. Aside from Emma, I have become especially close to Olivia, Rob's girlfriend, Charlotte, who is married to Nick, and Jane, who is Phil's sister. And the three of them have invited themselves for some pre-Christmas drinks to my house.

"Right, Maisie, are you ready to be passed around like an Oscar?" I coo and lift her from her baby gym into my arms. That thing definitely was the best investment ever. She can lie under it for ages and never gets bored.

Maisie looks so cute today in her little leggings and T-shirt saying "My dad rocks." I couldn't resist it when I saw it in the shop yesterday and as soon as it was dry after washing it, I had to put it on her.

I sent Dan a photo earlier and he replied with a voice note of just laughter. I feel a tight ball of anxiety in my belly when I think of Dan. The thought that he and Maisie could move down south again breaks my heart and my brain has been working overtime for the last couple of days.

What if this is the end of us? The thought makes me feel sick. I know he's only been back in my life for a few weeks but that doesn't change how I feel about him.

What if he asks me to move with him? I hate London. I also have my Bed & Breakfast here. But maybe—

My thoughts get interrupted by a knock on the door.

"Show time, miss," I say and tickle Maisie. I know the ladies will spoil her all afternoon.

After we have all said our hellos, we settle in with the party food and glasses of Prosecco. Charlotte has made a beeline for Maisie, and so far has defended giving her up from all attempts by the others. Maisie seemed a little unsure at the beginning but now she is lying on Charlotte's lap and watching her, mesmerised.

"So, have you shagged Dan yet?" Olivia blurts out. I choke on the sausage roll I had just taken a bite from.

"Olivia!" Charlotte, the eternal diplomat of the group, admonishes her.

"What, you all know that Christina made us promise to come back with the dirty gossip. I thought it would be easiest to ask," she chuckles, and I can feel my cheeks turn hot.

"Oh my god, you have," Jane says and leans forward in anticipation.

"I—" I just shrug. "Don't tell Emma. She'll tell Alex. Or Christina!" Christina is Emma's best friend and a gossip. The last thing I need is for Alex to find out about this from someone else. Especially not if Dan and I may be over before the relationship has even properly started.

"Fine, I'll try to avoid her calls because there's no way I can keep a secret from her." Olivia takes another sip of her drink. "And?"

"And what?" I ask.

"Jeez, Rose. Are you guys just boinking, or...?" Jane asks.

"I don't know," I reply honestly.

"Wait, are we ignoring the fact that Jane just said boinking?" Olivia laughs.

"I don't like being crude."

"What did I say? I said shagging. That is harmless. I didn't say fucking." Olivia laughs again.

"Shh," Jane says and puts her fingers over Maisie's ears.

"You're like Dan," I giggle. "He always turns into a Victorian virgin whenever I use a dirty word in front of Maisie."

"How's he getting on with her now?" Charlotte asks without looking up from Maisie who has grabbed onto her necklace.

"He's wonderful with her. You should see him. He's a born dad," I reply.

"So I take it that means there is more than boinking going on...," Olivia snorts, "... if you swoon over him like that."

I slide my fingers through my hair and take a deep breath.

"I'll tell you a secret, but you can't tell anyone. Swear."

"Oh, jeez, first boinking and now we have to make a pinkie swear," Olivia is laughing so hard and I am starting to wonder how much Prosecco she's had.

They all promise to keep my secret and I tell them everything that has happened, all the way back to our first night together over thirteen years ago.

"Well, fuck... I mean boink," Olivia says when I am finished.

"And the worst is, I'm sure I am in love with him." I put my face in my hands. As if feeling my distress, Maisie whines and wiggles in Charlotte's lap. On autopilot I reach out for her and she snuggles against my chest. "And I love this little one."

"Have you told him?" Charlotte asks and grabs a mini pizza.

"No, how can I? He has the job offer from down south."

"So? He needs to know the facts so he can make a decision," Jane chimes in.

"No, he needs to decide what is best for him and Maisie and not be swayed by me."

"Oh my god, Rose. You're not in a romance novel where you get points for noble deeds and it all ends up in a happily ever after. This is your fucking life. Tell him. And even if you do tell him, it doesn't mean he can't take the job. You said he could potentially commute or... maybe you could move with him?" Olivia claps excitedly.

I frown.

"Or maybe not?" Olivia asks.

"I hate London. But—"

"But if he'd ask you, you would rather say yes than lose him," Charlotte grins at me.

"I guess so. Argh. Why are we even talking about this? He hasn't said anything to that effect."

The girls polish off another two bottles of Prosecco, but I stopped drinking after one glass. I have Maisie after all.

"There he is, my gorgeous toy boy," Charlotte laughs and falls into Nick's arms when he steps into the living room. Nick has offered to pick them all up so they can have a drink, but looking at his expression, I don't think he expected his wife to be this pissed this early in the day.

"Babe, how much did you have to drink?"

"A tiny little bit," she giggles. Olivia is in fits of laughter on the floor as well. Jane looks rather sober, so I guess the three bottles of Prosecco were mainly drunk by Charlotte and Olivia.

I place Maisie in the playpen before helping Jane, who is trying to pull Olivia from the floor. Between the two of us, we manage to get her on her feet and we guide her out of the cottage. Nick, in the meanwhile, has placed his wife in the passenger seat.

When Olivia is safely strapped in on the backseat I give her one last hug and she whispers in my ear, "Tell him." I don't reply. I know I should talk to him but I am scared to hear him say that there is no place for me in his and Maisie's life.

I hug the other two goodbye and wave to Nick before rushing back into the cottage. *Fuck it's cold.*

"Well, Maisie Mouse, looks like it is just us again," I say as I step back into the living room. I quickly tidy up before preparing a bottle for Maisie.

When I sit down on the sofa with her to feed her, she seems to be looking around and searching for something. Or should I say someone. She restlessly wriggles in my arms but eventually she takes the bottle. When I give her a quick bath, she definitely knows something is different. She normally loves splashing around in the warm water and it's her and Dan's happy time. But today she keeps sticking her lip out at me, looking all sad. I am no substitute for her dad.

When I have her dressed in her pyjamas, I reach for my phone and see that I have a missed call from Dan.

"Your dad called, Maisie. Should we call him back?" I press the video call button and wait for it to connect.

"Thank fuck, Rose, I was worried. Is everything okay."

"Calm down, Dan," I giggle, "Maisie Mouse was just having a bath." Dan looks gloomy when I mention bath time.

"Maisie Mouse?" he asks after the new nickname I have given his daughter.

"It just slipped out this afternoon and I like it."

"I like it too," he chuckles and Maisie goes wild in my arms when she hears his voice.

"Look, Maisie, daddy." I turn the camera screen to her so she can see Dan. Frankly I am not sure if at her age she can actually make sense of what I am showing her.

She seems to be confused but when he says "There is Maisie, I missed you, baby girl," she starts happily kicking her arms and legs again.

"She missed you too," I say and a sad look appears on Dan's face.

"Right, should we read a bedtime story, Maisie Mouse?" He holds up one of her farm animal books. She loves it when he does the animal noises.

"Dan, where did you get that book from?" I ask.

"I packed it so I can read it to her tonight." He looks sheepish, but I can feel my eyes water.

I cradle Maisie in my arm and hold the phone out to her. Dan starts reading and when he makes the pig noises, she babbles with joy. But eventually I see her eyes drooping until they finally close.

"Is she sleeping?" Dan whispers.

"Yes, give me a second," I reply and walk towards my bedroom. This morning I cleared the little office next to my bedroom and set Maisie up in there. This way we have her closer to us. If Dan stays, that is.

"I'm back," I pick up the phone again. "So how was it?"

"Good. They're bending over backwards to get me back. Apparently a lot of my former clients have put pressure on and said they'll pull their portfolio unless I'll manage it."

"Great." I hope I sound sincere.

"Yeah. The only thing they won't agree to is remote working. I can shift my four days around but they want bums on chairs in the office." He sighs deeply.

"A bit old fashioned."

"Yeah." He sounds weird.

"Dan, what is it?"

"Rose, I... I told them I need to think about it over Christmas. They've given me until the new year to make up my mind."

"That's good." Not sure what else I can say.

"It's been a long day. I need get some sleep. I should be back around five tomorrow. I want us to talk about this properly. This affects all of us."

My heart starts hammering.

"Don't look so shocked, Rose."

"I'm not."

"I can see you on the camera. Of course I need to discuss this with you as well. I... We have started something and we can't just put it back in the box and ignore it for another twenty years. But... fuck, I don't want to do this over the phone."

"That's okay. We have my brother and Emma over tomorrow for Christmas Eve dinner, though."

"Shit, I forgot about that."

"You have until the new year. Let's have a nice Christmas and we can talk about this afterwards. How does that sound?" It's the coward's way out, but I'd rather have a lovely Christmas I can remember forever.

"Are you sure?"

"Yup."

"Okay. I can't wait to see you both tomorrow."

"We can't wait either." I hang up the phone and then a little sob escapes me. I can't lose him again.

Chapter 12

Dan

I step out of the small train station in Windermere and a car horn draws my attention. I walk over to where the Range Rover is parked when I recognise Alex and Emma in the car.

"Mate, what are you doing here?" I ask him as I climb into the backseat.

"I told Rose not to bother to come down to collect you as we are heading your way for the dinner anyway."

I bend between the two front seats and place a kiss on Emma's cheek as a greeting.

"And where is my kiss?" Alex jokes.

"Funny." I lean back against the soft seat as Alex pulls out of the car park.

"So, how was it?" Emma asks cautiously.

"It was okay."

"Rose made me swear that I wouldn't talk you into staying up here," Alex chuckles but his words hit me like a punch.

"Why's that?" I ask worried what the answer may be.

"Because she wants you to make the decision that's best for you and Maisie." Alex indicates to turn right and turns onto the road leading to the little hamlet where Rose's cottage is.

"But I will say as much: London sucks."

"Thanks, mate. Very subtle," I laugh. My eyes drift close as I didn't sleep much last night. I wasn't lying when I said the package they offered me is amazing. The salary is brilliant, but all the other extras they are willing to pay for, make it an incredibly generous offer. And the work hours don't sound too bad, if I can stick to them, that is.

As we approach Rose's cottage I take a deep breath. I am home and I will see my two girls in a minute. A smile lifts the corners of my mouth.

I lend Alex a hand in carrying the bags filled with groceries they brought. We both have our hands full when we follow Emma who has stepped into the warm cottage.

Rose must already be cooking something because it smells delicious. Christmas music fills the house and all of the thousands of Christmas lights she has are on. A fire is roaring in the fireplace, and then I see the one sight I have been missing the most.

Rose is dancing in the kitchen with Maisie in her arms. She stops and smirks embarrassed that we caught her.

"Maisie, look! Dad's here," she says softly to my daughter. I step up to them and lift Maisie in my arms. She squeals excitedly and gives me a smile before nuzzling against my shoulder.

"Hey, Maisie Mouse," I whisper. "I missed you so much." Her tiny hands grab my T-shirt when I plant my lips on her forehead. My eyes find Rose and she has tears in hers. *Fuck, I want to kiss her so much.*

"Merry Christmas, R," Alex greets his sister and pinches her in her side. She slaps him playfully.

"Merry Christmas, Alexander," she says, pronouncing his full name with glee.

"Don't call me that."

"Then don't call me R," she gives back

"Every fucking time," Emma chuckles and walks into the kitchen with the bags of food.

"No swearing around my daughter," I warn.

"Olivia said you turn into a, what did she call it... a Victorian virgin around Maisie," Emma chuckles and Alex throws his head back and laughs out loud, startling Maisie. Rose, on the other hand, turns pale at Emma's words.

"What else did she say?" she asks a little panicked.

"Just that," Emma shrugs. Rose's eyes find me and her look worries me.

"What else should she have told us?" Alex chuckles and pinches Rose again. She yelps and slaps him a little harder this time.

"You two are like little children. Maisie Mouse, don't pay any attention to them," I coo to my daughter and snuggle her closer. It's crazy how much I have missed her.

"Well, put her down now, we all have to help with the food," Alex orders and grabs a box of Scotch eggs.

I don't really want to let go of her, but I can't let them do all the work. When I place Maisie under her baby gym, she immediately reaches out with her little arms, babbling happily.

"Right, put me to work," I demand. Emma gives me some tomatoes and peppers to cut and I grab a chopping board.

We are invited to Rose and Alex's parents house for a proper Christmas dinner on Boxing Day, so for today we decided to just have our favourite party food. Between the four of us, it doesn't take long to get a selection of salads and nibbles ready.

"So, what did you guys do the whole time up here? We thought we might see you around the village after the snow cleared," Alex asks as he carries a platter with mini pizzas and sausage roles to the table.

"Nothing," Rose and I say in unison. My ears are burning and I can see the blush on Rose's cheeks, but what else could we have said? *Well, mate, I shagged your sister senseless*. Yup, didn't think so.

Alex puts his knife down. "Nothing?" he asks. "You must have done something." He has a weird smirk on his face and I'm not sure what that means.

"Well, we watched some films and stuff." Rose tries to sound nonchalant but I can hear the edge in her voice.

Maybe I should just rip the band aid off and tell him? But I wouldn't even know how to start.

"Let's eat," Rose announces and carries a small plate with pigs in blankets to the table, but in her attempt to escape her brother's interrogation she doesn't see the duffle bag on the floor.

"Watch out," Alex shouts but it's too late and Rose's foot gets caught in the shoulder strap making her trip. How she doesn't fall and how most of the pigs are still in their blanket is beyond me, but, somehow, she manages to regain her balance.

"Are you okay?" I ask worried and rush to her.

"I'm fine," she says as I slide my arm around her waist. Our eyes lock before we both take a cautious step apart.

"Sorry, Rose, let me put that away," I grab my duffle bag and take it to Rose's bedroom. I drop it in a corner and then quickly change from my suit into jeans and T-shirt. Although I have the room upstairs, over the last week, most of my clothes I wear regularly have found their way into Rose's room where I have spent every night.

I grab the little present I got Maisie and head back out.

"Maisie, look what daddy bought you," I say and hold out the little squishy teddy. Alex must have picked her up from the floor as she is now snuggled against him. She lifts her head from his shoulder and looks around until she sees me. Alex takes the toy from me and holds it out to Maisie who tries to grab it.

I take my seat next to Rose and reach for my pint of beer.

"Mate,..." Alex locks eyes with me, "why did you put your bag in Rose's bedroom?" *Oh shit!* Anyone who knows the layout of the cottage knows that the direction I took can only lead to Rose's bedroom. For all the other bedrooms, I would have had to leave the living room and take the stairs. And if anyone would know that, it would be Alex, who helped her refurbish the whole building.

"I... it was just quicker."

"Oh, okay.... and why were you in a rush?"

I can't read his facial expression but the silence in the room is adding to the tension. The only one breaking it is Maisie, who happily babbles at the toy that Alex is waving in front of her.

"Alex, what the fuck?" For once I forget to tell Rose off for swearing. Her brother's eyes are boring into me.

"Alex, I think we need to talk," I get up from my chair and take Maisie from him. Not that I am worried about her, more because it is less likely that he will punch me if I have her in my arms.

"I'm listening." He crosses his arms in front of his chest. That is his signature move when he wants your confession. And he is so bloody good at that. He waits you out until you crack under the silence and tell him all. I swear he missed his profession.

"Okay, so the thing is, that Rose and I are kind of... kind of dating."

"Kind of dating." He raises an eyebrow and puts the words in air quotes. "What does 'kind of' mean."

I look at Rose for help, but she is just fiddling with her napkin. Emma is staring at the table top with her hands folded in front of her mouth, but I swear it looks like her eyes are pulling up in laughter. Only Alex doesn't shy away from giving me a stern look.

"Rose and I are dating," I finally say. "I'm sorry, Alex. I should have told you sooner, but that doesn't change anything. Rose and I want to be together. You are my best friend, but I'll tell you now, I won't give her up." My voice is strong and determined, and I mean it.

"But you're moving to London," he says. There is no expression on his face and I can't read how he really feels.

"Maybe; Rose and I haven't decided yet."

"You're including my sister in the decision?" he asks and his shoulders seem to relax a little.

"Of course. I love her." Rose gasps next to me. *Oh fuck.*

"What?" She places a soft hand on my forearm to draw my attention to her.

"I love you. Maisie and I both love you." I give her small smile. A tear runs down her face and she plants a passionate kiss on my mouth.

"See, I told you," Alex says and grins at Emma.

Now it's my time to ask, "What?"

"Mate, you've fancied her since that summer when you came back from uni. I'm not a fucking idiot."

"So you're not angry?"

"Why would I be angry?" He looks at me confused.

"I'm your friend. And I'm, you know—" I wiggle my eyebrows and Alex frowns. "I remember how often we planned the best way to make Greg disappear."

"Greg was a wanker. Dan, you're one of my best mates. I trust you with my life, so of course I trust you to take care of my sister. And I kind of helped a little, didn't I?" He laughs cheerful and Emma giggles next to him.

"What do you mean?"

"Well, who came up with the idea for you to stay at Rose's."

"You lied?"

"No, we would have happily had you, but you know our cottage, it's tiny. So, sending you to Rose was the best option. But was I hoping that you'd both finally see sense? Maybe."

"I can't believe you," Rose whispers.

"Rose, you're my baby sister. It broke my heart to see you go through the divorce from that wanker and then withdraw from the world. You need someone like Dan in your life. Someone who can make you happy."

Rose stands up and rounds the table to pull Alex into a tight hug.

"So I worried for no fucking reason?" I shake my head.

"Language, mate. What are you teaching your daughter?" Alex teases before pulling his wife to his side. "Right, can we finally start eating?" he chuckles and breaks the tension. I put Maisie back under her baby gym in the hope that she will let us finish our meal before demanding our attention.

When I take my seat opposite Alex, he locks eyes with me again. There is a serious look on his face.

"Thanks, Alex." And that simple "Thank you" weighs heavy. *Thanks for trusting me, thanks for rooting for us. Thanks for everything.*

"Just don't hurt her!" He points at me.

Chapter 13

Rose

I reach out to the other side of the bed, but it's cold. I force my eyes open and the illuminated dials on my alarm clock tell me that it is just after six in the morning. Christmas Day. I immediately feel giddy until I remember that this means we're a day closer to having to make a decision.

As agreed, Dan and I didn't speak about it yesterday but that doesn't mean it wasn't at the back of my mind the whole time. Would I move with them? Sure. Would it hurt terribly to leave this life, my family, my friends behind? Abso-fucking-lutely.

I slip into my Christmas pyjamas and my thick Christmas socks, grab my Santa hat and tip toe from my room. I look like a Christmas lunatic, but I don't care. It's Christmas!

I pull the door shut behind me and hear Maisie's little squeals. She has become a lot more verbal in the last few days and there is no question anymore over the bond she has formed with Dan. He's her favourite person.

"Maisie, what are we going to do?" I hear Dan ask softly as if she could answer him. He's sitting on the sofa with Maisie lying on his knees. Her little fists hold onto his thumbs.

"I know you like it here. Daddy likes it here too. But think of all the things I can get you if we move back to London. Yeah, think about it," he coos. Something cold grips my heart. Maisie jiggles her little legs in joy clearly not understanding that he is talking about their future, our future.

"I can send you to the best school. And I can take you on holidays. And you... I don't know." He presses a soft kiss on her forehead, lifts her off his knees and nestles her against his chest.

"I don't know, Maisie, what I should do?" he finally says before humming a song I don't recognise. I push myself off the door frame I had been leaning against.

"Merry Christmas," I say softly. Dan locks eyes with me; his expression is serious.

"Merry Christmas," he replies, but doesn't sound very merry.

"How about some breakfast?" I walk to the stove and grab a frying pan. I think this calls for bacon. Everything looks better with a greasy bacon butty.

"Sure. Rose, did you hear what I said to Maisie?"

"Yes. However, I think the only advice she can give you is if it's milk time," I try to joke. Suddenly I feel his arms around me.

"Look at me," he demands. I turn and return his gaze. "I know we said we'll only talk about it after Christmas, but what are you thinking?" he sounds so unsure.

"Dan." I place a small kiss on the tip of his nose. "I love you. I'll come with you down south, I'll let you stay here, hell, I'll move to the moon with the two of you."

"But?" I take a deep breath. He knows me way to well already.

"But, let me ask you a question. When you think of your mum, what things do you wish she would have bought you that you missed out on?"

"None," he looks confused.

"Was there a particular trip she didn't take you on?"

"No. Rose, where are you going with this?"

"If you could turn back time, what would you like your mum to do differently?"

"Spend time with me. Be there for me. Sing happy birthday to me, read me a bedtime story. Give me a hug," he whispers. I can see his eyes tear up.

"Don't make the decision about moving to London about money. We'll be fine up here with the income from my Bed & Breakfast and whatever job you want to do. If you want to move to London because you miss the life there, because you miss your career, fine. I'll come. But don't do it just for the money."

He closes his eyes and a tear is dislodged. It slowly runs over his cheek and I wipe it away with my thumb.

"I don't want to move to London," he finally says. His voice has found strength again. "I love Fellside. I want to re-join FMR. I want to be surrounded by people I love. I met up with a few friends for dinner last night and I realised that they were never real friends. They were drinking buddies at best. I wouldn't want them around Maisie. But with Alex and the guys I know every single one of them will watch out for her. Frankly, I want to have this gossipy small-town life. I want Maisie to grow up in a community like this."

"Well, then..." I smile and my heart is almost jumping out of my chest in joy. "... fuck London."

Dan glances at Maisie in the playpen and then whispers, "Fuck London."

"Is she asleep?" I ask as Dan takes a seat next to me on the sofa.

"Yes. All the excitement over the wrapping paper has tired her out," he laughs. We had a small mountain of presents for her, but the only thing Maisie was interested in was the wrapping.

"Did you send a message to Kelly's parents?"

"Yes, I sent them a photo of Maisie in her little Christmas pyjamas." Dan pulls me in his arms. "I promised them that we would visit in the new year."

"That's a good idea."

"I want Maisie to have contact with them," he says seriously.

I nod. "That's definitely the right thing to do."

Dan leans over and kisses me. First on my lips and then moving along my neck down to my shoulder.

"Dan!" I mock warn.

"What?"

"It's three in the afternoon."

"So what? You want to watch the King's speech?" he chuckles before gently biting into my earlobe.

"No," I laugh, moaning loudly because he has decided to cup my pussy and slide his finger over the crotch area of my leggings.

"Well, in that case, how about some fuckin' under the Christmas tree," he paraphrases a famous song title.

"Dan!" I laugh and wiggle out of his arms. "I want to give you my present." I grab a box from under the tree. The minute I am within reach, he pulls me back into his lap.

"Can't I just unwrap you?"

"Nope. Here." I hold out the small rectangular box wrapped in Christmas paper.

"Fine," he sighs and gently pulls the ribbon off. He sucks his breath in sharply when the paper falls to the floor.

"I took this photo on Monday," I explain. In Dan's hand is a vintage picture frame with a photo of him and Maisie. He's fast asleep on the sofa topless and Maisie is cuddled against his chest. Dan's hand is protectively on her back. But the best thing about it is Maisie's expression; she isn't asleep. No. She has her blue eyes wide open, ear pressed against where his heart is beating, and there is a small, happy smile on her face.

"I love her so much," Dan whispers.

"I know you do." I place a soft kiss on his lips.

"Thank you! I love this gift." He gently places it on the coffee table before getting off the sofa. He walks to the tree and grabs the only present still left under it. The box is the length and width of an envelope but much thicker. I carefully untie the ribbon and then pull the lid off. Inside is a rectangular cookie with the words "Marry me?" written in icing. I gasp loudly.

"Dan. I love you and all, but are you insane? We've only been dating for three weeks."

"I know," he replies, "and it doesn't mean I want the wedding to be tomorrow. But we have known each other for almost our entire lives I want us to know that this is where this is leading and I have no doubt about that." He holds out the real ring. "Rose, please promise to be my wife in the not too distant future."

I can't hold back the tears any longer. This is all crazy, but I nod wildly before sobbing, "Yes, yes I will."

Epilogue

Dan

The little ghost wiggles in my arms as I step through the front door. Maisie's toothy little grin tells me that she had a blast first time trick or treating. We didn't go far, mainly to my FMR mates and a few other trusted neighbours, but the idea of people telling her how cute she is and then giving her chocolate does hold appeal to my one-year-old.

I place her on the floor and take my jacket off. It has almost been a year since Maisie came into my life and since I found my way back to Rose, and it has also been the best year of my life. I am still terrified every day that I am failing as a father, but then I look at my girl's face and see her big smile and I know we will be okay.

After I turned Naz down, I was at a loss as to what to do, but I didn't need to worry. In the mornings I help at the bed and breakfast. I'm a hit with the guests and it makes Rose's life a lot easier if she doesn't have to serve breakfast on her own. And, in the afternoons, I have one of only two paid positions at FMR. I am in charge of their finances and fundraising, and I am bloody good at it, if I may say so myself. I have plenty of time to spend with Maisie and Rose, and not for one second in the last year did I ever regret turning down Naz's offer.

"Boo," Maisie whispers. We taught her what to say as a ghost and she giggled like crazy when people pretended to be scared of her. My daughter has a tiny evil streak.

I grin and kneel down next to her so I can take her shoes off.

"Boo," I reply and she laughs. I take off the jacket she's wearing under the bedsheet that Rose had turned into a ghost costume. As I put the jacket on the hook I notice some plastic boxes in the corridor with a label saying "Christmas".

"Babe," I call out and lift Maisie back into my arms. She places her small palm on my cheek. It has become her signature move because she loves the feeling of my stubble.

"Babe," I call again, "I thought we had agreed, no Christmas deco until after Bonfire night." Rose has been itching to put some tinsel up for weeks.

"No, Mama," Maisie says with a frown on her face. She has started to tell me and Rose off when we do something she knows we shouldn't. It makes me giggle every time.

I step into the living room and freeze.

"What's this?" I ask. Strings are criss-crossing the room like dozens of washing lines. Photos are clipped to them. Photos of our little family. I see one of Maisie's second step; of course, we missed the chance to take a photo of the first one. Us hiking, us on holiday. So many memories.

"Hey, Maisie Mouse," Rose says from the kitchen before joining us.

"Rose, what is this?"

"A little surprise." Her cheeks are pink and her eyes are excited. She lifts Maisie from my arms and kisses her softly

"Mama, boo." Maisie giggles and Rose pretends to be scared.

"Why?" I point to all the photos. Rose just shrugs and moves further into the room ducking underneath the strings. I slowly follow her, trying to look at every photo.

"This is ama—" I swallow the sentence when I get to one I don't know yet. No, this is definitely a photo I have never seen before.

I take the little ultrasound scan from the washing line and hold it up to Rose.

Rose places Maisie on the floor in the little corner that has become her play area.

"I thought we should make sure everyone in the family is represented." Her voice is a whisper but every word echoes through me.

"You're—?"

"We're pregnant," she confirms with a small smile. A thousand different feelings fill me and the only way I can sum them up is by calling it complete happiness.

"We're pregnant," I whisper and place a kiss on her lips.

"Are you happy?" she asks carefully and I see her concern again.

"Indescribably happy. But you know what that means, right?"

"What's that?"

"You have to finally marry me," I gently stroke the engagement ring on her finger.

"How about at Christmas?" she grins and I love that she's no longer fighting me on it with her usual argument that it's too soon.

"Guess I was a very good boy this year, because Santa is making all my dreams come true," I reply before kissing her again.

"Wow, that was cheesy," she laughs.

Maybe it was, but it was also true. I definitely feel like the luckiest man on the planet.

Bonus Chapter

Dan

I take a deep breath.

"Dada," Maisie bends forward in my arms and draws my attention to her. She tugs on her little white dress. She hates it. I think I am raising a little tomboy.

"Just a little longer, Maisie Mouse," I whisper and grin sheepishly at the registrar standing next to me.

The music changes and everyone rises from their seats. When Rose turns the corner and walks down the aisle I gasp.

"Mama," Maisie shouts making everyone laugh, including Rose. She wiggles in my arms until I set her on the floor and then tumbles down the aisle towards Rose like a drunken person. Rose bends down and lifts Maisie into her arms before continuing her walk past our guests.

I wipe a small tear from my eye and I can see Alex, who is of course my best man and standing next to me, doing the same.

When Rose finally arrives at the end of the aisle, she gives me a shy smile. I know for sure that I won't remember what she wore today, but I also know for sure that I will always remember how beautiful she looked.

"Mama," Maisie whispers and pulls on her dress again.

"You look so beautiful, Maisie Mouse," Rose beams at her. That should keep my baby girl happy for a little while longer. She loves to hear that people think she is cute.

I gently lift Maisie from Rose's arms and pass her to Alex. I want her close by, but I also want to be able to give Rose my full attention.

"Are we ready," the nice registrar asks. I look out over the very small group of people we have invited. Just Rose's family, the guys from FMR and their families and, in the back, sit Kelly's parents. We usually visit them every three or four months. They saw what an amazing mother Rose has become to Maisie and they gave us their blessing wholeheartedly.

"Dan," Rose brings me back to the moment. I nod at the registrar, and she starts the proceedings.

"How drunk are you?" Rose calls out from the ensuite in our hotel room. We're spending our wedding night at Tommy's hotel where we also had our wedding. Maisie is with Alex and Emma tonight.

"Not at all. I only had lemonade," I shout back and unbutton my shirt.

"Why?" she asks as she steps out of the bathroom in a tiny little silk pyjama thingy. Her hair is down, and she is make-up free.

"Because you can't drink, I won't," I whisper and gently rub her tummy where our baby is growing. Rose places a kiss on one of my pecs and pushes the open shirt off my shoulders.

"You could have," she whispers

"I know. But I want to enjoy this night. The first night with my wife," I mumble and pull her closer for a deep kiss.

"I like that."

"What? When I call you 'my wife'?"

She smiles at me and nods.

"Yes, my husband. Some feminist is probably spinning in her grave somewhere, but I love the sound of it anyway."

"I don't care about other people. We know what we have and only we understand our love for each other." I lick my way along her neck before gripping the back of her thighs and lifting her in the air. I gently toss her onto the mattress and Rose laughs out loud. I just stand there a look at her. She is so beautiful. Her joy makes her appear radiant.

"Like what you see?" she sasses.

"I do," I nod and subconsciously rub my hard cock. Slowly, Rose parts her legs. She isn't wearing any underwear and I can see her glistening pussy. She parts her legs further and lets her fingers slide over her tits, still covered by silk, down to the apex of her legs. She gently plays with herself, her eyes locked on me. Then she drags her finger back up and in the process takes the silk top with her, exposing her stiff nipples.

I can't take it anymore. I swiftly move to her, unbuttoning my trousers. I cover her body with mine and kiss her deeply before dragging her to the edge of the bed.

"This is going to be fast and hard, baby. I'll give you slow later," I growl.

"Works for me," she moans before reaching for the zip of my trousers and pulling it down. I free my hard cock, not even bothering to take my trousers off properly. I align myself and enter her in one smooth trust. Rose cries out. Her hands push on my trousers and eventually we get them over my arse and they slide to the floor.

I bend forward, kiss her hard and whisper, "Hold on." She locks her hands behind my neck and that's my sign. I pull out and push in again. And again. She feels so good and warm and tight.

"Don't stop, Dan. Please!" Rose cries out and I can feel her tightening. I start to move a little faster, but I also reach between us and circle my thumb around her clit. She is panting and so am I. I pump into her hard. One time, two times. My body tenses up and I know I am only seconds away from exploding when her orgasm finds her. I let go and my release washes over me.

I collapse on top of her and try to slow my breathing.

"Do you know what the best thing of sex with you is?" I mumble against her neck.

"The orgasm," she chuckles and gently plays with the hair. I lift my head and look at her.

"No. The orgasm is great. But the best thing is that I am the closest I can get to you."

"I love you more with every day, Dan."

"I love you so much, Rose."

The End

Next in the Series is Ryan & Jane's story

Ride with Me

Dani Elias

Chapter 1

Ryan

I am soaked to my skin. Even the best mountaineering jacket can't keep you dry in torrential rain. Since Christmas we have had nothing but shit weather, so why anyone would venture into the hills in the first place is anyone's guess. Yet, here we are, on another rescue mission.

I wipe the water off my face, which is a mix of sweat and rain.

"Let's swap," Alex shouts and we gently put the basket stretcher onto the ground. This morning we got the call that a man in his fifties had slipped on Helvellyn and broken his leg. Luckily, it didn't take us long to find him as the accident happened on the main path up to the summit.

Once the guys had provided first aid we packed him up in an emergency bag and strapped him to the stretcher to carry him down into the valley. With Tommy, the team leader, still away on holiday in New Zealand, Alex called on Dan, his best friend and soon to be brother-in-law—if rumours are true—to make up the eighth member of our unit.

Alex is the unofficial second in command and the guy who got me onto the team. Aside from us and Tommy, there's also Nick, Phil, Rob, Chris and his wife Suzie. I've only known them for a few months but they've already become a kind of surrogate family to me.

"Fucking rain," Rob mumbles next to me. The wind's going bonkers, hitting you from every angle at once, and the rain's pounding down non-stop. It really is shit weather.

With the stretcher safely on the ground I wiggle my fingers because they are stiff from the cold. I'm wearing gloves but they are also soaked through and are no longer providing any warmth.

A second FMR unit takes over the stretcher for a while, allowing our team to rest and regain our strength.

"Ryan," Phil calls out before joining me. "Please can you do me a favour and sort this shit out between you and Jane?"

At the mention of her name, I stiffen. Jane is Phil's older sister and the bane of my existence. Ever since I opened my tattoo studio in the village, she has been trying to get me to close it again. All because she thinks the posh twats that come to her shop—she sells horse riding shit—could be upset by my display of tattoo art and piercings. Why they would be offended is beyond me. It's not like I display pictures of dicks with Jacob's ladders in my window. It's all PG.

But that doesn't matter for the prim princess. She tries to make my life hell whenever and however she can.

"Listen, all I do is run my studio. I can't help if she has nothing better to do than stick her nose in my business." I almost said pretty nose, but I caught myself. Oh, yes, aside from being an annoying little spitfire she is also fit, like gets-my-dick-hard fit. I would be lying if I said I hadn't imagined her sucking my cock in the shower more than once. But I can't really say that to her brother now, can I?

"What do you want me to do?" I ask.

Phil shrugs.

"I don't fucking know. I'm not even sure what her problem is, but I can tell you that the only thing she talked about at the family dinner on Boxing Day was you and how your business will destroy hers and how your bike is always parked in front of her shop—"

"That's where the parking spot is. I can't fucking move it," I growl, drawing the attention of the rest of the group.

"Jane got your back up again?" Nick chuckles. The guys have heard me and Phil bicker more than once about his sister.

"Yup, apparently she mouthed me off over her Christmas pudding," I smirk although I don't feel like I want to make light of this. I've invested all my savings into the shop and I really don't need her to ruin it for me. "Phil's trying to play mediator again."

"You and Jane don't need a mediator, you need a UN peacekeeping mission to stop you from fighting," Rob chuckles and slaps me on the back.

"Do you fancy Jane?" Suzie asks. We all stop and stare at her. She did not just ask me that.

"What the fuck?" Phil is the first to speak.

"What? I mean, they argue about insignificant little things and sometimes it feels like they're trying to find ways to provoke each other. There's a thin line between love and hate. That's all I'm saying." Suzie shrugs with a grin. That may be all she's saying, but I can see in her eyes that she has a theory.

"No. No!" I try to calm my voice. "The only interest I have in her is that she leaves me bloody well alone."

"And she's my sister," Phil protests like this is a valid argument.

"Hey, I'm in love with his sister and you don't see him complaining," Dan chuckles and points at Alex.

"Trust me, I have zero, nil, zilch, no interest at all in Jane," I try to shut down the conversation.

"Mate, you're denying it a little too hard," Nick smirks causing Phil to give me another side eye before we all move on down into the valley.

Fuck! Yes, she's hot as hell. But no, I definitely don't want her. No!

The coffee tastes rank as I swallow the last mouthful from my cup. I hate cold coffee but I'm shattered from this morning's rescue mission and I have three more clients booked in for a tattoo.

"Ry, her royal highness is out front with a parking attendant pointing at your bike," Leanne says as she guides a customer to her corner of the studio.

Leanne is the piercing stylist I employ two days a week. The rest of the week she works in a studio over in Penrith, because we don't have enough requests for piercings to employ someone full time. Neil, my other employee, works all week as a tattoo artist like me, but also does my accounts because he's a bloody genius with numbers.

"Why can she not leave me alone?" I groan as I place my coffee cup on the work bench. Leanne just laughs in reply. She and Neil have seen me fight with Jane enough times to know that hell will freeze over before the little princess will keep her nose out of my business.

As I walk towards the entrance of the studio, I can see Jane pointing animatedly at my bike and the parking attendant just shaking his head. Jane is wearing, as always, boring black trousers and a brown Polo shirt with her shop's logo right above her left nipple—okay, I may or may not have stared at that a little too much in the past. Her ginger hair is pinned up in a tight bun like flight attendants have. Come to think of it, I have never seen her with her hair down. The ugly polo shirt stretches tight on her curvy hips and that draws my eyes, as always, down to her round arse. *Get a grip!*

I pull the door open with force and the cold air hits me squarely in the face.

"What's the fucking problem now?" I try to sound calm but it comes out harshly and cold. I can feel my blood boiling already; that's the effect she has on me.

"This lady is complaining about this bike being parked here." The parking attendant glances at Jane. He looks like a kid but then anyone in their early twenties looks like a kid to me ever since I hit my forties.

"Have you told the lady...," I over-pronounce the word 'lady', "...that this parking spot is for bikes which means I can legally park here?" I cross my arms over my chest and stare at Jane.

"I did," he mumbles.

"Well, then, what's the problem?"

"The problem is that half of your bike is in my loading bay." Jane's voice sounds shaky as she points at the floor.

"Half my bike?" I shout. "That's five centimetres at most."

"But it's in my loading bay nevertheless," she screams back. Some people walking past give us curious looks.

"Fuck's sake, Princess," I growl, lift my bike and move it back a bit so it is now firmly within the parking spot.

"Stop calling me that," Jane hisses.

"Well, then get off your high horse and act like a normal person."

"I see all is sorted now—" The parking warden waves at us and scuttles away as fast as he can.

But Jane is not done. I can see it in her eyes. She is just looking for another reason to get to me.

"I'll complain about this parking spot. It's not good for the village image to have all these," she points vaguely at my Ducati, "around here."

"Seriously, how you and Phil are related is beyond me. He's a down-to-earth bloke and you are a snobbish princess with her knickers in a twist." Okay, I should not have said knickers because now I'm wondering what she is wearing underneath these fucking black trousers.

Jane gasps for air. "I... I—"

"You what?" I ask and step closer. This close I can see that the green of her eyes has a little blue in it.

"Are you threatening me?" She frowns but doesn't look scared.

"Fuck, Princess," I rub the back of my neck, "do you really think so little of me that you can imagine me threatening a woman?" My anger seems to evaporate at the thought that this is her opinion of me.

Jane looks at the floor before raising her gaze again and locking eyes with me. There is a faint blush on her cheeks underneath the cute little band of freckles.

"No. I don't think that," she finally says. She doesn't move for a few more seconds before turning on her heels and returning to her shop. *She is going to be the death of me.*

Chapter 2

Jane

He's here. Ryan's voice makes my stomach somersault. Of course he's here, what was I expecting? He is part of FMR now.

Chris and Suzie invited all of us to spend New Year's Eve with them on the farm. Chris's mum, who has a cottage nearby, has offered to watch the kids so that everyone can have a carefree evening. It sounded fun, but now that Ryan is here I'm no longer sure I should have come.

"Can you hold Lilly for a minute, please?" Christina, my sister-in-law, pulls me from my thoughts. She, my brother and I arrived half an hour ago and have been helping Suzie to get some of the food ready. We all brought something so it's going to be like a pot-luck supper.

"Sure," I hold out my hands and grab hold of Lilly. Lilly is Phil and Christina's one year old and I'm officially her favourite aunt. Okay, I might be her only aunt, but I'll take it anyway.

"Atty," Lilly cheers when I cuddle her to me. She can't say aunty properly yet, so until she does, I'm Atty.

"Hey, sweetheart, I missed you," I coo and she gives me a big grin.

"What can I do?" Ryan asks from behind me.

"Hey, Ry," Suzie greets him with a kiss on his cheek. He glances at me as he places a plastic pot on the kitchen counter.

"Hey, Suzie," he smiles at her and my stomach flips again. I hardly ever catch a glimpse of his smile, but given that all we seem to do is bicker, it's no wonder he doesn't save one of those smiles for me.

"Jane," he nods tensely.

"Hi." My reply is short and cold and I hate myself for it. Frankly, I hate myself for a lot of the interactions I've had with him over the last few months. When he appeared in Fellside with his tattoos and his chilled swagger, he became the talk of the village in no time. I didn't really mind.

That's until he opened his tattoo studio next to my tack shop.

Within days the complaints and comments from my clients started. We have a fair few snobs who own a holiday home in Fellside. The husbands usually have companies in London or Manchester and their stay-at-home wives spend their weeks riding up here. Although, the gossip is that they ride more than just horses.

But whatever I think of them, they're my customers. I need them and I can't lose them to one of the shops in Windermere or Keswick. I'm struggling to stay open as it is. I had to let my store assistant go recently and now I'm the only one in the shop. It's been a tough year, and Ryan's appearance hasn't made it any easier.

Sometimes I wonder if I'm projecting all my worries onto him. And maybe that's true. But then he does something that gets under my skin and the gloves come off. I just can't help it.

"Princess, I'm talking to you," Ryan pulls me from my thoughts.

"Don't call me that," I hiss back. God, I hate it when he calls me that.

"If the shoe fits," he mumbles. "I've asked if you can pass me the bowl." He nods towards a glass dish on the kitchen counter next to me. I grab it with the hand I'm not using to cradle Lilly and bang it in front of him. He just smirks.

"FYI, I've sent a letter to the council about the parking spot." That wipes the smirk off his face.

"What the fu—" he catches himself before adding in a more PG way, "is wrong with you. What harm does it do you?"

"It ruins the square which is a big tourist attraction."

"One motorbike?"

"Well..." I can't think of anything to say. Frankly, the whole thing started with Mrs Morton, one of my regulars, moaning at me again about the tattoo studio and it got me so riled up that I went way overboard. I don't seem to be able to help myself around him. Have you ever gotten yourself into a situation where you completely overreact and afterwards wonder why you did it? That's me every time I am near Ryan.

"One is just the start," I reply stubbornly. Yes, backing down is also not in my DNA.

"What? You think I'll have a motorbike gang joining me?" He crosses his arms in front of his chest.

"Well, maybe."

"I'm not in a motorbike gang. You are acting ridiculous," he says loudly, anger clearly showing on his face.

Before I can reply, Lilly looks at him with a frown. "No!" she says sternly.

"See, she agrees with me." *Oh fudge, I didn't just say that.*

"A child," he snorts and I know he's right. "Everyone else agrees with me."

Now that stings. I look around the room and Suzie, Olivia and Chris who have also been working on setting up the food all stare at me. I can see it in their faces. They agree with him. My throat constricts and tears burn in my eyes. The worst bit is, I know they're right.

"Excuse me," I whisper, hand Lilly over to Phil and then storm out of the kitchen.

As I leave the cottage, the house door slams shut behind me. "Argh," my scream echoes through the valley. I should really leave but I came with Phil and Christina as I don't drive, and the farm is too far out of Fellside to walk back. I also should have grabbed a jacket because it's freezing.

"Are you okay?" a voice makes me jump.

"Yes, I'm fine," I reply to Olivia. She is leaning against the entrance with her arms crossed. I can see her breath in the cold air despite there being no other light than that of the moon.

"What is this between you and him?"

I shrug. I'm not sure how to explain it to her.

"He's really nice. Why is his shop bothering you so much?"

I shrug again, causing Olivia to exhale loudly in frustration.

"Jane, I'm trying to be a friend here. I really am trying to help you but I don't get it. I mean who still cares about a tattoo studio. To be honest, I hear lots of people talk positively about it."

I pull my arms tighter around me against the cold, but also to give me some comfort.

"You know who my customers are."

"Stuffy people," she snorts.

"Conservative people."

"So, stuffy people. It's not like any of them will walk into the wrong shop." There is amusement in her voice and I know she right. But she is also wrong.

"Olivia, my shop is struggling. I can't afford to lose my regulars, and more than one has threatened to go to the new shop in Keswick."

"Jane, I'm sorry, but I still don't think Ryan's at fault. If anything, it's these snobs."

"Maybe," I blow out and a little cloud forms in front of my mouth.

"How bad is it?" she asks and slides an arm around my shoulder.

"I'm okay for another three months, but if I lose the Women's Institute group that's it. And Ruth has threatened to take her business somewhere else if I don't help the WI to get him out."

"She's a bitch. Have you spoken to your parents?"

"No! They already helped me so much to get the shop set up. If I can't make it on my own, I'd rather give up."

"Fine. Tell you what, come back in. Let's celebrate the end of this year and the start of a new one. And next year," she giggles when she says that, "we get together with the other girls and see if we can come up with some ideas. A few of them run their own businesses after all."

She's right. I need this year to be over. Surely, the new year can only get better.

I stare at the table in front of me. *Not me, not me!* We are only thirty minutes from midnight and in the middle of a game of truth and dare. So far, I have successfully blended into the background and been passed over.

Everyone is having a good time, some are more drunk than others, but aside from Suzie, who is breastfeeding, and me, most had more than their fair share of alcohol. They all drunk-called Tommy earlier, who is in New

Zealand with Ella, and those two shared their news that they got engaged. After the call, they all decided to play truth or dare. Most chose wisely truth, and I haven't laughed so much in a long time with all their confessions. Rob was the only brave soul who picked dare and Nick made him run to the end of the drive way and back in just his boxer shorts. The guys were like little children goading him.

"Jane," Ryan's voice cuts through the room and everyone goes quiet. *Why is he picking me?*

"Truth or dare," he asks and his dark eyes bore into me.

I sound shaky when I reply, "Dare." He raises an eyebrow in surprise. For me truth is a lot riskier than dare. If he asks me to tell him the truth of why I am so dead set on getting him out, I'll just ruin the evening. Rather have a dare. What's the worst thing he could ask me to do?

"Dare?"

"Yes. Dare."

"Okay, Princess, give us your best dirty talk."

"What?" My heart starts hammering like wild.

"Oh, that's going to be good. No boinking!" Olivia laughs. Everyone knows that I don't cuss and don't use the f word.

"You heard me," Ryan says completely ignoring everyone around us. He hasn't been drinking either so he is perfectly aware of what he's asking me. "Talk dirty to me." I notice that he doesn't say 'us.'

"I don't know how—" I am mesmerised by his eyes.

"Bullshit. Come on. It's not difficult. Say 'I want to fuck you hard.'" A small smirk flashes over his lips but his eyes are intense and focused.

"I want you to fu... fuck me hard," I whisper. Ryan licks his lips and I can feel the heat creeping into my cheeks.

"Louder," he growls and causes a shiver to run through me.

"I want you to fuck me," I reply with a firm voice. "I want you to take me and fuck me until I can't scream anymore." Blood is rushing in my ears as my eyes are glued to his. If this is possible, his dark eyes have taken on an even darker shade.

"Oh, come one, I don't need to hear this shit," Phil protests next to me. *Oh, deary me.* I feel my face turning beetroot red and I avert my eyes from Ryan. I can't believe I just did that. Everyone is laughing and clapping—well, aside from Phil who looks pained that he had to hear his older sister dirty talk. I want to sink into a hole, but all I can do is grab my glass and walk to the kitchen to refill it with water.

Ryan's eyes follow me and a shiver races down my back again. My breathing is still erratic, and I can't get the way he looked at me out of my head. *I'm in so much trouble!*

"Alright, everyone, it's almost midnight. Let's grab some Prosecco and we can watch the fireworks," Chris announces and everyone scrambles from the table. Chris and Suzie's farm is on a small hill overlooking the valley towards Fellside so the views will be good, especially on a clear night like today.

In a flurry of activity, we all grab a drink, put our jackets on and head outside. Naturally, the couples are all pairing up which leaves me and Ryan. I tug my woolly hat lower and slide further to the left to hide in the shadows. I love New Year's, but celebrating it with a whole bunch of couples does make you feel lonely.

"Ten...nine...," Charlotte starts to count down loudly and everyone joins in. On the dot of midnight, the firework starts.

"Happy New Year," Ryan's deep voice surprises me. He is just an arm's length away from me.

"Happy New Year, Ryan," I reply. Out of nowhere, his large hand gently slides into my hair, drawing me closer to him. His lips crash onto mine. Like it is the most natural thing in the world, my hands slide around his neck and he takes this as an invite to deepen the kiss. His tongue pushes into my mouth and the minute it slides alongside mine, fire spreads through my body and gathers in my core. A little moan escapes me when he nibbles on my bottom lip.

But then, as quick as it happened, he takes a step back and walks away leaving me a panting mess. *Well, happy New Year to me.*

Chapter 3

Ryan

The air mattress groans under me as I shift to my left side. I have been tossing and turning for an hour now and I am nowhere near close to falling asleep.

After midnight we called it a night fairly quickly and everyone went to their allocated rooms. But our group is large and there is only so much space in the cottage. Dan and Rose ended up sleeping in the barn whilst everyone else took either a kids' rooms or one of the guest bedrooms. I have been put in the kitchen on an air mattress and Jane is sleeping on the sofa in the living room. There is no door between the two rooms and I can hear every move she makes.

I shouldn't have kissed her earlier, but after her dare I couldn't think of anything else. I needed to know what it felt like to kiss her. When she melted into my arms and returned my kiss, I just didn't want to let her go; but eventually I came to my senses and pulled myself away. We have been fighting like cats and dogs for months. One kiss doesn't make up for that.

I turn again and the mattress hisses.

"Can you give it a rest!" Jane's voice makes me jump. *Fuck this!* In the dim light of the torch on my phone I crawl off the air bed and stalk to the arch separating the living room and kitchen. I flip the switch to turn on the kitchen light. Jane shoots up on the sofa and holds the blanket to her chest.

"What are you doing?" she whisper-shouts, but even in the semi-darkness, I can see that her eyes are travelling up and down my body. I am only wearing my black boxer briefs, but I don't care. I have dated my share of women, especially during my time as a professional motorbike racer. I don't get embarrassed easily.

"Like what you see?" I smirk and she avoids her eyes. "I'm going home." I turn my back to her as I pull on my jeans before grabbing my T-shirt from the kitchen stool.

"You can't." Jane's voice is much closer now. I almost swallow my tongue when I spot her in the archway. She's wearing grey pyjama shorts and a silky top that clings to her tear-shaped tits. She is clearly not wearing a bra and it takes every ounce of strength I have to not walk over to her and cup and suck them.

"Yes, I can," I reply and focus on putting on my socks and shoes.

"You've been drinking."

"No, I haven't. But I'm glad to hear that you are worried about me." I smirk at her but she ignores my dig.

"The others will wonder."

"I'll text Chris. This bed is too uncomfortable, I can't sleep on that." True, I wasn't able to sleep, but the bed had fuck all to do with it. It was all Jane.

"Can you take me with you?" she whispers. I drop my left shoe to the floor and look at her.

"You want to come with me?"

"Yes."

"On my bike?"

She pauses for a moment before replying, "Yes."

"Why?"

"I can't sleep on the sofa either. Being in my own bed allows me to get a proper night's rest before the event tomorrow. I have a stand at the New Year's jump in Ullswater."

"Have you ever ridden a bike before?" I ask as I put my second shoe on.

"Only horses," she giggles.

"Only horses, hm... How about a man?" *Oh, what the fuck did I say that for?* The minute the words leave my lips I can see her stiffening and a fire filling her eyes.

"How dare you," she yells.

"Shhh, you'll wake the others," I whisper. I wish I could take the words back. Why did I have to ruin the first moment where we talked like normal people?

"You are, you are..."

"I'm what? A pig? We both know you already thought I was scum." Although these are my own words, the idea of her thinking that about me does hit me hard.

"I do not," she protests and I laugh bitterly.

"Sure. Whatever. If you want a lift, get dressed; I'll wait outside." I grab my jacket and walk pass her without another look.

The cold air hits me in the face as I leave the cottage with my helmet under my arm. I suck in the winter air and it makes me feel awake. My bike is parked in Chris's garage next to his American pickup truck. I'm about to push my bike out onto the driveway when I notice a row of helmets along the back wall. I know Chris has a couple of quadbikes he and his team use when checking up on his sheep; I assume the helmets are for that. I grab a black one and hang it from the handlebar of my Ducati before leaving the garage.

"I thought you'd left," Jane whispers as I step out.

"I said I'd wait." What can I do for her to finally stop thinking the worst of me?

"I know. Sorry," she replies.

I study her for a moment. She's wearing a thick winter coat and leather gloves which should protect her from the cold air.

"Take that off," I point at the beanie she is wearing.

"Why?" Her eyes narrow suspiciously and I lift the helmet to show her. Cautiously she pulls the woolly hat off and stuffs it into her jacket pocket.

When I gently push her ginger locks from her face, a shudder races through her. I slide the helmet over her head and adjust it until it sits right.

"What about you?" she asks in a quiet voice, her eyes locked with mine.

"I have my own. This one belongs to Chris. I'll bring it back to him tomorrow." My fingers graze over her neck before I finally take a step back.

I straddle my motorbike needing some distance between us, even if it is just for a moment. I glance back at Jane and I can see a little fear but also some excitement in her eyes.

"Don't worry, I'll drive slowly." Leaning closer to her, I flash a reassuring smile and ask, "Are you ready?"

She nods nervously. I check her helmet one last time before pushing her visor down. Then, I gesture towards the bike.

"Alright, step over the seat and take a seat behind me. Keep your feet on the foot pegs, and put your arms around my waist."

"What?" The sound of her voice is muffled by the helmet.

"You'll be glad to have something to hold onto, believe me." She hesitates for a moment longer before following my instructions. I guide her until she settles behind me with her hands tentatively grabbing onto my jacket. I can't help but grin as I put on my own helmet.

With a gentle twist of the throttle I set the bike in motion, and slowly roll down the driveway towards the main road. The minute I speed up a little, Jane slides her arms around my waist and holds on tight. As we drive through the winter landscape, I lean carefully into each turn, with Jane instinctively following my lead. The road is empty this late at night and I speed up a little. In the distance I can already see the glow of the first streetlights of Fellside.

"Where do you live?" I call out over the noise of the wind.

Jane gives me her address. I just nod and guide the bike through the streets.

When we reach the block of flats, I cut the engine. Jane is clinging to me and doesn't move.

I take my helmet off before calling out to her, "We're here, Princess." The nickname she hates so much brings her back to reality.

"Don't call me that," she hisses as she sits up and clumsily moves off the bike. I hold out my hand to help her. When she is steady on her feet, I dismount as well. Jane fiddles with her helmet and eventually pushes it off. Her hair is sticking up wildly and I'm tempted to smooth it down.

"Thank you." She pushes the helmet against my chest, and stalks off towards the entrance to the building.

"You're welcome," I call after her. I'm about to get back on my bike when she gives me one last look. Our eyes meet and I almost forget to breathe. But just as quickly as the moment started, it's over again and she disappears into the building. Somehow my life has just gotten infinitely more complicated.

As I kill the motor the door to Chris's cottage opens. I've been meaning to return the helmet for two days but things kept coming up.

"Mate, I didn't expect you here." Chris strolls towards me.

"I had to return this," I hold up the helmet.

"You could have just given it to me at the FMR meeting next week," he chuckles.

"I know, but—" I hesitate. Why did I bother coming all the way out here? Chris lives the farthest from Fellside among my FMR buddies. It's only a twenty-minute drive, but still, it's outside the village.

"Want a beer?" he asks as if he knows I need someone to talk to.

"Sure." I dismount my Ducati before putting it on its kickstand.

"So, what really brings you here?" Chris asks as we enter the cottage.

"I kissed Jane."

"Okay," is all he replies, leading me into their kitchen. I's quiet in the house.

"Where are the kids?" I ask. Chris flips off the lid of one of the bottles of beer and holds it out to me.

"They're with Suzie and my mum at the library. Rob organised some kids' reading thingy." He takes a sip from his bottle and nods towards the kitchen table. "So? You and Jane, huh?" he asks as we take a seat.

I shake my head. *No, nope, there is no me and Jane. I think.*

"I shouldn't have kissed her. Why the fuck did I do that?"

"You're asking me?" he smirks. "You fancy her? Damn, I owe Suzie a trip to Manchester." I raise an eyebrow in question. "She bet me that you and Jane have the hots for each other because of your constant fighting. And I told her she's wrong. Now I have to take her to see a musical in Manchester. I hate that shit." He has a pained look on his face.

"Mate, I don't... how can I? She hates me."

"Did she snog you back?"

"So what?" In an instant, memories flood in—how her hair felt so soft, the taste of her, and the way she melted into my arms.

"Ry, what do you want me to say? Clearly you came here for a reason."

"I don't know." I slide the fingers of my hand through my hair. "How can I get her to stop fighting me?"

"Have you tried talking to her?" His eyes meet mine while he absentmindedly twists the beer bottle between his fingers.

"Whenever we talk, we argue."

"Or snog," he chuckles. "In all seriousness, Ry, just sit her down for a coffee or something and clear the air. You never have actual conversations. You just stumble from one moment to the next biting each other's heads off."

I sigh, as the front door opens and a little, blonde whirlwind storms into the kitchen.

"Uncle Ry!" Max calls out.

"Mate, shoes." Chris points at his son's feet. Max is his stepson, but don't let Chris hear you call him that. For him, Max is as much his child as baby Emma, the baby girl he and Suzie recently had together.

"Sorry Dad," Max winces. He toes his shoes off and puts them next to a set of wellies at the back door before sprinting back to us.

"Can you make me a tattoo? Pleeeaaasse!" He rolls up his sleeve and holds out his little pale arm.

"Sure, if you get your mum to give us her magic pen," I smile. Max loves my tattoos and a while back he was begging me to give him one. Who can resist the little squirt, so I drew him a pattern with one of Suzie's eyeliner, and now he wants one every time he sees me.

"Yes!" He pumps his little fist and storms off again. Chris just shakes his head.

"Seriously, mate, sit her down and talk for once."

"Who are you talking to? Hey, Ry." Suzie strolls into the kitchen, baby Emma in her arm and Max pulling on her handbag, probably trying to get her "magic pen". She hands Emma over to Chris and places a kiss on his lips.

"Max!" she says sternly and he lets go of her bag.

"Someone's stinky," Chris chuckles and lifts Emma's bottom to his nose. "Yup, someone needs a change." He takes Emma with him out of the kitchen.

"Uncle Ryan, I want a motorbike!" Max calls out after Suzie passes him the eyeliner.

"I don't know how you two do it," I laugh whilst the chaos continues around me. Chris returns and places baby Emma into the cot in the corner of the kitchen and shrugs.

"I wouldn't want it any other way." He slides his arm around Suzie's waist. I try to focus on drawing a bike on Max's arm just above his wrist. But I can't deny that I look at them and picture Jane in my arms. Just minus the children.

Don't get me wrong. I love being uncle to all the kids of my FMR buddies, but I don't think that's on the cards for me. It's not a responsibility I want. My mind drifts to Jane again. What if she wants children? Maybe we are just not meant to be. Or maybe I have lost my damn mind. Why am I even thinking about Jane and babies?

Chapter 4

Jane

The first thing I notice when I walk into the conservatory at the nursing home is how tired Grampy looks.

"Grampy are you okay?" I place the box of biscuits I brought for him on the table.

"Poppet, I'm almost ninety, of course I'm tired," he chuckles. "Now come and give me a kiss." He points at his cheek. When my lips touch the leathery skin on his cheek his trademark scent of Old Spice is unmissable.

"Is Phil not here?" I expected my brother to be around. He usually brings Lilly on a Friday afternoon.

"They were here earlier. Christina's singing tonight so they wanted to have an early dinner," he says and leans back in his chair. His thin legs are covered with a blanket.

"Now tell me about you and your man."

"Grampy, I don't have a man." I explain and open the box of biscuits.

"What about the lad you kept talking about on Boxing Day." I freeze.

"Ryan?"

"Yes." He replies with a smile, but waves away the biscuits.

"He's not my man. Haven't you been listening? He and I argue. He is a..." For some reason I can't call him an arsehole. Mainly because he isn't an arsehole.

"Now, now, Poppet, what did he do to you?"

"He... he—" He did nothing really. "Oh, Grampy!" I put my face in my hands and tell him all. How I turn into a hateful bitch every time he is around and just can't help it. How my customers want him gone and how I got sucked into Ruth's intrigue somehow. The only thing I don't tell him is how my business is currently suffering. I can live with him thinking that I'm crazy because of how I treat Ryan, but I can't live with him worrying about me, and he will if he knows my life's work is at risk.

"Oh, Poppet. You need to stop caring what other people think. If they don't want to come to your shop anymore just because of a tattoo studio being next door, they weren't very interested in the first place. Sounds like poppycock to me as an excuse." He pats my hand.

He's right though. It really does sound just like a stupid excuse.

"If it weren't for the shop, what would you think of him?"

That he is hot, hot, hot.

"I think we could be friends," I sigh.

"Just friends?" I feel my cheek blush.

"Grampy! It's okay to be a single woman, you know." I try to sound strong.

"Of course it is, Poppet. But you have so much love to give and I can see how you long to share your life. Don't get me wrong, the twerps you were dating in the past were no good." Well he's not wrong there. "But that's because you picked guys that you thought people would like you to pick. Jane, choose someone that challenges you, someone that gets you out of your comfort zone. You know what I loved on your grandmother the most?"

I shake my head.

"She surprised me almost every day. She wasn't the 'safe' woman my mother wanted me to marry. One that does the cooking, cleaning and raises the kids. No, she was one of the first female members of FMR. If the weather was nice, she would pick up your dad and your aunt Janet from school early and we would have lunch somewhere in the hills. The teachers kept complaining but she wanted to give them some freedom to enjoy life." There's a small smile on his face and it's obvious that he is still in love with her. My grandmother died five years ago, but his expression tells me that he doesn't love her any less than when she was still alive.

"Oh, Grampy," I sigh again.

"Poppet, I know your mother wants you to be this perfect person. Don't! Nobody is perfect. Be yourself, find yourself, and allow yourself to fall for the right man, not just a good man." I fiddle with the packet of biscuits but I don't know how to reply.

I wish it were that easy.

"Maybe start by apologising to Ryan." He grabs the box of biscuits and holds it out to me.

"They're yours. Besides, I don't think Ryan is a biscuit guy." I laugh.

"A man takes anything a beautiful woman offers him," he grins.

"Grampy, you old romantic," I giggle and place a kiss on his forehead. "Are you sure?" I ask. We normally play a few rounds of cards but for some reason I really want to get out of here and talk to Ryan.

"Absolutely. Go." He pats my hand again. I pull on my jacket and give him one last hug. My heart starts hammering faster. *Son of a biscuit, what am I going to say to him?*

I carefully balance a cardboard tray in my left hand and a bag with two sausage rolls in my other hand. I try to press my face against Ryan's studio window to see if he is in. The door is locked but I think I can see light in the back.

"What are you doing, Princess?" His voice makes me jump and I would have dropped the coffees if he hadn't placed his hands over mine and steadied me.

"Hi," I breathe.

"Hey." For a change there is no frown on his face when he looks at me.

"I brought you coffee and a sausage roll." I hold out my peace offering.

"Laced with poison?" he asks but before I can reply he adds, "Fuck! Sorry, Princess. Why do I deserve baked goods?" He gives me a small smile.

"Peace offering. I think maybe we should have a chat without shouting at each other. And I think coffee and sausage rolls put everyone in a good mood so we're less likely to have an argument." He stares at me for a few seconds before turning to the side. A small smile appears on his face as he rubs the back of his neck.

"Are these both the same coffees?" he asks.

"Yes" I reply confused. He takes them from my hand.

"Wait here." He points at me before unlocking the shop and disappearing into the back. Great. Here I am with my two sausage rolls. I guess if he doesn't come back at least I've got some greasy grub to cheer myself up

"Right, let's go." Ry steps back out of the shop. In one of his hands is a backpack, half open, with a flask in it. In his other are two helmets. "Put the food in here and then put it on, please."

"Why?"

"I'll take you for a ride. Let's have the coffee at my favourite place," he suggests and holds out the backpack to me. I shouldn't, but I want to. I slide the paper bag into the rucksack, zip it up and then put it on my shoulders. Ryan takes a step closer. He reaches out and gently strokes a strand of hair behind my ear. His eyes are trained on me and I suddenly find it difficult to breathe.

Eventually he breaks eye contact and helps me put my helmet on. Just like the first time, I slide behind him and my hands hold on to his sides.

The wind tousles the strands of hair that are sticking out from under my helmet as we speed along the A591 towards Keswick. He hasn't told me where his favourite place is, but at this moment in time, I don't care. Wherever he takes me will be great. I'm snug against him, feeling the vibrations of the bike as it eats up the miles. I slide my hands from his hips to his stomach which brings me closer to him. I can feel his tense muscles even through the jacket and I can't help but smile, thinking about how I could easily slide my fingers under his jacket and feel his skin. Something I have wanted to do ever since I saw him in nothing but his boxer shorts on New Year's.

Sheep graze lazily, casting indifferent glances our way. With each turn, I lean into the bends, the exhilaration building as we approach the top of the pass from where we get our first glimpse of Keswick. Rather than following the main road Ryan turns sharply right down a country lane. I know exactly where we are. I can already see the first glimpses of Castlerigg Stone Circle on the horizon. I love this place and I can't believe he's bringing me here. Maybe we have more in common than I thought.

Chapter 5

Ryan

I slow my bike when we get to the end of the lane and turn the corner, parking the Ducati next to the wooden gate marking the entrance to the field. I fell in love with this place the first time I came here. Imagine a small Stonehenge on top of a hill, smack bang in the middle of a valley surrounded by even higher mountains. The views are incredible.

The old monument sits in a farmer's sheep pasture. While it can get pretty crowded with tourists during the summer, right now in winter, especially near dusk, it looks like there's no one else around.

I help Jane balance as she climbs off the bike, before swinging my leg over the saddle myself.

"I love this place," she whispers and I'm not sure if she is talking to me or just to herself.

"I come here to think," I reply and she gives me a shy smile. "Ladies first." I push open the gate and let her pass. There are no sheep on the field today, but I can see a flock in the adjacent one.

Jane and I head towards the short distance to the stone circle quietly. The whole monument is around thirty metres in diameter, the largest stone not much taller than me. In the centre is a sandy spot where some people who believe in the mysticism leave offerings as part of rituals. I once watched a summer solstice ceremony up here, and although I'm not a spiritual person myself, I was surprisingly moved by it.

Jane and I walk over to a flat stone that has fallen over, on the north end of the circle. With the tourists and the sheep around, it's tough to pinpoint when or how it toppled over. But most visitors usually just plop down on it and soak in the view down into the valley, toward Thirlmere and Helvellyn.

"Here." Jane holds out the flask to me, pulling the sausage rolls from the backpack and taking a seat. I slide onto the rock next to her and unscrew the flask. The coffee is still steaming when I pour some into the cup that doubles up as the lid.

The hot liquid has a sweet aftertaste I can't place, but I feel the warmth of it spread through my chilled body. I really should get a car for the cold winter months up here.

"Want some?" I hold out the cup and Jane takes it. She wipes some crumbs away from her mouth before taking a sip. I grab a sausage roll from the bag in her hand and the smell alone makes my mouth water.

"So, what did you want to talk about?" I ask, going in for a big bite of the pastry in my hand. Jane avoids my gaze and stares into the distance.

"I am sorry I've been such a... bitch, is probably what you'd call me."

"I've never called you that."

"Well, I was. I'm sorry, Ryan. I just... I was worried about my business and I got sucked into this whole scheme by Ruth and her clique to get you out. I blamed you for my failing business and that wasn't fair. It was failing before you came to the village. But I worked so hard for it and I just can't bear the thought of losing it."

"I love my business too. And I've also worked hard for it." I stuff the last of the sausage roll in my mouth and crumple up the paper bag. A gentle breeze blows up from the valley and stirs the crows in the nearby trees. There is no reply from Jane so I turn and see a lone tear rolling over her cheek.

"Hey," I reach out and wipe the tear away with my thumb. She seems to press her face into my palm for a second before moving away and angrily rubbing her eyes. I don't think, however, that her anger is directed at me this time.

"I am so sorry Ryan." Her eyes are still filled with tears but she manages to contain them.

"Can we try to get along from now on?" I suggest. Wrong words. I don't just want to get along with her. I want to wrap her in my arms, devour her and bury myself so deep in her that she will never be able to think of another man.

"I'd like that," she whispers before taking another sip of coffee. Her eyes drift back to the valley but I can't look away from her. The wind has freed strands of her ginger hair and they are now framing her beautiful face.

"Want more?" she asks when she notices me looking at her. I hesitate but then take the cup.

"Thanks." The coffee is lukewarm by now but I force it down. I give the empty cup a shake to get the last drops out before flipping it upside down onto the flask. The ground's a bit wonky next to the rock we're sitting on, but I work it out and balance the flask so it won't tip over.

"What made you move to Fellside?" Jane's question breaks the silence and catches me a little off guard. I don't really talk a lot about my past.

"I... I was a professional motorbike racer in my twenties." She lifts her head in surprise.

"Like, in Silverstone?"

"That's Formula One," I chuckle, "but, yes professional, on TV and all. I raced in the Moto2 and Moto3 division for a few years and then did two seasons in MotoGP. I never won the championship, but I won a few races here and there. When I was twenty-nine I had an accident that almost cost me my life. After that, the racing had lost its appeal and I retired."

"Oh god," she whispers and places her hand gently on my arm.

"It's okay, Princess, I survived." I give her a smile. "I ended up with a bad scar and wanted to cover it up. That's how I got my first tattoo." I stand up, unzip my jacket, and pull my T-shirt up on the left side. Along the side of my stomach, almost all the way to my armpit, a thorny stem with roses covers the angry red scar. The cold wind bites at my skin and I am about to pull my shirt down again when Jane places her fingers on the tattoo. She traces the stem from where it starts under my arm down to where it disappears into my jeans. I try to keep my breathing in check because the simple gesture sends heatwaves through my body.

"Sorry," she says and withdraws her hand when she realises what she's doing. I zip up my jacket and sit down next to her again.

"Is that what got you into becoming a tattoo artist?"

"Yes, my dad was with me every step of the way during recovery and he encouraged me to find a new passion. I asked the guy who gave me my tattoo if I could become his apprentice and well, that was that."

"Where was that?" Her focus is on me and it's a little unnerving.

"Over in Sheffield, where my parents live. My dad took me on climbing holidays a lot when I was younger, usually here in the Lake District. Fellside was our favourite place to stay. So, when I thought of opening my own studio, I was determined to have it here. This is the place where I want to grow old."

"And now I've ruined it."

"You haven't ruined anything."

"You don't know Ruth. She's on a mission."

"Well, let her. I've done nothing wrong and I refuse to believe that she'll be able to get my shop closed down."

It's almost dark and the wind is stronger now, causing a shiver to race through Jane's body.

"Time to take you home, Princess." I announce. Jane just nods and grabs the backpack. "Maybe we can do this again some time?" I ask cautiously. Her eyes find mine and she studies me as if she wants to see if I am joking.

"I'd love that," she finally replies.

The ride back to Fellside doesn't take nearly long enough. I enjoy having her so close with her hands innocently (or maybe not so innocently?) roaming over my chest.

When we stop in front of the block of flats where she lives, she gets off the bike with much more confidence than she had the last two times. I slide the backpack onto my shoulders after she passes it to me.

"That's yours too." She holds out the helmet.

"Hold onto it for now. I have nowhere to store it on my bike and you'll need it the next time I take you out." I wink and a faint blush covers her cheeks.

"Okay," she grins, then spins around and heads for the flat door.

"Jane," I call out and pull my helmet off. In two strides I'm in front of her.

"Yes?"

"Thank you."

"What for?" She looks adorable when she is confused.

"For... be willing to try to be friends." *I need more. Tell her you want more!*

"Sure. And thank you for taking me to Castlerigg... and for forgiving me." She looks nervous.

"Okay."

"Okay," she whispers. "I should—" She points towards the block of flats.

"Yes, sure," I reply suddenly desperate to find a reason for her to stay.

"Night."

"Night." Neither of us is moving. My dick wants me to throw her over my shoulder and take her to her bedroom. My brain is telling me to slow down. We've only just agreed to try to be friends.

"Okay, right, night," she finally says, turns and walks to the entrance. *My princess.*

Chapter 6

Jane

I can't avoid yawning when I unlock the shop. It's been a long week and it has been ages since I had a proper day off. Today is the twenty-seventh, so that makes this my fourteenth day on the trot. But with no assistant, I can't help it. I tried to close early on Sundays a couple of times but of course that's exactly when a customer walked through the door. Did they buy anything? No, of course not.

"We're just looking," is usually the answer I get when I ask them if I can help. I see them taking pictures of stock and I guess they come to the shop to see things in real life before purchasing online. But there's nothing I can do about it. I can only watch the dwindling numbers in my bank account. Yesterday, I did some calculations, and the end is near for my shop. It's time to make some hard decisions.

I haven't seen Ryan since our trip either. When he said we should do this again, I was really hoping he would ask me out. I mean he lives and works next door. He must have made a real effort to avoid me for two weeks. Maybe I misread the whole situation?

It's not that I hadn't tried to bump into him accidently on purpose. But I didn't catch so much as a glimpse of him. *Argh, first I act like a nasty bitch and now like a desperate teenager.*

Honestly, it's been a long time since I went on a date, and my last serious relationship was two years ago. Grampy was right; the guys I used to date were always simple and safe. You know, the nine-to-five types who come home, expect a cooked meal, watch TV, and settle for some vanilla action twice a week. And, weirdly, that was fine by me. So why the sudden interest in someone different?

I blame the others—Olivia, Rob, Rose, Dan, and the rest of the gang. Watching them, I can't help but wonder if there's more to love than just settling.

Love. Ha. I'm not even sure if I've ever felt it, certainly not like the others do. Honestly, I think I've had warmer feelings for the heroes in romance novels than any of the guys I've dated.

The bell above the door chimes, drawing my attention.

Ruth. Fudge this! She is the last person I need to see today.

Ruth and I went to school together, but contrary to me, she is the perfect fortyish-year-old woman. Married, two children, runs her own small business and is the branch leader of the local WI—and she rules these ladies with an iron rod. I mean, nothing happens without her say. Her husband sits on the local council and I guess you could call them a power couple in our tiny world of Fellside.

"Jane, darling, why didn't you come to the meeting on Friday?"

Ruth has been trying to get me to join the WI for ages, but I already feel managed by her, I really don't need her involved in my life anymore.

"We discussed the unfortunate situation." She points in the direction of Ryan's studio.

"You know, lots of people talk really positively about Ryan," I cautiously object whilst nervously rearranging my pens on the counter.

"You missed the talk about the spring equestrian events in the area as well. Some of the ladies were talking of buying their new outfits online but I told them they can get much better service here. They were just not sure about how suitable it is for them to bring their daughters here." She pretends to ignore my objection but the thinly vailed threat in what she is saying is obvious.

Snobbish bitch! She has yet to explain to me why Ryan would be any danger to these precious daughters, but I doubt she could really give me a valid reason. I can feel anger rising in me. Not anger with Ruth, but with myself for letting her manipulate me for so long.

"Is there something I can get you, Ruth?" I ask coldly.

"No, pet. I just wanted to pop in and say that we think we found a solution. I can't say too much, but watch this space," she giggles although with her smoker's voice it sounds more like a witch cackling. With that, she blows a kiss in the air and struts out of my shop.

A cold feeling settles in my stomach. If they really found a way to get rid of Ryan then I'd be at fault as well. I complained about him to the council more than once and I... Argh.

As I grab my keys, I take a deep breath. It's almost five so nobody will mind if I close up my shop . On the way out I flip the sign to closed.

I have never been inside his studio so I am not sure what to expect. Black and velvet, or maybe some other kinky stuff. But I'm not prepared for the bright reception area that greets me. The walls are painted in a calming orange. There are large frames with artistic photographs of tattoos, and comfy chairs are arranged in small groups with coffee tables and plants. It looks more like a posh spa than what I had pictured.

"Hello?" I call out.

"Hi, how can I… Oh fuck, you!" A tall woman steps into the reception area. I recognise her as one of the employees, but I am not sure what her name is. Until now, I have kind of avoided his staff.

"Ry, her Majesty is here," she shouts before grabbing a backpack from the counter. "See ya," she smirks at me as she leaves. On her way out, she turns the sign on the door to closed.

"Jane." Ryan's voice makes me jump.

"I need to talk to you," is all I reply.

He exhales loudly and stuffs his hands in his jeans' pockets. He looks handsome today. No. Scratch that, handsome is the wrong word to describe him: he looks hot. His short, salt-and-pepper hair and nearly black eyes give him that dark, and dangerous vibe; but not in a scary way. He is wearing a white T-shirt with his tattoo covered arms on full display like an advert for his shop.

"What do you want?" So much for us trying to be friends.

"I... have information for you."

"Spit it out," he replies and there is hostility in his voice. I flinch and he must have noticed because he adds in a gentler voice, "Come to the back."

But instead of heading to the back, he walks past me and locks the door to the studio.

"You locked us in!" I can hear the panic in my voice.

"No need to get you knickers in a twist. The backdoor is unlocked. You can escape through there. I can't keep an eye on the front of the shop from the work room and we're closed for today, which is why I locked up."

"I'm still here!"

"You're not a client." He gently puts his hand on the small of my back and guides me in the direction he pointed. I feel heat emanating from his hand spreading through me and I hurry up and move away from his touch.

The backroom is large and separated into three sections with different workstations. A radio is playing a soft rock ballad I don't recognise.

Ryan turns the volume down but doesn't turn it off. Leaning against a cupboard displaying tools, he crosses his arms in front of his chest and I can't help admiring his flexed muscles.

"Jane!" He draws my attention and I feel heat in my cheeks.

"Do you know who Ruth is?"

He just shrugs like it's not important.

"Ruth is the leader of the local WI branch."

"Okay?"

"She is the one who has been trying to get you out."

"I'm pretty sure it was you that sent all the lovely letters to the council. FYI, I was informed that they are considering moving the motorbike parking spot."

I guess that explains the frosty welcome.

"Ryan, I'm sorry. I... I sent them another email asking them to disregard my letters. I guess I was too late. I'm truly sorry." No reply. He just looks at me with a frown.

"I...," I step closer. So close that I can smell a hint of aftershave and something more manly. *Stop it, Jane! Get your libido under control.* "I just wanted to warn you that Ruth mentioned that they have a plan to get you out."

"What plan?"

"I don't know. I'm sorry, she wouldn't tell me." I feel small under his stare. I avoid his gaze and instead my eyes dart around his workspace. I can see a frame with a certificate on the wall. "You have a certificate?" I ask.

"Princess, you won't believe it, but you can't just take a gun and tattoo people willy-nilly. You need to learn and practice the craft and you need a license before you can open a shop," he laughs but sounds bitter.

"I'm sorry. I just thought—"

"You just thought it's all so easy." He pushes off the cupboard and grabs one of the machines lying on it. He fiddles around with it for a bit and I guess that's me being dismissed.

"I probably should leave." I turn towards what looks to be the back entrance when Ryan takes a seat on the tattoo stool.

"Wait. Here." He holds out the contraption in his hand.

"What should I do with it?"

"It's a tattoo gun. Tattoo me. If you think it's that easy, this is your chance," he challenges me.

"Are you insane?" My heart is hammering like crazy. As mad as the idea sounds, something in me would like to do it, would like to know how it works. I've always been curious to learn new things and this is... exciting. "Ryan, you just said it needs lots of experience and —"

"Calm down, Princess. There's no needle. It's a practice gun with a pencil attached to it. See." He touches the tip with his finger.

Hesitantly, I take a step closer and reach for the metal contraption. It feels heavy in my hands.

"Whoa, what are you doing?" I protest and take a step back as Ryan pulls his T-shirt over his head.

"No need to get all Victorian. My arms are fully covered with tattoos. But you can try here," he points at his left pec, free of any ink. I feel a blush creeping up my cheeks. I've seen him half naked before, but I've never touched his bare chest. Sure, my hands have roamed over his muscles when riding on the back of the bike, but let's pretend that was all just in the name of safety. Plus, he was fully dressed.

I grin to myself at the memory and cautiously take a seat on the little stool next to him.

"What do I do first?"

"Use the can of soap and clean the area." His eyes are intense and focused on me. There's a noticeable shake in my hands as I place the tattoo gun on the little table next to us and grab the soap. I apply a bit of foam and rub it over his pec. *Oh my!* It's definitely getting hotter in here.

"Now use the razor to shave the area."

"What?" I heard him, but I'm not sure if I heard him right.

"You can't put a stencil on hair." His voice has lost all hostility. Instead, he patiently talks me through shaving off his dark hair, applying stencil solution and eventually the makeshift stencil of a flower he had prepared.

"Now, hold the gun like this," he places the machine into my hand, "and pull the skin as tight as you can."

I place my free hand on his pec. I can feel the heartbeat under his muscles. It's fast, almost as fast as mine. Ryan gently guides my hand in place. Here goes nothing.

Chapter 7

Ryan

Just like before the bike ride on New Year's Eve, Jane's eyes show a hint of fear, but also excitement as she lowers the tattoo gun to my chest. I have a suspicion that behind the prim and proper princess hides a little daredevil.

"Go on," I encourage her. A strand of hair has come loose from her usually perfect bun and my fingers itch to tuck it behind her ear. But before I can, she swipes it away herself and then focuses on my pec. She leans forward and cautiously places the tip of the pencil on the thin outline the stencil left on my skin. I mock flinch and Jane gasps. She pulls the machine back and stares at me with big eyes.

"It's just a pencil, remember?" I grin. She rolls her eyes and playfully slaps me.

"Don't do that," she demands but I can see a little smile playing on her lips.

Leaning forward again, she carefully stretches my skin like I showed her and starts tracing the stencil. She's totally focused, her face beaming with excitement. Every so often, her tongue pokes out between her lips and the sight causes my cock to harden. All sorts of dirty thoughts pop into my head. *Fuck, I need to get a grip!*

I lean back and just watch her face. Fuck, she's so beautiful. These damn freckles and the lush lips. I feel my dick twitch with excitement and it is getting harder to keep my hands to myself, the longer I'm watching her. This close I can smell that sweet scent of strawberries that I noticed when I kissed her on New Year's Eve.

"Is this okay?" She lifts her head and her blue eyes sparkle at me.

"Yes. Just pull the skin a bit tighter, this way you get a smoother line."

"Okay," she whispers but continues looking at me. The little strand of hair is framing her face again and this time I can't help myself. I reach out and tuck it behind her ear.

Her lips part and a little whimper escapes her. When she realises what she's done, she drops the tattoo gun on the side table.

"I should go. I... just watch out for Ruth," she mumbles and looks around my work area like she's checking for something. "Did I bring my handbag?" She is confused and flustered. Eventually she gives up her search and marches towards the back door without another word.

"Jane, wait." I slide an arm around her from behind and pull her against my chest. She freezes. "Why are you running?" I ask whilst gently pulling her hairband off, sending her ginger locks down over her shoulders.

"I'm not running," she replies, her voice barely audible.

"If you want to go, I'll let you go," I groan and attempt to release the arm still curled around her waist. She grabs it and pulls it back to rest on her stomach.

"What if I don't want to go?" Her head hits my chest as she leans back. I gently slide her hair to the side and place kisses along the column of her throat.

"Then, Princess, I'll take you for the best ride of your life." I pull her earlobe in my mouth and suck on it. She moans and starts to rub her arse against my dick. He really doesn't need the extra encouragement because he's been painfully hard for the last half an hour.

"Ryan," she whispers my name. I turn her in my arms and pull her in for a kiss. When our lips meet, a deep rumbling groan escapes me. I need her. I don't think I ever needed anyone as much as her. I walk her backwards and lift her onto the chest of drawers.

"Ry, what if someone comes in?" This is the first time she's used my nickname and I like it.

"Princess, the front is locked."

"But the back isn't," she whispers as I brush my lips over the sensitive skin of her neck. I step back and she looks at me with big eyes.

"Stay," I point at her before walking to the backdoor and flipping the key. "Now, nobody will interrupt us." My eyes are locked on hers as I return. She parts her legs and I step between them, cupping her face and capturing her lips with mine. Her fingers dig into my back and she pulls me closer.

When my tongue dips into her mouth I groan. I love her taste. I could kiss her for hours and not get bored. She slides her hand over my chest, down to the zip on my jeans.

"Wow, not so fast, Princess." My words cause her to blush and she avoids my eyes. Jane isn't much younger than me but at this moment she seems so innocent. I wonder how many men she's been with. The minute the thought hits me, jealousy fills my guts. *Yup, not thinking of her with other men.*

I cup her chin in my hand and turn her face so she looks at me.

"My dick can't wait to come out and play, sweetheart, but not here. First I'm going to make you come in my mouth on my workbench, so every time I look at it I'm reminded of you screaming my name. Then I'll take you upstairs and you can ride my cock."

A shiver races through her.

"Hm, do you like that dirty talk, Princess?" I chuckle.

"Yes," she whispers.

"I think there is little wildcat in you. Now be a good girl and take your shirt off." Her eyes turn a shade darker and she nervously licks her lips. Nevertheless, she reaches for the hem of her shirt and pulls it over her head.

She is wearing a simple black bra and yet she looks the sexiest I've ever seen her. My hands stroke over her tummy as my lips kiss a trail over the soft skin just above her tits. My cock feels like it's ready to burst through my jeans.

Her hands find their way into my short hair and the feel of her nails scratching gently over my scalp is almost too much for me to stick to my promise that she will come first.

I unbutton her trousers and pull them down. I don't need to tell her to lift her bum, she does it automatically.

Just like her bra, her knickers are plain and black, but when I stroke over them, they are damp.

"Hmm, someone's wet already," I growl and hook my fingers the material covering her hips, peeling her black knickers down.

She's breathing heavily with anticipation and I can't help but play with her a little longer.

I gently slide my fingers up and down the inside of her thighs.

"Ryan, I can't—"

"Can't what, Princess?" One look at her face tells me that she's not about to stop me. No, she is begging for me.

"I can't wait any longer, please touch me."

I remove my hands and place them on the cupboard either side of her, leaning forward and drawing her into a long, deep kiss.

"Touch you where, sweetheart? I need you to say it." I smirk.

"Ryan," she groans. "I need you to touch me down there."

"Knees? Toes?" *Heads, shoulders, knees and toes.* Great, now I have that song in my head.

"No," she protests.

"Say it!" This is torture for me just as much as for her.

"I want you to touch my pussy. I want you to make me come. I need you to make me come," she sighs.

"Your wish is my command." I grab her knees and pull her in place so her arse rests on the edge of the chest of drawers. Jane yelps and grips my arms to balance herself.

I slowly kiss my way down her chest and stomach to the soft skin of her mound. I can smell her arousal and it makes my mouth water. But before I give us both the satisfaction, I lift one of her legs, place it on my shoulder and kiss the inside of her thighs. One kiss. Then another. Jane's hands grip my hair and she gently pulls me higher.

"Patience, Princess."

"No, please, Ryan, please." Who can say no to such polite pleading? I finally take pity on her and swipe my tongue over the seam of her pussy. And again. She moans loudly and throws her head back.

"More!"

She doesn't need to ask twice. I let my tongue slide over her wet lips, up to her clit and back down before exploring her tight channel. Her moans turn into pants and I know she's close. I mould my lips around her clit and suck, and that's all it takes. She screams my name and grabs onto the edge of the chest of drawers. I can't take my eyes off her and I know the image of her coming apart in front of me will be forever burned into my memory.

"Son of a biscuit," she mumbles as she finally opens her eyes again.

"Princess, we need to work on your dirty talk," I chuckle and steal another kiss from her lips. I need to get her into my bed, like right now.

Chapter 8

Jane

I lower myself from the chest of drawers and cautiously put my feet on the ground. My legs still feel wobbly from the incredible orgasm he has just given me, but they seem to hold me up.

"Right, we're not done," Ryan says. Suddenly the world is upside down because he has put his shoulder into my tummy and lifted me up in the air. Ignoring my protests to let me down, he walks towards the staircase leading to the first floor.

Hanging of his shoulder I have a mighty fine view of his backside and I can't help but reach out and cup it.

"Did you just grab my arse?" Ryan chuckles.

"No... no, I was just... holding on," I stutter.

"Sure, Princess," he laughs as he pushes a door open. He drops me gently onto a firm mattress. In the dim light of the bedside lamp, I can see that his eyes are dark with desire. I've never had a man look at me like that. Nor did any of them ever push me onto the nearest piece of furniture and go down on me until I screamed their name. The thought of my earlier orgasm makes me blush.

"What are you thinking?" Ry asks as he moves his tall body over mine and darts kisses on my neck. I love the feel of it and don't want him to stop.

"Princess, what are you thinking?" he repeats his question with a chuckle, clearly aware of the effect he has on me.

"That I don't think any man has ever given me an orgasm like that."

"Good," he mumbles before nipping at my jaw. I lock my legs behind his back and pull him down to me until he is flush against my body. Despite him still wearing jeans I can feel his erection pressing into me.

"Can we take these off now?" My fingers find the buttons on his trousers and this time he doesn't stop me. Once the zip is down, he gets off the bed and strips off his remaining clothes. The only thing I'm still wearing is my bra and I cautiously open the hooks in the back and slid it off. I mean, I'm no longer in my twenties and gravity has done its thing. But before my insecurities can take over, Ryan is hovering over me.

"You are so beautiful," he whispers with his eyes locked on me and I know he's not just saying it. I can see in his expression that he means it.

When he swipes his tongue over my tight nipple, I moan loudly. Ryan licks and sucks them whilst he rubs my clit with his thumb. Just as he is about to push two of his fingers into me, I grab hold of his wrist.

"No more teasing, no more foreplay, Ry. I need you to...," *don't say boinking, don't say boinking,* " fu...fuck me." I plead with him.

"Nope," he replies in a growly voice before rolling off me, leaning against the headboard. "I need you to fuck me. I told you, you get to ride me; now move your pretty arse over here and take what you need, Princess." He gives me a smirk as he rolls on a condom.

Nervously, I get on all fours and crawl over to him. I see his erection twitch as I get closer. As I straddle him, he cups my behind with his large hands and manoeuvres me into position.

"Take what you need, Jane." He catches me off guard when he moans my name. I have got so used to him calling me Princess, but by saying my name it feels more real, that he wants me, plain Jane, Miss What-would-other-people-think. I suddenly realise that this is the first time in forever that I feel like myself. Not the persona I put on for others, no, this is me. Taking what I need.

I reach down between my legs and grab hold of his dick. There, I said it. I align myself and then slowly slide down. Okay, that's a tight fit. When he is fully seated in me, I pause to let my body adjust.

"That feels amazing," I tell him truthfully.

"Yes, it does and it will only get better." He slides an arm around me and pulls me closer. His mouth finds mine and we kiss passionately. With my mouth still on his, I start to move. I roll my hips back and forth, waves of pleasure emanating from my core. He rubs right up against my g-spot with every move.

"Holy moly," I whisper and speed up. I slide my arms around his neck and we end up in a tight embrace moving in unison.

I'm not sure how long I can keep going like this but just then, as if he can read my mind, Ryan flips me over so I'm underneath him. His lips have yet to leave mine, but he starts pumping into me like a man on a mission. I place my feet on the bed and lift my hips in the same rhythm to meet his strokes head on. One of my hands pushes against the headboard and the other is cupping Ryan's face.

"Fuck, this feels good," he groans and thrusts harder. Every stroke is hitting me at the right spot and an incredible pressure builds in me. I'm at the point where it feels so good, I don't want it to end but at the same time I need to come. I need to.

"Come for me now, Jane." My name, again. A shudder races through me and when Ryan gently bites my bottom lip, a second orgasm explodes through my body. It's more powerful than the one he gave me downstairs. I feel a burst of energy before I fall limply onto the mattress. Ryan calls out my name and stops moving.

"Oh wow," I whisper. Ryan slides his lips up and down my neck before taking one last kiss.

"I'll be back in a minute." His voice sounds distant. My eye lids feel heavy, and I can't get myself to open them. I feel deep relaxation spreading through me. I curl up and smile happily.

I blink once and twice, but I can't see much except for unfamiliar pieces of furniture in the dark. I must have fallen asleep. The last thing I remember was the best orgasm I have ever had.

I shift and become aware of the warm body spooning me. Ryan's arm is draped over my side with his hand cupping one of my breasts possessively.

Shit. What now? What was last night? A one-night-stand? More? My mother is going to have a fit. I should leave. I should sneak out and pretend it all never happened. I—

I carefully flip back the duvet to slide out of bed, but then I don't. I know he might want me to go, I know my mother definitely would want me to leave, but I want to stay.

I flip the duvet back down and soak in the warmth of his body. I can't remember when I ever felt so safe and so much like myself than I do lying here in his arms.

"Were you planning to do a runner, Princess?" Ryan's voice reverberates around the dark room.

"I thought maybe you'd want me gone by the time you wake up. Isn't that what men want from a one-night-stand?" Okay, this might be a thinly vailed attempt to hear that this is more for him.

Ry briefly shifts to switch on the bedside lamp.

"Jane, look at me." He leans over my shoulder to catch my eye. "If I wanted a one-night-stand, it wouldn't be with someone who I see almost every day and whose brother is a good friend of mine. You did get under my skin—"

"By acting like a bitch," I interrupt him.

"I wouldn't use that term, Princess, but you certainly had a stick up that beautiful backside of yours," he chuckles.

I move so I'm flat on my back and Ryan is hovering over me.

"Again, I'm so sorry Ryan." He tries to interrupt me, but I won't let him. "No, I'm sorry. I... my whole life I've always tried to please others. Growing up, I was always expected to behave properly, to do the right things and be a good example for Phil. I kind of slipped into that role and in the process I think I lost myself. I mean look at me. I'm forty-two years old and a minute ago I worried what my mother would think if she found me in bed with you. What's wrong with me?"

He gently swipes a strand of hair from my face.

"Sweetheart, we all play roles in our lives to fit in. Some more than others. I've met a lot of people who run around pretending to be 'true to themselves,' and it's just for show. But you know you've found your people when you feel relaxed enough to show your real self to them."

"This night, that was all me," I whisper.

"I know," is all he replies before kissing me deeply.

"Ry, I need to be up early."

"Why? It's Sunday. You open only at lunchtime." He nibbles on my ear. Okay, firstly, this man has a magic mouth. And secondly, looks like he has been paying very close attention to me if he knows my comings and goings.

"The family is taking Grampy out for breakfast," I explain and then I can't hold back a moan when he slides a finger inside me.

"I'll get you there on time, don't worry." *Yes, yes he will*, my mind flashes to the immediate need for another orgasm.

"Okay." I mean, who am I to argue with the man who has given me the best sex I've ever had?

Ryan stops his bike at the small car park next to the Cherry Pie bakery. They added a restaurant in the back and it has quickly become a favourite breakfast spot for locals and tourists.

I cautiously climb off the bike and remove the helmet. I could have walked really, but I had to get home and change first and my flat is on the other side of the village. It also didn't help that Ryan joined me in the shower and that turned into orgasm numbers four and five.

"Thanks for bringing me here." I hand over his spare helmet. I'm not sure what the protocol is after a night like we just had.

"Any time, Princess," he chuckles before sliding an arm around my waist and pulling me to him. His lips find mine and what starts of as a chaste kiss turns into an absolutely inappropriate public display of affection.

"Hey, there are children present." A harsh voice pulls me from the moment.

"Phil, what—"

"Grampy sent me out to tell you to bring Ryan in." My cheeks turn hot.

"How does he know about Ryan?" At my words, Phil points to the coffee house. *Fantastic.* The whole family is gathered around a table right at the entrance and they are all looking at us through the glass front. Mum looks incredulous, dad looks confused and Christina and Grampy wear matching grins. Christina is a well-known matchmaker, so I know why she's happy.

"Come on." Phil frowns at me before his eyes dart to Ryan.

"Mate, I hope you're okay with this." Ryan asks but his tone makes it clear that he won't back down if Phil isn't okay with it.

“What exactly is this?” Phil throws back. They’re both acting like I’m not here.

“I’m crazy about Jane.” *Oh wow, okay, maybe I’ll swoon a little here.*

“Don’t hurt her,” Phil growls and points at Ryan. To be honest that is laughable because my brother wouldn’t stand a chance against Ryan.

"Aw, Bambi," Generally, I reserve Christina's nickname for when I want to tease him. And this moment definitely calls for it. "I reckon I'm old enough to fend for myself. Still, thanks for looking out for me, little brother." I flash him a grin and playfully mess up his hair. Phil huffs in frustration, attempting to restore his locks.

As we step into the restaurant, Ryan intertwines our fingers. Somehow, this simple gesture banishes all the jittery butterflies, filling me with newfound confidence to confront my mum.

Chapter 9

Ryan

Jane's mother, Sharon, watches me like a hawk over breakfast. She isn't hostile per se, just careful. And every so often she'll throw in a comment that "Jane was always the good girl in school." It's not difficult to guess what she is implying. I'm not good enough for Jane.

I don't react because not only won't I give her the satisfaction of getting a rise out of me, but I also don't need to tell her that she knows nothing about her daughter. And let's not get me started on the fact that Jane left school twenty years ago. She's forty-two and not a girl anymore.

"So, tell me, Ryan, how did you woo my granddaughter? Did she take your breath away when you saw her the first time?" Her grandfather chuckles next to me.

Jane stiffens on my arm, but I try to comfort her by rubbing her back.

"Well, it wasn't quite that romantic. But she left a lasting impression when I saw her the first time at an FMR pub evening," I chuckle. Jane relaxes a little.

"Well, I believe my daughter has been trying to get your studio closed down for the last few months. I have to say I'm surprised to see you together now." At last, Jane's mom blurts out what's been bothering her since we sat down.

"That's not fair," Christina interjects, although we all know it isn't far from the truth.

"She—" Jane stops me with a gentle touch on my thigh.

"I told Grampy that I was an idiot and that I blamed you for my shop going under when really business had been shit for months."

"Jane! Don't swear! Lilly—" She points at the little girl in Phil's arms.

"Oh please, she hears way worse from me... occasionally," Christina objects sheepishly.

"I'm sorry, Jane, about the shop. You didn't tell me it was that serious," Grampy says and pats Jane's hand gently.

"We don't need the whole village to know that her shop is failing," her mum huffs and she is starting to annoy me.

"I'm not the whole village, I'm family," Grampy snaps at her. He's been the life of the party all morning, so I'm surprised about his change in character. "Jane, is there anything I can do to help?" He brings the attention back to Jane. She sniffles and sinks deeper into my side, like she is looking for some strength.

"Thanks, Grampy, but it would just be a temporary plaster. The market is changing and I can't compete with online platforms any longer. I've decided to close the shop in four weeks and use that time to sell off my stock. That way I will have some money left to tide me over until I find a job."

Everyone is staring at the table, avoiding Jane's gaze. I wish I could do something for her, but this is the first time she's told me how bad the situation is. *Fuck! I hate this for her.* I worked hard for my studio, which is why I was so angry when I thought she was trying to destroy it.

"That's a wise decision, Poppet. Give yourself some time, though, to work out what you want." He throws a pointed look at Sharon.

Jane grins, slipping out of my hug and chasing after Lilly, who's making a beeline for the tempting cakes on the other side of the room. Sharon shoots me a quick look before pulling her husband along to pick out their own cakes from the display.

"My grandchildren didn't have it easy with their mum. Appearances matter to her. Phil was always pushed to take centre stage, and Jane had to be perfect.

"I mean, she gave up on Phil after he peed his pants on stage at a school production. But my Poppet, she went all out trying to squeeze herself into the mould her mom envisioned for her." The old man looks at Jane and Lilly who are playing at a neighbouring table. His eyes are full of sadness. "I should have stood up for them more."

"I firmly believe everything happens for a reason. Imagine you had stepped in more when Phil was little. That could have changed the trajectory of his whole life and he and Christina may never have found each other."

He gives me a curious look. "That's very wise for someone so young."

"I'm over forty. I'm not young."

"Well, you're young to me. So, clever clogs, what about Jane? She hasn't found her happy ending yet. What if she doesn't? Still believe everything happens for a reason?"

"We crossed paths," I shrug, "and I hope that means she's found her happily ever after." My eyes are trained on my princess. For once she is wearing her curls not in a tight bun. The smile on her face reflects the love she has for her niece. I could watch her for hours.

"Good answer, son, good answer," Grampy grins at me. "Just be there for her and let her discover herself."

I nod. There is nothing I'd rather do.

"Ry, you are wanted," Neil calls out from the reception area. I put my phone on the chest of drawers. The same one that I had Jane propped up on when I made her come for the first time. I can't stop the smile from appearing on my lips at that thought.

Jane and I have been dating for three weeks and despite the tough time she has had closing down her shop—next week is the last day—she looks happier than ever. She is letting her hair down a lot more; literally and figurative speaking, and I even caught her saying 'fuck' when she dropped a box last week. We've spent almost every night together and I am addicted to her touch, scent and taste.

"How can I help you?" I say as I step into the reception area where three familiar-looking, older women greet me with a grin.

"Ryan, my boy, do you remember me?"

"Mrs Harris." I grin. Of course I remember Alex's grandmother. She handed out dick cookies at the Carol singing event. We had a tough time explaining that to the people that came to our stall.

"Pish posh. I told you before, call me Anna. And this is Mary Fuentes, Chris's mother, and Estelle, Emma's grandmother." I look at the three women and I have a suspicion they are powerhouses in the village.

"We're here to get tattoos," Mary says, although she doesn't look sure about it.

"We have appointments," Emma's Granny says, a lot more confidently.

Neil and I check them in and take them through to the studio. I watch with a grin as Neil tries to explain in the politest way possible that for senior skin we recommend specific areas on the body, and simpler designs without thin lines. I think Anna knows exactly what he means, but she's enjoying making him feel uncomfortable.

In the end, Anna goes ahead and gets her granddaughter Maisie's name tattooed, while Chris's mum settles on the names of her grandchildren.

I'm about to discuss a potential tattoo symbolising travel with Estelle when my phone rings.

"Excuse me," I tell her before snatching the landline phone from the side desk and answering.

"Ryan, hi, this is Mr Young." *My landlord?* "Listen, I have bad news. I'm cancelling the lease." Cold panic grips me. I try to take a deep breath.

"What do you mean? I have a three-year lease," I reply angrily. All eyes in the studio are on me, but I don't care.

"Well, there is a clause in it that if I need the premises for my own use I can cancel the lease with a three months' notice. I'm giving you three months. My lawyer will send you a formal letter today. I'm sorry." He doesn't sound bloody sorry. He doesn't sound sorry at all.

"What do you want to use it for?" I smell bullshit.

"Oh, a niece of mine is opening a coffee shop." Because that's what we need. Another fucking coffeeshop.

"I can't believe this." I have a sick feeling in my stomach.

"Sorry. My lawyer will be in touch." Those are his final words before he hangs up. My initial urge is to throw the phone.

"You know, his niece is Ruth's daughter." I look at Anna.

"I don't fucking believe this!" My voice booms through the shop.

"What's happened?" Jane is standing in the arch leading to the front of the studio, a tray with three take away coffees in her hands.

"My landlord cancelled my lease. I have three months to move out," I hiss. Jane flinches.

"Why?"

"Because he has a clause in the lease that says he can ask for the shop back if he needs it himself. And his niece wants to open a coffeeshop."

"Who's your landlord?"

"Stephen Young." I don't need to say more. Everyone knows him. He doesn't live here, he lives in Sheffield, but he owns a lot of the shops in the village and rents them out.

"Ruth's brother-in-law," Jane whispers.

"Apparently," I growl full of anger. Jane flinches again. I can see her hands shaking.

"I should go. I brought you coffee and pastries." She pulls a small box with logo of the Cherry Pie bakery from her large handbag and places it with the coffee on the nearest surface. "I'm sorry," she whispers and a tear runs down her face.

I don't reply. I turn away and stare at the wall. *What the fuck am I going to do?*

"Ryan!" Neil eventually pulls me from my thoughts.

"I think you should go after her." Estelle nods in direction of the front door.

"Why?" *Yup, I can hear that I sound like a wanker.*

"It's not her fault, but she blames herself," Anna says. "We actually came here today to show that not the whole WI is against you. Sadly, it looks like we're too late, but I can promise you that Ruth cooked that scheme up on her own. She's just a vicious bitch."

I rub my neck. "Fuck!" I shout before apologising for my outburst. "I need to talk to Jane. Can I leave you in Neil's capable hands?" I didn't really need to ask because the three ladies are basically shooing me out of the shop.

Jane doesn't drive so it doesn't take me long to catch up with her on her way to her flat.

"Princess, wait!" I call out. She slows her walk but doesn't stop. "Jane!" I gently grab her by her upper arm and swing her around.

"Ry, don't. It's my fault."

"Why do you think that?"

"If I hadn't played along with her for months she may have given up—"

"Princess, I have never even met this bitch and she has still made it her life's mission to destroy my business just because it doesn't fit into her pretentious world. She's just one of these people that are only happy if they ruin someone else. She would have done this with or without you." I gently wipe her tears away.

"What now?"

"I don't know." I drop my arms. "There's a big tattoo convention in London next week. I wasn't planning to go, but it might be a good idea to network and see if anyone is looking for tattoo artists up here. Jamie might also have some ideas."

"Who's Jamie?" she asks before blowing her nose in a tissue.

"My ex-girlfriend." I reply and my words cause Jane to freeze.

"You're meeting up with your ex?" New tears are forming in her eyes.

"Sweetheart," I cup her face, "Jamie is happily married and has two kids. She and I haven't been an item for ten years and even then we weren't very serious. But she and her husband have a chain of tattoo shops in Kent and West Sussex and they know everyone in the scene.

"Argh, I'm sorry, Ry. Fudge this! I'm behaving like a teenager. I'm a grown woman."

"Hey, it's okay to be vulnerable sometimes. Come here." I pull her into a hug. She is not the only vulnerable one here. Holding her in my arms makes me realise I need her in my life because she gives me strength. As long as she is with me, I can deal with anything.

Chapter 10

Jane

I could scream. I push hard again against the box, but it won't budge. This is the last of my stock and I'm currently trying to store it in my living room. I had to vacate the shop and now I have to try to shift this stuff online. The irony isn't lost on me

I push again, but the box sticking out from the pile of other boxes doesn't move. It must be caught on the one below somehow. Ryan is at the convention in London, otherwise I could have called him to help. Instead, I have to do it all on my own.

I'm not sure if it would have been easier to have him around or not for the shop closure; emotionally, I mean. No, that's a lie. Of course it would have been easier to have him here to comfort me. But instead of cuddling up in his arms at the end of the day, I sit in my crappy flat surrounded by the remnants of my career.

I'm about to lift the box and see what's going on when my phone rings. The display lights up with one of my favourite photos of Christina, Phil and Lilly. They're sharing an ice cream cone and they all look so happy. I pick up the phone and accept the call from my sister-in-law.

"Hey, Christina," I greet her and give the box another shove. I thought maybe by distracting it with my call it would magically move. Nothing.

"Jane." Christina's voice sounds pained. Immediately, alarm bells ring in my mind. Phil? Lilly!

"What's wrong?"

"Grampy died last night." Silence. I'm frozen to the spot. I try to breathe but it feels like I'm drowning. "He just fell asleep last night and didn't wake up this morning." No, no. No, no, no! I clear my throat trying to bring my voice back.

"Where's Phil?" Grampy wasn't just family; he was one of Phil's closest friends. Ignoring my own heartache about loosing Grampy, all I feel is the urgent need to be by my brother's side. His heart's gonna shatter, and I can't bear the thought of not being there for him.

"He's here." A little sob escapes her and I realise she is crying.

"I'll come to yours. I... I—"

"Emma's coming to get you, Jane."

"I can walk."

"No. Just give her five minutes and she'll be with you."

"Okay," I whisper. I still haven't moved.

"Do you want me to stay on the phone with you?" Her voice is quiet.

"No, no, go and be with Phil. Tell him I'll be there in a minute. Thanks, Christina." I disconnect the call and then drop the phone on the table.

I don't know what to do. I just stand there. And stand there a little longer. My mind is blank and I feel frozen and numb. *Grampy!*

Eventually the doorbell brings a little clarity. I grab my phone and purse and head to the door.

Emma's eyes are red rimmed. All of the FMR guys and their partners knew Grampy. And everyone loved him.

She pulls me into a hug and I briefly return it before demanding, "I need to get to Phil."

He is my little brother after all, and he will be hurting. He will be hurting so much.

The drive is short and I rush from the car the minute Emma parks. I notice that I'm shaking when I hug Christina.

"He's in the living room," she says and I push pass her. Phil is standing at the window looking out into the garden. I can only see his back. It is quiet in the room, too quiet.

"Phil." My voice startles him and he turns around. He's pale and suddenly looks older than he did a couple of days ago.

"I didn't get the chance to say goodbye" he whispers before a sob breaks through.

I cross the room and pull him into my arms. He's shaking and I don't know what hurts more, having lost Grampy or seeing my brother in this much pain.

"It's okay, it's okay," I say, but I know it's not. It's never going to be completely okay. Tears are now streaming down my face as well. I couldn't hold them in any longer.

I look over Phil's shoulder and see Alex sitting on the sofa. I didn't notice that he was there when I entered. He looks grief-stricken as well. Emma is curled up at his side, quietly crying.

Christina steps up to Phil and gently rubs his back. He let's go of me and hugs his wife. Nobody says a word. What can we say?

"Dada," Lilly's voice comes from the baby monitor in Christina's hand.

"I'll go." Before anyone can react, I leave the living room and head upstairs.

I gently push the door to Lilly's bedroom. The curtains are drawn, but Christina has left a nightlight on. As I enter I see Lilly, her chubby cheeks rosy from sleep. Her eyes, which are so much like Phil's, blink sleepily, and a slow, drowsy smile spreads across her face as she notices me. Her tousled hair sticks up in every direction and I involuntarily smile.

Her little arms reach out towards me.

"Atty!"

I lift her up and cuddle her close. She snuggles up against me and then it hits me. He won't see her grow up. He won't see how our lives go on, all the good and the not so good things that happen to us. He won't be around for all the highs and lows that life throws at us.

Yeah, Grampy was pushing into his eighties, and we all knew that time was slipping away. But it's funny how the day-to-day grind tricks you into thinking he'll always be there—a constant in the background.

"Atty?" Lilly mumbles again and swipes a tear from my face. She frowns and I try to pull myself together.

"How about a snack, Lilly?" I know Christina usually gives her some fruit after her afternoon nap. When she hears 'snack', she gives me a big smile and I want to cry again. I place a soft kiss on her forehead and take her downstairs.

As my flat door quietly clicks shut behind me, my knees start to feel weak, and I slump down in the middle of the hallway. The whole time I was at Phil's I tried to be strong. For him, for Christina, and for Lilly. In the end, all the FMR guys came over and they told stories about Grampy. We laughed and then we cried. Only Phil stayed quiet. I saw the guys watching him, and every so often one or another would talk to him quietly. With Christina and the guys, Phil has all the support he needs. Who do I have?

A sob escapes me and then I start crying. Not just tears rolling down my face, hysterical crying. My whole body is shaking. *My Grampy!* He was always there to build me up when I was down or felt like a loser. He never judged; he was just proud of me. As kids, we loved nothing more than spending time with him. And now I won't ever see him again. His cheeky grin and his warm hugs when you smell his aftershave that he insisted to put on "for the ladies" at the nursing home. Another of my wails echoes through the corridor. My nose is blocked with snot and I can't breathe, but the tears just won't stop.

The chime of the doorbell makes me jump. I ignore it. Whoever is at the door downstairs rings a few more times before giving up.

I get off the floor, and toe my shoes off before grabbing yet another tissue to blow my nose. As I do, a wave of sadness washes over me. A little glimpse of a memory of my Grampy holding out a tissue to me to blow my nose when I was a kid and I am sobbing again.

There's a knock on the door and I freeze.

"Jane, open up."

Ryan! It takes me a few more seconds before I move. I try to wipe my tears away, but I doubt I'll be able to hide that I've just cried my eyes out.

"Jane!" His voice sounds more urgent now. I slowly pull the door open and when the gap is big enough, Ryan pushes through. There is a deep frown on his face. He briefly looks at me, but before I can say anything, he pulls me into his arms.

"I'm so sorry," he whispers into my ear and that's all it takes for the last of my strength to go. I feel safe in his arms, safe enough to let go. My hands grab onto the back of his shirt and I start crying hysterically again.

Ryan lifts me up and carries me to the bedroom. He lays us both down on the bed with me curled up in his arms. His hand strokes my back soothingly, but neither of us says anything for a long time. He just lets me cry until I have no tears left.

The warmth of his embrace, the grief and the crying, it all makes me feel sleepy. My eyes start to droop and although I'm fighting it, it is a lost battle.

I suddenly startle and look around me, disoriented. I am still curled up against Ryan with my head on his chest. The small bedside lamp is on, bringing some light to the otherwise dark room.

I lift my head and find Ryan's eyes on me.

"What are you doing here?" My voice sounds hoarse from all the crying.

"Rob texted me. I tried to call to tell you that I'd come back."

"I switched my phone off when the whole bloomin' village started to text me." Okay, that is an exaggeration, but I just couldn't bear any more messages of condolence. A single tear roles over my cheek and Ryan wipes it away.

"That's okay." He pulls me back against his chest. "How are you feeling?"

"Ry, I... thank you for being here. I needed you so much." Another sob escapes me. I press myself as tight against him as I can.

"You didn't text me, or call me, so I wasn't sure if you wanted me here, but I just didn't like the idea of you being alone."

"I'm sorry, I didn't want to burden you. I wasn't sure if we were at a place where..."

"You weren't sure where we stand?" He tries to help me find my words.

"Kind of." I was also worried I'd scare him away by being needy, I guess. "And you have your own problems with the studio and the trip down south was supposed to help with that, and..."

I'm not making much sense.

"Jane." He puts a finger under my chin to make me look at him. "You're more important than anything else in the world to me. I love you."

My heart starts hammering faster.

"You love me?"

"I love you. And if anything or anyone hurts you, I want to know. I want to be there for you. I want to hold you in my arms and make sure you're safe. I can't take the pain away from losing Grampy, but I can be your strength when you need it. Let me be here for you!"

Chapter 11

Ryan

Jane presses a long kiss against my lips and curls up in my arms. My hand strokes her tense back.

When Rob texted me about what happened, the only thought I had was that I wanted to make sure she was okay. I couldn't get hold of her, so coming back home was a no-brainer. Jamie tried to caution me because we had an important meeting with a big tattoo studio chain scheduled for lunchtime, but I couldn't wait a minute longer.

It was the longest drive of my life and I only relaxed when I finally had her back in my arms. The whole trip to London was meant to help me find somewhere else to open my studio, but the need to be with her, to be there for her, showed me that I don't want to be anywhere but here.

I guess that if I moved Jane could come with me, but she loves it here. Her family is here in Fellside, and so are her friends. Hell, I love it here. *I won't leave without a fight.*

I know what I need to do now. I won't let that bitch Ruth drive me out of the village and away from the woman I love.

"Ry?" Jane draws my attention.

"Yes, Princess?"

"Make love to me."

"Jane, we don't have to. I came here to take care of you."

"Yes." She props herself and looks down at me. "And I need you to make love to me. Please, Ryan. I need to feel you close. I need to feel the connection." Her voice sounds desperate, and her eyes plead with me to give her want she needs.

I cup her face and pull her closer ,until my lips touch hers. I feather mine over hers and a sigh escapes her.

She lets me guide her so she lies flat with me hovering above her. Hearing her whimper and moan when I deepen the kiss has me hard in an instant. Those are officially my favourite sounds in the world.

"I need to feel your skin, Ryan," Jane moans and I know exactly how she feels. My fingers desperately pull on her shirt to get it off. We shed our clothes in between kisses and when I finally lower my naked body on to hers, all my earlier hesitation has disappeared.

I need this and she needs this. Nothing else matters. My lips find hers again and the feel of her tongue dancing with mine causes bolts of pleasure to shoot through me.

"I love you," I whisper as I push into her. The feeling of invading her warm pussy is probably the best feeling in the world. Nothing will ever compare to it. I still once I am fully seated in her. My lips find hers and I get lost in the kiss. She feels so familiar now, I can't imagine ever not having had her in my life.

When we finally break apart to catch our breath, I lock eyes with her and start to move. I link our fingers and place our hands on either side of her head. Never losing eye contact, I slowly withdraw and push back. Sliding my hard cock through her warm wetness feels so good. As my dick moves into her depths, she contracts her muscles and her pussy grips it hard.

"Jane, let's take it slow," I say through clenched teeth.

"No, let's not," she replies before pulling me down into a fierce kiss.

We move in a steady rhythm with neither of us saying anything. Occasionally one of us gasps or moans, but otherwise we are lost in each other's eyes.

Jane's are full of grief, but also trust and, although she hasn't said it yet, I believe there is love in there. Love for me.

"Harder, Ry. Give me more," she moans. I pull back and my aching dick slips from her warmth.

"What are you doing?" she protests. In reply I gently flip her onto her stomach before pushing a cushion underneath her hips. I cover her frame with my body, placing my head next to hers.

"Spread your legs for me, Princess," I whisper into her ear. When she parts for me, my hard cock slides through her wetness until my pelvis meets her mighty fine arse. "Now cross your legs.

"Ry, what?" she tries to turn her head.

"Cross your legs, darling." She finally does as I ask her and I start moving. With her legs crossed, her pussy has an iron grip on my dick and it is almost painful, but so good to pump in and out of her. I slide my hands over hers and lock out fingers.

"Oh, god, oh, wow," she moans. "Harder, Ry."

She is killing me here, but I give her what she needs. I move my hips faster and my cock slides ever deeper. We both groan before settling into a rhythm. I am as close as I can get to her with my body covering hers and I fucking love it.

"Don't stop. I am, I am—" she cries out and then her whole body stiffens, her pussy contracting around my dick. That's enough to make my own orgasm hit me like a freight train. I'm lost in the moment with all my sense being occupied by her. Then I slump over her. My breath is laboured and for a few seconds I don't move.

When I finally roll over, I drag Jane with me so she is cuddled against my chest.

"Ry?"

"Yes, Princess?"

"I quite like it when you call me that now," she muses.

"I do to. What did you want to say, though?"

She turns in my arms and looks up at me. One of her hands is placed over my scar; the other gently cups my jaw.

"I love you too."

It feels like an eternity before all the mourners have taken their seats. The family will follow the coffin into the crematorium and so we are all waiting outside in the rain. Jane insisted that I walk with her, and her parents didn't seem to mind.

We are sharing an umbrella, and she is curled up at my side. She's not crying, but she looks pale and like a shadow of herself. When we finally move into the crematorium she sways a little and I put my arm around her waist to keep her stable.

Her parents, her aunt and uncle lead the procession, followed by Phil and Christina, and then me and Jane. Phil cradles Lilly to his chest. He refused to leave her with anyone else and insisted she needed to stay with him.

When we get to the front we take our seats and the officiant starts the service. I find it difficult to follow the words of the readings because my whole focus is on Jane and what she could possibly need. I have never felt so protective of someone before.

She sits stiffly next to me fidgeting with her hands, and I get the sense she would prefer to get up and run away than stay here any longer. Her mum asked her to do a reading, but she refused. They almost had an argument when her mother kept insisting that's what people would expect, Jane shouting back that she doesn't fucking care what people want. Yes, she said 'fuck.'

"And now, Peter's grandson Philip wants to say a few words about his grandfather."

"Grampy," Phil corrects him as he steps up to the small lectern. He still has Lilly in his arms, her head resting against his shoulder as if she knows that he needs the happiness she gives him to get him through this day.

Phil has always looked like the baby of the FMR group but has aged in the last few days. Although he is nearing 34, you would have been forgiven to assume that he's in his mid-twenties. But now he carries a dark look on his face and grief seems to have added years in a single night.

"Grampy—Grampy was the best. Over the last week people have come up to me to tell me all about the wonderful things he has done. But I don't need people telling me all these great stories about him, like that he still holds the record for most goals scored for the local football team. Or the workers' protest he led when the mines were shut down." He swallows hard and briefly wipes his hand over his red-rimmed eyes.

"The moments I remember are him playing hide and seek with us and pretending he couldn't see our toes peeking out underneath the curtain. Or me visiting him in the nursing home, sitting on the grass eating ice cream and listening to him tell me about all the ladies he had been flirting with." His voice is shaky. Jane gives a little sob from next to me.

“I don’t need people telling me that at least he died in his sleep and didn't have to suffer. I’ll still miss him and nothing will take that away.” Phil almost sounds angry now. Lilly wipes a tear away from his face. “That’s the Grampy I know and I'll always remember. I will miss him every day. I’ll miss him whenever something big happens in my life because he can’t be there with us. I'll miss him when I have ice cream with my daughter Lilly because I know he would have loved to be there with us. We’ll miss you, Grampy.” He ends in a whisper and steps away from the microphone. Christina rushes to him and Lilly and they hug.

Jane is shaking next to me from crying and I gently pull her into my arms. I wish I could take that pain away from her but I can't and that's killing me.

Chapter 12

Jane

The sun hits my face when I step outside my parents' house.

"Hey!" I draw Phil's attention to me. He is sitting on the steps to the entrance feeding Lilly some cake.

"Hey," he replies quietly. The cold from the stairs seeps through the thin material of my skirt when I take a seat next to him. "How are you holding up?"

"Atty, cake!" Lilly shouts and holds up a piece of Victoria sponge. Crumbs cover the front of her little jacket. I give her a smile which is enough for her to stuff another piece in her mouth.

"I'm okay. How are you?" Phil replies.

"Same," and with 'Same' I mean I'm not okay, just like Phil's not okay.

"I want to leave. I can't talk with any of these strangers anymore," he says, his eyes gazing into the distance.

"Well, why are we still here then? Let's go."

"Christina said that mum and the people would expect us to hang around."

"Fuck the people. And with all due respect, fuck mum." Phil whips his head around.

"Jane!" he admonishes me, but there is a grin on his face. The first smile I have seen from him since it all happened.

"Fuck," Lilly giggles. *Oh shit.*

"Don't say that, Lilly. That is a mummy word," Phil chuckles. "Christina swears a lot so we had to find a way to not have Lilly copy her," he explains for my benefit.

"Let's go, Phil. Let's hang out with our friends rather than these people." A lot of the guests are acquaintances of our parents. These are all strangers who didn't really know Grampy.

"Okay, sure." He gets of the stairs and walks up to the entrance door. Before he pushes it open he turns to me. "You've changed, Jane. Ryan is good for you. I'm glad you two found each other."

Me and you both.

Ryan lifts me up onto the chest of drawers, just like he did when we slept together for the first time. His lips are needy, and he kisses me deeply.

It's been two weeks since Grampy's funeral and we are slowly falling back into our routine. One day you think you'll never be able to move on, the next you catch yourself whistling along to a tune, and when you realise what you're doing you feel angry with yourself because you forgot about your grief for a moment. But in the end, we have to live our lives, and I know Grampy would have wanted us to. But that doesn't mean I've stopped thinking of him every single day.

"Ry, what if a client comes in?" I protest with a laugh.

"I have no appointments until two," he replies with a groan before sliding his lips up and down my neck. I had only planned to pop by and bring him a coffee, but I might get a lot more.

"What about someone who doesn't have an appointment?" a voice booms through the studio.

"Fuck, mate, shit timing," Ryan greets Nick, who is leaning against the wall with a cocky smile on his lips.

“Hey, I am here on an important mission and you are going to apologise for that comment,” he chuckles before pushing of the wall and taking a seat on the little stool next to the tattoo chair.

“What’s this mission of yours then?” Ryan, still standing between my legs, turns his back to me and crosses his arms in front of his chest. I can’t resist sliding my arms around him and leaning my chin against his shoulder.

“What if I told you that Charlotte and I have the solution to your problem?”

“What problem?” Ryan asks. I don’t need to see his face to know that he is frowning at Nick’s cryptic declaration.

“This,” Nick points around the shop.

“You’re testing my patience, spit it out.”

“Fine, you have no flair for the dramatic,” Nick laughs again. “Charlotte and I spoke yesterday. Charlotte wants to cut back on her hours and so does Henry, her partner. So, we reckon the simplest solution would be for Charlotte to shut down the studio at the back of the gallery for a few years, giving them both the chance to concentrate on the gallery itself. They’ll sell for local artists, but won’t offer art classes or similar.”

“Okay?”

“Well, Charlotte owns the building, so she can do with it what she wants. Want to rent the workshop? It is at least as big as this place and it has Charlotte's old flat above it, which has been empty since she moved in with me. It's only accessible via the the studio, so we couldn't rent it out."

I feel Ryan's muscles tighten under my fingers.

"Are you serious?" he asks.

"Of course. We want someone we can trust in the place. Someone we know will work well with the gallery and we can rely on. And don't worry, if any of the snobs complain about it, Henry will tell them where to go to." I've met Henry a few times. He followed Charlotte up here with his husband and he is flamboyant and sassy and a total sweetheart.

"Mate, I don't—" Ryan rubs his face and his whole body seems to relax. He had been making light of the impending closure of the studio, but I know he has been worried. He has been adamant that he wants to stay in Fellside. I mean, I would have moved with him; it's not like I have a job that is keeping me here. But I would have missed the village, my brother, Christina, Lilly and the whole crazy FMR brood. Luckily Ryan loves it here too. Last time we talked he was considering applying for a job with the studio in Penrith. It wouldn't have been his and it would have involved an hour's commute but he assured me it would have been worth it.

Nick gives us a grin. “Glad I interrupted your canoodling now?”

“Not quite, but still some of the best news I’ve had in a while.” Ryan steps out from between my legs and gives Nick a hug.

“Wow, be careful with your boner,” Nick exclaims mockingly.

“Twat! I thought Rob was the joker. You’ve spent too much time with him,” Ryan laughs. “But, seriously mate, I’m not sure how to thank you.”

“Don’t thank me, thank Charlotte and Henry. Actually, don’t thank them either, because you are doing us a favour by taking it really. This way we don’t have to rent it to someone we don’t know and have no clue if they can be trusted.” He slaps Ryan on the back. “Charlotte would have told you herself, but she had an appointment and we wanted you to know as soon as possible.”

“I really appreciate it.”

“Well, I’ll leave you, but why don’t you both come over for dinner tomorrow and we can discuss details? The guys can help to move you.”

After walking Nick to the exit and thanking him one more time, Ryan comes back to the studio.

“Can you fucking believe it?” he screams with joy. I giggle and jump of the chest of drawers.

"Nope, but there is nothing Ruth can do now. You're staying!"

"I'm staying, and where do you think you're going?" In one swift move I am hoisted into the air and plonked back onto the chest of drawers. "I wasn't done kissing you," he mumbles before sucking my bottom lip into his mouth.

"Well, Mister, I only came to drop off the coffee. I need to job hunt, remember?" I am planning to drop off CVs in some local shops and restaurants. Not what I had hoped for, but I have no other plan.

"Tonight, you're mine. I'll make you come so often that you'll be hoarse from screaming tomorrow."

"I'll hold you to that." I pull him close for a long kiss before cutting it off just when his hands start exploring my body again. I wiggle from his embrace with a laugh and grab my bag.

"Make sure you don't come home too late or I might start without you." I wink at him but can feel the heat in my cheeks.

"Tease," he shouts after me, but his voice his laced with humour. I love this man. How could I ever have thought I hated him?

Epilogue

Ryan

There is a loud noise above me. I briefly lift the tattoo gun from the young woman's arm. She asked for a rose and I am almost done, but I would prefer to stop right now because I know my princess needs me. A door slams shut and that confirms what I had been dreading: Jane is in the flat upstairs and she has had another dreadful day at work.

For the last six months she has worked as a bartender in one of the local pubs and she hates it. Like, hates it with a passion. Although she only does day shifts, she constantly gets hit on by guys, which in return makes me hate her job as well. I have offered a number of times for her to move in with me, give up the job and take her time to find what brings her joy. But she refuses.

Since moving the tattoo studio to the back of the gallery, business is booming, and I make enough for her to take a few months off. But so far, my pleading has fallen on deaf ears. Instead, she suffers through a job she despises.

Another bang makes me jump, which is not a great thing when I am holding a needle that does six thousand strokes a minute.

"I think her majesty is having a bad day," Leanne comments from her corner. She is still calling Jane 'her majesty,' but it has become a cheeky nickname now.

"I'm done here, would you be able to do the bill for me, please?" I ask Leanne and she nods. I give the customer instructions on how to take care of her new tattoo and then snap my rubber gloves off.

The stairs to the flat are in reception. I had to cordon them off with a red velvet rope so customers wouldn't venture upstairs. For some reason people do not respect a sign saying PRIVATE, but they do respect the rope. I unhook it before putting it in place again once I have stepped through it.

There is another bang as I approach the flat door followed by a loud, "Poppycock!"

"Princess, what are you doing?" I ask when I find her sitting on the floor with pieces of wood surrounding her.

"I bought you a coffee table so I'm putting it together," she replies reaching for another wooden peg and what looks to be a meat tenderiser.

"That's not a hammer," I chuckle.

"No, I couldn't find one but this will do." As she grabs it her knuckles turn white because she's holding it so tightly. "See?" she says and smashes the metal meat tenderiser on the tiny wooden peg. The force behind her hit is so strong that the peg disappears completely into the table top, creating a split in the surrounding wood.

"Fuck," she exclaims and throws the tool on the floor.

Sitting down next to her, I pull her into my lap. "What happened at work?"

"Nothing."

"Not true."

"Just the same shit as every day," she leans her head against my shoulder. I have been a bad influence on her when it comes to swearing.

"Quit!"

"I can't quit." A tear trickles down her cheek. "I need the money."

"No, you don't. Give up your flat, move in here with me. Take a few months to get yourself sorted."

"You make it sound so easy." She sighs and places a small kiss on my lips.

"It is that easy," I reply. "I also found this," I pick up the envelope I had dropped on the floor next to us and hold it out to her.

"What's that?"

"Open it." I give her an encouraging smile. I don't care what she does in life as long as what she chooses gives her some joy. I love my job and I couldn't imagine doing anything else. As Charlotte owns this place, Ruth can't touch me. Besides, Alex's granny managed to get her voted from the WI leadership and when she tried to petition the council to stop me opening the studio in the gallery, the new council leader told her in clear terms that she could fuck off. Lucky for me he is a decent guy and not easily swayed by empty threats. All we need now is for Jane to also find what makes her happy.

"That's an application to university. And the course is offered here, in Fellside," I explain. The University of Cumbria has a small campus in our village.

"Ry, I can't afford that." I see longing in her eyes.

"Princess, for once in your life let someone else take care of you. You have been working since you were eighteen. It's time to do something for yourself and let me support you with that."

"I do have enough savings to pay for the course fee," she mumbles whilst thumbing through the brochure.

"Jane, look at me." Her eyes find mine. "Move in with me. Let me support you whilst you do this."

"Okay," she finally whispers.

"What?" I have heard her, but I need her to say it out loud.

"Okay." She grins and sniffles at the same time.

"Fuck, yes," I shout and pull my phone from my pocket. "Call your boss and quit."

"What? No, I'll still need to do some shifts to pay for food and utilities and—"

"Call. Your. Boss. And. Quit." I hold out my phone to her. "You can get some shift work with one of the girls or at Tommy's hotel or cover my reception. Hell, anything is better than that place. Please, Jane." We look at each other for a long minute before she finally takes my mobile.

"Yeah, hi, is John there?" she asks when someone answers the phone on the other end.

I take a deep breath before getting off the floor. I pick up the pieces of wood of what was supposed to be my new coffee table. Maybe Alex can rescue it for us. I'm starting to feel hungry, so I grab the frozen lasagne from the freezer and pop it into the oven when soft hands slide around my waist.

"Thank you," Jane whispers as I pull her in my arms.

"I love you, Princess, and all I care about is that you're happy."

"I'm very happy."

"Well, then I'm doing my job right." She grins and pulls me down for a kiss. What starts out slow turns steamy in a mere moment.

"Wait," she gently pushes me from her. "I love you too, Ryan."

I turn the oven off again. Fuck the lasagne! Now I am hungry for her.

The End

READ ON FOR AN EXCLUSIVE FAREWELL BONUS CHAPTER

Farewell Fellside

Dani Elias

Ryan

Chaos greets me as I enter the cottage. There are boxes everywhere. Boxes marked Christmas. It's August.

Jane and I moved into the cottage from the small flat above the tattoo studio a few months ago. We just wanted more space and the studio was doing so well, we could afford it. We turned the flat into an arts centre and Jane is offering classes again with help from Charlotte.

"Princess?" I call out, dropping my helmet on the side table beneath the coat hangers and slide my jacket on the hook above it. I

"I'm in the living room," Jane replies.

"What's going on?" I chuckle. She's on the living room floor, surrounded by ribbon and wrapping paper.

"I'm wrapping Max's birthday presents."

"And you needed the Christmas decorations because...?"

"The box with the wrapping material was underneath the Christmas deco boxes in the cupboard in the hall."

"Okay, great. Now, how many gifts are you wrapping?" I point to the ten different rolls of wrapping paper.

"I couldn't decide which one," she grins sheepishly.

"You know he's turning seven. He couldn't care less what paper you use." I place a soft kiss on her cheek.

"I know but I care," she is defiant.

"You smell amazing," I groan and slide my lips over her throat down to the little tattoo on her shoulder. I took her tattoo virginity two months ago and it turns me on to see her inked.

"Ry!" she protests with a giggle. "I smell no different to usual and we're already late."

"You always smell delicious." I don't give up easily, especially when she melts into my embrace rather than removing herself. I find the zip on the back of her dress and slowly draw it down.

"Ryan," she protests but then straddles my lap and pulls me into a passionate kiss. I just can't get enough of her. If anything, I need her more now than ever.

I pull her dress over her head and kiss my way to her bra. She unclips it at the back and drops it to the floor, giving me access to her pebbled nipples. When I close my lips around one, she whimpers. I know how much she loves it.

"More, Ryan, I need more. And I need it quick because we're late," she demands, making me laugh out loud.

"Your wish is my command!" I chuckle. I lay her down on the floor and kiss my way to her knickers, slowly peeling them off.

"We don't have time for this," she giggles and reaches for the buttons on my jeans.

"We'll make time for it." I move lower and lick along the seam of her pussy. And then another. Her hands find their way into my short hair and she pulls me down. I love it when she demands what she needs. I push two fingers into her warm cunt and at the same time draw small circles around her clit with the tip of my tongue. The taste is so uniquely her, it gets my aching cock even harder. I give her exactly what she wants and it doesn't take much for her to scream my name.

Her back arches and her fingernails dig into my scalp as her orgasm races through her. When her body collapses back on the floor I climb over her. Our eyes are locked as she frees my dick and pushes my jeans over my arse. I don't even bother taking them off. I just slide into her and groan. However, before I can move Jane pushes me backwards making me roll onto my back with her straddling me. I land on top of a roll of wrapping paper that flattens underneath me.

She sinks a little lower on my cock. *Fuck! I love when she rides me*. Looking up at her as she circles her hips with her tits swaying is my favourite sight.

"You're in charge, Princess," I say and slide my hands over her hips. She starts to roll her hips slowly alternating with moving up and down. Her eyes are closed and her lips are parted. I reach out and swipe my thumb over her bottom lip. She opens up and sucks it into her mouth. As she circles her tongue around the tip of my thumb, she locks eyes with me. They are full of lust and love.

She moves faster and I thrust upwards every time she lowers herself. I am so close, but I need her to come first. I withdraw my thumb from her mouth and place it on her clit. I rub the little nub, causing Jane to cry out in pleasure. Just when I think I can't hold it any longer, she explodes and I follow her over the edge. She slows her movements before collapsing onto my chest.

Eventually she lifts her head and kisses me. "That was so worth being late!"

Jane squeezes my jacket tightly, but I can't hear what she's saying over the wind. I don't need to. She's confused about where we're going, as I just drove past the turning to Chris's farm. Yup, we are going to be super late, but there's something I need to do first.

It's another fifteen minutes before we arrive at the entrance to Castlerigg Stone Circle.

"What're we doing here?" Jane asks as she pulls her helmet off.

"You'll see!" I grin and get off the bike. I link our fingers and drag her towards the stone circle. I was hoping there would be no one around but I can see a small group of people assembled. *Please leave, please leave!*

As we get closer I can see that it is a couple with their kids. The children are clearly bored of looking at large stones, and I can hear them whining. The August sun beats down on us and it is a scorcher of a day. When I hear the parents promising their kids an ice cream I "helpfully" point out that they can buy them at the climbing centre nearby. That's enough for the kids to run towards the car with their parents following them, but not before giving me an evil look. Hey, I do what I have to do.

"Come here," I pull Jane to the centre of the circle.

"Ry, what are we doing here?"

"I love you," I blurt out.

"I love you too, but—"

"Let me say this, Jane. I love you. I love you more than anyone or anything in my life before. I need you to know that you are my forever. I need the world to know that you are my forever. Will you marry me?" She gasps.

Jane and I have been together for less than two years and I hadn't really thought about marriage. That's until she went to London for a course last week. I woke up in the middle of the night, reaching for her, and when she wasn't next to me I panicked. The thought of not having her in my life was the most painful feeling I had ever experienced. I knew there and then that I wanted to say it out loud, in front of our friends, that I am hers forever. And I needed to know that she felt the same.

My heart is racing and my hand trembles as I hold out the ring,

"Ry, we've never spoken about this. We don't have to."

"I know, Princess. But that doesn't change the fact that I know I want to be with you for the rest of my life."

"Are you sure?" She sniffles and a small tear trickles down her cheek.

"One million percent."

"Then yes, I'll marry you." I pull her into my arms and kiss her long and hard before sliding the engagement ring on her finger.

I didn't know I could love her more, but what I feel in this moment beats every feeling I have ever had before.

Phil

Lilly wiggles in my arms.

"Hang on, baby girl," I chuckle as I carry her into the farm cottage.

"We are here, sorry we are late," Christina calls out, but it is quiet in the house. Too quiet, considering that all the FMR guys and their partners and children are supposed to be here.

"Hey, you're the first ones," Suzie smiles at us as we walk into the kitchen.

"How? We're thirty minutes late," I reply and greet Suzie with a quick kiss on her cheek.

"Aunty Sue!" Lilly calls out.

"Hey, Lilly. " She tickles my two-year-old. "Tommy had an emergency at the hotel and everyone else texted to say they are running late. But it's not an issue, because Chris took Max out on the quad bike to the sheep and they are not back yet either," she sighs.

Christina gives her a hug and we offer to help her get the food ready for Max's birthday party. I put Lilly in the playpen and tell her to read a story to Baby Emma, who is crawling around in it. Of course, my baby girl can't read yet, but she loves to pretend she can.

Suzie sends me outside to set up the large tables. I'm about to put one of the parasols up when I hear the distinct noise of quad bikes approaching. As the sound gets louder, I can see Chris on his quad with Max in front of him.

"Happy birthday, Max," I call out as the little squirt runs towards me.

"Thank you, Uncle Bambi," he grins. A while ago he heard Christina call me Bambi, and now I'm Uncle Bambi to him.

"Are you excited for your birthday party?"

"Yes! But we're late because Dad and I were chasing the sheep and the little buggers were lost on a steep slope."

"Max! Don't let your mum hear you say that," Chris says, wincing. Max gives him a thumbs up and runs off into the house.

"So, I take it he still loves helping you with the farm work."

"He would give up school and work fulltime with me if he could," Chris chuckles as Suzie joins us with a tray of glasses. She places them on a table before pulling me into a tight hug. *What's happening?*

"Congratulations," she whispers before releasing me. *Christina!*

"I think I need to have a word with my wife! But, thank you," I chuckle before heading back indoors. I find Christina in the kitchen chopping salad.

"What did we say?" I ask as I slide my arms around her waist. "We would not steal Max's thunder!"

"He'll still get plenty of attention," Christina whispers and leans back against me. Placing her hand over mine, she slides them both down onto her belly, where our new baby is growing. Peter. We found out yesterday that it's a boy. By the time we got home from the doctor's appointment, we had agreed to name him Peter. After Grampy.

I pull Christina closer. It's been over a year since he died, but I still miss him all the time. Knowing that my son will never meet him makes me sad. But then I remind myself that the last thing Grampy would have wanted was for me not to live and enjoy my life.

I have an amazing wife, a beautiful daughter, and will also soon have a son. I have the best friends a man can hope for and I love my life in Fellside. The best I can do to honour Grampy is to enjoy every minute.

"You know that we're getting to the second trimester," Christina whispers.

"Yes?"

"Remember what happened last time?" She flashes me a big grin.

"Uh oh." When Christina was pregnant with Lilly, her libido when through the roof. I mean, I was running the risk of chafing my dick because the amount of times she demanded sex.

"Exactly." She winks. "I'm feeling it already." She wiggles her arse against my crotch. I know she's playing with me but I also know that I might need to get Jane to babysit Lilly a few times.

"Behave," I whisper and nip her earlobe. "I love you, Christina."

"Oh Bambi, I'm glad too that I hunted you down." That little minx.

Chris

I pull Suzie in my arms. "What was that about?"

"Phil and Christina are expecting a baby boy." She grins at me.

"Jeez, I swear between the eight of us, we're raising the next generation of mountain rescuers."

"That's not a bad thing! You know Max will join as soon as we'll let him. He's already asked me if he can join the juniors."

"He asked me too. I guessed you'd said no, which is why he was trying his luck with me." I reply with a grin.

"No, I told him he can. I think he just wanted your opinion as well. He respects you, Chris." I swallow hard.

"I know." It's still overwhelming to me how Max accepted me and trusted me with his life despite everything he'd been through. We all moved past the kidnap attempt by Lucas, but I will never forget the fear I felt when I saw the car go over the edge of the hill road. A small part of me died on that day.

"Hey, we're here and we're safe." Suzie must know what I'm thinking, because she pulls me to her and places a soft kiss on my lips. We all went through therapy together and we learned to bring each other back from the dark thoughts that still invade our lives sometimes.

"Yes, we are." I hug her tightly. It was two years ago to the day that she opened up to me and allowed me to become part of her family. A little less than a year ago, baby Emma joined us and I seem to have ended up in one of these picture-perfect family lives. I sometimes worry I 'll wake up and it all was just a dream, but then I kiss Suzie and I know it's my reality.

"Right, should I fire up the barbecue?"

"Might as well, surely the others will be here soon." Suzie laughs before walking towards the house.

"Suz," I call her attention. She swings around, her blonde hair flying behind her. "I love you."

She walks towards me and smashes her lips to mine.

"I love you too. And tonight, I'll show you how much." I let out a groan when she walks away with a pronounced swing to her hips. She's killing me.

Rob

Olivia's gentle touch drives me wild.

"Please, Rob, move faster, we're late."

"Oh, if you are still thinking about a kid's birthday I must be doing something wrong." I thrust hard and Olivia lets out a loud moan. "Baby, look at me," I demand and Olivia opens her eyes. "Touch your clit, make yourself come."

She likes it when I talk to her like this.

"Yes," she hisses and her fingers reach between us. When she starts rubbing her little swollen nob, her breathing exhilarates and it doesn't take long for her to scream out as her orgasm hits her. I follow closely behind. Placing a soft kiss on her lips, I roll off her. I'm about to pull her in my arms when she stuffs a pillow under her bum and lifts her feet in the air.

"What are you doing?" I laugh.

"Your baby juice is going to stay in there as long as it takes for one of them to make it to my egg. I have enough of it. This needs to happen." She crosses her arms in front of her chest and stares at the ceiling.

"Baby, you heard the doctor. We're both healthy, we just need to be patient."

"Yup, patient, but we can help it along."

"I'm not sure that's how it works." I point at her legs which she is stretching towards the ceiling.

"Well, that's how they do it in the movies."

"Oh, yeah, because what we see on TV is always right," I chuckle and place a kiss on her forehead. She finally drops her legs, rolls over and cuddles into my chest.

"I want a baby, Rob."

"I know, and we'll have one. We've only been trying for a few months."

"You're right," she sighs.

"Hey, where're you going?" I ask when she jumps from the bed.

"We're late for Max's birthday. Let's go and have some cake and when we get back, you can put more of your baby juice in me."

"Can you stop calling it that?" I shout after her. I love this crazy woman. After our engagement last year we decided to get married in the spring and then start trying for a baby. She is impatient and even made us go and see a doctor when it didn't happen after one month, but he tested us and just told her to give it time.

The thought of having a tiny human that we created together does make me feel giddy. But I also know that if it were never to happen—not that we need to worry about that at this stage—I would still be the happiest man in the world just because I have my best friend at my side every day.

"Rob," Olivia steps back into the bedroom covered by just a towel. "I love you; you know that right?"

"Hey, I'm a lovable person," I chuckle.

"Don't joke. I love you, Rob. I know I shouldn't think this because we just started, but if it is not meant to be, I want you to know that I love you and nothing will change that."

"I love you too. Let's get ready and I'll give you more of my... squirty cream later."

"Ewww, now you've made it weird." she laughs before kissing me deeply. This is as perfect as it gets.

Tommy

"Ella! Ella!" I shout as I rip open the flat door. The sound of the fire alarm is almost deafening. My heart is beating like a jackhammer. My rational mind tells me that we have fire alarms in the hotel all the time. We actually had a few in the last three months, and almost always they are set off by guests smoking in their room or someone taking a shower so hot that the steam sets it off. But never before did I have my wife and new born in the building.

"Tommy?" Ella is trying to pull her jeans over her hips.

"What are you doing? It's a fire alarm. We need to get out." I sound almost hysterical. What has happened to me? I have done so many evacuations in my life and I am usually calm and collected.

"I was in the shower. I need to at least get dressed." She shrugs. I search the room for my baby girl.

"Nicky's in the bedroom," she shouts over the fire alarm, desperately trying to get her leg into the trousers. I rush past her and see Nicky crying her eyes out in her crib, scared of the noise. I gently lift her from her bed and place her against my shoulder, grabbing the nappy bag from the changing table and a blanket before rejoining Ella.

"I have her carrier, let's just put her in it when we get out," she says and I see her grab my car keys on the way out of the flat. In the corridor the alarm is even louder. So loud, I can barely hear Nicky's cries over it. On autopilot we move down the empty stairs. Hopefully by now Sheila will have evacuated the whole hotel. I can't smell any smoke and I try to convince myself this is due to there being no fire. Nevertheless, we walk as fast as we can.

We see a sea of confused looking people as we step through the fire exit.. We're fully booked today and have two events on; there was bound to be a lot of people out there.

In the distance I see the blue lights of the approaching fire engine. Our fire alarm is automatically linked to the fire station, which could be a lifesaver if we have a real fire but can be a pain in the arse if there isn't a fire and no need for them to attend.

"Let's put her in the car," Ella pulls me from my thoughts. I follow her to my BMW, parked under the trees. I calm Nicky down whilst Ella clicks the carrier in its place. All the excitement has tired our one-month-old baby out and she falls asleep quickly. She loves sleeping in my arms. I can't help grinning to myself like the proud dad I am.

"I take it the baby whisperer has done it again. Did she fall asleep?" Ella muses. I wink at her before carefully placing Nicky in her carrier and closing the car door so that the noise from all the people doesn't wake her.

"Let me check on Sheila," I say.

"Go. I'll text Suzie that we'll be late." I like her optimism, but if there is a fire I'm not sure I'll be able to leave. I pull her into my arms and press my lips against hers. Feeling her, tasting her, finally calms me down.

"That scared me," I whisper against her lips.

"Me too," she admits before kissing me again.

"Sorry, boss." John steps up to us. He finished his apprenticeship a few months ago and has been wearing his receptionist uniform with pride ever since.

"Is everything okay, John?"

"Yes, Sheila asked me tell you it was Mr Wilkinson who was smoking again."

I frown. "The fire chief won't be happy." This is the third time in as many months that the fire brigade has been called out because of a regular, Mr Wilkinson, who just doesn't want to get it into his head that he can't smoke in the rooms.

"Yeah, he's having it out with Sheila at the moment." John chuckles.

"Maybe I should help—" Ella stops me with her hand on my arm.

"Let Sheila deal with it. She knows what she's doing."

I grin. Every so often I need a reminder that I don't have to do everything myself anymore.

"You're right, let's go to Max's birthday party."

Dan

By the time we get to Chris and Suzie's farm most of the others are already there, but I can't see Alex anywhere, or Nick. The rest of the team, their partners and kids are all in the back garden.

"Sorry we're late," I greet Chris and Tommy who are standing by the barbecue. "This little one didn't want to leave the house." Maisie Mouse had a major tantrum earlier when we tried to get her ready for the birthday party. I'm not sure why or what was going on but it took us a while to get her dressed and into the car. She's now curled up in my arms, sulking.

Maisie is still adjusting to sharing the attention with her new little baby sister Anna. She loves playing with Anna, and Rose is amazing in making sure Maisie feels involved, but every so often she needs to demand our full attention.

"Hey, Maisie, don't you want some cake?" Tommy asks. rocking his tiny baby in his arms. It reminds me of Maisie when she came to me less than two years ago. I was so scared to fail as a dad.

At the words "cake" I can feel her lift her head, but the minute I look at her she curls up again pretending she hasn't heard it. Chris chuckles.

"That's a shame 'cause Max was so looking forward to you sitting with him and eating chocolate cake," Chris tries again.

"Maks!" Maisie shouts. She loves Max and he loves looking after her. He sees himself as the big brother to all the babies in the group. Rose and Emma have a bet going on about which baby girl he will date when he is older; Lilly or Maisie, Anna or Nicky. Phil, Tommy and I have agreed that the best option is none of them.

"Want to go and see Max?" Rose asks from my side and holds out her hands to Maisie. Suddenly all her sulking and bad moods are a thing of the past and she squeaks with joy as I pass her to Rose. Together they head to the table where Max is sitting with his mum and Olivia, who is rocking Anna.

"How's it going with the new baby?" Tommy asks.

"Mate, she's an angel. She, Maisie and Rose are the best thing that ever happened to me." I grin and look over to the three loves of my life.

"We're all bloody lucky," Alex says from behind me.

"His excuse for being late is a cranky child, what's yours for?" Chris slaps Alex on the shoulder in greeting.

"Adult fun; otherwise, I would have been the cranky one," he chuckles and wiggles his eyebrows.

"Damn, you and Emma have been married for two years now and you are still like bunnies in heat."

"And you know what the best thing is? We don't have kids so we can shag all day any day," he chuckles.

I mean, he's not wrong. Until Maisie started to sleep through the night, squeezing in some alone time was tough, but I have learned to make do with little sleep. Now it's getting easier. A small smile creeps over my face when I remember how Rose called out my name last night. Sometimes I wish I hadn't wasted so many years and told Rose how I felt when we were younger. But then I realise that this would mean Maisie Mouse wouldn't be in my life and the thought breaks my heart. No, it all was meant to happen the way it did. I strongly believe in that.

"Where's Nick?" Alex asks.

"Also late." Chris replies and I excuse myself.

When I get to the table where my two girls are sitting, I pull Rose up and into my arms. I kiss her long and hard.

"What's that for?"

"I love you. Is that reason enough?"

"More than enough. I love you too," she whispers.

"Dada, kiss," Maisie grins at me from the bench. I place a soft kiss on her forehead. Yes, this was definitely meant to be.

Nick

My heart's racing, and I swallow hard as I walk through Chris' cottage. Charlotte has a hand on my back and I draw strength from it. I am scared, excited, and happy, and a bit scared again. I feel like crying with happiness, but I am also full of fear that any minute someone will take my happiness away from me.

"Hi, everyone," I say as I step out into the sunshine. Everyone waves at me and then there's a stunned silence before all hell breaks loose.

Charlotte and I are swarmed and all the different questions thrown our way become just noise.

"Everyone, this is Jack," I introduce the little baby boy in my arms.

Charlotte and I had almost given up on creating our own family. We knew that Charlotte was not able to get pregnant so early on we decided to adopt a child. We made the difficult decision to apply to adopt a baby, a process that takes a lot longer and is a lot trickier than adopting an older child. Charlotte was desperate to be a mother and she wanted to experience motherhood as much as she could, even if she was not able to carry the baby herself.

We were promised a baby eighteen months ago and then a few weeks before we were supposed to collect the little girl, her mum decided against adoption. It nearly broke Charlotte, but we ploughed on. We had almost given up hope when we received another letter confirming that we had been chosen to adopt Jack. We didn't tell anyone. And we didn't believe it would happen until we collected him from the hospital in London two days ago. We don't know much about his parents, only that they don't want to be part of his life. But Charlotte and I have enough love to give this little boy, he will not miss anything.

Charlotte lifts the baby from my arms gently and holds him against her chest. She hasn't stopped smiling since we collected him, and seeing my wife this happy gives me joy I can't describe.

Everyone follows Charlotte to one of the tables where she takes a seat in the shade to protect Jack from the sun. I watch them from a distance and I can feel fear grow in me again. I take a deep breath and step away. I walk around the building and find a lone tree where I take a seat in the damp grass.

I'm not sure how long I am sitting there when a voice calls out to me.

"What are you doing here?" Alex strolls over to me.

"I... I just needed a minute."

He looks back at the house and then drops on the floor next to me.

"Jack's cute."

"Thanks," I reply. Alex and I have come a long way. I think back when we were almost sworn enemies... And now he is truly one of my best friends.

"So, why're you sitting here all alone?"

"Charlotte and I have been so busy, waiting and hoping and preparing for Jack that I had no time to even think what it means to have a child. And then when I picked him up for the first time, when they handed him over in the hospital, it hit me. What if I'm shit at this?"

"At being a father?"

"Yes!"

"Why would you be shit at it?" He kicks a stone with his foot.

"We both know that I was an arsehole in the past."

"Nick, none of us can change our past. Look at me and Rob. We shagged our way through the village. I hate the person I was back then."

"But you never hurt anyone. What if I do or say something that hurts Charlotte or Jack?"

"I don't believe that. Like I said, none of us can change our past, but we can learn from it. And I think we all learned from it and have grown as people. I trust you with my life, Nick. I trust all of the guys with my life. Jack is lucky to have you and Charlotte to take care of him. And I'll tell you something else: the fact that you're sitting here, worrying about what kind of father you will be, tells me you'll be a great one."

"Nick?" Charlotte calls as she walks around the corner of the cottage. Alex and I both get up from the floor and wipe the dirt from our jeans.

"You've got this, mate," Alex says before walking away.

Charlotte frowns when she steps up to me.

"What's wrong?" she asks.

"Nothing. I just had a little wobble. Where's Jack?" I reply and slide my arms around her waist.

"Olivia and Rob are playing with him. What are you worried about?"

"If I'll be a good dad."

"Nick!" She takes a step back and pulls her phone from her back pocket. "Look at this!" She holds out her phone and, on the screen, I can see a photo of me with Jack. She must have taken it yesterday. I'm asleep, and so is Jack; he is curled up on my chest and my hand is protectively on his back.

"Or this." She swipes her thumb over her phone and holds out another photo. It's me bathing Jack.

"Or this one." There is a tear in her eyes when she holds out the last photo. It's me standing over his crib watching him sleep. I stood there for an hour yesterday. I just couldn't make myself leave.

Charlotte cups my face. "You are an incredible man and you will be an even more incredible father." She says it with so much conviction.

"How do you know?"

"Because I love you and I have seen how fiercely you fight for those who you love."

"I love you too, Charlotte." I kiss her gently.

Alex

Just as the birthday boy is blowing out his candles, everyone's phones ring with a notification. I pull ming from my pocket and see that it is an alert from FMR for us to assemble for a mission.

"Fuck!" Ryan says. He and Jane turned up halfway through lunch with their own happy story to tell.

"Fuck!" little Lilly copies him.

This is followed by a chorus of "Ry!" from all the mothers around the table. Tommy steps away to make a call, I assume to the FMR call centre to find out the details of the mission.

"Emms." I grab my wife's hand and pull her with me into the kitchen.

"Rescue?" she asks. She has seen me receive these messages often enough to know what it means.

"Yup." I press a gentle kiss under her ear and then another one a little lower and the I kiss my way along her jaw.

"Alex!" she giggles but pulls me closer. Hm, the things I would like to do to her. Meeting Emma has been the best thing that ever happened to me. In the last four years, we have explored the world together and enjoyed life to the fullest. She opened my eyes to new experiences I never realised that I had I missed out on before meeting her.

"I'm going to take the car, if you can't get a lift back with one of the others, let me know and I'll pick you up when we are finished," I mumble against her neck as I brush my lips over it.

"Time to go, Romeo," Tommy shouts through the door.

"Be careful, Alex," Emma says, kissing me softly, "I'm quite fond of you," she chuckles.

"Just fond, huh," I chuckle and press a last kiss to her lips. "I love you."

"I love you too, Alex."

* * *

It's quiet in the FMR Range Rover. We took mine and Tommy's cars to the FMR centre where we picked up our equipment and changed to two of the FMR cars, as they are specially equipped to go off road and where we are heading, we will need it. Tommy, Ryan, Chris and Rob are in the first car, leaving Nick, Phil, Dan and myself in the second car. Suzie decided to stay with the birthday boy, given that eight of us is enough for a rescue.

The information we have is that a single person is in trouble on Devil's Pike. It is too windy today for the helicopter, so we will have to make our way up on foot. But first we'll take the cars as far as we can which will save us about an hour's walk. From the spot where the cars can't go any further we'll have another thirty minutes on foot to the point where the hikers noticed someone in trouble.

I can see the end of the gravel path in the distance when the sun hides behind the clouds. It looks like that's the end of the nice weather, as black clouds are forming in the distance.

I stop my car behind Tommy's and we all pile out of the Range Rover.

"Chris and Ryan, take the two sixty-metre-ropes. It sounded like the person in distress is lying in an area not accessible without a rope," Tommy instructs. We all grab backpacks with our gear, first aid equipment and other things we may need. Rob is strapping a folded-up basket stretcher to his back.

From where we parked the cars it is a steep ascent but we are all in good form, so we make it up the path fairly quickly. After the predicted thirty minutes, we reach a group of hikers who are pointing down into the valley.

"Did you make a call for mountain rescue?" Tommy asks.

"Yes, we think there's a person down there." The young man (he doesn't look older than twenty) points down a short rock face that ends on a steep slope. I can make out what looks like a pink bundle.

"That's not a person," Rob says next to me.

"Looks like a sleeping bag," Dan comments as he peers through binoculars.

"Fan-fucking-tastic, so I'm missing my son's birthday because of a sleeping bag," Chris mumbles and kicks a stone with his heavy hiking boot.

"Nick, gear up. Rob can belay, get down there and have a look," Tommy orders.

"You want me to rescue a sleeping bag?" Nick snorts.

"Yes, because that's your job. We need to make sure that it is just a sleeping bag. It's difficult to say from up here".

"Fine," Nick grumbles, but gets ready anyway. The hikers look on as Rob and Nick go through the process of roping up, checking each other's knots and setting up the belay.

"On belay," Nick calls out.

"Belay on," Rob confirms, and Nick steps over the edge. It doesn't take him long to abseil to the spot twenty meters below us, where the "sleeping bag in distress" is.

"FMR 6 to FMR 3, report," Tommy calls into the radio impatiently. Like all of us, he probably also thinks this is all a bit shit, but it's our job. We need at least check.

"Give me a minute, over," Nick replies. We see him shift through the sleeping bag and then traverse to the left and to the right before Tommy's radio crackles to life again.

"It's kittens, over." Tommy locks eyes with me. *What the fuck?*

"Repeat, over."

"It's kittens. One appears dead, two are in the sleeping bag with the dead one. They seem to be okay, although one has a damaged paw, I think. I found one more on the grass to the left. I can't see any—" His transmission stops.

"FMR3, come in. Over."

"Correction, I just found another one was hiding in the grass. Can you send down an empty backpack? Mine's full of gear. Over."

Thirty minutes later, Nick and a backpack full of kittens arrive safely back up on the ridge. Nick gently places the rucksack on the floor and we all try to peek into it. He had wrapped the dead kitten in a plastic bag, but the other four are peering up at us.

"Which kind of a twat throws kittens off a mountain?" Ryan growls.

"We're probably not going to find out," Tommy says matter-of-factly, and he is right. Nick brought the sleeping bag up with him and Tommy will report it to the police as it's a case of animal cruelty they're unlikely to do anything

By the time we get back to the FMR centre, Matthew, the local vet is waiting. We leave the kittens with him and head to the kitchen.

"So, Matt says, once he has pepped them up, the kittens will be fine. Who wants one?" Tommy says as he steps into the kitchen and accepts a cup of tea from Nick.

"Not me, mate, I have a newborn," Dan replies.

"Same applies to me," Nick shrugs. "Ry?"

"Sure, I'll take one," he grins.

"Emms and I can take two. They can keep each other company when we travel," I volunteer.

"Fine, Jane and I take two as well," Ryan shrugs, changing his mind.

"Excellent. I'll let Matt know." Tommy raises his mug as if he had given a toast.

"To the best Cat Mountain Rescue Team int he world," I chuckle and the others join in. These truly are my best friends.

* * *

Afterword

We have come to the end of the Fellside Mountain Rescue Series. Saying goodbye to Alex, Phil, Nick, Chris, Rob, Tommy, Dan and Ryan is harder than I thought it would be. They, just like their significant others, Emma, Christina, Charlotte, Suzie, Olivia, Ella, Rose and Jane, have become my friends and I will miss writing and reading about their lives.

I will also miss the small village of Fellside. But on that front, I have some good news. We will return to Fellside when we join the staff and guests of the Greenview Manor hotel in tales of lost loves, new passions, and hidden romances in five novellas, brimming with intense emotions and enough suspense to keep you on the edge of your seat.

And maybe, just maybe, some of the FMR guys will pop by.

Greenview Manor Tales will be released in 2024 and 2025.

Thank You

Thank you for taking the time to read Love at Fellside Vol. 2. Please spare a minute to leave a review on Amazon and Goodreads! Even a short sentence or two helps.

STAY IN TOUCH

Never miss a new release: Sign up for my newsletter to be the first to hear about free content, new releases, cover reveals, sales, and more: www.daniebooks.com/sign-up

You can also join the new reader Facebook group where you can meet other like-minded readers, pick up some exclusive giveaways and stay up-to-date with everything that is happening in my book world. I will have three big announcements in the next couple of months and you don't want to miss them!

You can join the Facebook group here:
https://bit.ly/3Cn5PQJ

More from Dani Elias

Fellside Mountain Rescue Series

Do you want to meet the guys from the Fellside Mountain Rescue Team? Get the series now:

Blossom with Me

Sing with Me

Paint with Me

Climb with Me

Read with Me

Build with Me

Wrap Up with Me

Ride with Me

Or binge the whole series:

Love at Fellside Vol. 1

Love at Fellside Vol. 2

Cat Ladies Rule The World

You know those "Cat Lady" myths? Forget 'em! These women are way more than meets the eye. They're not just crazy for cats – there's a whole lot more brewing beneath the surface. Picture this: romance, comedy, and a hint of kink. These books? They're like a rollercoaster ride through the love lives of forty-something ladies who redefine what it means to be a cat lover.

Valentine's Rebellion (Prequel Novella)

The Unnatural Habitat of a Cat Lady

The Unconventional Journey of a Cat Lady

Greenview Manor Tales

Get ready to meet the staff and guests of the **Greenview Manor Hotel**. Explore lost loves, new passions, and hidden romances in these five novellas, brimming with intense emotions and enough suspense to keep you on the edge of your seat.

Fierce Family
Alluring Adventure
Elusive Embrace
Wistful Whispers
Spellbinding Spirit

Aftermath

When aid workers Will, Melanie, and Jon find themselves tangled in an incident with devastating consequences, throwing them into a world of chaos and despair. Can their loved ones help them find their way back to life?

Mission
Escape
Rescue

Made in the USA
Middletown, DE
02 May 2024

53759950R00336